Henry James

STORIES OF
WRITERS AND
ARTISTS

Edited with an introduction
by F. O. Matthiessen

A NEW DIRECTIONS BOOK

FOURTH PRINTING

ACKNOWLEDGMENT

These stories are here reprinted by special arrangement with the Estate of Henry James and the original publishers holding copyrights. *Greville Fane, The Lesson of the Master, The Next Time, The Figure in the Carpet,* and *The Real Thing* were published by The Macmillan Company; *The Middle Years* and *The Death of the Lion* were published by Harper & Brothers; *Broken Wings* and *The Story in It* were published by Charles Scribner's Sons. The texts used are those of the Revised Editions, as published by Scribner's in 1907–1917 and Macmillan (London) 1921–1923. Mr. Matthiessen's introductory essay first appeared in *The Partisan Review*.

MANUFACTURED IN THE UNITED STATES OF AMERICA

New Directions Books are published for James Laughlin by New Directions Publishing Corporation, 333 Sixth Avenue, New York 14.

Contents

Publishing Statement:

This important reprint was made from an old and scarce book.

Therefore, it may have defects such as missing pages, erroneous pagination, blurred pages, missing text, poor pictures, markings, marginalia and other issues beyond our control.

Because this is such an important and rare work, we believe it is best to reproduce this book regardless of its original condition.

Thank you for your understanding and enjoy this unique book!

INTRODUCTION

Henry James' Portrait of the Artist

JAMES' prefaces have established themselves exactly as he envisaged them to Howells, as "a sort of comprehensive manual or *vademecum* for aspirants in our arduous profession." No other writer of fiction has bequeathed a comparable body of discourse for the understanding of his art. Two of his novels, *Roderick Hudson* and *The Tragic Muse,* have for their respective heroes a sculptor and a painter. But another grouping of James' work, to which far less consideration has been paid, presents even more intimately, if in the guise of fable, his portrait of the writer. He himself called attention to his stories dealing with the life of art by composing one of the volumes of his collected edition from them: *The Lesson of the Master, The Death of the Lion, The Next Time, The Figure in the Carpet,* and *The Coxon Fund.* But a single volume would not hold them all, and they ran part way through the next: *The Author of Beltraffio* and four shorter pieces, *The Middle Years, Greville Fane, Broken Wings,* and *The Tree of Knowledge.* The last of these shades off into the treatment characteristic of many other James stories: it is not primarily about the nature of art or of the artist; it uses the situation of a sculptor, whose family are in loyal conspiracy to hide from him his utter lack of talent, for the kind of psychological concealments and revelation so dear to James. *The Coxon Fund,* again, explicitly sets out to present the type of peculiarly helpless artistic temperament represented by Coleridge. But the center of reference in the others is to problems which James knew from the inside and whose urgency was ever with him, problems of the writer and his audience, of the lack of intelligent appreciation and of the demands of his craft. They also dramatize the issue which is still our issue, the relation of the artist to society.

The title stories of the two volumes, *The Lesson of the Master* (1888) and *The Author of Beltraffio* (1884), deal, in different ways, with the split between life and art. The one "lesson" which Henry St. George drills into young Paul Overt is not to be like him. The Master has reaped all the material rewards of a successful writer, but he has ceased to write important books and has come to look like "a lucky stockbroker." The choice that he insists upon between the world and the supremely exacting mistress of art may sound curiously dated to a generation whose most effective symbol of the artist has been a figure like Malraux, gathering the knowledge for his writing as he served in the air force for Loyalist Spain. But the half century since Henry St. George has known far more stream-lined ways of selling out than that smooth English gentleman ever dreamed of, and the choice still remains, even if not cast in James' monastic terms.

Equally dated is "the gospel of art" enunciated by Mark Ambient in the pages of his masterpiece Beltraffio. The donnée here, as James indicated in a still unpublished note-book, came to him from an anecdote he had heard about John Addington Symonds (not about Stevenson, as has long been the gossip). A situation was suggested by the reported cleavage between Symonds and his wife, who, in no sort of sympathy with his books, disapproved of their tone as "immoral, pagan, hyperaesthetic." The story which James invented to dramatize such a situation concentrated on the battle between Mark Ambient and his conventionally Christian wife over the control of their child, and reached its lurid climax in her deliberately letting the boy die from an attack of diphtheria rather than expose him to what she conceived to be the corruption of his pagan father.

James worked under two handicaps here. He made Mark Ambient so completely the correct English gentleman that he hardly succeeds in persuading us that he had really imagined him as a pagan sensualist. And increasing this unreality is the fact that he set himself to dramatize the aesthetic gospel of the eighties without quite indicating, perhaps without being quite sure at this stage of his development, exactly how much of it he accepted for himself. He was later to portray in The Tragic Muse (1890) the brilliant futility of the aesthete in the eerie figure of Gabriel Nash. In The Author of Beltraffio he made some fine humorous thrusts at the excesses of the movement. Nature faithfully copies art in Ambient's surroundings; even the creepers on the brown old walls appeared to have been borrowed from a pre-Raphaelite masterpiece. And as though a revenge for his aestheticism, Ambient's sister, who, in her faded velvet robe, seemed to have the notion that "she made up very well as a Rossetti," was a weirdly affected imitation of everything that in Ambient was original.

Ambient's own intense devotion to "every manifestation of human energy" is close to Pater's. And although James was to speak, a decade after this story, of Pater's having had "a phosphorescence, not a flame," there seems an inescapable kinship between Pater's aspiration to *be* the hard gem-like flame and Strether's famous exhortation to *live*, in *The Ambassadors*. Moreover, when Strether tries to convey the multiple-imaged fascination of Madame de Vionnet in likening her to a Renaissance medallion, "to a goddess still partly engaged in a morning cloud," "to a sea-nymph waist-high in the summer surge," to Cleopatra herself in her variety, we are not far from the elaborate spell of Pater's Mona Lisa. A further comparison would have to reckon with the fact that James' recurrent use of the word "morality" has a residue, quite foreign to Pater, of the values of James' transcendentalist father. For Pater, despite his debt to Arnold, would hardly have been able to rise to James' classic formulation, in the preface to *The Portrait of A Lady*, that there is "no more nutritive or suggestive truth . . . than that of the perfect dependence of the 'moral' sense of a work of art on the amount of felt life concerned in producing it." Yet Pater and James would be in accord with Mark Ambient's "passion for form," and likewise with his conviction that the artist must not falsify or smooth away details, but "must give the impression of life itself."

The stories where James is writing from the heart of his own aesthetic convictions are the rest of the group, most of which belong to the years 1893–6. These were crucial years for James. He had felt that with *The Tragic Muse* he had reached a dead-end with the long novel, and had turned to his anxious experiment with the stage. The failure of *Guy Domville*, early in 1895, marked the end of that chapter, and only a couple of weeks later he was writing to Howells: "I *have* felt, for a long time past, that I have fallen upon evil days—every sign or symbol of one's being in the least *wanted*, anywhere or by any one having so utterly failed. A new generation, that I know not, and mainly prize not, has taken universal possession." One great change from the old days was that James had now found that the magazines would hardly accept him any more, a serious matter for an artist now past fifty. He had only one answer: "Produce again—produce; produce better than ever, and all will yet be well." And even before the end of his letter to Howells he had rallied to the point of taking delight in the fact that he was "bursting with ideas and subjects."

He had already reached a partial resolution of his dilemma by dramatizing the problems over which he had been brooding, even though he could find for some of the resulting stories no more likely channel of publication than *The Yellow Book*. *The Death of the Lion* was printed by Harland with éclat as the leading item in his first issue (1894), though James was increasingly to feel the incongruity of having appeared among the newer aesthetes, the descendants of Pater; and was to take characteristic solace that his "comparatively so incurious text" had at least not provoked Beardsley into a perverse illustration.

How little characteristic it was of him to view his problems grimly is borne out by the tone of this story, where the situation is the reverse of James' own, that of the sudden fame of a heretofore unsuccessful writer. The whole is shot through with Flaubert's refrain about "the hatred of literature," as the admiring young critic who tells the story reflects that now Neil Paraday's rare talent is "to be squeezed into his horrible age." But though the "lion" is soon exhausted and thus killed by the violence with which he is taken up by Mrs. Weeks Wimbush, the handling of the theme is on a comic plane. No one at the country house where they are so ardently discussing his new book, while he lies sick upstairs, may have read beyond its twentieth page, and his hostess may end by losing his last manuscript, but still he has had the unique privilege of being brought into the sphere of his popular contemporaries, Guy Walsingham, the lady-author of *Obsessions*, and Dora Forbes, of *The Other Way Round*, who turns out to be a man with a big red moustache.

How clearly James observed the rôle played by the best-selling author of his day, and how little he envied it, may be read in the winning portrait he gives of Greville Fane, another lady whose pen dipped into gold. The reason why the critic—the most frequent narrator for these stories—liked her so much is that she rested him so from literature. He marvelled at her continued success, since her books were in no relation to life, until he reflected that "It's only real success that wanes, it's only solid things that melt." What endeared her to him, as she traced the loves of the duchesses beside the widowed cribs of her children, was her blind devotion to them alone. The plot of the story turns around the contrast between her and her son, who grows up to pretend to be a novelist, a fake disciple of form, and, while waiting for "inspiration," sponges on her generosity. James' tender handling of her character did not prevent him from commenting on the vulgarization of taste accomplished by a lady who could contribute volumes "to the diversion of her contemporaries," but who "couldn't write a page of English." He had similar authors in mind when, in *The American Scene*, he trained his eye upon "the little tales, mostly by ladies, and about and for children romping through the ruins of the Language, in the monthly magazines."

In *The Next Time* his approach to his own situation is no longer so oblique, though the tone is still that of high comedy. Here Mrs. Highmore, "one of the most voluminous writers" of the age, yearns to be like her brother-in-law Ralph Limbert, "but of course only once, an exquisite failure." He, on the other hand, had worn out his energies in the effort to sell. After *The Major Key* never even got the publisher's money back, he tried for every popular device, but the worst he could do couldn't escape from being "a shameless, merciless masterpiece" which only the critics read. It was the same to the end of his short career. Even *The Hidden Heart*, planned as an adventure story, turned out to be "but another female child." There was to be no next time for him any more than for Mrs. Highmore. As his critic friend, whose love was "the love that killed" with a popular audience, was to sum it up: "You can't make a sow's ear out of a silk purse."

The same phrase was turned by James about himself, immediately after the disastrous opening night of *Guy Domville*, in a letter to his brother William. But though he recounted the brutal shock of having been hissed and booed by the gallery after responding to the cry of "Author! Author!" he added: "Don't worry about me; I'm a Rock." Yet the problem of an audience was to bother him to the end. As he wrote in his note-book, *The Next Time* was suggested to him "really by all the little backward memories of one's own frustrated ambition;" and he recalled particularly how, in his early years, he had contracted to write some Paris letters for *The New York Tribune*, and how, despite every effort, he hadn't been able to make them bad enough to satisfy Whitelaw Reid. *Broken Wings*, written half a dozen years after the rest of the group, projected the situation of two writers, a man and a woman, who each had enjoyed a following in society, only to have it fall away, and to come to the realization that nothing was to be gained by an author in the country-house world, a world which simply took all one's cleverness and had no imagination to give. James said in his preface that he failed "to dis-inter again the buried germ" of this story, but went on to ask, "When had I been, as a fellow scribbler, closed to the general admonition of such adventures?" And thinking perhaps also of his own moment of popularity after *Daisy Miller*, he declared that "to dissimulate the grim realities of shrunken 'custom,' the felt chill of a lower professional temperature—any old note-book would show *that* laid away as a tragic 'value.' "

Where James draws most deeply on his own accumulated thoughts for these stories is in *The Middle Years*, in which the author-narrator is of the novelist's own age. Dencombe had been very sick, and picking up, in his convalescence, his book of the year before, he has a fresh impression of his own work. Like James he is "a passionate corrector" of his text, and thinking how much of his life it had taken to produce so little art, what he longs for most is "Ah for another go, ah for a better chance!" It is not necessary to force a too close parallel with James' life, since his own health, very precarious earlier, had developed by middle age considerable powers of endurance. Yet his sister's death in England in 1892, the year before this story, had heightened his feeling of isolation; and it is out of isolation that Dencombe cries: "I've outlived, I've lost by the way." Dencombe comes through to a renewed faith in creative possibilities, to the reassurance that there never is exhaustion in the abundance of material, but only "in the miserable artist." But he is not to have another chance. He recognizes that he is dying, and says with the eloquence of James' own urgency: "We work in the dark—we do what we can—we give what we have. Our doubt is our passion and our passion is our task. The rest is the madness of art."

The very conception of *The Figure in the Carpet* (1896) sprang from such passion. This was the story which James himself called "a significant fable"; and he said that what had stimulated him to write it was his acute impression of the Anglo-American's "so marked collective mistrust of anything like close or analytic appreciation." This story was designed as a plea for such mature criticism, as the prefaces were to be another. In it the ideal readers are those for whom "literature was a game of skill," since "skill meant courage, and courage meant honour, and honour meant passion, meant life."

In the view of the novelist Hugh Vereker life could be conveyed only indirectly, symbolically; his particular sense of it ran through all his books as their "exquisite scheme," "like a complex figure in a Persian carpet." James' title has given a phrase to the close textual criticism which he helped to inaugurate. Gide used it in his journal (1927) and Eliot, in introducing Wilson Knight's interpretation of Shakespeare's imaginative patterns (1930) held it up as the critic's goal. The impulse behind the phrase has quickened our awareness that the task of the critic today, after a century of historical accretion, is to see an artist's work not piece-meal but in its significant entirety, to find his compelling portrait in his works.

II

But the question that James' contemporaries might well ask was where he found, round about him at that hour, any models on which he could plead verisimilitude for his supersubtle Neil Faradays and Ralph Limberts and Hugh Verekers. He could simply answer that they had been "fathered but on his own intimate experience," that they had been "drawn preponderantly from the depths of the designer's own mind." But such an origin, he insisted, did not permit their being dismissed as unreal, since he had deliberately projected their situations as a form of what he called "operative irony," as a means of asserting that "if the life about us for the last thirty years refuses warrant for these examples, then so much the worse for that life."

If pressed further, he could have specified, as he did in his letters, how barren he found the sensibility of his milieu, in contrast with the analytic alertness of the French or of Turgenieff. There was no novelist in England with whom he could share his aims. He saw quite through the pointless elaborations of his somewhat older contemporary Meredith. On finishing *Lord Ormont and His Aminta* (1894) he was moved to declare to Gosse that he doubted "if any equal quantity of extravagant verbiage, or airs and graces, of phrases and attitudes, of obscurities and alembications, ever *started* less their subject . . ." He granted that he might be overstating the case, but he could not escape the conviction that many of Meredith's "profundities and tortuosities prove when threshed out to be only pretentious statements of the very simplest propositions." On the other hand, James was temperamentally at the opposite pole from Hardy, and never got closer to him than granting that *Tess* "is chock-full of faults and falsity, and yet has a singular beauty."

He continued to appreciate Howells and was in intermittent correspondence with him; but the one English practitioner of his craft with whom he felt a kinship was Stevenson, whom, unfortunately, he had come to know only a year before Stevenson left for the South Seas. But James' letters show the pitch of his admiration, which probably seems excessive to most readers now. What drew James to him was their common devotion to style. He also felt that he had at last found a reader who could understand what "an abject density and puerility" the current standards of criticism had fallen to. He was not blind to Stevenson's limitations, to his frequent mere "cleverness," to his "awfully jolly" side, but with Stevenson's departure he stated that he had "literally no one" left to share with, that he was "more and more shut up to the solitude inevitably the portion, in these islands, of him who would really try, even in so small a way as mine, to *do* it." Then, during the rehearsals of *Guy Domville,* came the news of Stevenson's death.

James was never to lose his avid curiosity in any potential incarnations of the artist, and, as late as 1914, in his essay on *The New Novel,* he was welcoming the promise of D. H. Lawrence, and, too generously, that of Hugh Walpole and Compton Mackenzie. Almost a quarter of a century before, he had been writing Stevenson that "the only news in literature" was "the infant monster of a Kipling." As though by the law of opposites James had been fascinated by the virility of his first stories, and thought that perhaps he contained "the seeds of an English Balzac." But as the years went on and James applied the demands of mature criticism, he wrote an incisive thumbnail critique to Grace Norton: "My view of his prose future has much shrunken in the light of one's increasingly observing how little of life he can make use of . . . He has come steadily from the less simple in subject to the more simple—from the Anglo-Indians to the natives, from the natives to the Tommies, from the Tommies to the quadrupeds, from the quadrupeds to the fish, and from the fish to the engines and the screws . . ." And the trouble with his handling of "steam and patriotism" was that it was so "mixed up with God."

Just at this time, near the close of the century, James' attention was attracted to a talent that he was to watch with interest for the rest of his life. No two writers could be farther apart in their aims than James and Wells, the apostle of craftsmanship and the greatest journalist of the great age of journalism. Their interchange deserves, therefore, more prominence than it has yet received as a symbolic landmark in modern critical debate. It constitutes also a kind of parable of the problems of the artist to put beside James' fictional creations and thus to add some further strokes to his self-portrait.

James' first letter is in appreciation of Wells' critical interest in *The Turn of the Screw*, and James' own statement that this story "is essentially a pot-boiler and *jeu d'esprit*" might serve as a check to our recent over-interpretation of it. What drew James to Wells was a more abundant energy than Kipling's, an ability to convey visible and audible life that he had so utterly missed in Meredith. After reading *Kipps* he declared: "You are, for me, more than ever, the most interesting 'literary man' of your generation—in fact, the only interesting one." He pronounced him in *Tono Bungay* to be "a very swagger performer" whose "vividness and colour" would have been the envy of Dickens. To be sure, James had to protest again and again, as of *The New Machiavelli*, against "that accurst autobiographic form which puts a premium on the loose, the improvised, the cheap and easy." He had known long since that their worlds were other, but, under the spell of Wells' force, he said: "I always read you . . . as I read no one else, with a complete abdication of all . . . 'principles of criticism,' canons of form, preconceptions of felicity, references to the idea of method or the sacred laws of composition." Of course, James could not do any such thing for long, and he had to comment to Mrs. Ward on the strange co-existence in Wells "of so much talent with so little art, so much life with (so to speak) so little living." This was always a basic criterion for James. But though he finally had to tell Wells that he found his persistent neglect of method to have become inexcusably "unconscious," he was still forced to add that there was no one else "who makes the whole apple-cart so run away that I don't care if I *don't* upset it and only want to stand out of its path and see it go."

But a jarring climax to their relation came in the year before James' death, when he was seventy-two and Wells forty-nine. Wells issued a facile catch-all volume, the alleged literary remains of *George Boon, The Mind of the Race*. This included an amateurish parody of James and some very heavy-handed discussion of him. *Boon* asserts that "James has never discovered that a novel isn't a

picture . . . that life isn't a studio." He goes on to take exception
to James' insistence upon composition and comes to the conclusion
that his people are all "eviscerated," that his books are of an "elaborate, copious emptiness." "The only living human motives left in
the novels of Henry James are a certain avidity and an entirely superficial curiosity . . . His people nose out suspicions, hint by hint,
link by link. Have you ever known living human beings do that?
The thing his novel is *about* is always there. It is like a church lit
but without a congregation to distract you, with every light and line
focused on the high altar. And on the altar, very reverently placed,
intensely there, is a dead kitten, an egg-shell, a bit of string."

James wrote at once, in profound bewilderment since, having enjoyed Wells so "enormously from far back," he had grown into "the
habit of taking some common meeting-ground . . . for granted,
and the falling away of this is like the collapse of a bridge which
made communication possible." "But," he went on, "I am by nature
more in dread of any fool's paradise, or at least of any bad misguid-
edness, than in love with the idea of a security proved, and the fact
that a mind as brilliant as yours *can* resolve me into such an unmitigated mistake, can't enjoy me in anything like the degree in which
I like to think I may be enjoyed, makes me greatly want to fix myself,
for as long as my nerves will stand it, with such a pair of eyes." The
defense that rose from such scrutiny rested its case squarely on "*my
measure of fullness—fullness* of life and of the projection of it, which
seems to you such an emptiness of both." Every sentence of this defense should be read in its slow dignified context, but since the issues
were sharpened by Wells' reply, we had better turn to it.

He pointed up their fundamental divergence in attitude by saying,
"To you literature like painting is an end, to me literature like architecture is a means, it has a use. Your view was, I felt, altogether
too prominent in the world of criticism and I assailed it in lines of
harsh antagonism. And writing that stuff about you was the first
escape I had from the obsession of this war. *Boon* is just a waste-paper
basket . . . I had rather be called a journalist than an artist, that is
the essence of it, and there was no other antagonist possible than
yourself. But since it was printed I have regretted a hundred times
that I did not express our profound and incurable contrast with a
better grace."

James' answer was immediate and forthright, not at all in the
manner with which *Boon* had charged him, the painful manner of

a hippopotamus trying to pick up a pea. "I am bound to tell you that I don't think your letter makes out any sort of case for the bad manners of *Boon*, as far as your indulgence in them at the expense of your poor old H.J. is concerned—I say 'your' simply because he has *been* yours, in the most liberal, continual, sacrificial, the most admiring and abounding critical way, ever since he began to know your writings: as to which you have had copious testimony." He took up Wells' case point by point. The comparison of a book to a wastebasket struck him "as the reverse of felicitous, for what one throws into that receptacle is exactly what one doesn't commit to publicity and make the affirmation of one's estimate of one's contemporaries by." He didn't have to elaborate his often expressed belief concerning the age's primary root of corruption: as he had remarked to Howells some years before, "The *faculty of attention* has utterly vanished from the general anglo-saxon mind, extinguished at its source by the big blatant Bayadère of Journalism." Nor did he see it anywhere evident that "my view of 'life and literature,'—or what you impute to me as such, is carrying everything before it and becoming a public menace—so unaware do I seem, on the contrary, that my products constitute an example in any measurable degree followed." The crux of the matter, however, was that he had no view of life and literature "other than that our form of the latter . . . is admirable exactly by its range and variety, its plasticity and liberality, its fairly living on the sincere and shining experience of the individual practitioner . . . Of course for myself I live, live intensely and am fed by life, and my value, whatever it be, is in my own kind of expression of that." No passage in his prefaces had rung more eloquently of his aims.

He was not in the least taken in by Wells' specious contrast between architecture and painting. His intimate knowledge of all the plastic arts told him that "there is no sense in which architecture is aesthetically 'for use' that doesn't leave any other art whatever exactly as much so . . . It is art that *makes* life, makes interest, makes importance . . . and I know of no substitute whatever for the force and beauty of its process. If I were *Boon* I should say that any pretence of such a substitute is helpless and hopeless humbug; but I wouldn't be *Boon* for the world, and am only, yours faithfully, Henry James."

To that Wells could only reply: "I don't clearly understand your concluding phrases—which shews no doubt how completely they define our difference. When you say 'it is art that makes life, makes interest, makes importance,' I can only read sense into it by assuming that you are using 'art' for every conscious human activity. I use the word for a research and attainment that is technical and special." That draws the central issue between them as sharply as possible, since the emptiness or living intricacy of the figure in James' carpet depends on whether he was using "art" as a mystical abracadabra or with verifiable comprehension of the enormous value he imputes to it.

III

Three other stories, written at widely spaced intervals, may be added to the group with which we started to give us James' answer most compactly. *The Madonna of the Future* (1873) can tell us why he saw so much value in art. *The Real Thing* (1893) is his most intimate fable of what that value consists in. *The Story in It* (1903) can demonstrate that art "makes life" only to the degree that it rises from, and, in turn, serves to heighten felt experience.

The Madonna of the Future is one of James' earliest real accomplishments, though it may seem still very "literary," with the detail of its unachieved canvas taken over from Balzac's *Le Chef-d'oeuvre inconnu,* and the speech of a Florentine painter quoted from Musset. But it puts very affectingly many of the problems of the beginning artist, and it vibrates with James' peculiarly high spiritual notes. It sprang from his own first immersion in Italian art, which had been followed by a reluctant return home. In part, therefore, the story dramatizes the special case of the American, as James had begun to feel the burden of it. The old Yankee painter, who has lived out his life in Florence, confesses sadly, and James' own anxiety is in his voice: "We're the disinherited of Art! We're condemned to be superficial! We're excluded from the magic circle! The soil of American perception is a poor little barren artificial deposit! Yes, we're wedded to imperfection! An American, to excel, has just ten times as much to learn as a European! We lack the deeper sense! We have neither tact nor force! How *should* we have them? Our crude and garish climate, our silent past, our deafening present . . . We poor aspirants must live in perpetual exile." To which the young narrator rejoins, speaking for James' hopes: "Nothing is so idle as to talk about our want of a nursing air, of a kindly soil, of opportunity, of the things that help. The only thing that helps is to do something fine. There's no law in our glorious Constitution against that. Invent, create, achieve."

The intensity with which Americans like James and Poe and Eliot have cared about art has been almost a compulsive reaction against its neglect in their surroundings. It is significant, as Harry Levin has said, that whereas Balzac's story emphasizes the essential vitality of life upon which art must be based, Hawthorne's *The Artist of the Beautiful* is concerned with the spiritual ideals which sustain the artist, and James insists that such ideals may themselves be a delusion and that the only health for the artist is in the constant practice of his craft. For James, at the outset of his career, there was an even deeper dread than that voiced by the old painter. He had seen in his father's generation, which was Emerson's generation, so many artists whose master canvases remained blanks, so many transcendental geniuses without the concentration of talent. His own father was a haunting case, possessing an amazing flair for style in individual sentences but absolutely no organizing form, without which his books remained unreadable. There was a further personal pressure behind this story: here was James himself, already at the verge of thirty, and with hardly a start in fiction. Was he to be yet another of Emerson's promising young men, afraid to take the plunge? Still, as he contemplated the old painter's fatal mistake in so idealizing art that he never brought it to earth, James could envisage an even worse fate in the opposite extreme, that of cynical talent without an ideal. His particular American heritage spoke through him as he created the Italian contriver of obscene animal figurines. To this heritage James was to owe his deepest tones, the blackest threads in his design, the rare ability to suggest the horror of spiritual death. Such horror comes out in this early story with the intensity of the narrator's revulsion from this sculptor's declaration: "Cats and monkeys—monkeys and cats—all human life is there!")

The rival claims of the real and the ideal in art, and the dread that he might never find his own way of reconciling talent and genius, had long since been resolved by James when an anecdote dropped by his friend Du Maurier stimulated him to one of the lightest and yet most searching affirmations of his aesthetic theory. He produced exactly what he hoped for in his note-book recording that *The Real Thing* "should be a little gem of bright quick vivid form." The fable here is so resiliently designed and brings out his ideas about art through so many deft symbols that nothing short of the whole can properly convey its effect. But James' main convictions may be suggested by recalling the situation. Major Monarch and his wife, the real social thing, are desperately out of funds and want to sit for illustrations for a modern society novel. The painter-narrator is touched by their plight and reluctantly takes them on, but is immediately faced with a whole series of problems. He has a detestation of the amateur in art, and an awareness of the stultification involved in type-casting—indeed, he is very like James in his deep-rooted desire for character instead of types. Moreover, he confesses to an innate preference for appearance over reality, for "the represented subject over the real one."

Does this mean that his art is an escape, a hollow evasion of experience as Wells found James? The answer involves James' wholehearted repudiation of realism as mere literal reporting. The painter's regular model, Miss Churm, is anything but the real thing. She is a freckled cockney, but a clever actress and so a constantly shifting challenge to fresh embodiment; whereas the Major's wife, a lady certainly, "is always the same lady" and soon comes to look "singularly like a bad illustration." The show-down occurs when a little Italian model turns up with the confident belief that he can pose for an English gentleman far better than the massive Major. He soon proves that he is as good as Miss Churm, "who could look, when requested, like an Italian." His brilliant mimetic gift illustrates the necessary doctrine of imitation for any branch of art. It tells the painter again what he already knew, that action must be heightened by stylization, if art is to convey the essence and not the accidents of life. And so he is forced to turn away the Monarchs, with James' experienced and now thoroughly anti-transcendental "lesson": "that in the deceptive atmosphere of art even the highest respectability may fail of being plastic."

A kind of grace note to this discussion, concentrating directly on the art of fiction, is sounded by The Story in It. One of the shortest of James' compositions, it amounts to another condensed parable of his material and method. Maud Blessingbourne's fondness for French novels and D'Annunzio is in contrast with the simple absorption in life of her hostess, Mrs. Dyott. An afternoon visit is paid by Colonel Voyt, who—though this has not been told to Maud,—is Mrs. Dyott's lover. The conversation centers on Maud's reading, on the contrast between Anglo-Saxon fiction and the French. The Colonel holds that "they do what they feel, and they feel more things than we." Granting the superior continental maturity, Maud holds that their fiction still lacks variety, that their lovers are all the same, that, for instance, they never portray "a decent woman." The Colonel contends that you must choose, since "the subject the novelist treats is the rise, the formation, the development, the climax and for the most part the decline of a relation . . . If a relation stops, where's the story? If it doesn't stop, where's the innocence?" If you don't choose, you're back in the floundering evasions of the English novel.

Maud doesn't argue, but she is not convinced. After the Colonel has left, she indicates why she feels so sure of her grounds. She herself is absorbed in the kind of inner drama which French fiction neglects. She is in love, but she will not say with whom; the man does not even suspect it, and she is determined, for unspoken reasons, that he should not. Mrs. Dyott tacitly guesses the truth, that Maud is in love with the Colonel, and when she next sees him, tells him so. He is astonished, but has then to grant that Maud's "consciousness, if they let it alone—as they of course after this mercifully must— was, in the last analysis, a kind of shy romance. Not a romance like their own, a thing to make the fortune of any author up to the mark —one who should have the invention or who *could* have the courage; but a small scared starved subjective satisfaction that would do her no harm and nobody else any good. Who but a duffer—he stuck to his contention—would see the shadow of a 'story' in it?"

Wells and his million followers would agree with the Colonel. I have deliberately ended James' plea on one of his special cases of scruples and renunciation, for such cases are recurrent threads in his carpet. The question, however, remains whether they are too special to make a living figure. Nothing could have shocked James worse than Wells' notion that the patiently projected essence of his stories amounted to nothing more than "a bit of string." For James, unlike the aesthetes of the nineties, always insisted on the supreme importance of subject, yet insisted also that what was important could not be legislated arbitrarily but must be determined by the artist's own seasoned vision of experience, and that substance could be produced only through form.

The split between James and Wells, between the inner and the outer world, between analytic subtlety and surface reporting, is a sign of one of the great cultural maladjustments of our age. Both James and Wells were damaged by it. The absence of critical appreciation forced James to his own extremes, to such overly ingenious effects as that in *The Figure in the Carpet* itself, where the breathless pursuit of Hugh Vereker's "meaning" ends as the kind of arid curiosity against which Wells protested. The failure of James' contemporaries to respond to Flaubert's challenge for composition compelled James to insist upon it to such lengths that he finally objected to Tolstoy and Dostoevsky as "fluid puddings" because of their "defiance of economy and architecture." Though Wells did not have that tragic blindness, his increasing indifference to any art is equally unbalanced. His novels have profited less and less by any of James' advice, and in his carelessly thrown together *Autobiography* he dismissed them altogether as of no lasting worth.

The consequences of this split between "highbrow" and "lowbrow" have been especially virulent in America, fed, on the one part, by the divorce between our educated minds and experience which Santayana named the genteel tradition; and, on the other, by the enormous premiums paid to any sensationalism. Despite the fact that he was himself the extreme case of a writer glutted by slabs of raw experience which he could not assimilate, Thomas Wolfe discerned one phase of our dilemma. At one extreme are "the laboring, farming sort of people" from which Wolfe came, who think of the writer as some one romantic and remote from their own lives. At the other extreme are "the university-going kind of people, and these people also become fascinated with the glamor and difficulty of writing, but in a different way. They get more involved or fancy than the most involved and fancy European people of this sort. They become more 'Flauberty' than Flaubert. They establish little magazines that not only split a hair with the best of them, but they split more hairs than Europeans think of splitting. The Europeans say: 'Oh God, where did these people, these aesthetic Americans, ever come from?' . . . I think all of us who have tried to write in this country may have fallen in between these two groups of well meaning and misguided people, and if we become writers finally, it is in spite of each of them."

Whitman escaped from one group, and James anticipated the other. It has been the fashion of recent criticism to dramatize the irreconcilable cleavage between the "lowbrows" and the "highbrows" in our literature as stemming symbolically from these two writers. But it is forgotten that James himself bridged the gap. At twenty-two, as the smartest of destructive young reviewers for the newly-launched *Nation*, he wrote his notorious apostrophe "from the intelligence to the bard" of *Drum Taps*. But in later years, as Edith Wharton has told us, he delighted in reciting Whitman's lines, "in a mood of subdued ecstasy"; and he took satisfaction too in what he called the "flat, familiar, affectionate, illiterate colloquy" of the letters to Pete Doyle. Such ripened appreciation does not in itself accomplish a reconciliation; but as Santayana observed, James in his own work overcame the genteel tradition "in the classic way, by understanding it."

The value of James' figure may be judged, as he insisted, only if it is sought out through his work as a whole. Only thus may be decided whether his scruples and renunciations are a sterile emptiness, or the guides to a peculiarly poignant suffering and inner triumph. One augury for life rather than death in his work has shone through his whole relationship with Wells. As he said, in his final letter in that interchange, it was when another "personal and intellectual history" had been determined "in the way most different" from his own that he most wanted to get at it—"precisely *for* the extension of life." It was the same with his relationship with his brother William, who from the time of *The Europeans* to *The Golden Bowl* was writing well-intentioned worried letters of uncomprehending counsel, only to have Henry reply at the end that he would "sooner descend to a dishonoured grave" than to have written such "things of the current age" as he had heard William express admiration for. "Yet," he added, "I can read *you* with rapture." We appear to have the case then that the seemingly special novelist is more outgoing in his interests than either the great journalist or the lively philosopher. Attention, perception, sympathy, are all on his side. His portrait of the artist would seem to challenge comparable qualities of our own.

F. O. Matthiessen

The Madonna of the Future

WE had been talking about the masters who had achieved but a single masterpiece—the artists and poets who but once in their lives had known the divine afflatus and touched the high level of perfection. Our host had shown us a charming little cabinet picture by a painter whose name we had never heard, and who, after this single spasmodic bid for fame, had appeared to relapse into obscurity and mediocrity. There was some discussion as to the frequency of this inconsequence; during which I noted H—— sit silent, finishing his cigar with a meditative air and looking at the picture, which was being handed round the table. "I don't know how common a case it is," he said at last, "but I've seen it. I've known a poor fellow who painted his one masterpiece, and who"—he added with a smile—"didn't even paint that. He made his bid for fame and missed it." We all knew H—— for a clever man who had seen much of men and manners and had a great stock of reminiscences. Some one immediately questioned him further, and while I was engrossed with the raptures of my neighbour over the precious object in circulation he was induced to tell his tale. If I were to doubt whether it would bear repeating, I should only have to remember how that charming woman our hostess, who had left the table, ventured back, in rustling rose-colour, to pronounce our lingering a want of gallantry, and, then finding us under the spell, sank into her chair in spite of our cigars and heard the story out so graciously that when the catastrophe was reached she glanced across and showed me a tear in each of her beautiful eyes.

It relates to my youth and to Italy: two very fine things! (H—— began.) I had arrived late in the evening at Florence and, while I finished my bottle of wine at supper, had fancied that, tired traveller though I was, I might pay such a place a finer compliment than by going vulgarly to bed. A narrow passage wandered darkly away out of the little square before my hotel and looked as if it bored into the heart of Florence. I followed it and at the end of ten minutes emerged upon a great piazza filled only with the mild autumn moonlight. Opposite rose the Palazzo Vecchio, like some huge civic fortress, with the great bell-tower springing from its embattled verge even as a mountain-pine from the edge of a cliff. At the base, in the great projected shadow, gleamed certain dim sculptures which I wonderingly approached. One of the images, on the left of the palace door, was a magnificent colossus who shone through the dusky air like a sentinel roused by some alarm and in whom I at once recognised Michael Angelo's famous David. I turned with a certain relief from his heroic sinister strength to a slender figure in bronze poised beneath the high light loggia which opposes the free and elegant span of its arches to the dead masonry of the palace; a figure supremely shapely and graceful, markedly gentle almost, in spite of his holding out with his light nervous arm the snaky head of the slaughtered Gorgon. His name—as, unlike the great David, he still stands there—is Perseus, and you may read his story not in the Greek mythology but in the memoirs of Benvenuto Cellini. Glancing from one of these fine fellows to the other, I probably uttered some irrepressible commonplace of praise, for, as if provoked by my voice, a man rose from the steps of the loggia, where he had been sitting in the shadow, and addressed me in proper English—a small slim personage clad in some fashion of black velvet tunic (as it seemed) and with a mass of auburn hair, which shimmered in the moonlight, escaping from a little beretto of the *cinquecento*. In a tone of the most insinuating deference he proceeded to appeal to me for my "impressions." He was romantic, fantastic, slightly unreal. Hovering in that consecrated neighbourhood he might have passed for the genius of esthetic hospitality—if the genius of esthetic hospitality wasn't commonly some shabby little custode who flourishes a calico pocket-handerchief and openly resents the divided franc. This analogy was made none the less complete by his breaking into discourse as I threw myself diffidently back upon silence.

"I've known Florence long, sir, but I've never known her so lovely as to-night. It's as if the ghosts of her past were abroad in the empty streets. The present is sleeping; the past hovers about us like a dream made visible. Fancy the old Florentines strolling up in couples to pass judgment on the last performance of Michael, of Benvenuto! We should come in for a precious lesson if we might overhear what they say. The plainest burgher of them, in his cap and gown, had a taken wings. No lovely human outline could charm it to vulgar fact. He saw the fair form made perfect; he rose to the vision without tremor, without effort of wing; he communed with it face to face and resolved into finer and lovelier truth the purity which completes it as the fragrance completes the rose. That's what they call idealism; the word's vastly abused, but the thing's good. It's my own creed at any rate. Lovely Madonna, model at once and muse, I call you to witness that I too am an idealist!"

"An idealist then"—and I really but wanted to draw him further out—"an idealist is a gentleman who says to Nature in the person of a beautiful girl: 'Go to, you're all wrong! Your fine's coarse, your bright's dim, your grace is *gaucherie.* This is the way you should have done it! Isn't the chance against him?"

He turned on me at first almost angrily—then saw that I was but sowing the false to reap the true. "Look at that picture," he said, "and cease your irreverent mockery! Idealism is *that!* There's no explaining it; one must feel the flame. It says nothing to Nature, or to any beautiful girl, that they won't both forgive. It says to the fair woman: 'Accept me as your artist-friend, lend me your beautiful face, trust me, help me, and your eyes shall be half my masterpiece.' No one so loves and respects the rich realities of nature as the artist whose imagination intensifies them. He knows what a fact may hold —whether Raphael knew, you may judge by his inimitable portrait, behind us there, of Tommaso Inghirami—but his fancy hovers above it as Ariel in the play hovers above the sleeping prince. There's only one Raphael, but an artist may still be an artist. As I said last night, the days of illumination are gone; visions are rare; we've to look long to have them. But in meditation we may still cultivate the ideal; round it, smooth it, perfect it. The result, the result"—here his voice faltered suddenly and he fixed his eyes for a moment on the picture; when they met my own again they were full of tears—"the result may be less than this, but still it may be good, it may be *great!*" he cried with vehemence. "It may hang somewhere, through all the years, in goodly company, and keep the artist's memory warm. Think of being known to mankind after some such fashion as this; of keeping pace with the restless centuries and the changing world; of living on and on in the cunning of an eye and a hand that belong to the dust of ages, a delight and a law to remote generations; of making beauty more and more a force and purity more and more an example!'

tourist? But I wasn't called to defend myself. A great brazen note broke suddenly from the far-off summit of the bell-tower above us and sounded the first stroke of midnight. My companion started, apologised for detaining me and prepared to retire. But he seemed to offer so lively a promise of further entertainment that I was loth to part with him and suggested we should proceed homeward together. He cordially assented; so we turned out of the Piazza, passed down before the statued arcade of the Uffizi and came out upon the Arno. What course we took I hardly remember, but we roamed far and wide for an hour, my companion delivering by snatches a positively moon-touched esthetic lecture. I listened in puzzled fascination, wondering who the deuce he might be. He confessed with a melancholy but all-respectful headshake to an origin identical with my own. "We're the disinherited of Art! We're condemned to be superficial! We're excluded from the magic circle! The soil of American perception is a poor little barren artificial deposit! Yes, we're wedded to imperfection! An American, to excel, has just ten times as much to learn as a European! We lack the deeper sense! We have neither taste nor tact nor force! How *should* we have them? Our crude and garish climate, our silent past, our deafening present, the constant pressure about us of unlovely conditions, are as void of all that nourishes and prompts and inspires the artist as my sad heart is void of bitterness in saying so! We poor aspirants must live in perpetual exile."

"You seem fairly at home in exile," I made answer, "and Florence seems to me a very easy Siberia. But do you know my own thought? Nothing is so idle as to talk about our want of a nursing air, of a kindly soil, of opportunity, of inspiration, of the things that help. The only thing that helps is to do something fine. There's no law in our glorious Constitution against that. Invent, create, achieve. No matter if you've to study fifty times as much as one of these. What else are you an artist for? Be you our Moses," I added, laughing and laying my hand on his shoulder, "and lead us out of the house of bondage!"

"Golden words, golden words, young man!"—my friend rose to it beautifully. " 'Invent, create, achieve'! Yes, that's our business; I know it well. Don't take me, in heaven's name, for one of your —barren complainers, of the falsely fastidious, who have neither talent nor faith! I'm at work!"—and he glanced about him and lowered his voice as if this were quite a peculiar secret—"I'm at work night and day. I've undertaken, believe me, a creation. I'm no Moses; I'm only a poor patient artist; but it would be a fine thing if I were to cause some slender stream of beauty to flow in our thirsty land! Don't think me a monster of conceit," he went on as he saw me smile at the avidity with which he adopted my illustration; "I confess that I *am* in one of those moods when great things seem possible. This is one of my—shall I say inspired?—nights: I dream waking. When the south wind blows over Florence at midnight it seems to coax the soul from all the fair things locked away in her churches and galleries; it comes into my own little studio with the moonlight; it sets my heart beating too deeply for rest. You see I'm always adding a thought to my conception. This evening I felt I couldn't sleep unless I had communed with the genius of Buonarotti!"

He seemed really to know his Florence through and through and had no need to tell me he loved her. I saw he was an old devotee and had taken her even from the first to his heart. "I owe her everything," he put it—"it's only since I came here that I've really lived, intellectually and esthetically speaking. One by one all profane desires, all mere worldly aims, have dropped away from me and left me nothing but my pencil, my little note-book"—he tapped his breast pocket— "and the worship of the pure masters, those who were pure because they were innocent and those who were pure because they were strong!"

"And have you been very productive all this time?" I found myself too interested to keep from asking.

He was silent a while before replying. "Not in the vulgar sense! I've chosen never to manifest myself by imperfection. The good in every performance I've reabsorbed into the generative force of new creations; the bad—there's always plenty of that—I've religiously destroyed. I may say with some satisfaction that I've not added a grain to the rubbish of the world. As a proof of my conscientiousness"—and he stopped short, eyeing me with extraordinary candour, as if the proof were to be overwhelming—"I've never sold a picture! 'At least no merchant traffics in my heart!' Do you remember that divine line in Browning? My little studio has never been profaned by superficial feverish mercenary work. It's a temple of labour but of leisure! Art is long. If we work for ourselves of course we must hurry. If we work for *her* we must often pause. She can wait!"

This had brought us to my hotel door, somewhat to my relief, I confess, for I had begun to feel unequal to the society of a genius

of this heroic strain. I left him, however, not without expressing
a friendly hope that we should meet again. The next morning my
curiosity had not abated; I was anxious to see him by common daylight. I counted on meeting him in one of the many art-haunts of
the so rich little city, and I was gratified without delay. I found him
in the course of the morning in the Tribune of the Uffizi—that little
treasure-chamber of world-famous things. He had turned his back
on the Venus de' Medici and, with his arms resting on the rail that
protects the pictures and his head buried in his hands, was lost in
the contemplation of that superb neighbouring triptych of Andrea
Mantegna—a work which has neither the material splendour nor the
commanding force of some of its neighbours, but which, glowing
there with the loveliness of patient labour, suits possibly a more constant need of the soul I looked at the picture for some time over his
shoulder; at last, with a heavy sigh, he turned away and our eyes met.
As he recognised me he coloured for the consciousness of what I
brought back: he recalled perhaps that he had made a fool of himself overnight. But I offered him my hand with a frankness that assured him I was no scoffer. I knew him by his great nimbus of red
hair; otherwise he was much altered. His midnight mood was over,
and he looked as haggard as an actor by daylight. He was much older
than I had supposed, and had less bravery of costume and attitude.
He seemed quite the poor patient artist he had proclaimed himself,
and the fact that he had never sold a picture was more conceivable
doubtless than commendable. His velvet coat was threadbare and
his short slouched hat, of an antique pattern, revealed a rustiness
that marked it an "original" and not one of the picturesque reproductions that members of his craft sometimes affect. His eye was mild
and heavy, and his expression singularly gentle and acquiescent; the
more so for a certain pale facial spareness which I hardly knew
whether to refer to the consuming fire of genius or to a meagre
diet. A very little talk, however, cleared his brow and brought back
his flow.

"And this is your first visit to these enchanted halls?" he cried.
"Happy, thrice happy youth!"—with which, taking me by the arm,
he prepared to lead me to each of the pre-eminent works in turn
and show me the flower of the array. Before we left the Mantegna,
however, I felt him squeeze me and give it a loving look. "*He* was not
in a hurry," he murmured. "*He* knew nothing of 'raw Haste, half-
sister to Delay'!" How sound a critic he might have been didn't seem

to me even then to concern me—it so served that he was an amusing one; overflowing with opinions and theories, sympathies and aversions, with disquisition and gossip and anecdote. He inclined more than I approved to the sentimental proposition, was too fond, I thought, of superfine shades and of discovering subtle intentions and extracting quintessences. At moments too he plunged into the sea of metaphysics and floundered a while in waters that were not for my breasting. But his abounding knowledge and frequent felicities told a touching story of long attentive hours in all such worshipful companies; there was a reproach to my wasteful saunterings in his systematic and exhaustive attack. "There are two moods," I remember his saying, "in which we may walk through galleries—the critical and the ideal. They seize us at their pleasure, and we can never tell which is to take its turn. The critical, oddly, is the genial one, the friendly, the condescending. It relishes the pretty trivialities of art, its vulgar cleverness, its conscious graces. It has a kindly greeting for anything which looks as if, according to his light, the painter had enjoyed doing it—for the little Dutch cabbages and kettles, for the taper fingers and breezy mantles of late-coming Madonnas, for the little blue-hilled, broken-bridged, pastoral, classical landscapes. Then there are the days of fierce, fastidious longing—solemn church-feasts of the taste or the faith—when all vulgar effort and all petty success is a weariness and everything but the best, the best of the best, disgusts. In these hours we're relentless aristocrats of attitude. We'll not take Michael for granted, we'll not swallow Raphael whole!"

The gallery of the Uffizi is not only rich in its possessions, but peculiarly fortunate in that fine architectural accident or privilege which unites it—with the breadth of river and city between them —to the princely extent of the Pitti. The Louvre and the Vatican hardly give you such a sense of sustained enclosure as those long passages projected over street and stream to establish an inviolate transition between the two palaces of art. We paced the clear tunnel in which those precious drawings by eminent hands hang chaste and grey above the swirl and murmur of the yellow Arno, and reached the grand-ducal, the palatial saloons. Grand-ducal as they are, they must be pronounced imperfect show-rooms, since, thanks to their deep-set windows and their massive mouldings, it is rather a broken light that reaches the pictured walls. But here the masterpieces hang thick, so that you see them in a deep diffused lustre of their own.

And the great chambers, with their superb dim ceilings, their outer wall in splendid shadow and the sombre opposite glow of toned canvas and gleaming gold, make themselves almost as fine a picture as the Titians and Raphaels they imperfectly reveal. We lingered briefly before many a Raphael and Titian; but I saw my friend was impatient and I suffered him at last to lead me directly to the goal of our journey—the most tenderly fair of Raphael's virgins, the Madonna of the Chair. Of all the fine pictures of the world, it was to strike me at once as the work with which criticism has least to do. None betrays less effort, less of the mechanism of success and of the irrepressible discord between conception and result that sometimes faintly invalidates noble efforts. Graceful, human, near to our sympathies as it is, it has nothing of manner, of method, nothing almost of style; it blooms there in a softness as rounded and as instinct with harmony as if it were an immediate exhalation of genius. The figure imposes on the spectator a spell of submission which he scarce knows whether he has given to heavenly purity or to earthly charm. He is intoxicated with the fragrance of the tenderest blossom of maternity that ever bloomed among men.

"That's what I call a fine picture," said my companion after we had gazed a while in silence. "I've a right to say so, for I've copied it so often and so carefully that I could repeat it now with my eyes shut. Other works are of Raphael: this is Raphael himself. Others you can praise, you can qualify, you can measure, explain, account for: this you can only love and admire. I don't know in what seeming he walked here below while this divine mood was upon him; but after it surely he could do nothing but die—this world had nothing more to teach him. Think of it a while, my friend, and you'll admit that I'm not raving. Think of his seeing that spotless image not for a moment, for a day, in a happy dream or a restless fever-fit, not as a poet in a five minutes' frenzy—time to snatch his phrase and scribble his immortal stanza; but for days together, while the slow labour of the brush went on, while the foul vapours of life interposed and the fancy ached with tension, fixed, radiant, distinct, as we see it now! What a master, certainly! But ah what a seer!"

"Don't you imagine," I fear I profanely asked, "that he had a model, and that some pretty young woman—"

"As pretty a young woman as you please! It doesn't diminish the miracle. He took his hint of course, and the young woman possibly sat smiling before his canvas. But meanwhile the painter's idea had taken wings. No lovely human outline could charm it to vulgar fact. He saw the fair form made perfect; he rose to the vision without tremor, without effort of wing; he communed with it face to face and resolved into finer and lovelier truth the purity which completes it as the fragrance completes the rose. That's what they call idealism; the word's vastly abused, but the thing's good. It's my own creed at any rate. Lovely Madonna, model at once and muse, I call you to witness that I too am an idealist!"

"An idealist then"—and I really but wanted to draw him further out—"an idealist is a gentleman who says to Nature in the person of a beautiful girl: 'Go to, you're all wrong! Your fine's coarse, your bright's dim, your grace is *gaucherie*. This is the way you should have done it! Isn't the chance against him?"

He turned on me at first almost angrily—then saw that I was but sowing the false to reap the true. "Look at that picture," he said, "and cease your irreverent mockery! Idealism is *that!* There's no explaining it; one must feel the flame. It says nothing to Nature, or to any beautiful girl, that they won't both forgive. It says to the fair woman: 'Accept me as your artist-friend, lend me your beautiful face, trust me, help me, and your eyes shall be half my masterpiece.' No one so loves and respects the rich realities of nature as the artist whose imagination intensifies them. He knows what a fact may hold —whether Raphael knew, you may judge by his inimitable portrait, behind us there, of Tommaso Inghirami—but his fancy hovers above it as Ariel in the play hovers above the sleeping prince. There's only one Raphael, but an artist may still be an artist. As I said last night, the days of illumination are gone; visions are rare; we've to look long to have them. But in meditation we may still cultivate the ideal; round it, smooth it, perfect it. The result, the result"—here his voice faltered suddenly and he fixed his eyes for a moment on the picture; when they met my own again they were full of tears—"the result may be less than this, but still it may be good, it may be *great!*" he cried with vehemence. "It may hang somewhere, through all the years, in goodly company, and keep the artist's memory warm. Think of being known to mankind after some such fashion as this; of keeping pace with the restless centuries and the changing world; of living on and on in the cunning of an eye and a hand that belong to the dust of ages, a delight and a law to remote generations; of making beauty more and more a force and purity more and more an example!'

"Heaven forbid," I smiled, "that I should take the wind out of your sails! But doesn't it occur to you that besides being strong in his genius Raphael was happy in a certain good faith of which we've lost the trick? There are people, I know, who deny that his spotless Madonnas are anything more than pretty blondes of that period, enhanced by the Raphaelesque touch, which they declare to be then as calculating and commercial as any other. Be that as it may, people's religious and esthetic needs went arm in arm, and there was, as I may say, a demand for the Blessed Virgin, visible and adorable, which must have given firmness to the artist's hand. I'm afraid there's no demand now.

My friend momentarily stared—he shivered and shook his ears under this bucketful of cold water. But he bravely kept up his high tone. "There's always a demand—that ineffable type is one of the eternal needs of man's heart; only pious souls long for it in silence, almost in shame. Let it appear and their faith grows brave. How *should* it appear in this corrupt generation? It can't be made to order. It could indeed when the order came trumpet-toned from the lips of the Church herself and was addressed to genius panting with inspiration. But it can spring now only from the soil of passionate labour and culture. Do you really fancy that while from time to time a man of complete artistic vision is born into the world such an image can perish? The man who paints it has painted everything. The subject admits of every perfection—form, colour, expression, composition. It can be as simple as you please and yet as rich; as broad and free and yet as full of delicate detail. Think of the chance for flesh in the little naked nestling child, irradiating divinity; of the chance for drapery in the chaste and ample garment of the mother. Think of the great story you compress into that simple theme. Think above all of the mother's face and its ineffable suggestiveness, of the mingled burden of joy and trouble, the tenderness turned to worship and the worship turned to far-seeing pity. Then look at it all in perfect line and lovely colour, breathing truth and beauty and mastery."

"*Anch' io son pittore!*" I laughed. "Unless I'm mistaken *you* have a masterpiece on the stocks. If you put all that in, you'll do more than Raphael himself did. Let me know when your picture's finished, and wherever in the wide world I may be I'll post back to Florence and pay my respects to—the *Madonna of the future!*"

His face, at this, had a flush of consciousness, and he seemed to sigh half in protest, half in resignation. "I don't often mention picture by name. I detest this modern custom of premature publicity. A great work needs silence, privacy, mystery. And then, do you know, people are so cruel, so frivolous, so unable to imagine a man's wishing to paint a Madonna at this time of day, that I've been laughed at, positively laughed at, sir!"—and his poor, guilty blush deepened. "I don't know what has prompted me to be so frank and trustful with you. You look as if you wouldn't laugh at me. My dear young man"—and he laid his hand on my arm—"I'm worthy of respect. Whatever my limitations may be, I'm honest. There's nothing grotesque in a pure ambition or in a life devoted to it."

II

There was something so admirably candid in his look and tone that further questions seemed to savour just then of indiscretion. I had repeated opportunity to put as many as I would, however, for after this we spent much time together. Daily, for a fortnight, we met under agreement that he should help me to intimacy with the little treasure-city. He knew it so well and had studied it with so pious a patience, he was so deeply versed both in its greater and its minor memories, he had become in short so fond and familiar a Florentine, that he was an ideal *valet de place* and I was glad enough to leave dryer documents at home and learn what I wanted from his lips and his example. He talked of Florence as a devoted old lover might still speak of an old incomparable mistress who remained proof against time; he liked to describe how he had lost his heart to her at first sight. "It's the fashion to make all cities of the feminine gender, but as a rule it's a monstrous mistake. Is Florence of the same sex as New York, as Chicago, as London, as Liverpool? She's the sole perfect lady of them all; one feels toward her as some sensitive aspiring youth feels to some beautiful older woman with a 'history.' She fills you with a presumptuous gallantry." This disinterested passion seemed to stand my friend instead of the common social ties; he led a lonely life and cared for nothing but his work. I was duly flattered by his having taken my uninstructed years into his favour and by his generous sacrifice of precious hours to my society. We spent them in historic streets and consecrated nooks, in churches and convents and galleries, spent them above all in study of those early paintings in which Florence is so rich, returning ever and anon, with restless sympathies, to find in these tender blossoms of art a fragrance and savour more precious than the full-fruited knowledge of the later works. We lingered often in the mortuary chapel of San Lorenzo, where we watched Michael Angelo's dim-visaged warrior sit like some awful Genius of Doubt and brood behind his eternal mask upon the mysteries of life. We stood more than once in the little convent chambers where Fra Angelico wrought as if an angel indeed had held his hand, and gathered that sense of scattered dews and early bird-notes which makes an hour among his relics resemble a morning stroll in some monkish garden. We did all this and much more—wandered into obscure shrines, damp courts, and dusty palace-rooms, in quest of lingering hints of fresco and lurking treasures of sculpture.

I was more and more impressed with my companion's remarkable singleness of purpose. Everything became a pretext for one of his high-flown excursions. Nothing could be seen or said that didn't lead him sooner or later to a glowing discourse on the true, the beautiful and the good. If my friend was not a genius, he was certainly a natural rhapsodist, or even a harmless madman; and I found the play of his temper, his humour, and his candid and unworldly character as quaint as if he had been a creature from another planet. He seemed indeed to know very little of this one, and lived and moved altogether in his boundless province of art. A creature more unsullied by the accidents of life it's impossible to conceive, and I sometimes questioned the reality of an artistic virtue, an esthetic purity, on which some profane experience hadn't rubbed off a little more. It was hard to have to accept him as of our own hard-headed stock; but after all there could be no better sign of his American star than the completeness of his reaction in favour of vague profits. The very heat of his worship was a mark of conversion; those born within sight of the temple take their opportunities more for granted. He had, moreover, all our native mistrust for intellectual discretion and our native relish for sonorous superlatives. As a critic he rather ignored proportion and degree; his recognitions had a generous publicity, his discriminations were all discoveries. The small change of appreciation seemed to him in fine no coin for a gentleman to handle; and yet with all this overflow of opinion and gesture he remained in himself a mystery. His professions were practically, somehow, all masks and screens, and his personal allusions, as to his ambiguous background, mere wavings of the dim lantern. He was modest and proud, in other words, and never spoke of his domestic matters. He was evidently poor, and yet must have had some slender independence, since he could afford to make so merry over the fact that his culture of ideal beauty had never brought him a penny, His poverty, I supposed, was his motive for neither inviting me to his lodging nor mentioning its whereabouts. We met either in some public place or at my hotel, where I entertained him as freely as I might without appearing to be prompted by charity. He appeared for the most part hungry, and this was his nearest approach to human grossness. I made a point of never seeming to cross a certain line with him, but, each time we met, I ventured to make some respectful allusion to the *magnum opus*, to inquire, if I might, as to its health and progress. "We're getting on, with the Lord's help," he would say with a bravery that never languished; "I think we can't be said not to be doing well. You see I've the grand advantage that I lose no time. These hours I spend with you are pure profit. They bring me in a harvest of incentives. Just as the truly religious soul is always at worship, the genuine artist is always in labour. He takes his property wherever he finds it—he learns some precious secret from every object that stands up in the light. If you but knew—in connexion with something to be done—of the rapture of observing and remembering, of applying one's notes. I take in at every glance some hint for light, for colour, for style. When I get home I pour out my treasures into the lap of my Madonna. Oh, I'm not idle! *Nulla dies sine linea.*"

III

I had been introduced meanwhile to an American lady whose drawing-room had long formed an attractive place of reunion for strangers of supposed distinction. She lived on a fourth floor and was not rich; but she offered her visitors very good tea, little cakes at option, and conversation not quite to match. Her conversation had mainly a high esthetic pitch, for Mrs. Coventry was famously "artistic." Her apartment was a sort of miniature Pitti Palace. She possessed "early masters" by the dozen—a cluster of Peruginos in her dining room, a Giotto in her boudoir, an Andrea del Sarto over her drawing-room chimney-piece. Surrounded by these treasures and by innumerable bronzes, mosaics, majolica dishes, and little worm-eaten diptychs covered with angular saints on gilded backgrounds, she enjoyed the dignity of a social high-priestess of the arts. She always wore on her bosom a huge, if reduced, copy of the Madonna della Seggiola. Gaining her ear quietly one evening I asked her whether she knew among our compatriots in the place of a certain eccentric but charming Mr. Theobald.

"Know him, know poor Theobald?"—her answer was as public as if I had owed it to the bell-crier. "All Florence knows him, his flamed-coloured locks, his black velvet coat, his interminable harangues on the Beautiful and his wondrous Madonna that mortal eye has never seen and that mortal patience has quite given up expecting."

"Really," I asked, "you don't believe in his wondrous Madonna?"

"My dear ingenuous youth," rejoined my shrewd friend, "has he made a convert of you? Well, we all believed in him once; he came down upon Florence—that is on our little colony here—and took the town by storm. Another Raphael, at the very least, had been born among men, and our poor dear barbarous country was to have the credit of him. Hadn't he the very hair of Raphael flowing down on his shoulders? The hair, alas—it's his difficulty—appears to have to do duty for the head! We swallowed him whole, however; we hung on his lips and proclaimed his genius from the house-tops. The women were dying to sit to him for their portraits and be made immortal like Leonardo's Gioconda. We decided that his manner was a good deal like Leonardo's—'esoteric' and indescribable and fascinating. Well, it has all remained esoteric, and nobody can describe what nobody has ever seen. The months, the years have passed and the miracle has hung fire; our master has never produced his masterpiece. He has passed hours in the galleries and churches, posturing, musing, and gazing; he has talked more about his subject—about every subject—than any human being before has ever talked about anything, but has never put brush to canvas. We had all subscribed, as it were, to the great performance; but as it never came off people began to ask for their money again. I was one of the last of the faithful; I carried devotion so far as to sit to him for my head. If you could have seen the horrible creature he made of me, you'd recognise that even a woman with no more vanity than will tie her bonnet straight must have cooled off then. The man didn't know the very alphabet of drawing. His strong point, he intimated, was his sentiment; but is it a consolation, when one has been painted a fright, to know that the man has particularly enjoyed doing it? One by one, I confess, we fell away from the faith, and Mr. Theobald didn't

lift his little finger to preserve us. At the first hint that we were tired
of waiting and that we should like the show to begin he was off in
a huff. 'Great work requires time, contemplation, privacy, mystery!
O ye of little faith!' We answered that we didn't insist on a great
work; that the five-act tragedy might come at his convenience; that
we merely asked for something to keep us from yawning, some light
little *lever de rideau*. On that the poor dear man took his stand as
a genius misconceived and persecuted, a martyr to his opinions, and
washed his hands of us from that hour! No, I believe he does me the
honour to consider me the head and front of the conspiracy formed
to nip his glory in the bud—a bud that has taken twenty years to
blossom. Ask him if he knows me, and he'll tell you I'm a horribly
ugly old woman who has vowed his destruction because he doesn't
see his way to paint her in the style of Titian's Flora. I'm afraid that
since then he has had none but chance followers, innocent strangers
like yourself, who have taken him at his word. The mountain's still
in labour; I haven't heard that the mouse has been born. I pass him
once in a while in the galleries, and he fixes his great dark eyes on
me with a sublimity of indifference, as if I were a bad copy of a
Sassoferrato! It's ever so long now since I heard that he was making
studies for a Madonna who was to be a *résumé* of all the other Madonnas of the Italian school—like that antique Venus who borrowed
a nose from one great image and an ankle from another. It's certainly
a grand idea. The parts may be fine, but when I think of my unhappy portrait I tremble for the whole. He has communicated this
trouvaille, under pledge of solemn secrecy, to fifty chosen spirits, to
every one he has ever been able to buttonhole for five minutes. I suppose he wants to get an order for it, and he's not to blame; for goodness knows how he lives. I see by your blush"—my friend freely
proceeded—"that you've been honoured with his confidence. You
needn't be ashamed, my dear young man; a man of your age is none
the worse for a certain generous credulity. Only allow me this word
of advice: keep your credulity out of your pockets! Don't pay for
the picture till it's delivered. You haven't been treated to a peep at
it, I imagine? No more have your fifty predecessors in the faith. There
are people who doubt there's any picture to be seen. I shouldn't myself be surprised if, when one runs him to earth, one finds scarce
more than in that terrible little tale of Balzac's—a mere mass of in-
coherent scratches and daubs, a jumble of dead paint!"

I listened to this bold sketch in silent wonder. It had a painfully

plausible sound, it set the seal on shy suspicions of my own. My
hostess was satirical, but was neither unveracious nor vindictive. I
determined to let my judgment wait upon events. Possibly she was
right, but if she was wrong she was cruelly wrong. Her version of
my friend's eccentricities made me impatient to see him again and
examine him in the light of public opinion. On our next meeting
I at once asked him if he knew Mrs. Coventry. He laid his hand on
my arm with a sadder, though perhaps sharper, look than had ever
yet come into his face. "Has she got *you* into training? She's a most
vain woman. She's empty and scheming, and she pretends to be
serious and kind. She prattles about Giotto's second manner and
Vittoria Colonna's liaison with 'Michael'—one would suppose Michael lived across the way and was expected in to take a hand at
whist—but she knows as little about art, and about the conditions
of production, as I know about the stock-market. She profanes sacred
things," he more vehemently went on. "She cares for you only as
someone to hand teacups in that horrible humbugging little parlor
with its trumpery Peruginos! If you can't dash off a new picture
every three days and let her hand it round among her guests, she
tells them you're a low fraud and that they must have nothing to
do with you."

This attempt of mine to test Mrs. Coventry's understanding of
our poor friend was made in the course of a late afternoon walk to
the quiet old church of San Miniato, on one of the hill-tops which
directly overlook the city, from whose gates you are guided to it by
a stony and cypress-bordered walk, the most fitting of avenues to a
shrine. No spot is more propitious to rest and thought than the broad
terrace in front of the church, where, lounging against the parapet,
you may glance in slow alternation from the black and yellow
marbles of the church-façade, seamed and cracked with time and
wind-sown with a tender flora of their own, down to the full domes
and slender towers of Florence and over to the blue sweep of the
wide-mouthed cup of mountains in whose hollow this choicest handful of the spoils of time has been stored away for keeping. I had
proposed, as a diversion from the painful memories evoked by Mrs.
Coventry's name, that Theobald should go with me the next evening
to the opera, where some work rarely played was to be given. He
declined, as I half-expected, for I had noted that he regularly kept
his evenings in reserve and never alluded to his manner of passing
them. "You've reminded me before," I put to him, "of that charm-

ing speech of the Florentine painter in Alfred de Musset's *Loren-zaccio*: '*I do no harm to any one. I pass my days in my studio. On Sunday I go to the Annunziata or to Santa Maria; the monks think I have a voice; they dress me in a white gown and a red cap, and I take a share in the choruses; sometimes I do a little solo: these are the only times I go into public. In the evening, I visit my sweetheart; when the night is fine, we pass it on her balcony.*' I don't know whether you've a sweetheart or whether she has a balcony. But if you *are* so happy it's certainly better than trying to hold out against a third-rate prima donna."

He made no immediate answer, but at last he turned to me solemnly. "Can you look upon a beautiful woman with reverent eyes?"

"Really," I said, "I don't pretend to be sheepish, but I should be sorry to think myself impudent." And I asked him what in the world he meant. When at last I had assured him that if the question was of his giving me such an exhibition I would accept it on the terms he should impose, he made known to me—with an air of religious mystery—that it was in his power to introduce me to the most beautiful woman in Italy: "A beauty with a beautiful soul."

"Upon my word," I said, "you're extremely fortunate. I'm not less so, but you do keep cards up your sleeve."

"This woman's beauty," he returned, "is a revelation, a lesson, a morality, a poem! It's my daily study." Of course after this I lost no time in reminding him of what, before we parted, had taken the shape of a promise. "I feel somehow," he had said, "as if it were a violation of that privacy in which I've always studied and admired her. Therefore what I'm doing for you—well, my friend, is friendship. No hint of her existence has ever fallen from my lips. But with too great a familiarity we're apt to lose a sense of the real value of things, and you'll perhaps throw some new light on what I show you and offer a fresher appreciation."

We went accordingly by appointment to a certain ancient house in the heart of Florence—the precinct of the Mercato Vecchio—and climbed a dark, steep staircase to its highest flight. Theobald's worshipped human type seemed hung as far above the line of common vision as his artistic ideal was lifted over the usual practice of men. He passed without knocking into the dark vestibule of a small apartment where, opening an inner door, he ushered me into a small saloon. The room affected me as mean and sombre, though I caught a glimpse of white curtains swaying gently at an open window. At a table, near a lamp, sat a woman dressed in black, working at a piece of embroidery. As my guide entered she looked up with a serene smile; then, seeing me, she made a movement of surprise and rose with stately grace. He stepped nearer, taking her hand and kissing it with an indescribable air of immemorial usage. As he bent his head she looked at me askance and had, I thought, a perfectly human change of colour.

"This is the sublime Serafina!"—Theobald frankly waved me forward. "And this is a friend and a lover of the arts," he added, introducing me. I received a smile, a curtsey, and a request to be seated.

The most beautiful woman in Italy was a person of a generous Italian type and of a great simplicity of demeanour. Seated again at her lamp with her embroidery, she seemed to have nothing whatever to say. Theobald, bending to her in a sort of Platonic ecstasy, asked her a dozen paternally tender questions about her health, her state of mind, her occupations and the progress of her needlework, which he examined minutely and summoned me to admire. It was one of the pieces of some ecclesiastical vestment—ivory satin wrought with an elaborate design of silver and gold. She made answer in a full rich voice, but with a brevity I couldn't know whether to attribute to native reserve or to the profane constraint of my presence. She had been that morning to confession; she had also been to market and had bought a chicken for dinner. She felt very happy; she had nothing to complain of except that the people for whom she was making her vestment and who furnished her materials should be willing to put such rotten silver thread into the garment, as one might say, of the Lord. From time to time, as she took her slow stitches, she raised her eyes and covered me with a glance which seemed at first to express but a placid curiosity, but in which, as I saw it repeated, I thought I perceived the dim glimmer of an attempt to establish an understanding with me at the expense of our companion. Meanwhile, as mindful as possible of Theobald's injunction of reverence, I considered the lady's personal claims to the fine compliment he had paid her.

That she was indeed a beautiful woman I recognised as soon as I had recovered from the surprise of finding her without the freshness of youth. Her appearance was of the sort which, in losing youth, loses little of its greater merit, expressed for the most part as it was in form and structure and, as Theobald would have said, in "composition." She was broad and ample, low-browed and large-eyed, dark and pale. Her thick brown hair hung low beside her cheek and ear and seemed to drape her head with a covering as chaste and formal as the veil of a nun. The poise and carriage of this head were admirably free and noble, and all the more effective that their freedom was at moments discreetly corrected by a little sanctimonious droop which harmonised admirably with the level gaze of her dark and quiet eye. A strong serene physical nature, with the placid temper which comes of no nerves and no troubles, seemed this lady's comfortable portion. She was dressed in plain dull black, save for a dark blue kerchief which was folded across her bosom and exposed a glimpse of her massive throat. Over this kerchief was suspended a little silver cross. I admired her greatly, yet with a considerable reserve. A certain mild intellectual apathy was the very mark of her complexion and form, and always seemed to round and enrich them; but this bourgeoise Egeria, if I viewed her right, betrayed rather a vulgar stagnation of mind. There might have once been a dim spiritual light in her face, but it had long since begun to wane. And furthermore, in plain prose, she was growing stout. My disappointment amounted very nearly to complete disenchantment when Theobald, as if to facilitate my covert inspection, declaring that the lamp was very dim and that she would ruin her eyes without more light, rose and addressed himself to a couple of candles on the mantelpiece, which he lighted and transferred to the table. In this improved clearness I made our hostess out a very mature person. She was neither haggard nor worn nor grey, but she was thick and coarse. The beautiful soul my friend had promised me seemed scarce worth making such a point of; it dwelt in no deeper principle than some accident of quietude, some matronly mildness of lip and brow. I should have been ready even to pronounce her sanctified bend of the head nothing more inward than the trick of a person always working at embroidery. It might have been even a slightly more sinister symptom, for in spite of her apparently admirable dullness this object of our all-candid homage practically dropped a hint that she took the situation rather less seriously than her friend. When he rose to light the candles she looked across at me with a quick intelligent smile and tapped her forehead with her forefinger; then, as from a sudden feeling of compassionate loyalty to poor Theobald I preserved a blank face, she gave a little shrug and resumed her work.

What was the relation of this singular couple? Was he the most ardent of friends or the most discreet of lovers? Did she regard him as an eccentric swain whose benevolent admiration of her beauty — she was not ill-pleased to humour at the small cost of having him climb into her little parlour and gossip of summer nights? With her decent and sombre dress, her simple gravity and that fine piece of priestly stitching, she looked like some pious lay-member of a sister-hood living by special permission outside her convent walls. Or was she maintained here aloft by her admirer in comfortable leisure, so that he might have before him the perfect eternal type, uncorrupted and untarnished by the struggle for existence? Her shapely hands, I observed, were very fair and white; they lacked the traces of what is called honest toil.

"And the pictures, how do they come on?" she asked of Theobald after a long pause.

"Oh, in their own fine, quiet way! I've here a friend whose sym-pathy and encouragement give me new faith and ardour."

Our hostess turned to me, gazed at me a moment rather in-scrutably, and then, repeating the vivid reference to the contents of our poor friend's head she had used a minute before, "He has a magnificent genius!" she said with perfect gravity.

"I'm inclined to think so"—I was amused in spite of myself.

"Eh, why do you smile?" she cried. "If you doubt what I say, you must see the *santo bambino!*" And she took the lamp and conducted me to the other side of the room, where, on the wall, in a plain black frame, hung a large drawing in red chalk. Beneath it was attached a little bowl for holy-water. The drawing represented a very young child, entirely naked, half-nestling back against his mother's gown, but with his two little arms outstretched as in the act of benediction. It had been thrown off with singular freedom and directness, but was none the less vivid with the sacred bloom of infancy. A dimpled elegance and grace, which yet didn't weaken its expression, recalled the touch of Correggio. "That's what he can do!" said my hostess. "It's the blessed little boy I lost. It's his very image, and the Signor Teobaldo, a generous person if there ever was one, gave it me as a gift. He has given me many things besides!"

I looked at the picture for some time—certainly it had a charm. Turning back to our friend I assured him that if it were hung amid the drawings in the Uffizi and labelled with a glorious name it would bravely hold its own. My praise seemed to give him joy; he pressed my hands—his eyes filled with tears. I had apparently quickened his desire to expatiate on the history of the drawing, for he rose and took leave of our companion, kissing her hand with the same mild ardour as before. It occurred to me that the offer of a similar piece of gallantry on my own part might help me to know what manner of woman she was. When she felt my intention she withdrew her hand, dropped her eyes solemnly, and made me a severe curtsey. Theobald took my arm and led me rapidly into the street.

"And what do you think of the sublime Serafina?" he cried with anxiety.

"She's certainly a fine figure of a woman," I answered without ceremony.

He eyed me an instant askance and then seemed hurried along by the current of remembrance. "You should have seen the mother and the child together, seen them as I first saw them—the mother with her head draped in a shawl, a divine trouble in her face and the bambino pressed to her bosom. You'd have said, I'm sure, that Raphael had found his match in common chance. I was coming back one summer night from a long walk in the country when I met this apparition at the city gate. The woman held out her hand and I hardly knew whether to say 'What do you want?' or to fall down and worship. She asked for a little money and received what I gave her with the holy sweetness with which the Santissima Vergine receives the offerings of the faithful. I saw she was beautiful and pale—she might have stepped out of the stable of Bethlehem! I gave her money and helped her on her way into the town. I had guessed her story. She too was a maiden mother, but she had been turned out into the world in her shame. I felt in all my pulses that here was my subject marvellously realised. It was as if I had had like one of the monkish artists of old a miraculous vision. I rescued the poor creatures, cherished them, watched them as I would have done some precious work of art, some lovely fragment of fresco discovered in a mouldering cloister. In a month—as if to deepen and sanctify the sadness and sweetness of it all—the poor little child died. When she felt he was going she lifted him up to me for ten minutes—so as not to lose him *all*—and I made that sketch. You saw a feverish haste in it, I suppose; I wanted to spare the poor little mortal the pain of his position. After that I doubly valued the mother. She's the simplest, sweetest, most natural creature that ever bloomed in this brave old land of Italy. She lives in the memory of her child, in her gratitude for the scanty kindness I've been able to show her, and in her simple instinctive imperturbable piety. She's not even conscious of her beauty; my admiration has never made her vain. Heaven yet knows that I've made no secret what I think of it. You must have taken in the extraordinary clearness and modesty of her look. Was there ever such a truly virginal brow, such a natural classic elegance in the wave of the hair and the arch of the forehead? I've studied her; I may say I know her. I've absorbed her little by little, I've made her my own, my mind's stamped and imbued, and I've determined now to clinch the — impression. I shall at last invite her to sit for me!"

" 'At last—at last'?" I repeated in amazement. "Do you mean she has never done so yet?"

"I've not really—since that first time—made her *pose*," he said with a shade of awkwardness. "I've taken notes, you know; I've got my grand fundamental impression. That's the great thing! But I've not actually put her to the inconvenience—so to call it—to which I'd have put a common model."

What had become for the moment of my perception and my tact I'm at a loss to say; in their absence I was unable to repress a headlong exclamation. I was destined to regret it. We had stopped at a turning and beneath a lamp. "My poor friend," I exclaimed, laying my hand on his shoulder, "you've *dawdled!* She's an old, old woman —for a maiden mother."

It was as if I had brutally struck him; I shall never forget the long slow almost ghastly look of pain with which he answered me. "Dawdled?—old, old?" he stammered. "Are you joking?"

"Why, my dear fellow, I suppose you don't take her for anything *but* mature?"

He drew a long breath and leaned against a house, looked at me with questioning, protesting, reproachful eyes. At last starting forward and grasping my arm: "Answer me solemnly: does she seem to you really and truly old? Is she wrinkled, is she faded—am I blind?" he demanded.

Then at last I understood the immensity of his illusion; how, one by one, the noiseless years had ebbed away and left him brooding in charmed inaction, for ever preparing for a work for ever deferred. It struck me almost as a kindness now to tell him the plain truth. "I should be sorry to say you're blind," I returned, "but I think you're rather unfortunately deceived. You've lost time in effortless contemplation. Your friend was once young and fresh and virginal; but you see that must have been some years ago. Still, she has fine things left. By all means make her sit for you." But I broke down; his face was too horribly reproachful.

He took off his hat and stood passing his handkerchief mechanically over his forehead. " 'Fine things left'?" he stared. "Do you speak as if other people had helped themselves—?"

"Why, my dear man," I smiled, "the years have helped themselves! But she has what the French call—don't they?—*de beaux restes?*"

Oh, how he gaped and how something seemed to roll over him! "I must make my Madonna out of *de beaux restes!* What a masterpiece she'll be! Old—old! Old—old!" he re-echoed.

"Never mind her age," I cried, revolted by what I had done; "never mind my impression of her! You have your memory, your notes, your genius. Finish your picture in a month. I pronounce it beforehand a masterpiece and hereby offer you for it any sum you may choose to ask."

He kept staring, but seemed scarce to understand me. "Old—old!" he kept stupidly repeating. "If she's old what am I? If her beauty has faded where, where is my strength? Has life been a dream? Have I worshipped too long? Have I loved too well?" The charm in truth was broken. That the chord of illusion should have snapped at my light accidental touch showed how it had been weakened by excessive tension. The poor fellow's sense of wasted time, of vanished opportunity, surged in upon his soul in waves of darkness. He suddenly dropped his head and burst into tears.

I led him homeward with all possible tenderness, but I attempted neither to check his grief, to restore his equanimity nor to unsay the hard truth. When we reached my hotel I tried to induce him to come in. "We'll drink a glass of wine," I smiled, "to the completion of the Madonna."

With a violent effort he held up his head, mused for a moment with a formidably sombre frown and then, giving me his hand, "I'll finish it," he vowed, "in a month! No, no, in a fortnight! After all I have it *here!*" And he smote his forehead. "Of course she's old! She can afford to have it said of her—a woman who has made twenty years pass like a twelvemonth! Old—old! Why, sir, she shall be eternal!"

I wished to see him safely to his own door, but he waved me back and walked away with an air of resolution, whistling and swinging his cane. I waited a moment—then followed him at a distance and saw him proceed to cross the Santa Trinità Bridge. When he reached the middle he suddenly paused, as if his strength had deserted him, and leaned upon the parapet gazing over into the Arno. I was careful to keep him in sight; I confess I passed ten very nervous minutes. He recovered himself at last and went his way slowly and with hanging head.

That I had really startled him into a bolder use of his long-garnered stores of knowledge and taste, into the vulgar effort and hazard of production, seemed at first reason enough for his continued silence and absence; but as day followed day without his either calling or sending me a line and without my meeting him in his customary haunts, in the galleries, in the chapel at San Lorenzo, or even strolling between the Arno-side and the great hedge-screen of verdure — which, along the drive of the Cascine, throws the fair occupants of the open carriages into such becoming relief—as for more than a week I got neither tidings nor sight of him, I began to fear I might have fatally offended him and that instead of giving a wholesome push to his talent, or at least to his faith, I had done it a real harm. I had a wretched suspicion I might have made him ill. My stay at Florence was drawing to a close, and it was important that before resuming my journey I should assure myself of the truth. Theobald had to the last kept his lodging a secret, and I was at a loss how to follow him up. The simplest course was to make inquiry of the object of his homage who neighboured with the Mercato Vecchio, and I confess that unsatisfied curiosity as to the lady herself counselled it as well. Perhaps I had done her injustice, perhaps she was as immortally fresh and fair as he conceived her. I was at any rate anxious to set eyes once more on the ripe enchantress who had made twenty years, as he had said, pass like a twelvemonth. I repaired accordingly one morning to her abode, climbed the interminable staircase, and reached her door. It stood ajar, and, while I hesitated to enter, a little serving-maid came clattering out with an empty cooking-pot, as if she had just performed some savoury errand. The inner door too was open; so I crossed the little vestibule and reached the room in which I had formerly been received. It hadn't its evening aspect. The table, or one end of it, was spread for a late breakfast, before which sat a gentleman—an individual at least of the male sex—doing execution upon a beefsteak and onions and a bottle of wine. At his elbow, in intimate nearness, was placed the lady of the house. Her attitude, as I arrived, was not that of an enchantress. With one hand she held in her lap a plate of smoking maccaroni; with the other she had lifted high in air one of the pendulous filaments of this succulent compound and was in the act of slipping it gently down her throat. On the uncovered end of the table, facing her companion, were ranged half-a-dozen small statuettes, of some snuff-coloured substance resembling terra-cotta. He, brandishing his knife with ardour, was apparently descanting on their merits.

Evidently I darkened the door. My hostess dropped her maccaroni —into her mouth, and rose hastily with a harsh exclamation and a flushed face. I forthwith felt sure that the sublime Serafina's secret was still better worth knowing than I had supposed, and that the way to learn it was to take it for granted. I summoned my best Italian, I smiled and bowed and apologised for my intrusion; and in a moment, whether or no I had dispelled the lady's irritation, I had at least made her prudent. I must put myself at my ease; I must take a seat. This was another friend of hers—also an artist, she declared with a smile that had turned to the gracious. Her companion wiped his moustache and bowed with great civility. I saw at a glance that he was equal to the situation. He was presumably the author of the statuettes on the table and knew a money-spending *forestiere* when he saw one. He was a small active man, with a clever, impudent tossed-up nose, a sharp little black eye, conscious of many things at once, and the cocked-up moustache of a trooper. On the side of his head he wore jauntily one of the loose velvet caps affected by sculptors in damp studios, and I observed that his feet were encased in bright "worked" slippers. On Serafina's remarking with dignity that I was the friend of Mr. Theobald he broke out into the fantastic French of which Italians are sometimes so insistently lavish, declaring without reserve that Mr. Theobald was a magnificent genius.

"I am sure I don't know," I answered with a shrug. "If you're in a position to affirm it you've the advantage of me. I've seen nothing from his hand but the bambino yonder, which certainly is fine."

He had it that the bambino was a masterpiece—in the maniera Correggiesca. It was only a pity, he added with a knowing laugh, that the sketch hadn't been made on some good bit of honeycombed old panel. The sublime Serafina hereupon protested that Mr. Theobald was the soul of honour and didn't lend himself to that style of manufacture. "I'm not a judge of genius," she said, "and I know nothing of pictures. I'm a poor, simple widow; but I'm sure *nostro signore* has the heart of an angel and the virtue of a saint. He's my great benefactor," she made no secret of it. The after-glow of the somewhat sinister flush with which she had greeted me still lingered in her cheek and perhaps didn't favour her beauty; I couldn't but judge it a wise custom of Theobald's to visit her only by candle-light. She was coarse and her poor adorer a poet.

"I've the greatest esteem for him," I stated; "it's for that reason I've been so uneasy at not seeing him for ten days. Have you seen him? Is he perhaps ill?"

"Ill? Heaven forbid!" cried Serafina with genuine vehemence.

Her companion uttered a rapid expletive and reproached her with not having been to see him. She hesitated a moment, then simpered the least bit and bridled. "He comes to see me—without reproach! But it wouldn't be the same for me to go to him, though indeed you may almost call him a man of holy life."

"He has the greatest admiration for you," I said. "He'd have been honoured by your visit."

She looked at me a moment sharply. "More admiration than you. Admit that!" Of course I protested with all the eloquence at my command, and my ambiguous hostess then confessed that she had taken no fancy to me on my former visit and that, our friend not having returned, she believed I had poisoned his mind against her. "It would be no kindness to the poor gentleman, I can tell you that," she said. "He has come to see me every evening for years. It's a long friendship! No one knows him as I do."

"I don't pretend to know him or to understand him. I can only esteem and—I think I may say—love him. Nevertheless he seems to me 'a little—!" And I touched my forehead and waved my hand in the air.

Serafina glanced at her companion as for inspiration. He contented himself with shrugging his shoulders while he filled his glass again. The padrona hereupon treated me to a look of more meaning than quite consorted with her noble blankness. "Ah, but it's for that that *I* love him! The world has so little kindness for such persons. It laughs at them and despises them and cheats them. He's too good for this wicked life. It's his blest imagination that he finds a little Paradise up here in my poor apartment. If he thinks so, how can I help it? He has a strange belief—really I ought to be ashamed to tell you—that I resemble the Madonna Santissima, heaven forgive me! I let him think what he pleases so long as it makes him happy. He was very kind to me once and I'm not one who forgets a favour. So I receive him every evening civilly, and ask after his health, and let him look at me on this side and that. For that matter, I may say it without vanity, I was worth looking at once. And he's not always amusing, *poveretto!* He sits sometimes for an hour without speaking a word, or else he talks away, without stopping, about art and nature and beauty and duty, about fifty fine things that are all so much Latin to me. I beg you to understand that he has never said a word to me I mightn't honourably listen to. He may be a little cracked, but he's one of the blessed saints."

"Eh, eh," cried the man, "the blessed saints were all a little cracked!"

Serafina, I surmised, left part of her story untold; what she said sufficed to make poor Theobald's own statement still more affecting than I had already found its strained simplicity. "It's a strange fortune, certainly," she went on, "to have such a friend as this dear man—a friend who's less than a lover, yet more than a brother." I glanced at her comrade, who continued to smirk in a mystifying manner while he twisted the ends of his moustache between his copious mouthfuls. Was *he* less than a lover? "But what will you have?" Serafina pursued. "In this hard world one mustn't ask too many questions; one must take what comes and keep what one gets. I've kept my *amoroso* for twenty years, and I do hope that, at this time of day, signore, you've not come to turn him against me!"

I assured her I had no such intention, and that I should vastly regret disturbing Mr. Theobald's habits or convictions. On the contrary I was alarmed about him and would at once go in search of him. She gave me his address and a florid account of her sufferings at his non-appearance. She had not been to him for various reasons; chiefly because she was afraid of displeasing him, as he had always made such a mystery of his home. "You might have sent this gentleman!" I however ventured to suggest.

"Ah," cried the gentleman, "he admires Madonna Serafina, but he wouldn't admire me whom he doesn't take for Saint Joseph!" And then confidentially, his finger on his nose: "His taste's terribly severe!"

I was about to withdraw after having promised that I would inform our hostess of my friend's condition, when her companion, who had risen from table and girded his loins apparently for the onset, grasped me gently by the arm and led me before the row of statuettes. "I perceive by your conversation, signore, that you're a patron of the arts. Allow me to request your honourable attention for these modest products of my own ingenuity. They are brand-new, fresh from my atelier, and have never been exhibited in public. I have brought them here to receive the verdict of this dear lady, who's a good critic, for all she may pretend to the contrary. I'm the inventor of this peculiar style of statuette—of subject, manner, material, everything. Touch them, I pray you; handle them freely—you needn't fear. Delicate as they look, it's impossible they should break! My various creations have met with great success. They're especially admired by the American *conoscenti*. I've sent them all over Europe—to London, Paris, Vienna! You may have noticed some little specimens in Paris, on the *grand boulevard*"—he aimed at the French sound of the words—"in a shop of which they constitute the specialty. There's always a crowd about the window. They form a very pleasing ornament for the mantel-shelf of a gay young bachelor, for the boudoir of a pretty woman. You couldn't make a prettier present to a person with whom you should wish to exchange a harmless joke. It's not classic art, signore, of course; but, between ourselves, isn't classic art sometimes rather a bore? Caricature, burlesque, *la charge,* has hitherto been confined to paper, to the pen and pencil. Now it has been my inspiration to introduce it into statuary. For this purpose I've invented a peculiar plastic compound which you will permit me not to divulge. That's my secret, signore! It's as light, you perceive, as cork, and yet firm as alabaster! I frankly confess that I really pride myself as much on this little stroke of chemical ingenuity as upon the other element of novelty in my creations—my types. What do you say to my types, signore? The idea's bold; does it strike you as happy? Cats and monkeys—monkeys and cats—all human life is there! Human life, of course I mean, viewed with the eye of the satirist! To combine sculpture and satire, signore, has been my unprecedented ambition. I flatter myself I've not egregiously failed."—

As this jaunty Juvenal of the chimney-piece thus persuasively proceeded he took up his little groups successively from the table, held them aloft, turned them about, rapped them with his knuckles and gazed at them lovingly, his head on one side. They consisted each, with a vengeance, of a cat and a monkey, occasionally draped, in some preposterously sentimental conjunction. They exhibited a certain sameness of motive and illustrated chiefly the different phases of what, in fine terms, might have been called the amorous advance and the amorous alarm; but they were strikingly clever and expressive, and were at once very dreadful little beasts and very natural

men and women. I confess, however, that they failed to amuse me.
I was doubtless not in a mood to enjoy them, for they seemed to me
peculiarly cynical and vulgar. Their imitative felicity was revolting.
As I looked askance at the complacent little artist, brandishing them
between finger and thumb and caressing them with the fondest eye,
he struck me as himself little more than an exceptionally intelligent
ape. I mustered an admiring grin, however, and he blew another
blast. "My figures are studied from life! I've a little menagerie of
monkeys whose frolics I follow by the hour. As for the cats, one has
only to look out of one's back window! Since I've begun to examine
these expressive little brutes I've made many profound observations.
Speaking, signore, to a man of imagination, I may say that my little
designs are not without a philosophy of their own. Truly, I don't
know whether the cats and monkeys imitate us, or whether it's we
who imitate them." I congratulated him on his philosophy, and he
resumed: "You'll do me the honour to admit that I've handled my
subjects with delicacy. Eh, it was needed, *signore mio*. I've been just
a bit free, but not too free—eh, *dica*? Just a scrap of a hint, you
know! You may see as much or as little as you please. These little
groups, however, are no measure of my invention. If you'll favour
me with a call at my studio I think you'll admit that my combinations are really infinite. I likewise execute figures to command.
You've perhaps some little motive—the fruit of your philosophy of
life, signore—which you'd like to have interpreted. I can promise to
work it up to your satisfaction; it shall have as many high lights and
sharp accents as you please! Allow me to present you with my card
and to remind you that my prices are moderate. Only sixty francs
for a little group like that. My statuettes are as durable as bronze—
aere perennius, signore—and, between ourselves, I think they're
more amusing!"

As I pocketed his card I turned an eye on Madonna Serafina, wondering whether she had a sense for contrasts. She had picked up one
of the little couples and was tenderly dusting it with a feather broom.

What I had just seen and heard had so deepened my compassionate
interest in my deluded friend that I took a summary leave, making
my way directly to the house designated by this remarkable woman.
It was in an obscure corner of the opposite side of the town and
presented a sombre and squalid appearance. A withered crone, in
the doorway, on my inquiring for Theobald, welcomed me with a
mumbled blessing and an expression of relief at the poor gentleman's

having at last a caller. His lodging appeared to consist of a single room at the top of the house. On getting no answer to my knock I opened the door, supposing him absent; so that it gave me a certain shock to find him but seated helpless and dumb. His chair was near the single window, facing an easel which supported a large canvas. On my entering he looked up at me blankly, without changing his position, which was that of absolute lassitude and dejection, his arms loosely folded, his legs stretched before him, his head hanging on his breast. Advancing into the room I saw how vividly his face answered to his attitude. He was pale, haggard, and unshaven, and his dull and sunken eye gazed at me without a spark of recognition. My fear had been that he would greet me with fierce reproaches, as the cruelly officious patron who had turned his contentment to bitterness, and I was relieved to find my appearance excite no visible resentment. "Don't you know me?"—I put out my hand. "Have you already forgotten me?"

He made no response, but kept his position stupidly and left me staring about the room. It spoke, the poor place, all plaintively for itself. Shabby, sordid, naked, it contained, beyond the wretched bed, but the scantiest provision for personal comfort. It was bedroom at once and studio—a grim ghost of a studio. A few dusty casts and prints on the walls, three or four old canvases turned face inward and a rusty-looking colour-box formed, with the easel at the window, the sum of its appurtenances. The whole scene savoured horribly of indigence. Its only wealth was the picture on the easel, presumably the famous Madonna. Averted as this was from the door I was unable to see its face; but at last, sickened by my impression of vacant misery, I passed behind Theobald eagerly and tenderly. I can scarcely say I was surprised at what I found—a canvas that was a mere dead blank cracked and discoloured by time. This was his immortal work! Though not surprised, I confess I was powerfully moved, and I think that for five minutes I couldn't have trusted myself to speak. At last my silent nearness affected him; he stirred and turned and then rose, looking at me with a slow return of intelligence. I murmured some kind ineffective nothings about his being ill and needing advice and care, but he seemed absorbed in the effort to recall distinctly what had last passed between us. "You were right," he said with a pitiful smile, "I'm a dawdler! I'm a failure! I shall do nothing more in this world. You opened my eyes, and though the truth is bitter I bear you no grudge. Amen! I've been sitting here for a week face to face with it, the terrible truth, face to face with the past, with my weakness and poverty and nullity. I shall never touch a brush! I believe I've neither eaten nor slept. Look at that canvas!" he went on as I relieved my emotion by an urgent request that he would come home with me and dine. "That was to have contained my masterpiece! Isn't it a promising foundation? The elements of it are all *here*." And he tapped his forehead with that mystic confidence which had so often marked the gesture for me before. "If I could only transpose them into some brain that has the hand, the will! Since I've been sitting here taking stock of my intellects, I've come to believe that I've the material for a hundred masterpieces. But my hand's paralysed now and they'll never be painted. I never began! I waited and waited to be worthier to begin—I wasted my life in preparation. While I fancied my creation was growing it was only dying. I've taken the whole business too hard. Michael Angelo didn't when he went at the Lorenzo. He did his best at a venture, and his venture's immortal. *That's* mine!" And he pointed with a gesture I shall never forget at the empty canvas. "I suppose we're a genus by ourselves in the providential scheme—we talents that can't act, that can't do nor dare! We take it out in talk, in study, in plans and promises, in visions! But our visions, let me tell you," he cried with a toss of his head, "have a way of being brilliant, and a man has not lived in vain who has seen the things *I've* seen. Of course you won't believe in them when that bit of worm-eaten cloth is all I have to show for them; but to convince you, to enchant and astound the world, I need only the hand of Raphael. His brain I already have. A pity, you'll say, that I haven't his modesty! Ah, let me boast and babble now—it's all I have left! I'm the half of a genius! Where in the wide world is my other half? Lodged perhaps in the vulgar soul, the cunning ready fingers of some dull copyist or some trivial artisan who turns out by the dozen his easy prodigies of touch! But it's not for me to sneer at him; he at least does something. He's not a dawdler. Well for me if I had been vulgar and clever and reckless, if I could have shut my eyes and taken my leap."

What to say to the poor fellow, what to do for him, seemed hard to determine; I chiefly felt I must break the spell of his present in-action and draw him out of the haunted air of the little room it was such cruel irony to call a studio. I can't say I persuaded him to come forth with me; he simply suffered himself to be led, and when we began to walk in the warm light of day I was able to appreciate his great weakness. Nevertheless he seemed in a manner to revive; he even murmured to me at last that he should like to go to the Pitti Gallery. I shall never forget our melancholy stroll through those gorgeous halls, every picture on whose walls glowed, to my stricken sight, with an insolent renewal of strength and lustre. The eyes and lips of the great portraits reflected for me a pitying scorn of the dejected pretender who had dreamed of competing with their triumphant authors. The celestial candour even of the Madonna of the Chair, as we paused in perfect silence before her, broke into the strange smile of the women of Leonardo. Perfect silence indeed marked our whole progress—the silence of a deep farewell; for I felt in all my pulses, as Theobald, leaning on my arm, dragged one heavy foot after the other, that he was looking his last. When we came out he was so exhausted that instead of taking him to my hotel to dine I called a cab and drove him straight to his own poor lodging. He had sunk into the deepest lethargy; he lay back in the vehicle with his eyes closed, as pale as death, his faint breathing interrupted at intervals by a gasp like a smothered sob or a vain attempt to speak. With the help of the old woman who had admitted me before and who emerged from a dark back court I contrived to lead him up the long, steep staircase and lay him on his wretched bed. To her I gave him in charge while I prepared in all haste to call a doctor. But she followed me out of the room with a pitiful clasping of her hands.

"Poor dear blessed gentleman," she wailed—"is he dying?"

"Possibly. How long has he been so bad?"

"Since a certain night he passed ten days ago. I came up in the morning to make his poor bed, and found him sitting up in his clothes before that great dirty canvas he keeps there. Poor dear strange man, he says his prayers to it! He hadn't been to bed—nor even since then, as you may say. What has happened to him? Has he found out about *quella cattiva donna?*" she panted with a glittering eye and a toothless grin.

"Prove at least that one old woman can be faithful," I said, "and watch him well till I come back." My return was delayed through the absence of the English physician, who was away on a round of visits and whom I vainly pursued from house to house before I overtook him. I brought him to Theobald's bedside none too soon. A violent fever had seized our patient, whose case was evidently grave. A couple of hours later on I knew he had brain-fever. From this moment I was with him constantly, but I am far from wishing fully to report his illness. Excessively painful to witness, it was happily brief. Life burned out in delirium. One night in particular that I passed at his pillow, listening to his wild snatches of regret, of aspiration, of rapture and awe at the phantasmal pictures with which his brain seemed to swarm, comes back to my memory now like some stray page from a lost masterpiece of tragedy. Before a week was over we had buried him in the little Protestant cemetery on the way to Fiesole. Madonna Serafina, whom I had caused to be informed of his state, had come in person, I was told, to inquire about its progress; but she was absent from his funeral, which was attended but by a scanty concourse of mourners. Half-a-dozen old Florentine sojourners, in spite of the prolonged estrangement that had preceded his death, had felt the kindly impulse to honour his grave. Among them was my friend Mrs. Coventry, whom I found, on my departure, waiting in her carriage at the gate of the cemetery.

"Well," she said, relieving at last with a significant smile the solemnity of our immediate greeting, "and the greatest of all Madonnas? Have you seen her after all?"

"I've seen her," I said; "she's mine—by bequest. But I shall never show her to you."

"And why not, pray?"

"Because you wouldn't understand her!"

She rather glared at me. "Upon my word you're polite!"

"Pardon me—I'm sad and vexed and bitter." And with reprehensible rudeness I marched away. I was impatient to leave Florence; my friend's blighted spirit met my eyes in all aspects. I had packed my trunk to start for Rome that night, and meanwhile, to beguile my unrest, I aimlessly paced the streets. Chance led me at last to the church of San Lorenzo. Remembering poor Theobald's phrase about Michael Angelo—"He did his best at a venture"—I went in and turned my steps to the chapel of the tombs. Viewing in sadness the sadness of its immortal treasures, I could say to myself while I stood there that they needed no ampler commentary than those simple words. As I passed through the church again to leave it, a woman, turning away from one of the side-altars, met me face to face. The black shawl depending from her head draped becomingly the handsome face of Madonna Serafina. She stopped as she recognised me, and I saw she wished to speak. Her brow was lighted and her ample bosom heaved in a way that seemed to portend a certain sharpness of reproach. But some expression of my own then drew the sting from her resentment, and she addressed me in a tone in which bitterness was tempered by an acceptance of anticlimax that had been after all so long and so wondrously postponed. "I know it was you, now, who separated us," she said. "It was a pity he ever brought you to see me! Of course, you couldn't think of me as he did. Well, the Lord gave him, the Lord has taken him. I've just paid for a nine days' mass for his soul. And I can tell you this, signore—I never deceived him. Who put it into his head that I was made to live on holy thoughts and fine phrases? It was his own imagination, and it pleased him to think so. Did he suffer much?" she added more softly and after a pause.

"His sufferings were great, but they were short."

"And did he speak of me?" She had hesitated and dropped her eyes; she raised them with her question, and revealed in their sombre stillness a gleam of feminine confidence which for the moment revived and enhanced her beauty. Poor Theobald! Whatever name he had given his passion it was still her fine eyes that had charmed him.

"Be contented, madam," I answered gravely.

She lowered her lids again and was silent. Then exhaling a full rich sigh as she gathered her shawl together: "He was a magnificent genius!"

I bowed assent and we separated.

Passing through a narrow side street on my way back to my hotel, I noted above a doorway a sign that it seemed to me I had read before. I suddenly remembered it for identical with the superscription of a card that I had carried for an hour in my waistcoat-pocket. On the threshold stood the ingenious artist whose claims to public favour were thus distinctly signalised, smoking a pipe in the evening air and giving the finishing polish with a bit of rag to one of his inimitable "combinations." I caught the expressive curl of a couple of tails. He recognized me, removed his little red cap with an obsequious bow, and motioned me to enter his studio. I returned his salute and passed on, vexed with the apparition. For a week afterwards, whenever I was seized among the ruins of triumphant Rome with some peculiarly poignant memory of Theobald's transcendent illusions and deplorable failure, I seemed to catch the other so impertinent and so cynical echo: "Cats and monkeys, monkeys and cats—all human life is there!"

The Author of Beltraffio

*M*UCH as I wished to see him I had kept my letter of introduction three weeks in my pocket-book. I was nervous and timid about meeting him—conscious of youth and ignorance, convinced that he was tormentēd by strangers, and especially by my country-people, and not exempt from the suspicion that he had the irritability as well as the dignity of genius. Moreover, the pleasure, if it should occur—for I could scarcely believe it was near at hand—would be so great that I wished to think of it in advance, to feel it there against my breast, not to mix it with satisfactions more superficial and usual. In the little game of new sensations that I was playing with my ingenuous mind I wished to keep my visit to the author of "Beltraffio" as a trump-card. It was three years after the publication of that fascinating work, which I had read over five times and which now, with my riper judgement, I admire on the whole as much as ever. This will give you about the date of my first visit—of any duration—to England; for you will not have forgotten the commotion, I may even say the scandal, produced by Mark Ambient's masterpiece. It was the most complete presentation that had yet been made of the gospel of art; it was a kind of esthetic war-cry. People had endeavoured to sail nearer to "truth" in the cut of their sleeves and the shape of their sideboards; but there had not as yet been, among English novels, such an example of beauty of execution and "intimate" importance of theme. Nothing had been done in that line from the point of view of art for art. That served me as a fond formula, I may mention, when I was twenty-five; how much it still serves I won't take upon myself to say—especially as the discerning reader will be able to judge for himself. I had been in England, briefly, a twelve-month before the time to which I began by alluding, and had then learned that Mr. Ambient was in distant lands—was making a considerable tour in the East; so that there was nothing to do but to keep my letter till I should be in London again. It was of little use to me to hear that his wife had not left England and was, with her little boy, their only child, spending the period of her husband's absence—a good many months—at a small place they had down in Surrey. They had a house in London, but actually in the occupation of other persons. All this I had picked up, and also that Mrs. Ambient was charming—my friend the American poet, from whom I had my introduction, had never seen her, his relations with the great man confined to the exchange of letters; but she wasn't, after all, though she had lived so near the rose, the author of "Beltraffio," and I didn't go down into Surrey to call on her. I went to the Continent, spent the following winter in Italy and returned to London in May. My visit to Italy had opened my eyes to a good many things, but to nothing more than the beauty of certain pages in the works of Mark Ambient. I carried his productions about in my trunk—they are not, as you know, very numerous, but he had preluded to "Beltraffio" by some exquisite things—and I used to read them over in the evening at the inn. I used profoundly to reason that the man who drew those characters and wrote that style understood what he saw and knew what he was doing. This is my sole ground for mentioning my winter in Italy. He had been there much in former years—he was saturated with what painters call the "feeling" of that classic land. He expressed the charm of the old hill-cities of Tuscany, the look of certain lonely grass-grown places which, in the past, had echoed with life; he understood the great artists, he understood the spirit of the Renaissance; he understood everything. The scene of one of his earlier novels was laid in Rome, the scene of another in Florence, and I had moved through these cities in company with the figures he set so firmly on their feet. This is why I was now so much happier even than before in the prospect of making his acquaintance.

At last, when I had dallied with my privilege long enough, I dispatched to him the missive of the American poet. He had already gone out of town; he shrank from the rigour of the London "season," and it was his habit to migrate on the first of June. Moreover I had heard he was this year hard at work on a new book, into which some of his impressions of the East were to be wrought, so that he desired nothing so much as quiet days. That knowledge, however, didn't prevent me—*cet âge est sans pitié*—from sending with my friend's letter a note of my own, in which I asked his leave to come down and see him for an hour or two on some day to be named by himself. My proposal was accompanied with a very frank expression of my sentiments, and the effect of the entire appeal was to elicit from the great man the kindest possible invitation. He would be delighted to see me, especially if I should turn up on the following Saturday and would remain till the Monday morning. We would take a walk over the Surrey commons, and I could tell him all about the other great man, the one in America. He indicated to me the best train, and it may be imagined whether on the Saturday afternoon I was punctual at Waterloo. He carried his benevolence to the point of coming to meet me at the little station at which I was to alight, and my heart beat very fast as I saw his handsome face, surmounted with a soft wide-awake and which I knew by a photograph long since enshrined on my mantel-shelf, scanning the carriage-windows as the train rolled up. He recognised me as infallibly as I had recognised himself; he appeared to know by instinct how a young American of critical pretensions, rash youth, would look when much divided between eagerness and modesty. He took me by the hand and smiled at me and said: "You must be—a—*you*, I think!" and asked if I should mind going on foot to his house, which would take but a few minutes. I remember feeling it a piece of extraordinary affability that he should give directions about the conveyance of my bag; I remember feeling altogether very happy and rosy, in fact quite transported, when he laid his hand on my shoulder as we came out of the station.

I surveyed him, askance, as we walked together; I had already, I had indeed instantly, seen him as all delightful. His face is so well known that I needn't describe it; he looked to me at once an English gentleman and a man of genius, and I thought that a happy combination. There was a brush of the Bohemian in his fineness; you would easily have guessed his belonging to the artist guild. He was addicted to velvet jackets, to cigarettes, to loose shirt-collars, to looking a little dishevelled. His features, which were firm but not perfectly regular, are fairly enough represented in his portraits; but no portrait I have seen gives any idea of his expression. There were innumerable things in it, and they chased each other in and out of his face. I have seen people who were grave and gay in quick alternation; but Mark Ambient was grave and gay at one and the same moment. There were other strange oppositions and contradictions in his slightly faded and fatigued countenance. He affected me somehow as at once fresh and stale, at once anxious and indifferent. He had evidently had an active past, which inspired one with curiosity;

yet what was that compared to his obvious future? He was just
enough above middle height to be spoken of as tall, and rather lean
and long in the flank. He had the friendliest frankest manner possible, and yet I could see it cost him something. It cost him small
spasms of the self-consciousness that is an Englishman's last and dearest treasure—the thing he pays his way through life by sacrificing
small pieces of even as the gallant but moneyless adventurer in
"Quentin Durward" broke off links of his brave gold chain. He had
been thirty-eight years old at the time "Beltraffio" was published.
He asked me about his friend in America, about the length of my
stay in England, about the last news in London and the people I
had seen there; and I remember looking for the signs of genius in
the very form of his questions and thinking I found it. I liked his
voice as if I were somehow myself having the use of it.

There was genius in his house too I thought when we got there;
there was imagination in the carpets and curtains, in the pictures
and books, in the garden behind it, where certain old brown walls
were muffled in creepers that appeared to me to have been copied
from a masterpiece of one of the pre-Raphaelites. That was the way
many things struck me at that time, in England—as reproductions
of something that existed primarily in art or literature. It was not
the picture, the poem, the fictive page, that seemed to me a copy;
these things were the originals, and the life of happy and distinguished people was fashioned in their image. Mark Ambient called
his house a cottage, and I saw afterwards he was right; for if it
hadn't been a cottage it must have been a villa, and a villa, in England at least, was not a place in which one could fancy him at home.
But it was, to my vision, a cottage glorified and translated; it was
a palace of art, on a slightly reduced scale—and might besides have
been the dearest haunt of the old English *genius loci*. It nestled
under a cluster of magnificent beeches, it had little creaking lattices
that opened out of, or into, pendent mats of ivy, and gables, and
old red tiles, as well as a general aspect of being painted in water-
colours and inhabited by people whose lives would go on in chapters and volumes. The lawn seemed to me of extraordinary extent,
the garden-walls of incalculable height, the whole air of the place
delightfully still, private, proper to itself. "My wife must be somewhere about," Mark Ambient said as we went in. "We shall find
her perhaps—we've about an hour before dinner. She may be in
the garden. I'll show you my little place."

We passed through the house and into the grounds, as I should
have called them, which extended into the rear. They covered scarce
three or four acres, but, like the house, were very old and crooked
and full of traces of long habitation, with inequalities of level and
little flights of steps—mossy and cracked were these—which connected the different parts with each other. The limits of the place,
cleverly dissimulated, were muffled in the great verdurous screens.
They formed, as I remember, a thick loose curtain at the further
end, in one of the folds of which, as it were, we presently made out
from afar a little group. "Ah there she is!" said Mark Ambient; "and
she has got the boy." He noted that last fact in a slightly different
tone from any in which he yet had spoken. I wasn't fully aware of
this at the time, but it lingered in my ear and I afterwards understood it.

"Is it your son?" I inquired, feeling the question not to be brilliant.

"Yes, my only child. He's always in his mother's pocket. She coddles
him too much." It came back to me afterwards too—the sound of
these critical words. (They weren't petulant; they expressed rather a
sudden coldness, a mechanical submission.) We went a few steps
further, and then he stopped short and called the boy, beckoning to
him repeatedly.

"Dolcino, come and see your daddy!" There was something in the
way he stood still and waited that made me think he did it for a
purpose. Mrs. Ambient had her arm round the child's waist, and he
was leaning against her knee; but though he moved at his father's
call she gave no sign of releasing him. A lady, apparently a neighbour, was seated near her, and before them was a garden-table on
which a tea-service had been placed.

Mark Ambient called again, and Dolcino struggled in the maternal
embrace; but, too tightly held, he after two or three fruitless efforts
jerked about and buried his head deep in his mother's lap. There
was a certain awkwardness in the scene; I thought it odd Mrs. Ambient should pay so little attention to her husband. But I wouldn't
for the world have betrayed my thought and, to conceal it, I began
loudly to rejoice in the prospect of our having tea in the garden.
"Ah she won't let him come!" said my host with a sigh; and we went
our way till we reached the two ladies. He mentioned my name to
his wife, and I noticed that he addressed her as "My dear," very
genially, without a trace of resentment at her detention of the child.
The quickness of the transition made me vaguely ask myself if he

were perchance henpecked—a shocking surmise which I instantly
dismissed. Mrs. Ambient was quite such a wife as I should have expected him to have; slim and fair, with a long neck and pretty eyes
and an air of good breeding. She shone with a certain coldness and
practised in intercourse a certain bland detachment, but she was
clothed in gentleness as in one of those vaporous redundant scarves
that muffle the heroines of Gainsborough and Romney. She had also
a vague air of race, justified by my afterwards learning that she
was "connected with the aristocracy." I have seen poets married to
women of whom it was difficult to conceive that they should gratify
the poetic fancy—women with dull faces and glutinous minds, who
were none the less, however, excellent wives. But there was no
obvious disparity in Mark Ambient's union. My hostess—so far as
she could be called so—delicate and quiet, in a white dress, with
her beautiful child at her side, was worthy of the author of a work
so distinguished as "Beltraffio." Round her neck she wore a black
velvet ribbon, of which the long ends, tied behind, hung down her
back, and to which, in front, was attached a miniature portrait of
her little boy. Her smooth shining hair was confined in a net. She
gave me an adequate greeting and Dolcino—I thought this small
name of endearment delightful—took advantage of her getting up
to slip away from her and go to his father, who seized him in silence
and held him high for a long moment, kissing him several times.

I had lost no time in observing that the child, not more than seven
years old, was extraordinarily beautiful. He had the face of an angel
—the eyes, the hair, the smile of innocence, the more than mortal
bloom. There was something that deeply touched, that almost
alarmed, in his beauty, composed, one would have said, of elements
too fine and pure for the breath of this world. When I spoke to him
and he came and held out his hand and smiled at me I felt a sudden
strange pity for him—quite as if he had been an orphan or a
changeling or stamped with some social stigma. It was impossible to
be in fact more exempt from these misfortunes, and yet, as one kissed
him, it was hard to keep from murmuring all tenderly "Poor little
devil!" though why one should have applied this epithet to a living
cherub is more than I can say. Afterwards indeed I knew a trifle
better; I grasped the truth of his being too fair to live, wondering
at the same time that his parents shouldn't have guessed it and have
been in proportionate grief and despair. For myself I had no doubt
of his evanescence, having already more than once caught in the

fact the particular infant charm that's as good as a death-warrant.

The lady who had been sitting with Mrs. Ambient was a jolly ruddy personage in velveteen and limp feathers, whom I guessed to be the vicar's wife—our hostess didn't introduce me—and who immediately began to talk to Ambient about chrysanthemums. This was a safe subject, and yet there was a certain surprise for me in seeing the author of "Beltraffio" even in such superficial communion with the Church of England. His writings implied so much detachment from that institution, expressed a view of life so profane, as it were, so independent and so little likely in general to be thought edifying, that I should have expected to find him an object of horror to vicars and their ladies—of horror repaid on his own part by any amount of effortless derision. This proved how little I knew as yet of the English people and their extraordinary talent for keeping up their forms, as well as of some of the mysteries of Mark Ambient's hearth and home. I found afterwards that he had, in his study between nervous laughs and free cigar-puffs, some wonderful comparisons for his clerical neighbours; but meanwhile the chrysanthemums were a source of harmony, as he and the vicaress were equally attached to them, and I was surprised at the knowledge they exhibited of this interesting plant. The lady's visit, however, had presumably been long, and she presently rose for departure and kissed Mrs. Ambient. Mark started to walk with her to the gate of the grounds, holding Dolcino by the hand.

"Stay with me, darling," Mrs. Ambient said to the boy, who had surrendered himself to his father.

Mark paid no attention to the summons, but Dolcino turned and looked at her in shy appeal. "Can't I go with papa?"

"Not when I ask you to stay with me."

"But please don't ask me, mamma," said the child in his small clear new voice.

"I must ask you when I want you. Come to me, dearest." And Mrs. Ambient, who had seated herself again, held out her long slender slightly too osseous hands.

Her husband stopped, his back turned to her, but without releasing the child. He was still talking to the vicaress, but this good lady, I think, had lost the thread of her attention. She looked at Mrs. Ambient and at Dolcino, and then looked at me, smiling in a highly amused cheerful manner and almost to a grimace.

"Papa," said the child, "mamma wants me not to go with you."

"He's very tired—he has run about all day. He ought to be quiet till he goes to bed. Otherwise he won't sleep." These declarations fell successively and very distinctly from Mrs. Ambient's lips.

Her husband, still without turning round, bent over the boy and looked at him in silence. The vicaress gave a genial irrelevant laugh and observed that he was a precious little pet. "Let him choose," said Mark Ambient. "My dear little boy, will you go with me or will you stay with your mother?"

"Oh it's a shame!" cried the vicar's lady with increased hilarity.

"Papa, I don't think I can choose," the child answered, making his voice very low and confidential. "But I've been a great deal with mamma to-day," he then added.

"And very little with papa! My dear fellow, I think you *have* chosen!" On which Mark Ambient walked off with his son, accompanied by re-echoing but inarticulate comments from my fellow-visitor.

His wife had seated herself again, and her fixed eyes, bent on the ground, expressed for a few moments so much mute agitation that anything I could think of to say would be but a false note. Yet she none the less quickly recovered herself, to express the sufficiently civil hope that I didn't mind having had to walk from the station. I reassured her on this point, and she went on: "We've got a thing that might have gone for you, but my husband wouldn't order it." After which and another longish pause, broken only by my plea that the pleasure of a walk with our friend would have been quite what I would have chosen, she found for reply: "I believe the Americans walk very little."

"Yes, we always run," I laughingly allowed.

She looked at me seriously, yet with an absence in her pretty eyes. "I suppose your distances are so great."

"Yes, but we break our marches! I can't tell you the pleasure to me of finding myself here," I added. "I've the greatest admiration for Mr. Ambient."

"He'll like that. He likes being admired."

"He must have a very happy life then. He has many worshippers."

"Oh yes, I've seen some of them," she dropped, looking away, very far from me, rather as if such a vision were before her at the moment. It seemed to indicate, her tone, that the sight was scarcely edifying, and I guessed her quickly enough to be in no great intellectual sympathy with the author of "Beltraffio." I thought the fact strange, but somehow, in the glow of my own enthusiasm, didn't think it important: it only made me wish rather to emphasise that homage.

"For me, you know," I returned—doubtless with a due *suffisance*—"he's quite the greatest of living writers."

"Of course I can't judge. Of course he's very clever," she said with a patient cheer.

"He's nothing less than supreme, Mrs. Ambient! There are pages in each of his books of a perfection classing them with the greatest things. Accordingly for me to see him in this familiar way, in his habit as he lives, and apparently to find the man as delightful as the artist—well, I can't tell you how much too good to be true it seems and how great a privilege I think it." I knew I was gushing, but I couldn't help it, and what I said was a good deal less than what I felt. I was by no means sure I should dare to say even so much as this to the master himself, and there was a kind of rapture in speaking it out to his wife which was not affected by the fact that, as a wife, she appeared peculiar. She listened to me with her face grave again and her lips a little compressed, listened as if in no doubt, of course, that her husband was remarkable, but as if at the same time she had heard it frequently enough and couldn't treat it as stirring news. There was even in her manner a suggestion that I was so young as to expose myself to being called forward—an imputation and a word I had always loathed; as well as a hinted reminder that people usually got over their early extravagance. "I assure you that for me this is a red-letter day," I added.

She didn't take this up, but after a pause, looking round her, said abruptly and a trifle dryly: "We're very much afraid about the fruit this year."

My eyes wandered to the mossy mottled garden-walls, where plum-trees and pears, flattened and fastened upon the rusty bricks, looked like crucified figures with many arms. "Doesn't it promise well?"

"No, the trees look very dull. We had such late frosts."

Then there was another pause. She addressed her attention to the opposite end of the grounds, kept it for her husband's return with the child. "Is Mr. Ambient fond of gardening?" it occurred to me to ask, irresistibly impelled as I felt myself, moreover, to bring the conversation constantly back to him.

"He's very fond of plums," said his wife.

"Ah well then I hope your crop will be better than you fear. It's a lovely old place," I continued. "The whole impression's that of certain places he has described. Your house is like one of his pictures."

She seemed a bit frigidly amused at my glow. "It's a pleasant little place. There are hundreds like it."

"Oh it has his *tone*," I laughed, but sounding my epithet and insisting on my point the more sharply that my companion appeared to see in my appreciation of her simple establishment a mark of mean experience.

It was clear I insisted too much. "His tone?" she repeated with a harder look at me and a slightly heightened colour.

"Surely he has a tone, Mrs. Ambient."

"Oh yes, he has indeed! But I don't in the least consider that I'm living in one of his books at all. I shouldn't care for that in the least," she went on with a smile that had in some degree the effect of converting her really sharp protest into an insincere joke. "I'm afraid I'm not very literary. And I'm not artistic," she stated.

"I'm very sure you're not ignorant, not stupid," I ventured to reply, with the accompaniment of feeling immediately afterwards that I had been both familiar and patronising. My only consolation was in the sense that she had begun it, had fairly dragged me into it. She had thrust forward her limitations.

"Well, whatever I am I'm very different from my husband. If you like him you won't like me. You needn't say anything. Your liking me isn't in the least necessary!"

"Don't defy me!" I could but honourably make answer.

She looked as if she hadn't heard me, which was the best thing she could do; and we sat some time without further speech. Mrs. Ambient had evidently the enviable English quality of being able to be mute without unrest. But at last she spoke—she asked me if there seemed many people in town. I gave her what satisfaction I could on this point, and we talked a little of London and of some of its characteristics at that time of the year. At the end of this I came back irrepressibly to Mark.

"Doesn't he like to be there now? I suppose he doesn't find the proper quiet for his work. I should think his things had been written for the most part in a very still place. They suggest a great stillness following on a kind of tumult. Don't you think so?" I laboured on. "I suppose London's a tremendous place to collect impressions, but a refuge like this, in the country, must be better for working them up. Does he get many of his impressions in London, should you say?" I proceeded from point to point in this malign inquiry simply because my hostess, who probably thought me an odious chattering person, gave me time; for when I paused—I've not represented my pauses—she simply continued to let her eyes wander while her long fair fingers played with the medallion on her neck. When I stopped altogether, however, she was obliged to say something, and what she said was that she hadn't the least idea where her husband got his impressions. This made me think her, for a moment, positively disagreeable; delicate and proper and rather aristocratically fine as she sat there. But I must either have lost that view a moment later or been goaded by it to further aggression, for I remember asking her if our great man were in a good vein of work and when we might look for the appearance of the book on which he was engaged. I've every reason now to know that she found me insufferable.

She gave a strange small laugh as she said: "I'm afraid you think I know much more about my husband's work than I do. I haven't the least idea what he's doing," she then added in a slightly different, that is a more explanatory, tone and as if from a glimpse of the enormity of her confession. "I don't read what he writes."

She didn't succeed, and wouldn't even had she tried much harder, in making this seem to me anything less than monstrous. I stared at her and I think I blushed. "Don't you admire his genius? Don't you admire 'Beltraffio'?"

She waited, and I wondered what she could possibly say. She didn't speak, I could see, the first words that rose to her lips; she repeated what she had said a few minutes before. "Oh of course he's very clever!" And with this she got up; our two absentees had reappeared.

II

Mrs. Ambient left me and went to meet them; she stopped and had a few words with her husband that I didn't hear and that ended in her taking the child by the hand and returning with him to the house. Her husband joined me in a moment, looking, I thought, the least bit conscious and constrained, and said that if I would come in with him he would show me my room. In looking back upon these first moments of my visit I find it important to avoid the error of appearing to have at all fully measured his situation from the first or made out the signs of things mastered only afterwards. This later knowledge throws a backward light and makes me forget that, at least on the occasion of my present reference—I mean that first afternoon—Mark Ambient struck me as only enviable. Allowing for this he must yet have failed of much expression as we walked back to the house, though I remember well the answer he made to a remark of mine on his small son.

"That's an extraordinary little boy of yours. I've never seen such a child."

"Why," he asked while we went, "do you call him extraordinary?"

"He's so beautiful, so fascinating. He's like some perfect little work of art."

He turned quickly in the passage, grasping my arm. "Oh don't call him that, or you'll—you'll—!" But in his hesitation he broke off suddenly, laughing at my surprise. Immediately afterwards, however, he added: "You'll make his little future very difficult."

I declared that I wouldn't for the world take any liberties with his little future—it seemed to me to hang by threads of such delicacy. I should only be highly interested in watching it.

"You Americans are very keen," he commented on this. "You notice more things than we do."

"Ah if you want visitors who aren't struck with you," I cried, "you shouldn't have asked me down here!"

He showed me my room, a little bower of chintz, with open windows where the light was green, and before he left me said irrelevantly: "As for my small son, you know, we shall probably kill him between us before we've done with him!" And he made this assertion as if he really believed it, without any appearance of jest, his fine near-sighted expressive eyes looking straight into mine.

"Do you mean by spoiling him?"

"No, by fighting for him!"

"You had better give him to me to keep for you," I said. "Let me remove the apple of discord!"

It was my extravagance of course, but he had the air of being perfectly serious. "It would be quite the best thing we could do. I should be all ready to do it."

"I'm greatly obliged to you for your confidence."

But he lingered with his hands in his pockets. I felt as if within a few moments I had, morally speaking, taken several steps nearer to him. He looked weary, just as he faced me then, looked preoccupied and as if there were something one might do for him. I was terribly conscious of the limits of my young ability, but I wondered what such a service might be, feeling at bottom nevertheless that the only thing I could do for him was to like him. I suppose he guessed this and was grateful for what was in my mind, since he went on presently "I haven't the advantage of being an American, but I also notice a little, and I've an idea that"—here he smiled and laid his hand on my shoulder—"even counting out your nationality you're not destitute of intelligence. I've only known you half an hour, but—!" For which again he pulled up. "You're very young after all."

"But you may treat me as if I could understand you!" I said; and before he left me to dress for dinner he had virtually given me a promise that he would.

When I went down into the drawing-room—I was very punctual —I found that neither my hostess nor my host had appeared. A lady rose from a sofa, however, and inclined her head as I rather surprisedly gazed at her. "I dare say you don't know me," she said with the modern laugh. "I'm Mark Ambient's sister." Whereupon I shook hands with her, saluting her very low. Her laugh was modern—by which I mean that it consisted of the vocal agitation serving between people who meet in drawing-rooms as the solvent of social disparities, the medium of transitions; but her appearance was—what shall I call it?—medieval. She was pale and angular, her long thin face was inhabited by sad dark eyes and her black hair intertwined with golden fillets and curious clasps. She wore a faded velvet robe which clung to her when she moved and was "cut," as to the neck and sleeves, like the garments of old Italians. She suggested a symbolic picture, something akin even to Dürer's Melancholia, and was so perfect an image of a type which I, in my ignorance, supposed to be extinct, that while she rose before me I was almost as much startled as if I had seen a ghost. I afterwards concluded that Miss Ambient wasn't incapable of deriving pleasure from this weird effect, and I now believe that reflexion concerned in her having sunk again to her seat with her long lean but not ungraceful arms locked together in an archaic manner on her knees and her mournful eyes addressing me a message of intentness which foreshadowed what I was subsequently to suffer. She was a singular fatuous artificial creature, and I was never more than half to penetrate her motives and mysteries. Of one thing I'm sure at least: that they were considerably less insuperable than her appearance announced. Miss Ambient was a restless romantic disappointed spinster, consumed with the love of Michael-Angelesque attitudes and mystical robes; but I'm now convinced she hadn't in her nature those depths of unutterable thought which, when you first knew her, seemed to look out from her eyes and to prompt her complicated gestures. Those features in especial had a misleading eloquence; they lingered on you with a far-off dimness, an air of obstructed sympathy, which was certainly not always a key to the spirit of their owner; so that, of a truth, a young lady could scarce have been so dejected and disillusioned without having committed a crime for which she was consumed with remorse, or having parted with a hope that she couldn't sanely have entertained. She had, I believe, the usual allowance of rather vain motives: she wished to be looked at, she wished to be married, she wished to be thought original.

It costs me a pang to speak in this irreverent manner of one of Ambient's name, but I shall have still less gracious things to say before I've finished my anecdote, and moreover—I confess it—I owe the young lady a bit of a grudge. Putting aside the curious cast of her face she had no natural aptitude for an artistic development, had little real intelligence. But her affectations rubbed off on her brother's renown, and as there were plenty of people who darkly disapproved of him they could easily point to his sister as a person formed by his influence. It was quite possible to regard her as a warning, and she had almost compromised him with the world at large. He was the original and she the inevitable imitation. I suppose him scarce aware of the impression she mainly produced, beyond having a general idea that she made up very well as a Rossetti; he was used to her and was sorry for her, wishing she would marry and observing how she didn't. Doubtless I take her too seriously, for she did me no harm, though I'm bound to allow that I can only half-account for her. She wasn't so mystical as she looked, but was a strange indirect uncomfortable embarrassing woman. My story gives the reader at best so very small a knot to untie that I needn't hope to excite his curiosity by delaying to remark that Mrs. Ambient hated her sister-in-law. This I learned but later on, when other matters came to my knowledge. I mention it, however, at once, for I shall perhaps not seem to count too much on having beguiled him if I say he must promptly have guessed it. Mrs. Ambient, a person of conscience, put the best face on her kinswoman, who spent a month with her twice a year; but it took no great insight to recognise the very different personal paste of the two ladies, and that the usual feminine hypocrisies would cost them on either side much more than the usual effort. Mrs. Ambient, smooth-haired, thin-lipped, perpetually fresh, must have regarded her crumpled and dishevelled visitor as an equivocal joke; she herself so the opposite of a Rossetti, she herself a Reynolds or a Lawrence, with no more far-fetched note in her composition than a cold ladylike candour and a well-starched muslin dress.

It was in a garment and with an expression of this kind that she made her entrance after I had exchanged a few words with Miss Ambient. Her husband presently followed her and, there being no other company, we went to dinner. The impressions I received at that repast are present to me still. The elements of oddity in the air hovered, as it were, without descending—to any immediate check of my delight. This came mainly of course from Ambient's talk, the easiest and richest I had ever heard. I mayn't say to-day whether he laid himself out to dazzle a rather juvenile pilgrim from over the sea; but that matters little—it seemed so natural to him to shine. His spoken wit or wisdom, or whatever, had thus a charm almost beyond his written; that is if the high finish of his printed prose be really, as some people have maintained, a fault. There was such a kindness in him, however, that I've no doubt it gave him ideas for me, or about me, to see me sit as open-mouthed as I now figure myself. Not so the two ladies, who not only were very nearly dumb from beginning to end of the meal, but who hadn't even the air of being struck with such an exhibition of fancy and taste. Mrs. Ambient, detached, and inscrutable, met neither my eye nor her husband's; she attended to her dinner, watched her servants, arranged the puckers in her dress, exchanged at wide intervals a remark with her sister-in-law and, while she slowly rubbed her lean white hands between the courses, looked out of the window at the first signs of evening—the long June day allowing us to dine without candles. Miss Ambient appeared to give little direct heed to anything said by her brother; but on the other hand she was much engaged in watching its effect upon me. Her "die-away" pupils continued to attach themselves to my countenance, and it was only her air of belonging to another century that kept them from being importunate. She seemed to look at me across the ages, and the interval of time diminished for me the inconvenience. It was as if she knew in a general way that he must be talking very well, but she herself was so at home among such allusions that she had no need to pick them up and was at liberty to see what would become of the exposure of a candid young American to a high esthetic temperature.

The temperature was esthetic certainly, but it was less so than I could have desired, for I failed of any great success in making our friend abound about himself. I tried to put him on the ground of his own genius, but he slipped through my fingers every time and shifted the saddle to one or other of his contemporaries. He talked about Balzac and Browning, about what was being done in foreign countries, about his recent tour in the East and the extraordinary forms of life to be observed in that part of the world. I felt he had reasons for holding off from a direct profession of literary faith, a full consistency or sincerity, and therefore dealt instead with certain social topics, treating them with extraordinary humour and with a due play of that power of ironic evocation in which his books abound. He had a deal to say about London as London appears to the observer who has the courage of some of his conclusions during the high-pressure time—from April to July—of its gregarious life. He flashed his faculty of playing with the caught image and liberating the wistful idea over the whole scheme of manners or conception of intercourse of his compatriots, among whom there were evidently not a few types for which he had little love. London in short was grotesque to him, and he made capital sport of it; his only allusion that I can remember to his own work was his saying that he meant some day to do an immense and general, a kind of epic, social satire. Miss Ambient's perpetual gaze seemed to put to me: Do you perceive how artistic, how very strange and interesting, we are? Frankly now is it possible to be *more* artistic, *more* strange and interesting, than this? You surely won't deny that we're remarkable. I was irritated by her use of the plural pronoun, for she had no right to pair herself with her brother; and moreover, of course, I couldn't see my way to—at all genially—include Mrs. Ambient. Yet there was no doubt they were, taken together, unprecedented enough, and, with all allowances, I had never been left, or condemned, to draw so many rich inferences.

After the ladies had retired my host took me into his study to smoke, where I appealingly brought him round, or so tried, to some disclosure of fond ideals. I was bent on proving I was worthy to listen to him, on repaying him for what he had said to me before dinner, by showing him how perfectly I understood. He liked to talk; he liked to defend his convictions and his honour (not that I attacked them); he liked a little perhaps—it was a pardonable weakness—to bewilder the youthful mind even while wishing to win it over. My ingenuous sympathy received at any rate a shock from three or four of his professions—he made me occasionally gasp and stare. He couldn't help forgetting, or rather couldn't know, how little, in another and dryer clime, I had ever sat in the school in which he was master; and he promoted me as at a jump to a sense of its penetralia. My trepidations, however, were delightful; they were just what I had hoped for, and their only fault was that they passed away too quickly; since I found that for the main points I was essentially, I was quite constitutionally, on Mark Ambient's "side." This was the taken stand of the artist to whom every manifestation of human energy was a thrilling spectacle and who felt for ever the desire to resolve his experience of life into a literary form. On that high head of the passion for form—the attempt at perfection, the quest for which was to his mind the real search for the holy grail—he said the most interesting, the most inspiring things. He mixed with them a thousand illustrations from his own life, from other lives he had known, from history and fiction, and above all from the annals of the time that was dear to him beyond all periods, the Italian cinquecento. It came to me thus that in his books he had uttered but half his thought, and that what he had kept back—from motives I deplored when I made them out later—was the finer, and braver part. It was his fate to make a great many still more "prepared" people than me not inconsiderably wince; but there was no grain of bravado in his ripest things (I've always maintained it, though often contradicted), and at bottom the poor fellow, disinterested to his finger-tips and regarding imperfection not only as an esthetic but quite also as a social crime, had an extreme dread of scandal. There are critics who regret that having gone so far he didn't go further; but I regret nothing—putting aside two or three of the motives I just mentioned —since he arrived at a noble rarity and I don't see how you can go beyond that. The hours I spent in his study—this first one and the few that followed it; they were not after all so numerous—seem to glow, as I look back on them, with a tone that is partly that of the brown old room, rich, under the shaded candle-light where we sat and smoked, with the dusky delicate bindings of valuable books; partly that of his voice, of which I still catch the echo, charged with the fancies and figures that came at his command. When we went

back to the drawing-room we found Miss Ambient alone in possession and prompt to mention that her sister-in-law had a quarter of
an hour before been called by the nurse to see the child, who appeared rather unwell—a little feverish.

"Feverish! how in the world comes he to be feverish?" Ambient
asked. "He was perfectly right this afternoon."

"Beatrice says you walked him about too much—you almost killed
him."

"Beatrice must be very happy—she has an opportunity to triumph!" said my friend with a bright bitterness which was all I could
have wished it.

"Surely not if the child's ill," I ventured to remark by way of pleading for Mrs. Ambient.

"My dear fellow, you aren't married—you don't know the nature
of wives!" my host returned with spirit.

I tried to match it. "Possibly not; but I know the nature of moth-
ers."

"Beatrice is perfect as a mother," sighed Miss Ambient quite
tremendously and with her fingers interlaced on her embroidered
knees.

"I shall go up and see my boy," her brother went on. "Do you suppose he's asleep?"

"Beatrice won't let you see him, dear"—as to which our young
lady looked at me, though addressing our companion.

"Do you call that being perfect as a mother?" Ambient asked.

"Yes, from her point of view."

"Damn her point of view!" cried the author of "Beltraffio." And he
left the room; after which we heard him ascend the stairs.

I sat there for some ten minutes with Miss Ambient, and we naturally had some exchange of remarks, which began, I think, by my
asking her what the point of view of her sister-in-law could be.

"Oh it's so very odd. But we're so very odd altogether. Don't you
find us awfully unlike others of our class?—which indeed mostly, in
England, is awful. We've lived so much abroad. I adore 'abroad.'
Have you people like us in America?"

"You're not all alike, you interesting three—or, counting Dolcino,
four—surely, surely; so that I don't think I understand your question. We've no one like your brother—I may go so far as that."

"You've probably more persons like his wife," Miss Ambient deso-
lately smiled.

"I can tell you that better when you've told me about her point of view."

"Oh yes—oh yes. Well," said my entertainer, "she doesn't like his ideas. She doesn't like them for the child. She thinks them undesirable."

Being quite fresh from the contemplation of some of Mark Ambient's *arcana* I was particularly in a position to appreciate this announcement. But the effect of it was to make me, after staring a moment, burst into laughter which I instantly checked when I remembered the indisposed child above and the possibility of parents nervously or fussily anxious.

"What has that infant to do with ideas?" I asked. "Surely he can't tell one from another. Has he read his father's novels?"

"He's very precocious and very sensitive, and his mother thinks she can't begin to guard him too early." Miss Ambient's head drooped a little to one side and her eyes fixed themselves on futurity. Then of a sudden came a strange alteration; her face lighted to an effect more joyless than any gloom, to that indeed of a conscious insincere grimace, and she added: "When one has children what one writes becomes a great responsibility."

"Children are terrible critics," I prosaically answered. "I'm really glad I haven't any."

"Do you also write then? And in the same style as my brother? And do you like that style? And do people appreciate it in America? I don't write, but I think I feel." To these and various other inquiries and observations my young lady treated me till we heard her brother's step in the hall again and Mark Ambient reappeared. He was so flushed and grave that I supposed he had seen something symptomatic in the condition of his child. His sister apparently had another idea; she gazed at him from afar—as if he had been a burning ship on the horizon—and simply murmured "Poor old Mark!"

"I hope you're not anxious," I as promptly pronounced.

"No, but I'm disappointed. She won't let me in. She has locked the door, and I'm afraid to make a noise." I dare say there might have been a touch of the ridiculous in such a confession, but I liked my new friend so much that it took nothing for me from his dignity. "She tells me—from behind the door—that she'll let me know if he's worse."

"It's very good of her," said Miss Ambient with a hollow sound.

I had exchanged a glance with Mark in which it's possible he read

that my pity for him was untinged with contempt, though I scarce
know why he should have cared; and as his sister soon afterward got
up and took her bedroom candlestick he proposed we should go
back to his study. We sat there till after midnight; he put himself
into his slippers and an old velvet jacket, he lighted an ancient pipe,
but he talked considerably less than before. There were longish
pauses in our communion, but they only made me feel we had advanced in intimacy. They helped me further to understand my
friend's personal situation and to imagine it by no means the happiest possible. When his face was quiet it was vaguely troubled,
showing, to my increase of interest—if that was all that was wanted!
—that for him too life was the same struggle it had been for so many
another man of genius. At last I prepared to leave him, and then, to
my ineffable joy, he gave me some sheets of his forthcoming book—
which, though unfinished, he had indulged in the luxury, so dear
to writers of deliberation, of having "set up," from chapter to chapter, as he advanced. These early pages, the *prémices*, in the language
of letters, of that new fruit of his imagination, I should take to my
room and look over at my leisure. I was in the act of leaving him
when the door of the study noiselessly opened and Mrs. Ambient
stood before us. She observed us a moment, her candle in her hand,
and then said to her husband that as she supposed he hadn't gone
to bed she had come down to let him know Dolcino was more quiet
and would probably be better in the morning. Mark Ambient made
no reply; he simply slipped past her in the doorway, as if for fear
she might seize him in his passage, and bounded upstairs to judge
for himself of his child's condition. She looked so frankly discomfited
that I for a moment believed her about to give him chase. But she
resigned herself with a sigh and her eyes turned, ruefully and without a ray, to the lamplit room where various books at which I had
been looking were pulled out of their places on the shelves and the
fumes of tobacco hung in midair. I bade her good-night and then,
without intention, by a kind of fatality, a perversity that had already
made me address her overmuch on that question of her husband's
powers, I alluded to the precious proof-sheets with which Ambient
had entrusted me and which I nursed there under my arm. "They're
the opening chapters of his new book," I said. "Fancy my satisfaction
at being allowed to carry them to my room!"

    She turned away, leaving me to take my candlestick from the table
in the hall; but before we separated, thinking it apparently a good

occasion to let her know once for all—since I was beginning, it would seem, to be quite "thick" with my host—that there was no fitness in my appealing to her for sympathy in such a case; before we separated, I say, she remarked to me with her quick fine well-bred inveterate curtness: "I dare say you attribute to me ideas I haven't got. I don't take that sort of interest in my husband's proof-sheets. I consider his writings most objectionable!"

III

I had an odd colloquy the next morning with Miss Ambient, whom I found strolling in the garden before breakfast. The whole place looked as fresh and trim, amid the twitter of the birds, as if, an hour before, the housemaids had been turned into it with their dust-pans and feather-brushes. I almost hesitated to light a cigarette and was doubly startled when, in the act of doing so, I suddenly saw the sister of my host, who had, at the best, something of the weirdness of an apparition, stand before me. She might have been posing for her photograph. Her sad-coloured robe arranged itself in serpentine folds at her feet; her hands locked themselves listlessly together in front; her chin rested on a cinque-cento ruff. The first thing I did after bidding her good-morning was to ask her for news of her little nephew—to express the hope she had heard he was better. She was able to gratify this trust—she spoke as if we might expect to see him during the day. We walked through the shrubberies together and she gave me further light on her brother's household, which offered me an opportunity to repeat to her what his wife had so startled and distressed me with the night before. *Was* it the sorry truth that she thought his productions objectionable?

"She doesn't usually come out with that so soon!" Miss Ambient returned in answer to my breathlessness.

"Poor lady," I pleaded, "she saw I'm a fanatic."

"Yes, she won't like you for that. But you mustn't mind, if the rest of us like you! Beatrice thinks a work of art ought to have a 'purpose.' But she's a charming woman—don't you think her charming? I find in her quite the grand air."

"She's very beautiful," I produced with an effort; while I reflected that though it was apparently true that Mark Ambient was mismated it was also perceptible that his sister was perfidious. She assured me her brother and his wife had no other difference but this one—that she thought his writings immoral and his influence pernicious. It was a fixed idea: she was afraid of these things for the child. I answered that it was in all conscience enough, the trifle of a woman's regarding her husband's mind as a well of corruption, and she seemed much struck with the novelty of my remark. 'But there hasn't been any of the sort of trouble that there so often is among married people," she said. "I suppose you can judge for yourself that Beatrice isn't at all —well, whatever they call it when a woman kicks over! And poor Mark doesn't make love to other people either. You might think he would, but I assure you he doesn't. All the same of course, from her point of view, you know, she has a dread of my brother's influence on the child—on the formation of his character, his 'ideals,' poor little brat, his principles. It's as if it were a subtle poison or a contagion—something that would rub off on his tender sensibility when his father kisses him or holds him on his knee. If she could she'd prevent Mark from even so much as touching him. Every one knows it—visitors see it for themselves; so there's no harm in my telling you. Isn't it excessively odd? It comes from Beatrice's being so religious and so tremendously moral—so à cheval on fifty thousand riguardi. And then of course we mustn't forget," my companion added, a little unexpectedly, to this polyglot proposition, "that some of Mark's ideas are—well, really—rather impossible, don't you know?"

I reflected as we went into the house, where we found Ambient unfolding *The Observer* at the breakfast-table, that none of them were probably quite so "impossible, don't you know?" as his sister. Mrs. Ambient, a little "the worse," as was mentioned, for her ministrations, during the night, to Dolcino, didn't appear at breakfast. Her husband described her, however, as hoping to go to church. I afterwards learnt that she did go, but nothing naturally was less on the cards than that we should accompany her. It was while the church-bell droned near at hand that the author of "Beltraffio" led me forth for the ramble he had spoken of in his note. I shall attempt here no record of where we went or of what we saw. We kept to the fields and copses and commons, and breathed the same sweet air as the nibbling donkeys and the browsing sheep, whose woolliness seemed to me, in those early days of acquaintance with English objects, but part of the general texture of the small dense landscape, which looked as if the harvest were gathered by the shears and with all nature bleating and braying for the violence. Everything was full of expression for Mark Ambient's visitor—from the big bandy-legged geese whose whiteness was a "note" amid all the tones of green as they wandered beside a neat little oval pool, the foreground of a thatched and whitewashed inn, with a grassy approach and a pictorial sign—from these humble wayside animals to the crests of high woods which let a gable or a pinnacle peep here and there and looked even at a distance like trees of good company, conscious of an individual profile. I admired the hedge-rows, I plucked the faint-hued heather, and I was for ever stopping to say how charming I thought the threadlike footpaths across the fields, which wandered in a diagonal of finer grain from one smooth stile to another. Mark Ambient was abundantly good-natured and was as much struck, dear man, with some of my observations as I was with the literary allusions of the landscape. We sat and smoked on stiles, broaching paradoxes in the decent English air; we took short cuts across a park or two where the bracken was deep and my companion nodded to the old woman at the gate; we skirted rank coverts which rustled here and there as we passed, and we stretched ourselves at last on a heathery hillside where if the sun wasn't too hot neither was the earth too cold, and where the country lay beneath us in a rich blue mist. Of course I had already told him what I thought of his new novel, having the previous night read every word of the opening chapters before I went to bed.

"I'm not without hope of being able to make it decent enough," he said as I went back to the subject while we turned up our heels to the sky. "At least the people who dislike my stuff—and there are plenty of them, I believe—will dislike this thing (if it does turn out well) most." This was the first time I had heard him allude to the people who couldn't read him—a class so generally conceived to sit heavy on the consciousness of the man of letters. A being organised for literature as Mark Ambient was must certainly have had the normal proportion of sensitiveness, or irritability; the artistic *ego*, capable in some cases of such monstrous development, must have been in his composition sufficiently erect and active. I won't therefore go so far as to say that he never thought of his detractors or that he had any illusions with regard to the number of his admirers—he could never so far have deceived himself as to believe he was popular, but I at least then judged (and had occasion to be sure later on) that stupidity ruffled him visibly but little, that he had an air of thinking it quite natural he should leave many simple folk, tasting of him,

as simple as ever he found them, and that he very seldom talked
about the newspapers, which, by the way, were always even abnormally vulgar about him. Of course he may have thought them
over—the newspapers—night and day; the only point I make is that
he didn't show it; while at the same time he didn't strike one as a
man actively on his guard. I may add that, touching his hope of
making the work on which he was then engaged the best of his books,
it was only partly carried out. That place belongs incontestably to
"Beltraffio," in spite of the beauty of certain parts of its successor.
I quite believe, however, that he had at the moment of which I speak
no sense of having declined; he was in love with his idea, which was
indeed magnificent, and though for him, as I suppose for every sane
artist, the act of execution had in it as much torment as joy, he
saw his result grow like the crescent of the young moon and promise
to fill the disk. "I want to be truer than I've ever been," he said,
settling himself on his back with his hands clasped behind his head;
"I want to give the impression of life itself. No, you may say what
you will, I've always arranged things too much, always smoothed
them down and rounded them off and tucked them in—done everything to them that life doesn't do. I've been a slave to the old superstitions."

"You a slave, my dear Mark Ambient? You've the freest imagination of our day!"

"All the more shame to me to have done some of the things I have!
The reconciliation of the two women in 'Natalina,' for instance,
which could never really have taken place. That sort of thing's ignoble—I blush when I think of it! This new affair must be a golden
vessel, filled with the purest distillation of the actual; and oh how
it worries me, the shaping of the vase, the hammering of the metal!
I have to hammer it so fine, so smooth; I don't do more than an
inch or two a day. And all the while I have to be so careful not to
let a drop of the liquor escape! When I see the kind of things Life
herself, the brazen hussy, does, I despair of ever catching her peculiar
trick. She has an impudence, Life! If one risked a fiftieth part of the
effects she risks! It takes ever so long to believe it. You don't know yet,
my dear youth. It isn't till one has been watching her some forty years
that one finds out half of what she's up to! Therefore one's earlier
things must inevitably contain a mass of rot. And with what one
sees, on one side, with its tongue in its cheek, defying one to be real
enough, and on the other the *bonnes gens* rolling up their eyes at

one's cynicism, the situation has elements of the ludicrous which the poor reproducer himself is doubtless in a position to appreciate better than any one else. Of course one mustn't worry about the *bonnes gens*," Mark Ambient went on while my thoughts reverted to his ladylike wife as interpreted by his remarkable sister.

"To sink your shaft deep and polish the plate through which people look into it—that's what your work consists of," I remember ingeniously observing.

"Ah polishing one's plate—that's the torment of execution!" he exclaimed, jerking himself up and sitting forward. "The effort to arrive at a surface, if you think anything of that decent sort necessary —some people don't, happily for them! My dear fellow, if you could see the surface I dream of as compared with the one with which I've to content myself. Life's really too short for art—one hasn't time to make one's shell ideally hard. Firm and bright, firm and bright is very well to say—the devilish thing has a way sometimes of being bright, and even of being hard, as mere tough frozen pudding is hard, without being firm. When I rap it with my knuckles it doesn't give the right sound. There are horrible sandy stretches where I've taken the wrong turn because I couldn't for the life of me find the right. If you knew what a dunce I am sometimes! Such things figure to me now base pimples and ulcers on the brow of beauty!"

"They're very bad, very bad," I said as gravely as I could.

"Very bad? They're the highest social offence I know; it ought— it absolutely ought; I'm quite serious—to be capital. If I knew I should be publicly thrashed else I'd manage to find the true word. The people who can't—some of them don't so much as know it when they see it—would shut their inkstands, and we shouldn't be deluged by this flood of rubbish!"

I shall not attempt to repeat everything that passed between us, nor to explain just how it was that, every moment I spent in his company, Mark Ambient revealed to me more and more the consistency of his creative spirit, the spirit in him that felt all life as plastic material. I could but envy him the force of that passion, and it was at any rate through the receipt of this impression that by the time we returned I had gained the sense of intimacy with him that I have noted. Before we got up for the homeward stretch he alluded to his wife's having once—or perhaps more than once—asked him whether he should like Dolcino to read "Beltraffio." He must have been unaware at the moment of all that this conveyed to me—as well doubtless of my extreme curiosity to hear what he had replied. He had said how much he hoped Dolcino would read *all* his works—when he was twenty; he should like him to know what his father had done. Before twenty it would be useless; he wouldn't understand them.

"And meanwhile do you propose to hide them—to lock them up in a drawer?" Mrs. Ambient had proceeded.

"Oh no—we must simply tell him they're not intended for small boys. If you bring him up properly after that he won't touch them."

To this Mrs. Ambient had made answer that it might be very awkward when he was about fifteen, say; and I asked her husband if it were his opinion in general, then, that young people shouldn't read novels.

"Good ones—certainly not!" said my companion. I suppose I had had other views, for I remember saying that for myself I wasn't sure it was bad for them if the novels were "good" to the right intensity of goodness. "Bad for *them*, I don't say so much!" my companion returned. "But very bad, I'm afraid, for the poor dear old novel itself." That oblique accidental allusion to his wife's attitude was followed by a greater breadth of reference as we walked home. "The difference between us is simply the opposition between two distinct ways of looking at the world, which have never succeeded in getting on together, or in making any kind of common household, since the beginning of time. They've borne all sorts of names, and my wife would tell you it's the difference between Christian and Pagan. I may be a pagan, but I don't like the name; it sounds sectarian. She thinks me at any rate no better than an ancient Greek. It's the difference between making the most of life and making the least, so that you'll get another better one in some other time and place. Will it be a sin to make the most of that one too, I wonder; and shall we have to be bribed off in the future state as well as in the present? Perhaps I care too much for beauty—I don't know, I doubt if a poor devil *can*; I delight in it, I adore it, I think of it continually, I try to produce it, to reproduce it. My wife holds that we shouldn't cultivate or enjoy it without extraordinary precautions and reserves. She's always afraid of it, always on her guard. I don't know what it can ever have done to her, what grudge it owes her or what resentment rides. And she's so pretty, too, herself! Don't you think she's lovely? She was at any rate when we married. At that time I wasn't aware of that difference I speak of—I thought it all came to the same thing: in the end, as they say. Well, perhaps it will in the end. I don't know what the end will be. Moreover, I care for seeing things as they are; that's the way I try to show them in any professed picture. But you mustn't talk to Mrs. Ambient about things as they are. She has a moral dread of things as they are."

"She's afraid of them for Dolcino," I said: surprised a moment afterward at being in a position—thanks to Miss Ambient—to be so explanatory; and surprised even now that Mark shouldn't have shown visibly that he wondered what the deuce I knew about it. But he didn't; he simply declared with a tenderness that touched me: "Ah nothing shall ever hurt *him!*"

He told me more about his wife before we arrived at the gate of home, and if he be judged to have aired overmuch his grievance I'm afraid I must admit that he had some of the foibles as well as the gifts of the artistic temperament; adding, however, instantly that hitherto, to the best of my belief, he had rarely let this particular cat out of the bag. "She thinks me immoral—that's the long and short of it," he said as we paused outside a moment and his hand rested on one of the bars of his gate; while his conscious expressive perceptive eyes—the eyes of a foreigner, I had begun to account them, much more than of the usual Englishman—viewing me now evidently as quite a familiar friend, took part in the declaration. "It's very strange when one thinks it all over, and there's a grand comicality in it that I should like to bring out. She's a very nice woman, extraordinarily well-behaved, upright and clever and with a tremendous lot of good sense about a good many matters. Yet her conception of a novel—she has explained it to me once or twice, and she doesn't do it badly as exposition—is a thing so false that it makes me blush. It's a thing so hollow, so dishonest, so lying, in which life is so blinked and blinded, so dodged and disfigured, that it makes my ears burn. It's two different ways of looking at the whole affair," he repeated, pushing open the gate. "And they're irreconcilable!" he added with a sigh. We went forward to the house, but on the walk, halfway to the door, he stopped and said to me: "If you're going into this kind of thing there's a fact you should know beforehand; it may save you some disappointment. There's a hatred of art, there's a hatred of literature—I mean of the genuine kinds. Oh the shams—*those* they'll swallow by the bucket!" I looked up at the charming house, with its genial colour and crookedness, and I answered with a smile that those evil passions might exist, but that I should never have expected to find them there. "Ah it doesn't matter after all," he a bit nervously laughed; which I was glad to hear, for I was reproaching myself with having worked him up.

If I had it soon passed off, for at luncheon he was delightful; strangely delightful considering that the difference between himself and his wife was, as he had said, irreconcilable. He had the art, by his manner, by his smile, by his natural amenity, of reducing the importance of it in the common concerns of life; and Mrs. Ambient, I must add, lent herself to this transaction with a very good grace. I watched her at table for further illustrations of that fixed idea of which Miss Ambient had spoken to me; for in the light of the united revelations of her sister-in-law and her husband she had come to seem to me almost a sinister personage. Yet the signs of a sombre fanaticism were not more immediately striking in her than before; it was only after a while that her air of incorruptible conformity, her tapering monosyllabic correctness, began to affect me as in themselves a cold thin flame. Certainly, at first, she resembled a woman with as few passions as possible; but if she had a passion at all it would indeed be that of Philistinism. She might have been (for there are guardian-spirits, I suppose, of all great principles) the very angel of the pink of propriety—putting the pink for a principle, though I'd rather put some dismal cold blue. Mark Ambient, apparently, ten years before, had simply and quite inevitably taken her for an angel, without asking himself of what. He had been right in calling my attention to her beauty. In looking for some explanation of his original surrender to her I saw more than before that she was, physically speaking, a wonderfully cultivated human plant—that he might well have owed her a brief poetic inspiration. It was impossible to be more propped and pencilled, more delicately tinted and petalled.

If I had had it in my heart to think my host a little of a hypocrite for appearing to forget at table everything he had said to me in our walk, I should instantly have cancelled such a judgement on reflecting that the good news his wife was able to give him about their little boy was ground enough for any optimistic reaction. It may have come partly too from a certain compunction at having breathed to me at all harshly on the cool fair lady who sat there—a desire to prove himself not after all so mismated. Dolcino continued to be much better, and it had been promised him he should come downstairs after his dinner. As soon as we had risen from our own meal Mark slipped away, evidently for the purpose of going to his child;

and no sooner had I observed this than I became aware his wife had simultaneously vanished. It happened that Miss Ambient and I, both at the same moment, saw the tail of her dress whisk out of a doorway; an incident that led the young lady to smile at me as if I now knew all the secrets of the Ambients. I passed with her into the garden and we sat down on a dear old bench that rested against the west wall of the house. It was a perfect spot for the middle period of a Sunday in June, and its felicity seemed to come partly from an antique sun-dial which, rising in front of us and forming the centre of a small intricate parterre, measured the moments ever so slowly and made them safe for leisure and talk. The garden bloomed in the suffused afternoon, the tall beeches stood still for an example, and, behind and above us, a rose-tree of many seasons, clinging to the faded grain of the brick, expressed the whole character of the scene in a familiar exquisite smell. It struck me as a place to offer genius every favour and sanction—not to bristle with challenges and checks. Miss Ambient asked me if I had enjoyed my walk with her brother and whether we had talked of many things.

"Well, of most things," I freely allowed, though I remembered we hadn't talked of Miss Ambient.

"And don't you think some of his theories are very peculiar?"

"Oh I guess I agree with them all." I was very particular, for Miss Ambient's entertainment, to guess.

"Do you think art's everything?" she put to me in a moment.

"In art, of course I do!"

"And do you think beauty's everything?"

"Everything's a big word, which I think we should use as little as possible. But how can we not want beauty?"

"Ah there you are!" she sighed, though I didn't quite know what she meant by it. "Of course it's difficult for a woman to judge how far to go," she went on. "I adore everything that gives a charm to life. I'm intensely sensitive to form. But sometimes I draw back— don't you see what I mean?—I don't quite see where I shall be landed. I only want to be quiet, after all," Miss Ambient continued as if she had long been baffled of this modest desire. "And one must be good, at any rate, must not one?" she pursued with a dubious quaver—an intimation apparently that what I might say one way or the other would settle it for her. It was difficult for me to be very original in reply, and I'm afraid I repaid her confidence with an unblushing plat- itude. I remember moreover attaching to it an inquiry, equally destitute of freshness and still more wanting perhaps in tact, as to whether she didn't mean to go to church, since that was an obvious way of being good. She made answer that she had performed this duty in the morning, and that for her, of Sunday afternoons, supreme virtue consisted in answering the week's letters. Then suddenly and without transition she brought out: "It's quite a mistake about Dolcino's being better. I've seen him and he's not at all right."

I wondered, and somehow I think I scarcely believed. "Surely his mother would know, wouldn't she?"

She appeared for a moment to be counting the leaves on one of the great beeches. "As regards most matters one can easily say what, in a given situation, my sister-in-law will, or would, do. But in the present case there are strange elements at work."

"Strange elements? Do you mean in the constitution of the child?"

"No, I mean in my sister-in-law's feelings."

"Elements of affection of course; elements of anxiety," I concurred. "But why do you call them strange?"

She repeated my words. "Elements of affection, elements of anxiety. She's very anxious."

Miss Ambient put me indescribably ill at ease; she almost scared me, and I wished she would go and write her letters. "His father will have seen him now," I said, "and if he's not satisfied he will send for the doctor."

"The doctor ought to have been here this morning," she promptly returned. "He lives only two miles away."

I reflected that all this was very possibly but a part of the general tragedy of Miss Ambient's view of things; yet I asked her why she hadn't urged that view on her sister-in-law. She answered me with a smile of extraordinary significance and observed that I must have very little idea of her "peculiar" relations with Beatrice; but I must do her the justice that she re-enforced this a little by the plea that any distinguishable alarm of Mark's was ground enough for a difference of his wife's. He was always nervous about the child, and as they were predestined by nature to take opposite views, the only thing for the mother was to cultivate a false optimism. In Mark's absence and that of his betrayed fear she would have been less easy. I remembered what he had said to me about their dealings with their son— that between them they'd probably put an end to him; but I didn't repeat this to Miss Ambient: the less so that just then her brother emerged from the house, carrying the boy in his arms. Close behind him moved his wife, grave and pale; the little sick face was turned over Ambient's shoulder and toward the mother. We rose to receive the group, and as they came near us Dolcino twisted himself about. His enchanting eyes showed me a smile of recognition, in which, for the moment, I should have taken a due degree of comfort. Miss Ambient, however, received another impression, and I make haste to say that her quick sensibility, which visibly went out to the child, argues that in spite of her affectations she might have been of some human use. "It won't do at all—it won't do at all," she said to me under her breath. "I shall speak to Mark about the Doctor."

Her small nephew was rather white, but the main difference I saw in him was that he was even more beautiful than the day before. He had been dressed in his festal garments—a velvet suit and a crimson sash—and he looked like a little invalid prince too young to know condescension and smiling familiarly on his subjects.

"Put him down, Mark, he's not a bit at his ease," Mrs. Ambient said.

"Should you like to stand on your feet, my boy?" his father asked.

He made a motion that quickly responded. "Oh, yes; I'm remarkably well."

Mark placed him on the ground; he had shining pointed shoes with enormous bows. "Are you happy now, Mr. Ambient?"

"Oh yes, I'm particularly happy," Dolcino replied. But the words were scarce out of his mouth when his mother caught him up and, in a moment, holding him on her knees, took her place on the bench where Miss Ambient and I had been sitting. This young lady said something to her brother, in consequence of which the two wandered away into the garden together.

IV

I remained with Mrs. Ambient, but as a servant had brought out a couple of chairs I wasn't obliged to seat myself beside her. Our conversation failed of ease, and I, for my part, felt there would be a shade of hypocrisy in my now trying to make myself agreeable to the partner of my friend's existence. I didn't dislike her—I rather admired her; but I was aware that I differed from her inexpressibly. Then I suspected, what I afterwards definitely knew and have already intimated, that the poor lady felt small taste for her husband's so undisguised disciple; and this of course was not encouraging. She thought me an obtrusive and designing, even perhaps a depraved, young man whom a perverse Providence had dropped upon their quiet lawn to flatter his worst tendencies. She did me the honour to say to Miss Ambient, who repeated the speech, that she didn't know when she had seen their companion take such a fancy to a visitor; and she measured apparently my evil influence by Mark's appreciation of my society. I had a consciousness, not oppressive but quite sufficient, of all this; though I must say that if it chilled my flow of small-talk it yet didn't prevent my thinking the beautiful mother and beautiful child, interlaced there against their background of roses, a picture such as I doubtless shouldn't soon see again. I was free, I supposed, to go into the house and write letters, to sit in the drawing-room, to repair to my own apartment and take a nap; but the only use I made of my freedom was to linger still in my chair and say to myself that the light hand of Sir Joshua might have painted Mark Ambient's wife and son. I found myself looking perpetually at the latter small mortal, who looked constantly back at me, and that was enough to detain me. With these vaguely-amused eyes he smiled, and I felt it an absolute impossibility to abandon a child with such an expression. His attention never strayed; it attached itself to my face as if among all the small incipient things of his nature throbbed a desire to say something to me. If I could have taken him on my own knee he perhaps would have managed to say it; but it would have been a critical matter to ask his mother to give him up, and it has remained a constant regret for me that on that strange Sunday afternoon I didn't even for a moment hold Dolcino in my arms. He had said he felt remarkably well and was especially happy; but though peace may have been with him as he pillowed his charming head on his mother's breast, dropping his little crimson silk legs from her lap, I somehow didn't think security was. He made no attempt to walk about; he was content to swing his legs softly and strike one as languid and angelic.

Mark returned to us with his sister; and Miss Ambient, repeating her mention of the claims of her correspondence, passed into the house. Mark came and stood in front of his wife, looking down at the child, who immediately took hold of his hand and kept it while he stayed. "I think Mackintosh ought to see him," he said; "I think I'll walk over and fetch him."

"That's Gwendolen's idea, I suppose," Mrs. Ambient replied very sweetly.

"It's not such an out-of-the-way idea when one's child's ill," he returned.

"I'm not ill, papa; I'm much better now," sounded in the boy's silver pipe.

"Is that the truth, or are you only saying it to be agreeable? You've a great idea of being agreeable, you know."

The child seemed to meditate on this distinction, this imputation, for a moment; then his exaggerated eyes, which had wandered, caught my own as I watched him. "Do *you* think me agreeable?" he inquired with the candour of his age and with a look that made his father turn round to me laughing and ask, without saying it, "Isn't he adorable?"

"Then why don't you hop about, if you feel so lusty?" Ambient went on while his son swung his hand.

"Because mamma's holding me close!"

"Oh yes; I know how mamma holds you when I come near!" cried Mark with a grimace at his wife.

She turned her charming eyes up to him without deprecation or concession. "You can go for Mackintosh if you like. I think myself it would be better. You ought to drive."

"She says that to get me away," he put to me with a gaiety that I thought a little false; after which he started for the Doctor's.

I remained there with Mrs. Ambient, though even our exchange of twaddle had run very thin. The boy's little fixed white face seemed, as before, to plead with me to stay, and after a while it produced still another effect, a very curious one, which I shall find it difficult to express. Of course I expose myself to the charge of an attempt to justify by a strained logic after the fact a step which may have been on my part but the fruit of a native want of discretion; and indeed the traceable consequences of that perversity were too lamentable to leave me any desire to trifle with the question. All I can say is that I acted in perfect good faith and that (Dolcino's friendly little gaze gradually kindled the spark of my inspiration.) What helped it to glow were the other influences—the silent suggestive garden-nook, the perfect opportunity (if it was not an opportunity for that it was an opportunity for nothing) and the plea I speak of, which issued from the child's eyes and seemed to make him say: "The mother who bore me and who presses me here to her bosom—sympathetic little organism that I am—has really the kind of sensibility she has been represented to you as lacking, if you only look for it patiently and respectfully. How is it conceivable she shouldn't have it? How is it possible that *I* should have so much of it—for I'm quite full of it, dear strange gentleman—if it weren't also in some degree in her? I'm my great father's child, but I'm also my beautiful mother's, and I'm sorry for the difference between them!" So it shaped itself before me, the vision of reconciling Mrs. Ambient with her husband, of putting an end to their ugly difference. The project was absurd of course, for had I not had his word for it—spoken with all the bitterness of experience—that the gulf dividing them was well-nigh bottomless? Nevertheless, a quarter of an hour after Mark had left us, I observed to my hostess that I couldn't get over what she had told me the night before about her thinking her husband's compositions "objectionable." I had been so very sorry to hear it, had thought of it constantly and wondered whether it mightn't be possible to make her change her mind. She gave me a great cold stare, meant apparently as an admonition to me to mind my business. I wish I had taken this mute counsel, but I didn't take it. I went on to remark that it seemed an immense pity so much that was interesting should be lost on her.

"Nothing's lost upon me," she said in a tone that didn't make the contradiction less. "I know they're very interesting."

"Don't you like papa's books?" Dolcino asked, addressing his mother but still looking at me. Then he added to me: "Won't you read them to me, American gentleman?"

"I'd rather tell you some stories of my own," I said. "I know some that are awfully good."

"When will you tell them? To-morrow?"

"To-morrow with pleasure, if that suits you."

His mother took this in silence. Her husband, during our walk, had asked me to remain another day; my promise to her son was an implication that I had consented, and it wasn't possible the news could please her. This ought doubtless to have made me more careful as to what I said next, but all I can plead is that it didn't. I soon mentioned that just after leaving her the evening before, and after hearing her apply to her husband's writings the epithet already quoted, I had on going up to my room sat down to the perusal of those sheets of his new book that he had been so good as to lend me. I had sat entranced till nearly three in the morning—I had read them twice over. "You say you haven't looked at them. I think it's such a pity you shouldn't. Do let me beg you to take them up. They're so very remarkable. I'm sure they'll convert you. They place him in—really —such a dazzling light. All that's best in him is there. I've no doubt it's a great liberty, my saying all this; but pardon me, and *do* read them!"

"Do read them, mamma!" the boy again sweetly shrilled. "Do read them!"

She bent her head and closed his lips with a kiss. "Of course I know he has worked immensely over them," she said; after which she made no remark, but attached her eyes thoughtfully to the ground. The tone of these last words was such as to leave me no spirit for further pressure, and after hinting at a fear that her husband mightn't have caught the Doctor I got up and took a turn about the grounds. When I came back ten minutes later she was still in her place watching her boy, who had fallen asleep in her lap. As I drew near she put her finger to her lips and a short time afterwards rose, holding him; it being now best, she said, that she should take him upstairs. I offered to carry him and opened my arms for the purpose; but she thanked me and turned away with the child still in her embrace, his head on her shoulder. "I'm very strong," was her last word as she passed into the house, her slim flexible figure bent backward with the filial weight. So I never laid a longing hand on Dolcino.

I betook myself to Ambient's study, delighted to have a quiet hour to look over his books by myself. The windows were open to the garden; the sunny stillness, the mild light of the English summer, filled the room without quite chasing away the rich dusky tone that was a part of its charm and that abode in the serried shelves where old morocco exhaled the fragrance of curious learning, as well as in the brighter intervals where prints and medals and miniatures were suspended on a surface of faded stuff. The place had both colour and quiet; I thought it a perfect room for work and went so far as to say to myself that, if it were mine to sit and scribble in, there was no knowing but I might learn to write as well as the author of "Beltraffio." This distinguished man still didn't reappear, and I rummaged freely among his treasures. At last I took down a book that detained me a while and seated myself in a fine old leather chair by the window to turn it over. I had been occupied in this way for half an hour —a good part of the afternoon had waned—when I became conscious of another presence in the room and, looking up from my quarto, saw that Mrs. Ambient, having pushed open the door quite again in the same noiseless way marking or disguising her entrance the night before, had advanced across the threshold. On seeing me she stopped; she had not, I think, expected to find me. But her hesitation was only of a moment; she came straight to her husband's writing-table as if she were looking for something. I got up and asked her if I could help her. She glanced about an instant and then put her hand upon a roll of papers which I recognised, as I had placed it on that spot at the early hour of my descent from my room.

"Is this the new book?" she asked, holding it up.

"The very sheets," I smiled; "with precious annotations."

"I mean to take your advice"—and she tucked the little bundle under her arm. I congratulated her cordially and ventured to make of my triumph, as I presumed to call it, a subject of pleasantry. But she was perfectly grave and turned away from me, as she had presented herself, without relaxing her rigour; after which I settled down to my quarto again with the reflexion that Mrs. Ambient was truly an eccentric. My triumph, too, suddenly seemed to me rather vain. A woman who couldn't unbend at a moment exquisitely indicated would never understand Mark Ambient. He came back to us at last in person, having brought the Doctor with him. "He was away from home," Mark said, "and I went after him to where he was supposed to be. He had left the place, and I followed him to two or three others, which accounts for my delay." He was now with Mrs. Ambient, looking at the child, and was to see Mark again before leaving the house. My host noticed at the end of two minutes that the proof-sheets of his new book had been removed from the table; and when I told him, in reply to his question as to what I knew about them, that Mrs. Ambient had carried them off to read he turned almost pale with surprise. "What has suddenly made her so curious?" he cried; and I was obliged to tell him that I was at the bottom of the mystery; I had had it on my conscience to assure her that she really ought to know of what her husband was capable. "Of what I'm capable? Elle ne s'en doute que trop!" said Ambient with a laugh; but he took my meddling very good-naturedly and contented himself with adding that he was really much afraid she would burn up the sheets, his emendations and all, of which latter he had no duplicate. The Doctor paid a long visit in the nursery, and before he came down I retired to my own quarters, where I remained till dinner-time. On entering the drawing-room at this hour I found Miss Ambient in possession, as she had been the evening before.

"I was right about Dolcino," she said, as soon as she saw me, with an air of triumph that struck me as the climax of perversity. "He's really very ill."

"Very ill! Why when I last saw him, at four o'clock, he was in fairly good form."

"There has been a change for the worse, very sudden and rapid, and when the Doctor got here he found diphtheritic symptoms. He ought to have been called, as I knew, in the morning, and the child oughtn't to have been brought into the garden."

"My dear lady, he was very happy there," I protested with horror.

"He would be very happy anywhere. I've no doubt he's very happy now, with his poor little temperature—!" She dropped her voice as her brother came in, and Mark let us know that as a matter of course Mrs. Ambient wouldn't appear. It was true the boy had developed diphtheritic symptoms, but he was quiet for the present and his mother earnestly watching him. She was a perfect nurse, Mark said, and Mackintosh would come back at ten. Our dinner wasn't very gay—with my host worried and absent; and his sister annoyed me by her constant tacit assumption, conveyed in the very way she nibbled her bread and sipped her wine, of having "told me so." I had had no disposition to deny anything she might have told me, and I couldn't see that her satisfaction in being justified by the event relieved her little nephew's condition. The truth is that, as the sequel was to prove, Miss Ambient had some of the qualities of the sibyl and had therefore perhaps a right to the sibylline contortions. Her brother was so preoccupied that I felt my presence an indiscretion and was sorry I had promised to remain over the morrow. I put it to Mark that clearly I had best leave them in the morning; to which he replied that, on the contrary, if he was to pass the next days in the fidgets my company would distract his attention. The fidgets had already begun for him, poor fellow; and as we sat in his study with our cigars after dinner he wandered to the door whenever he heard the sound of the Doctor's wheels. Miss Ambient, who shared this apartment with us, gave me at such moments significant glances; she had before rejoining us gone upstairs to ask about the child. His mother and his nurse gave a fair report, but Miss Ambient found his fever high and his symptoms very grave. The Doctor came at ten o'clock, and I went to bed after hearing from Mark that he saw no present cause for alarm. He had made every provision for the night and was to return early in the morning.

I quitted my room as eight struck the next day and when I came downstairs saw, through the open door of the house, Mrs. Ambient standing at the front gate of the grounds in colloquy with Mackintosh. She wore a white dressing-gown, but her shining hair was carefully tucked away in its net, and in the morning freshness, after a night of watching, she looked as much "the type of the lady" as her sister-in-law had described her. Her appearance, I suppose, ought to have reassured me; but I was still nervous and uneasy, so that I shrank from meeting her with the necessary challenge. None the less, however, was I impatient to learn how the new day found him; and as Mrs. Ambient hadn't seen me I passed into the grounds by a round-about way and, stopping at a further gate, hailed the Doctor just as he was driving off. Mrs. Ambient had returned to the house before he got into his cart.

"Pardon me, but as a friend of the family I should like very much to hear about the little boy."

The stout sharp circumspect man looked at me from head to foot and then said: "I'm sorry to say I haven't seen him."

"Haven't seen him?"

"Mrs. Ambient came down to meet me as I alighted, and told me he was sleeping so soundly, after a restless night, that she didn't wish him disturbed. I assured her I wouldn't disturb him, but she said he was quite safe now and she could look after him herself."

"Thank you very much. Are you coming back?"

"No sir; I'll be hanged if I come back!" cried the honest practitioner in high resentment. And the horse started as he settled beside his man.

I wandered back into the garden, and five minutes later Miss Ambient came forth from the house to greet me. She explained that breakfast wouldn't be served for some time and that she desired a moment herself with the doctor. I let her know that the good vexed man had come and departed, and I repeated to her what he had told me about his dismissal. This made Miss Ambient very serious, very serious indeed, and she sank into a bench, with dilated eyes, hugging her elbows with crossed arms. She indulged in many strange signs, she confessed herself immensely distressed, and she finally told me what her own last news of her nephew had been. She had sat up very late—after me, after Mark—and before going to bed had knocked at the door of the child's room, opened to her by the nurse. This good woman had admitted her and she had found him quiet, but flushed and "unnatural," with his mother sitting by his bed. "She held his hand in one of hers," said Miss Ambient, "and in the other —what do you think?—the proof-sheets of Mark's new book! She was reading them there intently: did you ever hear of anything so extraordinary? Such a very odd time to be reading an author whom she never could abide!" In her agitation Miss Ambient was guilty of this vulgarism of speech, and I was so impressed by her narrative that only in recalling her words later did I notice the lapse. Mrs. Ambient had looked up from her reading with her finger on her lips —I recognised the gesture she had addressed me in the afternoon— and, though the nurse was about to go to rest, had not encouraged her sister-in-law to relieve her of any part of her vigil. But certainly at that time the boy's state was far from reassuring—his poor little breathing so painful; and what change could have taken place in him in those few hours that would justify Beatrice in denying Mackintosh access? This was the moral of Miss Ambient's anecdote, the moral for herself at least. The moral for me, rather, was that it *was* a very singular time for Mrs. Ambient to be going into a novelist she had never appreciated and who had simply happened to be recommended to her by a young American she disliked. I thought of her sitting there in the sick-chamber in the still hours of the night and after the nurse had left her, turning and turning those pages of genius and wrestling with their magical influence.

I must be sparing of the minor facts and the later emotions of this sojourn—it lasted but a few hours longer—and devote but three words to my subsequent relations with Ambient. They lasted five years—till his death—and were full of interest, of satisfaction and, I may add, of sadness. The main thing to be said of these years is that I had a secret from him which I guarded to the end. I believe he never suspected it, though of this I'm not absolutely sure. If he had so much as an inkling the line he had taken, the line of absolute negation of the matter to himself, shows an immense effort of the will. I may at last lay bare my secret, giving it for what it is worth; now that the main sufferer has gone, that he has begun to be alluded to as one of the famous early dead and that his wife has ceased to survive him; now too that Miss Ambient, whom I also saw at intervals during the time that followed, has, with her embroideries and her attitudes, her necromantic glances and strange intuitions, retired to a Sisterhood, where, as I am told, she is deeply immured and quite lost to the world.

Mark came in to breakfast after this lady and I had for some time been seated there. He shook hands with me in silence, kissed my companion, opened his letters and newspapers and pretended to drink his coffee. But I took these movements for mechanical and was little surprised when he suddenly pushed away everything that was before him and, with his head in his hands and his elbows on the table, sat staring strangely at the cloth.

"What's the matter, *caro fratello mio?*" Miss Ambient quavered, peeping from behind the urn.

He answered nothing, but got up with a certain violence and strode to the window. We rose to our feet, his relative and I, by a common impulse, exchanging a glance of some alarm; and he continued to stare into the garden. "In heaven's name what has got possession of Beatrice?" he cried at last, turning round on us a ravaged face. He looked from one of us to the other—the appeal was addressed to us alike.

Miss Ambient gave a shrug. "My poor Mark, Beatrice is always—Beatrice!"

"She has locked herself up with the boy—bolted and barred the door. She refuses to let me come near him!" he went on.

"She refused to let Mackintosh see him an hour ago!" Miss Ambient promptly returned.

"Refused to let Mackintosh see him? By heaven I'll smash in the door!" And Mark brought his fist down upon the sideboard, which he had now approached, so that all the breakfast-service rang.

I begged Miss Ambient to go up and try to have speech of her sister-in-law, and I drew Mark out into the garden. "You're exceedingly nervous, and Mrs. Ambient's probably right," I there undertook to plead. "Women know; women should be supreme in such a situation. Trust a mother—a devoted mother, my dear friend!" With such words as these I tried to soothe and comfort him, and, marvellous to relate, I succeeded, with the help of many cigarettes, in making him walk about the garden and talk, or suffer me at least to do so for near an hour. When about that time had elapsed his sister reappeared, reaching us rapidly and with a convulsed face while she held her hand to her heart.

"Go for the Doctor, Mark—go for the Doctor this moment!"

"Is he dying? Has she killed him?" my poor friend cried, flinging away his cigarette.

"I don't know what she has done! But she's frightened, and now she wants the Doctor."

"He told me he'd be hanged if he came back!" I felt myself obliged to mention.

"Precisely—therefore Mark himself must go for him, and not a messenger. You must see him and tell him it's to save your child. The trap has been ordered—it's ready."

"To save him? I'll save him, please God!" Ambient cried, bounding with his great strides across the lawn.

As soon as he had gone I felt I ought to have volunteered in his place, and I said as much to Miss Ambient; but she checked me by grasping my arm while we heard the wheels of the dog-cart rattle away from the gate. "He's off—he's off—and now I can think! To get him away—while I think—while I think!"

"While you think of what, Miss Ambient?"

"Of the unspeakable thing that has happened under this roof!"

Her manner was habitually that of such a prophetess of ill that I at first allowed for some great extravagance. But I looked at her hard, and the next thing felt myself turn white. "Dolcino *is* dying then—he's dead?"

"It's too late to save him. His mother has let him die! I tell you that because you're sympathetic, because you've imagination," Miss Ambient was good enough to add, interrupting my expression of horror. "That's why you had the idea of making her read Mark's new book!"

"What has that to do with it? I don't understand you. Your accusation's monstrous."

"I see it all—I'm not stupid," she went on, heedless of my emphasis. "It was the book that finished her—it was that decided her!"

"Decided her? Do you mean she has murdered her child?" I demanded, trembling at my own words.

"She sacrificed him; she determined to do nothing to make him live. Why else did she lock herself in, why else did she turn away the Doctor? The book gave her a horror; she determined to rescue him —to prevent him from ever being touched. He had a crisis at two o'clock in the morning. I know that from the nurse, who had left her then, but whom, for a short time, she called back. The darling got much worse, but she insisted on the nurse's going back to bed, and after that she was alone with him for hours."

I listened with a dread that stayed my credence, while she stood there with her tearless glare. "Do you pretend then she has no pity, that she's cruel and insane?"

"She held him in her arms, she pressed him to her breast, not to see him; but she gave him no remedies; she did nothing the Doctor ordered. Everything's there untouched. She has had the honesty not even to throw the drugs away!"

I dropped upon the nearest bench, overcome with my dismay—quite as much at Miss Ambient's horrible insistence and distinctness as at the monstrous meaning of her words. Yet they came amazingly straight, and if they did have a sense I saw myself too woefully figure in it. Had I been then a proximate cause—? "You're a very strange woman and you say incredible things," I could only reply.

She had one of her tragic headshakes. "You think it necessary to protest, but you're really quite ready to believe me. You've received an impression of my sister-in-law—you've guessed of what she's capable."

I don't feel bound to say what concession on this score I made to Miss Ambient, who went on to relate to me that within the last half-hour Beatrice had had a revulsion, that she was tremendously frightened at what she had done; that her fright itself betrayed her; and that she would now give heaven and earth to save the child. "Let us hope she will!" I said, looking at my watch and trying to time poor Ambient; whereupon my companion repeated all portentously "Let us hope so!" When I asked her if she herself could do nothing, and whether she oughtn't to be with her sister-in-law, she replied: "You had better go and judge! She's like a wounded tigress!"

I never saw Mrs. Ambient till six months after this, and therefore can't pretend to have verified the comparison. At the latter period she was again the type of the perfect lady. "She'll treat him better after this," I remember her sister-in-law's saying in response to some quick outburst, on my part, of compassion for her brother. Though I had been in the house but thirty-six hours this young lady had treated me with extraordinary confidence, and there was therefore a certain demand I might, as such an intimate, make of her. I extracted from her a pledge that she'd never say to her brother what she had just said to me, that she'd let him form his own theory of his wife's conduct. She agreed with me that there was misery enough in the house without her contributing a new anguish, and that Mrs. Ambient's proceedings might be explained, to her husband's mind, by the extravagance of a jealous devotion. Poor Mark came back with the Doctor much sooner than we could have hoped, but we knew five minutes afterwards that it was all too late. His sole, his adored little son was more exquisitely beautiful in death than he had been in life. Mrs. Ambient's grief was frantic; she lost her head and said strange things. As for Mark's—but I won't speak of that. *Basta, basta,* as he used to say. Miss Ambient kept her secret—I've already had occasion to say that she had her good points—but it rankled in her conscience like a guilty participation and, I imagine, had something to do with her ultimately retiring from the world. And, apropos of consciences, the reader is now in a position to judge of my compunction for my effort to convert my cold hostess. I ought to mention that the death of her child in some degree converted her. When the new book came out (it was long delayed) she read it over as a whole, and her husband told me that during the few supreme weeks before her death—she failed rapidly after losing her son, sank into a consumption and faded away at Mentone—she even dipped into the black "Beltraffio."

The Lesson of the Master

*H*E had been told the ladies were at church, but this was corrected by what he saw from the top of the steps—they descended from a great height in two arms, with a circular sweep of the most charming effect—at the threshold of the door which, from the long bright gallery, overlooked the immense lawn. Three gentlemen, on the grass, at a distance, sat under the great trees, while the fourth figure showed a crimson dress that told as a "bit of colour" amid the fresh rich green. The servant had so far accompanied Paul Overt as to introduce him to this view, after asking him if he wished first to go to his room. The young man declined that privilege, conscious of no disrepair from so short and easy a journey and always liking to take at once a general perceptive possession of a new scene. He stood there a little with his eyes on the group and on the admirable picture, the wide grounds of an old country house near London—that only made it better—on a splendid Sunday in June. "But that lady, who's *she?*" he said to the servant before the man left him.

"I think she's Mrs. St. George, sir."

"Mrs. St. George, the wife of the distinguished—" Then Paul Overt checked himself, doubting if a footman would know.

"Yes, sir—probably, sir," said his guide, who appeared to wish to intimate that a person staying at Summersoft would naturally be, if only by alliance, distinguished. His tone, however, made poor Overt himself feel for the moment scantly so.

"And the gentlemen?" Overt went on.

"Well, sir, one of them's General Fancourt."

"Ah, yes, I know; thank you." General Fancourt was distinguished, there was no doubt of that, for something he had done, or perhaps even hadn't done—the young man couldn't remember which—some years before in India. The servant went away, leaving the glass doors open into the gallery, and Paul Overt remained at the head of the wide double staircase, saying to himself that the place was sweet and promised a pleasant visit, while he leaned on the balustrade of fine

old ironwork which, like all the other details, was of the same period
as the house. It all went together and spoke in one voice—a rich
English voice of the early part of the eighteenth century. It might
have been church-time on a summer's day in the reign of Queen
Anne: the stillness was too perfect to be modern, the nearness
counted so as distance, and there was something so fresh and sound
in the originality of the large smooth house, the expanse of beautiful
brickwork that showed for pink rather than red and that had been
kept clear of messy creepers by the law under which a woman with a
rare complexion disdains a veil. When Paul Overt became aware that
the people under the trees had noticed him he turned back through
the open doors into the great gallery which was the pride of the
place. It marched across from end to end and seemed—with its
bright colours, its high panelled windows, its faded flowered chintzes,
its quickly-recognised portraits and pictures, the blue-and-white
china of its cabinets and the attenuated festoons and rosettes of its
ceiling—a cheerful, upholstered avenue into the other century.
Our friend was slightly nervous; that went with his character as
a student of fine prose, went with the artist's general disposition to
vibrate; and there was a particular thrill in the idea that Henry
St. George might be a member of the party. For the young aspirant
he had remained a high literary figure, in spite of the lower range of
production to which he had fallen after his three first great successes,
the comparative absence of quality in his later work. There had been
moments when Paul Overt almost shed tears for this; but now that
he was near him—he had never met him—he was conscious only of
the fine original source and of his own immense debt. After he had
taken a turn or two up and down the gallery he came out again and
descended the steps. He was but slenderly supplied with a certain
social boldness—it was really a weakness in him—so that, conscious
of a want of acquaintance with the four persons in the distance, he
gave way to motions recommended by their not committing him to a
positive approach. There was a fine English awkwardness in this—
he felt that too as he sauntered vaguely and obliquely across the lawn,
taking an independent line. Fortunately there was an equally fine
English directness in the way one of the gentlemen presently rose
and made as if to "stalk" him, though with an air of conciliation and
reassurance. To this demonstration Paul Overt instantly responded,
even if the gentleman were not his host. He was tall, straight and
elderly and had, like the great house itself, a pink smiling face, and

into the bargain a white moustache. Our young man met him half-way while he laughed and said: "Er—Lady Watermouth told us you were coming; she asked me just to look after you." Paul Overt thanked him, liking him on the spot, and turned round with him to walk toward the others. "They've all gone to church—all except us," the stranger continued as they went; "we're just sitting here—it's so jolly." Overt pronounced it jolly indeed: it was such a lovely place. He mentioned that he was having the charming impression for the first time.

"Ah, you've not been here before?" said his companion. "It's a nice little place—not much to *do*, you know." Overt wondered what he wanted to "do"—he felt that he himself was doing so much. By the time they came to where the others sat he had recognised his initiator for a military man and—such was the turn of Overt's imagination—had found him thus still more sympathetic. He would naturally have a need for action, for deeds at variance with the pacific pastoral scene. He was evidently so good-natured, however, that he accepted the inglorious hour for what it was worth. Paul Overt shared it with him and with his companions for the next twenty minutes; the latter looked at him and he looked at them without knowing much who they were, while the talk went on without much telling him even what it meant. It seemed indeed to mean nothing in particular; it wandered, with casual pointless pauses and short terrestrial flights, amid names of persons and places—names which, for our friend, had no great power of evocation. It was all sociable and slow, as was right and natural of a warm Sunday morning.

His first attention was given to the question, privately considered, of whether one of the two younger men would be Henry St. George. He knew many of his distinguished contemporaries by their photographs, but had never, as happened, seen a portrait of the great misguided novelist. One of the gentlemen was unimaginable—he was too young; and the other scarcely looked clever enough, with such mild, undiscriminating eyes. If those eyes were St. George's the problem presented by the ill-matched parts of his genius would be still more difficult of solution. Besides, the deportment of their proprietor was not, as regards the lady in the red dress, such as could be natural, toward the wife of his bosom, even to a writer accused by several critics of sacrificing too much to manner. Lastly, Paul Overt had a vague sense that if the gentleman with the expressionless eyes bore the name that had set his heart beating faster (he also had contradictory, conventional whiskers—the young admirer of the celebrity had never in a mental vision seen *his* face in so vulgar a frame) he would have given him a sign of recognition or of friendliness, would have heard of him a little, would know something about "Ginistrella," would have an impression of how that fresh fiction had caught the eye of real criticism. Paul Overt had a dread of being grossly proud, but even morbid modesty might view the authorship of "Ginistrella" as constituting a degree of identity. His soldierly friend became clear enough: he was "Fancourt," but was also "the General"; and he mentioned to the new visitor in the course of a few moments that he had but lately returned from twenty years' service abroad.

"And now you remain in England?" the young man asked.

"Oh, yes; I've bought a small house in London."

"And I hope you like it," said Overt, looking at Mrs. St. George.

"Well, a little house in Manchester Square—there's a limit to the enthusiasm *that* inspires."

"Oh, I meant being at home again—being back in Piccadilly."

"My daughter likes Piccadilly—that's the main thing. She's very fond of art and music and literature and all that kind of thing. She missed it in India and she finds it in London, or she hopes she'll find it. Mr. St. George has promised to help her—he has been awfully kind to her. She has gone to church—she's fond of that too—but they'll all be back in a quarter of an hour. You must let me introduce you to her—she'll be so glad to know you. I daresay she has read every blest word you've written."

"I shall be delighted—I haven't written so very many," Overt pleaded, feeling, and without resentment, that the General at least was vagueness itself about that. But he wondered a little why, expressing this friendly disposition, it didn't occur to the doubtless eminent soldier to pronounce the word that would put him in relation with Mrs. St. George. If it was a question of introductions Miss Fancourt—apparently as yet unmarried—was far away, while the wife of his illustrious confrère was almost between them. This lady struck Paul Overt as altogether pretty, with a surprising juvenility and a high smartness of aspect, something that—he could scarcely have said why—served for mystification. St. George certainly had every right to a charming wife, but he himself would never have imagined the important little woman in the aggressively Parisian dress the partner for life, the *alter ego,* of a man of letters. That partner in general, he knew, that second self, was far from presenting herself in a single type: observation had taught him that she was not inveterately, not necessarily plain. But he had never before seen her look so much as if her prosperity had deeper foundations than an ink-spotted study-table littered with proof-sheets. Mrs. St. George might have been the wife of a gentleman who "kept" books rather than wrote them, who carried on great affairs in the City and made better bargains than those that poets mostly make with publishers. With this she hinted at a success more personal—a success peculiarly stamping the age in which society, the world of conversation, is a great drawing-room with the City for its antechamber. Overt numbered her years at first as some thirty, and then ended by believing that she might approach her fiftieth. But she somehow in this case juggled away the excess and the difference—you only saw them in a rare glimpse, like the rabbit in the conjuror's sleeve. She was extraordinarily white, and her every element and item was pretty: her eyes, her ears, her hair, her voice, her hands, her feet—to which her relaxed attitude in her wicker chair gave a great publicity—and the numerous ribbons and trinkets with which she was bedecked. She looked as if she had put on her best clothes to go to church and then had decided they were too good for that and had stayed at home. She told a story of some length about the shabby way Lady Jane had treated the Duchess, as well as an anecdote in relation to a purchase she had made in Paris—on her way back from Cannes; made for Lady Egbert, who had never refunded the money. Paul Overt suspected her of a tendency to figure great people as larger than life, until he noticed the manner in which she handled Lady Egbert, which was so sharply mutinous that it reassured him. He felt he should have understood her better if he might have met her eye; but she scarcely so much as glanced at him. "Ah, here they come—all the good ones!" she said at last; and Paul Overt admired at his distance the return of the churchgoers—several persons, in couples and threes, advancing in a flicker of sun and shade at the end of a large green vista formed by the level grass and the overarching boughs.

"If you mean to imply that *we're* bad, I protest," said one of the gentlemen—"after making one's self agreeable all the morning!"

"Ah, if they've found you agreeable—!" Mrs. St. George gaily cried. "But if we're good the others are better."

"They must be angels then," said the amused General.

"Your husband was an angel, the way he went off at your bidding," the gentleman who had first spoken declared to Mrs. St. George.

"At my bidding?"

"Didn't you make him go to church?"

"I never made him do anything in my life but once—when I made him burn up a bad book. That's all!" At her "That's all!" our young friend broke into an irrepressible laugh; it lasted only a second, but it drew her eyes to him. His own met them, though not long enough to help him to understand her; unless it were a step towards this that he saw on the instant how the burnt book—the way she alluded to it!—would have been one of her husband's finest things.

"A bad book?" her interlocutor repeated.

"I didn't like it. He went to church because your daughter went," she continued to General Fancourt. "I think it my duty to call your attention to his extraordinary demonstrations to your daughter."

"Well, if you don't mind them I don't!" the General laughed.

"*Il s'attache à ses pas*. But I don't wonder—she's so charming."

"I hope she won't make him burn any books!" Paul Overt ventured to exclaim.

"If she'd make him write a few it would be more to the purpose," said Mrs. St. George. "He has been of a laziness of late—!"

Our young man stared—he was so struck with the lady's phraseology. Her "Write a few" seemed to him almost as good as her "That's all." Didn't she, as the wife of a rare artist, know what it was to produce *one perfect work of art?* How in the world did she think they were turned off? His private conviction was that, admirably as Henry St. George wrote, he had written for the last ten years, and especially for the last five, only too much, and there was an instant during which he felt inwardly solicited to make this public. But before he had spoken a diversion was effected by the return of the absentees. They strolled up dispersedly—there were eight or ten of them—and the circle under the trees rearranged itself as they took their place in it. They made it much larger, so that Paul Overt could feel—he was always feeling that sort of thing, as he said to himself—that if the company had already been interesting to watch the interest would now become intense. He shook hands with his hostess, who welcomed him without many words, in the manner of a woman able to trust him to understand and conscious that so pleasant an occasion would in every way speak for itself. She offered him no particular facility for sitting by her, and when they had all subsided again he found himself still next General Fancourt, with an unknown lady on his other flank.

"That's my daughter—that one opposite," the General said to him without loss of time. Overt saw a tall girl, with magnificent red hair, in a dress of a pretty grey-green tint and of a limp silken texture, a garment that clearly shirked every modern effect. It had therefore somehow the stamp of the latest thing, so that our beholder quickly took her for nothing if not contemporaneous.

"She's very handsome—very handsome," he repeated while he considered her. There was something noble in her head, and she appeared fresh and strong.

Her good father surveyed her with complacency, remarking soon: "She looks too hot—that's her walk. But she'll be all right presently. Then I'll make her come over and speak to you."

"I should be sorry to give you that trouble. If you were to take me over *there*—!" the young man murmured.

"My dear sir, do you suppose I put myself out that way? I don't mean for you, but for Marian," the General added.

"*I* would put myself out for her soon enough," Overt replied; after which he went on: "Will you be so good as to tell me which of those gentlemen is Henry St. George?"

"The fellow talking to my girl. By Jove, he *is* making up to her—they're going off for another walk."

"Ah, is that he—really?" Our friend felt a certain surprise, for the personage before him seemed to trouble a vision which had been vague only while not confronted with the reality. As soon as the reality dawned, the mental image, retiring with a sigh, became substantial enough to suffer a slight wrong. Overt, who had spent a considerable part of his short life in foreign lands, made now, but not for the first time, the reflexion that whereas in those countries he had almost always recognised the artist and the man of letters by his personal "type," the mould of his face, the character of his head, the expression of his figure, and even the indications of his dress, so in England this identification was as little as possible a matter of course, thanks to the greater conformity, the habit of sinking the profession instead of advertising it, the general diffusion of the air of the gentleman—the gentleman committed to no particular set of ideas. More than once, on returning to his own country, he had said to himself about people met in society: "One sees them in this place and that, and one even talks with them; but to find out what they *do* one would really have to be a detective." In respect to several individuals whose work he was the opposite of "drawn to"—perhaps he was wrong—he found himself adding, "No wonder they conceal it— when it's so bad!" He noted that oftener than in France and in Germany his artist looked like a gentleman—that is, like an English one —while, certainly outside a few exceptions, his gentleman didn't look like an artist. St. George was not one of the exceptions; that circumstance he definitely apprehended before the great man had turned his back to walk off with Miss Fancourt. He certainly looked better behind than any foreign man of letters—showed for beautifully correct in his tall black hat and his superior frock coat. Somehow, all the same, these very garments—he wouldn't have minded them so much on a weekday—were disconcerting to Paul Overt, who forgot for the moment that the head of the profession was not a bit better dressed than himself. He had caught a glimpse of a regular face, a fresh colour, a brown moustache, and a pair of eyes surely never visited by a fine frenzy, and he promised himself to study these denotements on the first occasion. His superficial sense was that their owner might have passed for a lucky stockbroker—a gentleman driving eastward every morning from a sanitary suburb in a smart dog-cart. That carried out the impression already derived from his wife. Paul's glance, after a moment, travelled back to this lady, and he saw how her own had followed her husband as he moved off with Miss Fancourt. Overt permitted himself to wonder a little if she were jealous when another woman took him away. Then he made out that Mrs. St. George wasn't glaring at the indifferent maiden. Her eyes rested but on her husband, and with unmistakable serenity. That was the way she wanted him to be—she liked his conventional uniform. Overt longed to hear more about the book she had induced him to destroy.

II

As they all came out from luncheon General Fancourt took hold of him with an "I say, I want you to know my girl!" as if the idea had just occurred to him and he hadn't spoken of it before. With the other hand he possessed himself all paternally of the young lady. "You know all about him. I've seen you with his books. She reads everything—everything!" he went on to Paul. The girl smiled at him and then laughed at her father. The General turned away and his daughter spoke—"Isn't papa delightful?"

"He is indeed, Miss Fancourt."

"As if I read you because I read 'everything'!"

"Oh, I don't mean for saying that, said Paul Overt. "I liked him from the moment he began to be kind to me. Then he promised me this privilege."

"It isn't for you he means it—it's for me. If you flatter yourself that he thinks of anything in life but me you'll find you're mistaken. He introduces everyone. He thinks me insatiable."

"You speak just like him," laughed our youth.

"Ah, but sometimes I want to"—and the girl coloured. "I don't read everything—I read very little. But I *have* read you."

"Suppose we go into the gallery," said Paul Overt. She pleased him greatly, not so much because of this last remark—though that of course was not too disconcerting—as because, seated opposite to him at luncheon, she had given him for half an hour the impression of her beautiful face. Something else had come with it—a sense of generosity, of an enthusiasm which, unlike many enthusiasms, was not all manner. That was not spoiled for him by his seeing that the repast had placed her again in familiar contact with Henry St. George. Sitting next her this celebrity was also opposite our young man, who had been able to note that he multiplied the attentions lately brought by his wife to the General's notice. Paul Overt had gathered as well that this lady was not in the least discomposed by these fond excesses and that she gave every sign of an unclouded spirit. She had Lord Masham on one side of her and on the other the accomplished Mr. Mulliner, editor of the new high-class lively evening paper which was expected to meet a want felt in circles increasingly conscious that Conservatism must be made amusing, and unconvinced when assured by those of another political colour that it was already amusing enough. At the end of an hour spent in her company Paul Overt thought her still prettier than at the first radiation, and if her profane allusions to her husband's work had not still rung in his ears he should have liked her—so far as it could be a question of that in connexion with a woman to whom he had not yet spoken and to whom probably he should never speak if it were left to her. Pretty women were a clear need to this genius, and for the hour it was Miss Fancourt who supplied the want. If Overt had promised himself a closer view the occasion was now of the best, and it brought consequences felt by the young man as important. He saw more in St. George's face, which he liked the better for its not having told its whole story in the first three minutes. That story came out

as one read, in short instalments—it was excusable that one's analogies should be somewhat professional—and the text was a style
considerably involved, a language not easy to translate at sight.
There were shades of meaning in it and a vague perspective of history
which receded as you advanced. Two facts Paul had particularly
heeded. The first of these was that he liked the measured mask much
better at inscrutable rest than in social agitation; its almost convul-
sive smile above all displeased him (as much as any impression from
that source could), whereas the quiet face had a charm that grew in
proportion as stillness settled again. The change to the expression of
gaiety excited, he made out, very much the private protest of a person sitting gratefully in the twilight when the lamp is brought in too
soon. His second reflexion was that, though generally adverse to the
flagrant use of ingratiating arts by a man of age "making up" to a
pretty girl, he was not in this case too painfully affected: which
seemed to prove either that St. George had a light hand or the air
of being younger than he was, or else that Miss Fancourt's own
manner somehow made everything right.

Overt walked with her into the gallery, and they strolled to the
end of it, looking at the pictures, the cabinets, the charming vista,
which harmonised with the prospect of the summer afternoon, resembling it by a long brightness, with great divans and old chairs
that figured hours of rest. Such a place as that had the added merit
of giving those who came into it plenty to talk about. Miss Fancourt
sat down with her new acquaintance on a flowered sofa, the cushions
of which, very numerous, were tight ancient cubes of many sizes, and
presently said: "I'm so glad to have a chance to thank you."

"To thank me—?" He had to wonder.

"I liked your book so much. I think it splendid."

She sat there smiling at him, and he never asked himself which
book she meant; for after all he had written three or four. That
seemed a vulgar detail, and he wasn't even gratified by the idea of
the pleasure she told him—her handsome bright face told him—he
had given her. The feeling she appealed to, or at any rate the feeling
she excited, was something larger, something that had little to do
with any quickened pulsation of his own vanity. It was responsive
admiration of the life she embodied, the young purity and richness
of which appeared to imply that real success was to resemble that,
to live, to bloom, to present the perfection of a fine type, not to have
hammered out headachy fancies with a bent back at an ink-stained

table. While her grey eyes rested on him—there was a widish space between these, and the division of her rich-coloured hair, so thick that it ventured to be smooth, made a free arch above them—he was almost ashamed of that exercise of the pen which it was her present inclination to commend. He was conscious he should have liked better to please her in some other way. The lines of her face were those of a woman grown, but the child lingered on in her complexion and in the sweetness of her mouth. Above all she was natural—that was indubitable now; more natural than he had supposed at first, perhaps on account of her esthetic toggery, which was conventionally unconventional, suggesting what he might have called a tortuous spontaneity. He had feared that sort of thing in other cases, and his fears had been justified; for, though he was an artist to the essence, the modern reactionary nymph, with the brambles of the woodland caught in her folds and a look as if the satyrs had toyed with her hair, made him shrink, not as a man of starch and patent leather, but as a man potentially himself a poet or even a faun. The girl was really more candid than her costume, and the best proof of it was her supposing her liberal character suited by any uniform. This was a fallacy, since if she was draped as a pessimist he was sure she liked the taste of life. He thanked her for her appreciation—aware at the same time that he didn't appear to thank her enough and that she might think him ungracious. He was afraid she would ask him to explain something he had written, and he always winced at that— perhaps too timidly—for to his own ear the explanation of a work of art sounded fatuous. But he liked her so much as to feel a confidence that in the long run he should be able to show her he wasn't rudely evasive. Moreover, she surely wasn't quick to take offence, wasn't irritable; she could be trusted to wait. So when he said to her, "Ah, don't talk of anything I've done, don't talk of it *here; there's* another man in the house who's the actuality!"—when he uttered this short sincere protest it was with the sense that she would see in the words neither mock humility nor the impatience of a successful man bored with praise.

"You mean Mr. St. George—isn't he delightful?"

Paul Overt met her eyes, which had a cool morning light that would have half-broken his heart if he hadn't been so young. "Alas, I don't know him. I only admire him at a distance."

"Oh, you *must* know him—he wants so to talk to you," returned Miss Fancourt, who evidently had the habit of saying the things that, by her quick calculation, would give people pleasure. Paul saw how she would always calculate on everything's being simple between others.

"I shouldn't have supposed he knew anything about me," he professed.

"He does then—everything. And if he didn't I should be able to tell him."

"To tell him everything?" our friend smiled.

"You talk just like the people in your book," she answered.

"Then they must all talk alike."

She thought a moment, not a bit disconcerted. "Well, it must be so difficult. Mr. St. George tells me it *is*—terribly. I've tried too—and I find it so. I've tried to write a novel."

"Mr. St. George oughtn't to discourage you," Paul went so far as to say.

"You do much more—when you wear that expression."

"Well, after all, why try to be an artist?" the young man pursued. "It's so poor—so poor!"

"I don't know what you mean," said Miss Fancourt, who looked grave.

"I mean as compared with being a person of action—as living your works."

"But what's art but an intense life—if it be real?" she asked. "I think it's the only one—everything else is so clumsy!" Her companion laughed, and she brought out with her charming serenity what next struck her. "It's so interesting to meet so many celebrated people."

"So I should think—but surely it isn't new to you."

"Why, I've never seen anyone—anyone: living always in Asia."

The way she talked of Asia somehow enchanted him. "But doesn't that continent swarm with great figures? Haven't you administered provinces in India and had captive rajahs and tributary princes chained to your car?"

It was as if she didn't care even *should* he amuse himself at her cost. "I was with my father, after I left school to go out there. It was delightful being with him—we're alone together in the world, he and I—but there was none of the society I like best. One never heard of a picture—never of a book, except bad ones."

"Never of a picture? Why, wasn't all life a picture?"

She looked over the delightful place where they sat. "Nothing to compare to this. I adore England!" she cried.

It fairly stirred in him the sacred chord. "Ah, of course I don't deny that we must do something with her, poor old dear, yet!"

"She hasn't been touched, really," said the girl.

"Did Mr. St. George say that?"

There was a small and, as he felt, harmless spark of irony in his question; which, however, she answered very simply, not noticing the insinuation. "Yes, he says England hasn't been touched—not considering all there is," she went on eagerly. "He's so interesting about our country. To listen to him makes one want so to do something."

"It would make *me* want to," said Paul Overt, feeling strongly, on the instant, the suggestion of what she said and that of the emotion with which she said it, and well aware of what an incentive, on St. George's lips, such a speech might be.

"Oh, you—as if you hadn't! I should like so to hear you talk together," she added ardently.

"That's very genial of you; but he'd have it all his own way. I'm prostrate before him."

She had an air of earnestness. "Do you think, then, he's so perfect?"

"Far from it. Some of his later books seem to me of a queerness—!"

"Yes, yes—he knows that."

Paul Overt stared. "That they seem to me of a queerness—?"

"Well, yes, or at any rate that they're not what they should be. He told me he didn't esteem them. He has told me such wonderful things—he's so interesting."

There was a certain shock for Paul Overt in the knowledge that the fine genius they were talking of had been reduced to so explicit a confession and had made it, in his misery, to the first comer; for though Miss Fancourt was charming what was she after all but an immature girl encountered at a country-house? Yet precisely this was part of the sentiment he himself had just expressed: he would make way completely for the poor peccable great man, not because he didn't read him clear, but altogether because he did. His consideration was half composed of tenderness for superficialities which he was sure their perpetrator judged privately, judged more ferociously than anyone, and which represented some tragic intellectual secret. He would have his reasons for his psychology *à fleur de peau,* and these reasons could only be cruel ones, such as would make him dearer to those who already were fond of him. "You excite my envy. I have my reserves, I discriminate—but I love him," Paul said in a moment. "And seeing him for the first time this way is a great event for me."

"How momentous—how magnificent!" cried the girl. "How delicious to bring you together!"

"*Your* doing it—that makes it perfect," our friend returned.

"He's as eager as you," she went on. "But it's so odd you shouldn't have met."

"It's not really so odd as it strikes you. I've been out of England so much—made repeated absences all these last years."

She took this in with interest. "And yet you write of it as well as if you were always here."

"It's just the being away perhaps. At any rate the best bits, I suspect, are those that were done in dreary places abroad."

"And why were they dreary?"

"Because they were health-resorts—where my poor mother was dying."

"Your poor mother?"—she was all sweet wonder.

"We went from place to place to help her to get better. But she never did. To the deadly Riviera (I hate it!), to the high Alps, to Algiers, and far away—a hideous journey—to Colorado."

"And she isn't better?" Miss Fancourt went on.

"She died a year ago."

"Really?—like mine! Only that's years since. Some day you must tell me about your mother," she added.

He could at first, on this, only gaze at her. "What right things you say! If you say them to St. George I don't wonder he's in bondage."

It pulled her up for a moment. "I don't know what you mean. He doesn't make speeches and professions at all—he isn't ridiculous."

"I'm afraid you consider, then, that I am."

"No, I don't"—she spoke it rather shortly. And then she added: "He understands—understands everything."

The young man was on the point of saying jocosely: "And I don't —is that it?" But these words, in time, changed themselves to others slightly less trivial. "Do you suppose he understands his wife?"

Miss Fancourt made no direct answer, but after a moment's hesitation put it: "Isn't she charming?"

"Not in the least!"

"Here he comes. Now you must know him," she went on. A small group of visitors had gathered at the other end of the gallery and had been there overtaken by Henry St. George, who strolled in from a neighbouring room. He stood near them a moment, not falling into the talk but taking up an old miniature from a table and vaguely regarding it. At the end of a minute he became aware of Miss Fancourt and her companion in the distance; whereupon, laying down his miniature, he approached them with the same procrastinating air, his hands in his pockets and his eyes turned, right and left, to the pictures. The gallery was so long that this transit took some little time, especially as there was a moment when he stopped to admire the fine Gainsborough. "He says Mrs. St. George has been the making of him," the girl continued in a voice slightly lowered.

"Ah, he's often obscure!" Paul laughed.

"Obscure?" she repeated as if she heard it for the first time. Her eyes rested on her other friend, and it wasn't lost upon Paul that they appeared to send out great shafts of softness. "He's going to speak to us!" she fondly breathed. There was a sort of rapture in her voice, and our friend was startled. "Bless my soul, does she care for him like *that?*—is she in love with him?" he mentally inquired. "Didn't I tell you he was eager?" she had meanwhile asked of him.

"It's eagerness dissimulated," the young man returned as the subject of their observation lingered before his Gainsborough. "He edges toward us shyly. Does he mean that she saved him by burning that book?"

"That book? what book did she burn?" The girl quickly turned her face to him.

"Hasn't he told you, then?"

"Not a word."

"Then he doesn't tell you everything!" Paul had guessed that she pretty much supposed he did. The great man had now resumed his course and come nearer; in spite of which his more qualified admirer risked a profane observation. "St. George and the Dragon is what the anecdote suggests!"

His companion, however, didn't hear it; she smiled at the dragon's adversary. "He *is* eager—he is!" she insisted.

"Eager for you—yes."

But meanwhile she had called out: "I'm sure you want to know Mr. Overt. You'll be great friends, and it will always be delightful to me to remember I was here when you first met and that I had something to do with it."

There was a freshness of intention in the words that carried them off; nevertheless our young man was sorry for Henry St. George, as he was sorry at any time for any person publicly invited to be responsive and delightful. He would have been so touched to believe that a man he deeply admired should care a straw for him that he wouldn't play with such a presumption if it were possibly vain. In a single glance of the eye of the pardonable master he read —having the sort of divination that belonged to his talent—that this personage had ever a store of friendly patience, which was part of his rich outfit, but was versed in no printed page of a rising scribbler. There was even a relief, a simplification, in that: liking him so much already for what he had done, how could one have liked him any more for a perception which must at the best have been vague? Paul Overt got up, trying to show his compassion, but at the same instant he found himself encompassed by St. George's happy personal art— a manner of which it was the essence to conjure away false positions. It all took place in a moment. Paul was conscious that he knew him now, conscious of his handshake and of the very quality of his hand; of his face, seen nearer and consequently seen better, of a general fraternising assurance, and in particular of the circumstance that St. George didn't dislike him (as yet at least) for being imposed by a charming but too gushing girl, attractive enough without such danglers. No irritation at any rate was reflected in the voice with which he questioned Miss Fancourt as to some project of a walk—a general walk of the company round the park. He had soon said something to Paul about a talk—"We must have a tremendous lot of talk; there are so many things, aren't there?"—but our friend could see this idea wouldn't in the present case take very immediate effect. All the same he was extremely happy, even after the matter of the walk had been settled—the three presently passed back to the other part of the gallery, where it was discussed with several members of the party; even when, after they had all gone out together, he found himself for half an hour conjoined with Mrs. St. George. Her husband had taken the advance with Miss Fancourt, and this pair were quite out of sight. It was the prettiest of rambles for a summer afternoon—a grassy circuit, of immense extent, skirting the limit of the park within. The park was completely surrounded by its old mottled but perfect red wall, which, all the way on their left, constituted in itself an object of interest. Mrs. St. George mentioned to him the surprising number of acres thus enclosed, together with numerous other facts relating to the property and the family, and the family's other properties: she couldn't too strongly urge on him the importance of seeing their other houses. She ran over the names of these and rang the changes on them with the facility of practice, making them appear an almost endless list. She had received Paul Overt very amiably on his breaking ground with her by the mention of his joy in having just made her husband's acquaintance, and struck him as so alert and so accommodating a little woman that he was rather ashamed of his *mot* about her to Miss Fancourt; though he reflected that a hundred other people, on a hundred occasions, would have been sure to make it. He got on with Mrs. St. George, in short, better than he expected; but this didn't prevent her suddenly becoming aware that she was faint with fatigue and must take her way back to the house by the shortest cut. She professed that she hadn't the strength of a kitten and was a miserable wreck; a character he had been too preoccupied to discern in her while he wondered in what sense she could be held to have been the making of her husband. He had arrived at a glimmering of the answer when she announced that she must leave him, though this perception was of course provisional. While he was in the very act of placing himself at her disposal for the return, the situation underwent a change; Lord Masham had suddenly turned up, coming back to them, overtaking them, emerging from the shrubbery—Overt could scarcely have said how he appeared—and Mrs. St. George had protested that she wanted to be left alone and not to break up the party. A moment later she was walking off with Lord Masham. Our friend fell back and joined Lady Watermouth, to whom he presently mentioned that Mrs. St. George had been obliged to renounce the attempt to go further.

"She oughtn't to have come out at all," her ladyship rather grumpily remarked.

"Is she so very much of an invalid?"

"Very bad indeed." And his hostess added with still greater austerity: "She oughtn't really to come to one!" He wondered what was implied by this, and presently gathered that it was not a reflexion on the lady's conduct or her moral nature: it only represented that her strength was not equal to her aspirations.

III

The smoking-room at Summersoft was on the scale of the rest of the place—high light commodious and decorated with such refined old carvings and mouldings that it seemed rather a bower for ladies who should sit at work at fading crewels than a parliament of gentlemen smoking strong cigars. The gentlemen mustered there in considerable force on the Sunday evening, collecting mainly at one end, in front of one of the cool fair fireplaces of white marble, the entablature of which was adorned with a delicate little Italian "subject." There was another in the wall that faced it, and, thanks to the mild summer night, a fire in neither; but a nucleus for aggregation was furnished on one side by a table in the chimney-corner laden with bottles, decanters and tall tumblers. Paul Overt was a faithless smoker; he would puff a cigarette for reasons with which tobacco had nothing to do. This was particularly the case on the occasion of which I speak; his motive was the vision of a little direct talk with Henry St. George. The "tremendous" communion of which the great man had held out hopes to him earlier in the day had not yet come off, and this saddened him considerably, for the party was to go its several ways immediately after breakfast on the morrow. He had, however, the disappointment of finding that apparently the author of "Shadowmere" was not disposed to prolong his vigil. He wasn't among the gentlemen assembled when Paul entered, nor was he one of those who turned up, in bright habiliments, during the next ten minutes. The young man waited a little, wondering if he had only gone to put on something extraordinary; this would account for his delay as well as contribute further to Overt's impression of his tendency to do the approved superficial thing. But he didn't arrive—he must have been putting on something more extraordinary than was probable. Our hero gave him up, feeling a little injured, a little wounded, at this loss of twenty coveted words. He wasn't angry, but he puffed his cigarette sighingly, with the sense of something rare possibly missed. He wandered away with his regret and moved slowly round the room, looking at the old prints on the walls. In this attitude he presently felt a hand on his shoulder and a friendly voice in his ear: "This is good. I hoped I should find you. I came down on purpose." St. George was there without a change of dress and with a fine face—his graver one—to which our young

man all in a flutter responded. He explained that it was only for the
Master—the idea of a little talk—that he had sat up, and that, not
finding him, he had been on the point of going to bed.

"Well, you know, I don't smoke—my wife doesn't let me," said
St. George, looking for a place to sit down. "It's very good for me
—very good for me. Let us take that sofa."

"Do you mean smoking's good for you?"

"No, no—her not letting me. It's a great thing to have a wife who's
so sure of all the things one can do without. One might never find
them out one's self. She doesn't allow me to touch a cigarette." They
took possession of a sofa at a distance from the group of smokers,
and St. George went on: "Have you got one yourself?"

"Do you mean a cigarette?"

"Dear no—a wife!"

"No; and yet I'd give up my cigarette for one."

"You'd give up a good deal more than that," St. George returned.
"However, you'd get a great deal in return. There's a something
to be said for wives," he added, folding his arms and crossing his
outstretched legs. He declined tobacco altogether and sat there without returning fire. His companion stopped smoking, touched by his
courtesy; and after all they were out of the fumes, their sofa was in
a faraway corner. It would have been a mistake, St. George went
on, a great mistake for them to have separated without a little chat;
"for I know all about you," he said, "I know you're very remarkable.
You've written a very distinguished book."

"And how do you know it?" Paul asked.

"Why, my dear fellow, it's in the air, it's in the papers, it's everywhere." St. George spoke with the immediate familiarity of a confrère—a tone that seemed to his neighbour the very rustle of the
laurel. "You're on all men's lips and, what's better, on all women's.
And I've just been reading your book."

"Just? You hadn't read it this afternoon," said Overt.

"How do you know that?"

"I think you should know how I know it," the young man laughed.

"I suppose Miss Fancourt told you."

"No indeed—she led me rather to suppose you had."

"Yes—that's much more what she'd do. Doesn't she shed a rosy
glow over life? But you didn't believe her?" asked St. George.

"No, not when you came to us there."

"Did I pretend? did I pretend badly?" But without waiting for an answer to this St. George went on: "You ought always to believe such a girl as that—always, always. Some women are meant to be taken with allowances and reserves, but you must take *her* just as she is."

"I like her very much," said Paul Overt.

Something in his tone appeared to excite on his companion's part a momentary sense of the absurd; perhaps it was the air of deliberation attending this judgement. St. George broke into a laugh to reply. "It's the best thing you can do with her. She's a rare young lady! In point of fact, however, I confess I hadn't read you this afternoon."

"Then you see how right I was in this particular case not to believe Miss Fancourt."

"How right? how can I agree to that when I lost credit by it?"

"Do you wish to pass exactly for what she represents you? Certainly you needn't be afraid," Paul said.

"Ah, my dear young man, don't talk about passing—for the likes of me! I'm passing away—nothing else than that. She has a better use for her young imagination (isn't it fine?) than in 'representing' in any way such a weary wasted used-up animal!" The Master spoke with a sudden sadness that produced a protest on Paul's part; but before the protest could be uttered he went on, reverting to the latter's striking novel: "I had no idea you were so good—one hears of so many things. But you're surprisingly good."

"I'm going to be surprisingly better," Overt made bold to reply.

"I see that, and it's what fetches me. I don't see so much else—as one looks about—that's going to be surprisingly better. They're going to be consistently worse—most of the things. It's so much easier to be worse—heaven knows I've found it so. I'm not in a great glow, you know, about what's breaking out all over the place. But you *must* be better, you really must keep it up. I haven't, of course. It's very difficult—that's the devil of the whole thing, keeping it up. But I see you'll be able to. It will be a great disgrace if you don't."

"It's very interesting to hear you speak of yourself; but I don't know what you mean by your allusions to your having fallen off," Paul Overt observed with pardonable hypocrisy. He liked his companion so much now that the fact of any decline of talent or of care had ceased for the moment to be vivid to him.

"Don't say that—don't say that," St. George returned gravely, his head resting on the top of the sofa-back and his eyes on the ceiling.

"You know perfectly what I mean. I haven't read twenty pages of your book without seeing that you can't help it."

"You make me very miserable," Paul ecstatically breathed.

"I'm glad of that, for it may serve as a kind of warning. Shocking enough it must be, especially to a young fresh mind, full of faith—the spectacle of a man meant for better things sunk at my age in such dishonour." St. George, in the same contemplative attitude, spoke softly but deliberately, and without perceptible emotion. His tone indeed suggested an impersonal lucidity that was practically cruel—cruel to himself—and made his young friend lay an argumentative hand on his arm. But he went on while his eyes seemed to follow the graces of the eighteenth-century ceiling: "Look at me well, take my lesson to heart—for it *is* a lesson. Let that good come of it at least that you shudder with your pitiful impression, and that this may help to keep you straight in the future. Don't become in your old age what I have in mine—the depressing, the deplorable illustration of the worship of false gods!"

"What do you mean by your old age?" the young man asked.

"It has made me old. But I like your youth."

Paul answered nothing—they sat for a minute in silence. They heard the others going on about the governmental majority. Then "What do you mean by false gods?" he inquired.

His companion had no difficulty whatever in saying, "The idols of the market; money and luxury and 'the world'; placing one's children and dressing one's wife; everything that drives one to the short and easy way. Ah, the vile things they make one do!"

"But surely one's right to want to place one's children."

"One has no business to have any children," St. George placidly declared. "I mean, of course, if one wants to do anything good."

"But aren't they an inspiration—an incentive?"

"An incentive to damnation, artistically speaking."

"You touch on very deep things—things I should like to discuss with you," Paul said. "I should like you to tell me volumes about yourself. This is a great feast for *me!*"

"Of course it is, cruel youth. But to show you I'm still not incapable, degraded as I am, of an act of faith, I'll tie my vanity to the stake for you and burn it to ashes. You must come and see me—you must come and see us," the Master quickly substituted. "Mrs. St. George is charming; I don't know whether you've had any opportunity to talk with her. She'll be delighted to see you; she likes great celebrities, whether incipient or predominant. You must come and dine—my wife will write to you. Where are you to be found?"

"This is my little address"—and Overt drew out his pocket-book and extracted a visiting-card. On second thoughts, however, he kept it back, remarking that he wouldn't trouble his friend to take charge of it but would come and see him straightway in London and leave it at his door if he should fail to obtain entrance.

"Ah, you'll probably fail; my wife's always out—or when she isn't out is knocked up from having *been* out. You must come and dine —though that won't do much good either, for my wife insists on big dinners." St. George turned it over further, but then went on: "You must come down and see us in the country, that's the best way; we've plenty of room and it isn't bad."

"You've a house in the country?" Paul asked enviously.

"Ah, not like this! But we have a sort of place we go to—an hour from Euston. That's one of the reasons."

"One of the reasons?"

"Why my books are so bad."

"You must tell me all the others!" Paul longingly laughed.

His friend made no direct rejoinder to this, but spoke again abruptly. "Why have I never seen you before?"

The tone of the question was singularly flattering to our hero, who felt it to imply the great man's now perceiving he had for years missed something. "Partly, I suppose, because there has been no particular reason why you should see me. I haven't lived in the world —in your world. I've spent many years out of England, in different places abroad."

"Well, please don't do it any more. You must do England—there's such a lot of it."

"Do you mean I must write about it?"—and Paul struck the note of the listening candour of a child.

"Of course you must. And tremendously well, do you mind? That takes off a little of my esteem for this thing of yours—that it goes on abroad. Hang 'abroad'! Stay at home and do things here—do subjects we can measure."

"I'll do whatever you tell me," Overt said, deeply attentive. "But pardon me if I say I don't understand how you've been reading my book," he added. "I've had you before me all the afternoon, first in that long walk, then at tea on the lawn, till we went to dress for dinner, and all the evening at dinner and in this place."

St. George turned his face about with a smile. "I gave it but a quarter of an hour."

"A quarter of an hour's immense, but I don't understand where you put it in. In the drawing-room after dinner you weren't reading—you were talking to Miss Fancourt."

"It comes to the same thing, because we talked about 'Ginistrella.' She described it to me—she lent me her copy."

"Lent it to you?"

"She travels with it."

"It's incredible," Paul blushed.

"It's glorious for you, but it also turned out very well for me. When the ladies went off to bed she kindly offered to send the book down to me. Her maid brought it to me in the hall, and I went to my room with it. I hadn't thought of coming here, I do that so little. But I don't sleep early, I always have to read an hour or two. I sat down to your novel on the spot, without undressing, without taking off anything but my coat. I think that's a sign my curiosity had been strongly aroused about it. I read a quarter of an hour, as I tell you, and even in a quarter of an hour I was greatly struck."

"Ah, the beginning isn't very good—it's the whole thing!" said Overt, who had listened to this recital with extreme interest. "And you laid down the book and came after me?" he asked.

"That's the way it moved me. I said to myself, 'I see it's off his own bat, and he's there, by the way, and the day's over, and I haven't said twenty words to him.' It occurred to me that you'd probably be in the smoking-room and that it wouldn't be too late to repair my omission. I wanted to do something civil to you, so I put on my coat and came down. I shall read your book again when I go up."

Our friend faced round in his place—he was touched as he had scarce ever been by the picture of such a demonstration in his favour. "You're really the kindest of men. *Cela s'est passé comme ça?*—and I've been sitting here with you all this time and never apprehended it and never thanked you!"

"Thank Miss Fancourt—it was she who wound me up. She has made me feel as if I had read your novel."

"She's an angel from heaven!" Paul declared.

"She is indeed. I've never seen anyone like her. Her interest in literature's touching—something quite peculiar to herself; she takes it all so seriously. She feels the arts and she wants to feel them more. To those who practise them it's almost humiliating—her curiosity, her sympathy, her good faith. How can anything be as fine as she supposes it?"

"She's a rare organisation," the younger man sighed.

"The richest I've ever seen—an artistic intelligence really of the first order. And lodged in such a form!" St. George exclaimed.

"One would like to represent such a girl as that," Paul continued.

"Ah, there it is—there's nothing like life!" said his companion. "When you're finished, squeezed dry and used up and you think the sack's empty, you're still appealed to, you still get touches and thrills, the idea springs up—out of the lap of the actual—and shows you there's always something to be done. But I shan't do it—she's not for me!"

"How do you mean, not for you?"

"Oh, it's all over—she's for you, if you like."

"Ah, much less!" said Paul. "She's not for a dingy little man of letters; she's for the world, the bright rich world of bribes and rewards. And the world will take hold of her—it will carry her away."

"It will try—but it's just a case in which there may be a fight. It would be worth fighting, for a man who had it in him, with youth and talent on his side."

These words rang not a little in Paul Overt's consciousness—they held him briefly silent. "It's a wonder she has remained as she is; giving herself away so—with so much to give away."

"Remaining, you mean, so ingenuous—so natural? Oh, she doesn't care a straw—she gives away because she overflows. She has her own feelings, her own standards; she doesn't keep remembering that she must be proud. And then she hasn't been here long enough to be spoiled; she has picked up a fashion or two, but only the amusing ones. She's a provincial—a provincial of genius," St. George went on; "her very blunders are charming, her mistakes are interesting. She has come back from Asia with all sorts of excited curiosities and unappeased appetites. She's first-rate herself and she expends herself on the second-rate. She's life herself and she takes a rare interest in imitations. She mixes all things up, but there are none in regard to which she hasn't perceptions. She sees things in a perspective—as if from the top of the Himalayas—and she enlarges everything she touches. Above all she exaggerates—to herself, I mean. She exaggerates you and me!"

There was nothing in that description to allay the agitation caused in our younger friend by such a sketch of a fine subject. It seemed to him to show the art of St. George's admired hand, and he lost himself in gazing at the vision—this hovered there before him—of a woman's figure which should be part of the glory of a novel. But at the end of a moment the thing had turned into smoke, and out of the smoke—the last puff of a big cigar—proceeded the voice of General Fancourt, who had left the others and come and planted himself before the gentlemen on the sofa. "I suppose that when you fellows get talking you sit up half the night."

"Half the night?—*jamais de la vie!* I follow a hygiene"—and St. George rose to his feet.

"I see—you're hothouse plants," laughed the General. "That's the way you produce your flowers."

"I produce mine between ten and one every morning—I bloom with a regularity!" St. George went on.

"And with a splendour!" added the polite General, while Paul noted how little the author of "Shadowmere" minded, as he phrased it to himself, when addressed as a celebrated story-teller. The young man had an idea *he* should never get used to that; it would always make him uncomfortable—from the suspicion that people would think they had to—and he would want to prevent it. Evidently his great colleague had toughened and hardened—had made himself a surface. The group of men had finished their cigars and taken up their bedroom candlesticks; but before they all passed out Lord Watermouth invited the pair of guests who had been so absorbed together to "have" something. It happened that they both declined; upon which General Fancourt said: "Is that the hygiene? You don't water the flowers?"

"Oh, I should drown them!" St. George replied; but, leaving the room still at his young friend's side, he added whimsically, for the latter's benefit, in a lower tone: "My wife doesn't let me."

"Well, I'm glad I'm not one of you fellows!" the General richly concluded.

The nearness of Summersoft to London had this consequence, chilling to a person who had had a vision of sociability in a railway carriage, that most of the company, after breakfast, drove back to town, entering their own vehicles, which had come out to fetch them, while their servants returned by train with their luggage. Three or four young men, among whom was Paul Overt, also availed themselves of the common convenience; but they stood in the portico of the house and saw the others roll away. Miss Fancourt got into a victoria with her father after she had shaken hands with our hero and said, smiling in the frankest way in the world, "I *must* see you more. Mrs. St. George is so nice; she has promised to ask us both to dinner together." This lady and her husband took their places in a perfectly appointed brougham—she required a closed carriage—and as our young man waved his hat to them in response to their nods and flourishes he reflected that, taken together, they were an honourable image of success, of the material rewards and the social credit of literature. Such things were not the full measure, but he nevertheless felt a little proud for literature.

IV

Before a week had elapsed he met Miss Fancourt in Bond Street, at a private view of the works of a young artist in "black-and-white" who had been so good as to invite him to the stuffy scene. The drawings were admirable, but the crowd in the one little room was so dense that he felt himself up to his neck in a sack of wool. A fringe of people at the outer edge endeavoured by curving forward their backs and presenting, below them, a still more convex surface of resistance to the pressure of the mass, to preserve an interval between their noses and the glazed mounts of the pictures; while the central body, in the comparative gloom projected by a wide horizontal screen hung under the skylight and allowing only a margin for the day, remained upright, dense, and vague, lost in the contemplation of its own ingredients. This contemplation sat especially in the sad eyes of certain female heads, surmounted with hats of strange convolution and plumage, which rose on long necks above the others. One of the heads, Paul perceived, was much the most beautiful of the collection, and his next discovery was that it belonged to Miss Fancourt. Its beauty was enhanced by the glad smile she sent him across surrounding obstructions, a smile that drew him to her as fast as he could make his way. He had seen for himself at Summersoft that the last thing her nature contained was an affectation of indifference: yet even with this circumspection he took a fresh satisfaction in her not having pretended to await his arrival with composure. She smiled as radiantly as if she wished to make him hurry, and as soon as he came within earshot she broke out in her voice of joy: "He's here—he's here; he's coming back in a moment!"

"Ah, your father?" Paul returned as she offered him her hand.

"Oh, dear no, this isn't in my poor father's line. I mean Mr. St. George. He has just left me to speak to someone—he's coming back. It's he who brought me—wasn't it charming?"

"Ah that gives him a pull over me—I couldn't have 'brought' you, could I?"

"If you had been so kind as to propose it—why not you as well as he?" the girl returned with a face that, expressing no cheap coquetry, simply affirmed a happy fact.

"Why he's a *père de famille.* They've privileges," Paul explained. And then quickly: "Will you go to see places with *me?*" he asked.

"Anything you like," she smiled. "I know what you mean, that girls have to have a lot of people—!" Then she broke off: "I don't know; I'm free. I've always been like that—I can go about with anyone. I'm so glad to meet you," she added with a sweet distinctness that made those near her turn around.

"Let me at least repay that speech by taking you out of this squash," her friend said. "Surely people aren't happy here!"

"No, they're awfully *mornes,* aren't they? But I'm very happy indeed and I promised Mr. St. George to remain on this spot till he comes back. He's going to take me away. They send him invitations for things of this sort—more than he wants. It was so kind of him to think of me."

"They also send me invitations of this kind—more than *I* want. And if thinking of *you* will do it—!" Paul went on.

"Oh, I delight in them—everything that's life, everything that's London!"

"They don't have private views in Asia, I suppose," he laughed. "But what a pity that for this year, even in this gorged city, they're pretty well over."

"Well, next year will do, for I hope you believe we're going to be friends always. Here he comes!" Miss Fancourt continued before Paul had time to respond.

He made out St. George in the gaps of the crowd, and this perhaps led to his hurrying a little to say: "I hope that doesn't mean I'm to wait till next year to see you."

"No, no—aren't we to meet at dinner on the twenty-fifth?" she panted with an eagerness as happy as his own.

"That's almost next year. Is there no means of seeing you before?"

She stared with all her brightness. "Do you mean you'd *come?*"

"Like a shot, if you'll be so good as to ask me!"

"On Sunday then—this next Sunday?"

"What have I done that you should doubt it?" the young man asked with delight.

Miss Fancourt turned instantly to St. George, who had now joined them, and announced triumphantly: "He's coming on Sunday—this next Sunday!"

"Ah, my day—my day too!" said the famous novelist, laughing, to their companion.

"Yes, but not yours only. You shall meet in Manchester Square; you shall talk—you shall be wonderful!"

"We don't meet often enough," St. George allowed, shaking hands with his disciple. "Too many things—ah, too many things! But we must make it up in the country in September. You won't forget you've promised me that?"

"Why, he's coming on the twenty-fifth—you'll see him then," said the girl.

"On the twenty-fifth?" St. George asked vaguely.

"We dine with you; I hope you haven't forgotten. He's dining out that day," she added gaily to Paul.

"Oh, bless me, yes—that's charming! And you're coming? My wife didn't tell me," St. George said to him. "Too many things—too many things!" he repeated.

"Too many people—too many people!" Paul exclaimed, giving ground before the penetration of an elbow.

"You oughtn't to say that. They all read you."

"Me? I should like to see them! Only two or three at most," the young man returned.

"Did you ever hear anything like that? He knows, haughtily, how good he is!" St. George declared, laughing, to Miss Fancourt. "They read me, but that doesn't make me like them any better. Come away from them, come away!" And he led the way out of the exhibition.

"He's going to take me to the Park," Miss Fancourt observed to Overt with elation as they passed along the corridor that led to the street.

"Ah, does he go there?" Paul asked, taking the fact for a somewhat unexpected illustration of St. George's mœurs.

"It's a beautiful day—there'll be a great crowd. We're going to look at the people, to look at types," the girl went on. "We shall sit under the trees; we shall walk by the Row."

"I go once a year—on business," said St. George, who had overheard Paul's question.

"Or with a country cousin, didn't you tell me? I'm the country cousin!" she continued over her shoulder to Paul as their friend drew her toward a hansom to which he had signalled. The young man watched them get in; he returned, as he stood there, the friendly wave of the hand with which, ensconced in the vehicle beside her, St. George took leave of him. He even lingered to see the vehicle start away and lose itself in the confusion of Bond Street. He followed it with his eyes; it put to him embarrassing things. "She's not for me!" the great novelist had said emphatically at Summersoft; but his manner of conducting himself toward her appeared not quite in harmony with such a conviction. How could he have behaved differently if she *had* been for him? An indefinite envy rose in Paul Overt's heart as he took his way on foot alone; a feeling addressed alike, strangely enough, to each of the occupants of the hansom. How much he should like to rattle about London with such a girl! How much he should like to go and look at "types" with St. George!

The next Sunday at four o'clock he called in Manchester Square, where his secret wish was gratified by his finding Miss Fancourt alone. She was in a large bright friendly occupied room, which was painted red all over, draped with the quaint cheap florid stuffs that are represented as coming from southern and eastern countries, where they are fabled to serve as the counterpanes of the peasantry, and bedecked with pottery of vivid hues, ranged on casual shelves, and with many water-colour drawings from the hand (as the visitor learned) of the young lady herself, commemorating with a brave breadth the sunsets, the mountains, the temples and palaces of India. He sat an hour—more than an hour, two hours—and all the while no one came in. His hostess was so good as to remark, with her liberal humanity, that it was delightful they weren't interrupted: it was so rare in London, especially at that season, that people got a good talk. But luckily now, of a fine Sunday, half the world went out of town, and that made it better for those who didn't go, when these others were in sympathy. It was the defect of London—one of two or three, the very short list of those she recognised in the teeming world city she adored—that there were too few good chances for talk: you never had time to carry anything far.

"Too many things, too many things!" Paul said, quoting St. George's exclamation of a few days before.

"Ah, yes, for him there are too many—his life's too complicated."

"Have you seen it *near?* That's what I should like to do; it might explain some mysteries," the visitor went on. She asked him what mysteries he meant, and he said: "Oh, peculiarities of his work, in-equalities, superficialities. For one who looks at it from the artistic point of view it contains a bottomless ambiguity."

She became at this, on the spot, all intensity. "Ah, do describe that more—it's so interesting. There are no such suggestive questions. I'm so fond of them. He thinks he's a failure—fancy!" she beautifully wailed.

"That depends on what his ideal may have been. With his gifts it ought to have been high. But till one knows what he really proposed to himself—! Do *you* know by chance?" the young man broke off.

"Oh, he doesn't talk to me about himself. I can't make him. It's too provoking."

Paul was on the point of asking what, then, he did talk about, but discretion checked it and he said instead: "Do you think he's unhappy at home?"

She seemed to wonder. "At home?"

"I mean in his relations with his wife. He has a mystifying little way of alluding to her."

"Not to me," said Marian Fancourt with her clear eyes. "That wouldn't be right, would it?" she asked gravely.

"Not particularly; so I'm glad he doesn't mention her to you. To praise her might bore you, and he has no business to do anything else. Yet he knows you better than me."

"Ah, but he respects *you!*" the girl cried as with envy.

Her visitor stared a moment, then broke into a laugh. "Doesn't he respect you?"

"Of course, but not in the same way. He respects what you've done—he told me so the other day."

Paul drank it in, but retained his faculties. "When you went to look at types?"

"Yes—we found so many: he has such an observation of them! He talked a great deal about your book. He says it's really im-portant."

"Important! Ah the grand creature!"—and the author of the work in question groaned for joy.

"He was wonderfully amusing, he was inexpressibly droll, while we walked about. He sees everything; he has so many comparisons and images, and they're always exactly right. *C'est d'un trouvé,* as they say!"

"Yes, with his gifts, such things as he ought to have done!" Paul sighed.

"And don't you think he *has* done them?"

Ah, it was just the point. "A part of them, and of course even that part's immense. But he might have been one of the greatest. However, let us not make this an hour of qualifications. Even as they stand," our friend earnestly concluded, "his writings are a mine of gold."

To this proposition she ardently responded, and for half an hour the pair talked over the Master's principal productions. She knew them well—she knew them even better than her visitor, who was struck with her critical intelligence and with something large and bold in the movement in her mind. She said things that startled him and that evidently had come to her directly; they weren't picked-up phrases—she placed them too well. St. George had been right about her being first-rate, about her not being afraid to gush, not remembering that she must be proud. Suddenly something came back to her, and she said: "I recollect that he did speak of Mrs. St. George to me once. He said, apropos of something or other, that she didn't care for perfection."

"That's a great crime in an artist's wife," Paul returned.

"Yes, poor thing!" and the girl sighed with a suggestion of many reflexions, some of them mitigating. But she presently added: "Ah perfection, perfection—how one ought to go in for it! I wish *I* could."

"Every one can in his way," her companion opined.

"In *his* way, yes—but not in hers. Women are so hampered—so condemned! Yet it's a kind of dishonour if you don't, when you want to *do* something, isn't it?" Miss Fancourt pursued, dropping one train in her quickness to take up another, an accident that was common with her. So these two young persons sat discussing high themes in their eclectic drawing-room, in their London "season" —discussing, with extreme seriousness, the high theme of perfection. It must be said in extenuation of this eccentricity that they were interested in the business. Their tone had truth and their emotion beauty; they weren't posturing for each other or for someone else.

The subject was so wide that they found themselves reducing it; the perfection to which for the moment they agreed to confine their speculations was that of the valid, the exemplary work of art. Our young woman's imagination, it appeared, had wandered far in that direction, and her guest had the rare delight of feeling in their conversation a full interchange. This episode will have lived for years in his memory and even in his wonder; it had the quality that fortune distils in a single drop at a time—the quality that lubricates many ensuing frictions. He still, whenever he likes, has a vision of the room, the bright red sociable talkative room with the curtains that, by a stroke of successful audacity, had the note of vivid blue. He remembers where certain things stood, the particular book open on the table and the almost intense odour of the flowers placed, at the left, somewhere behind him. These facts were the fringe, as it were, of a fine special agitation which had its birth in those two hours and of which perhaps the main sign was in its leading him inwardly and repeatedly to breathe, "I had no idea there was any one like this—I had no idea there was any one like this!" Her freedom amazed him and charmed him—it seemed so to simplify the practical question. She was on the footing of an independent personage—a motherless girl who had passed out of her teens and had a position and responsibilities, who wasn't held down to the limitations of a little miss. She came and went with no dragged duenna, she received people alone, and, though she was totally without hardness, the question of protection or patronage had no relevancy in regard to her. She gave such an impression of the clear and the noble combined with the easy and the natural that in spite of her eminent modern situation she suggested no sort of sisterhood with the "fast" girl. Modern she was indeed, and made Paul Overt, who loved old colour, the golden glaze of time, think with some alarm of the muddled palette of the future. He couldn't get used to her interest in the arts he cared for; it seemed too good to be real—it was so unlikely an adventure to tumble into such a well of sympathy. One might stray into the desert easily—that was on the cards and that was the law of life; but it was too rare an accident to stumble on a crystal well. Yet if her aspirations seemed at one moment too extravagant to be real they struck him at the next as too intelligent to be false. They were both high and lame, and, whims for whims, he preferred them to any he had met in a like relation. It was probable enough she would leave them behind—exchange them for politics or "smartness" or mere prolific maternity, as was the custom of scribbling daubing educated flattered girls in an age of luxury and a society of leisure. He noted that the water-colours on the walls of the room she sat in had mainly the quality of being naïves, and reflected that naïveté in art is like a zero in a number: its importance depends on the figure it is united with. Meanwhile, however, he had fallen in love with her. Before he went away, at any rate, he said to her: "I thought St. George was coming to see you today, but he doesn't turn up."

For a moment he supposed she was going to cry "*Comment donc?* Did you come here only to meet him?" But the next he became aware of how little such a speech would have fallen in with any note of flirtation he had as yet perceived in her. She only replied: "Ah, yes, but I don't think he'll come. He recommended me not to expect him." Then she gaily but all gently added: "He said it wasn't fair to you. But I think I could manage two."

"So could I," Paul Overt returned, stretching the point a little to meet her. In reality his appreciation of the occasion was so completely an appreciation of the woman before him that another figure in the scene, even so esteemed a one as St. George, might for the hour have appealed to him vainly. He left the house wondering what the great man had meant by its not being fair to him; and, still more than that, whether he had actually stayed away from the force of that idea. As he took his course through the Sunday solitude of Manchester Square, swinging his stick and with a good deal of emotion fermenting in his soul, it appeared to him he was living in a world strangely magnanimous. Miss Fancourt had told him it was possible she should be away, and that her father should be, on the following Sunday, but that she had the hope of a visit from him in the other event. She promised to let him know should their absence fail, and then he might act accordingly. After he had passed into one of the streets that open from the Square he stopped, without definite intentions, looking sceptically for a cab. In a moment he saw a hansom roll through the place from the other side and come a part of the way toward him. He was on the point of hailing the driver when he noticed a "fare" within; then he waited, seeing the man prepare to deposit his passenger by pulling up at one of the houses. The house was apparently the one he himself had just quitted; at least he drew that inference as he recognised Henry St. George in the person who stepped out of the hansom. Paul turned off as quickly as if he had been caught in the act of spying. He gave up his cab— he preferred to walk; he would go nowhere else. He was glad St.

George hadn't renounced his visit altogether—that would have been too absurd. Yes, the world was magnanimous, and even he himself felt so as, on looking at his watch, he noted but six o'clock, so that he could mentally congratulate his successor on having an hour still to sit in Miss Fancourt's drawing-room. He himself might use that hour for another visit, but by the time he reached the Marble Arch the idea of such a course had become incongruous to him. He passed beneath that architectural effort and walked into the Park till he had got upon the spreading grass. Here he continued to walk; he took his way across the elastic turf and came out by the Serpentine. He watched with a friendly eye the diversions of the London people, he bent a glance almost encouraging on the young ladies paddling their sweethearts about the lake and the guardsmen tickling tenderly with their bearskins the artificial flowers in the Sunday hats of their partners. He prolonged his meditative walk; he went into Kensington Gardens, he sat upon the penny chairs, he looked at the little sail-boats launched upon the round pond and was glad he had no engagement to dine. He repaired for this purpose, very late, to his club, where he found himself unable to order a repast and told the waiter to bring whatever there was. He didn't even observe what he was served with, and he spent the evening in the library of the establishment, pretending to read an article in an American magazine. He failed to discover what it was about; it appeared in a dim way to be about Marian Fancourt.

Quite late in the week she wrote to him that she was not to go into the country—it had only just been settled. Her father, she added, would never settle anything, but put it all on her. She felt her responsibility—she had to—and since she was forced this was the way she had decided. She mentioned no reasons, which gave our friend all the clearer field for bold conjecture about them. In Manchester Square on this second Sunday he esteemed his fortune less good, for she had three or four other visitors. But there were three or four compensations; perhaps the greatest of which was that, learning how her father had after all, at the last hour, gone out of town alone, the bold conjecture I just now spoke of found itself becoming a shade more bold. And then her presence was her presence, and the personal red room was there and was full of it, whatever phantoms passed and vanished, emitting incomprehensible sounds. Lastly, he had the resource of staying till every one had come and gone and of believing this grateful to her, though she gave no particular sign.

When they were alone together he came to his point. "But St. George did come—last Sunday. I saw him as I looked back."

"Yes, but it was the last time."

"The last time?"

"He said he would never come again."

Paul Overt stared. "Does he mean he wishes to cease to see you?"

"I don't know what he means," the girl bravely smiled. "He won't at any rate see me here."

"And pray why not?"

"I haven't the least idea," said Marian Fancourt, whose visitor found her more perversely sublime than ever yet as she professed this clear helplessness.

V

"Oh, I say, I want you to stop a little," Henry St. George said to him at eleven o'clock the night he dined with the head of the profession. The company—none of it indeed *of* the profession—had been numerous and was taking its leave; our young man, after bidding good-night to his hostess, had put out his hand in farewell to the master of the house. Besides drawing from the latter the protest I have cited, this movement provoked a further priceless word about their chance now to have a talk, their going into his room, his having still everything to say. Paul Overt was all delight at this kindness; nevertheless he mentioned in weak jocose qualification the bare fact that he had promised to go to another place which was at a considerable distance.

"Well, then, you'll break your promise, that's all. You quite awful humbug!" St. George added in a tone that confirmed our young man's ease.

"Certainly I'll break it—but it was a real promise."

"Do you mean to Miss Fancourt? You're following her?" his friend asked.

He answered by a question. "Oh, is *she* going?"

"Base impostor!" his ironic host went on. "I've treated you handsomely on the article of that young lady: I won't make another concession. Wait three minutes—I'll be with you." He gave himself to his departing guests, accompanied the long-trained ladies to the door. It was a hot night, the windows were open, the sound of the quick carriages and of the linkmen's call came into the house. The affair had rather glittered; a sense of festal things was in the heavy air: not only the influence of that particular entertainment, but the suggestion of the wide hurry of pleasure which in London on summer nights fills so many of the happier quarters of the complicated town. Gradually Mrs. St. George's drawing-room emptied itself; Paul was left alone with his hostess, to whom he explained the motive of his waiting. "Ah, yes, some intellectual, some *professional*, talk," she leered; "at this season doesn't one miss it? Poor dear Henry, I'm so glad!" The young man looked out of the window a moment, at the called hansoms that lurched up, at the smooth broughams that rolled away. When he turned round Mrs. St. George had disappeared; her husband's voice rose to him from below—he was laughing and talking, in the portico, with some lady who awaited her carriage. Paul had solitary possession, for some minutes, of the warm deserted rooms where the covered tinted lamplight was soft, the seats had been pushed about, and the odour of flowers lingered. They were large, they were pretty, they contained objects of value; everything in the picture told of a "good house." At the end of five minutes a servant came in with a request from the Master that he would join him downstairs; upon which, descending, he followed his conductor through a long passage to an apartment thrown out, in the rear of the habitation, for the special requirements, as he guessed, of a busy man of letters.

St. George was in his shirt-sleeves in the middle of a large high room—a room without windows, but with a wide skylight at the top, that of a place of exhibition. It was furnished as a library, and the serried bookshelves rose to the ceiling, a surface of incomparable tone produced by dimly gilt "backs" interrupted here and there by the suspension of old prints and drawings. At the end furthest from the door of admission was a tall desk, of great extent, at which the person using it could write only in the erect posture of a clerk in a counting-house; and stretched from the entrance to this structure was a wide plain band of crimson cloth, as straight as a garden path and almost as long, where, in his mind's eye, Paul at once beheld the Master pace to and fro during vexed hours—hours, that is, of admirable composition. The servant gave him a coat, an old jacket with a hang of experience, from a cupboard in the wall, retiring afterwards with the garment he had taken off. Paul Overt welcomed the coat; it was a coat for talk, it promised confidences—having visibly received so many—and had tragic literary elbows. "Ah, we're practical

—we're practical!" St. George said as he saw his visitor look the place over. "Isn't it a good big cage for going round and round? My wife invented it and she locks me up here every morning."

Our young man breathed—by way of tribute—with a certain oppression. "You don't miss a window—a place to look out?"

"I did at first awfully; but her calculation was just. It saves time, it has saved me many months in these ten years. Here I stand, under the eye of day—in London of course, very often, it's rather a bleared old eye—walled in to my trade. I can't get away—so the room's a fine lesson in concentration. I've learnt the lesson, I think; look at that big bundle of proof and acknowledge it." He pointed to a fat roll of papers, on one of the tables, which had not been undone.

"Are you bringing out another—?" Paul asked in a tone the fond deficiencies of which he didn't recognise till his companion burst out laughing, and indeed scarce even then.

"You humbug, you humbug!"—St. George appeared to enjoy caressing him, as it were, with that opprobrium. "Don't I know what you think of them?" he asked, standing there with his hands in his pockets and with a new kind of smile. It was as if he were going to let his young votary see him all now.

"Upon my word in that case you know more than I do!" the latter ventured to respond, revealing a part of the torment of being able neither clearly to esteem nor distinctly to renounce him.

"My dear fellow," said the more and more interesting Master, "don't imagine I talk about my books specifically; they're not a decent subject—*il ne manquerait plus que ça!* I'm not so bad as you may apprehend. About myself, yes, a little, if you like; though it wasn't for that I brought you down here. I want to ask you something—very much indeed; I value this chance. Therefore sit down. We're practical, but there *is* a sofa, you see—for she does humour my poor bones so far. Like all really great administrators and disciplinarians she knows when wisely to relax." Paul sank into the corner of a deep leathern couch, but his friend remained standing and explanatory. "If you don't mind, in this room, this is my habit. From the door to the desk and from the desk to the door. That shakes up my imagination gently; and don't you see what a good thing it is that there's no window for her to fly out of? The eternal standing as I write (I stop at that bureau and put it down, when anything comes, and so we go on) was rather wearisome at first, but we adopted it with an eye to the long run: you're in better order—if your legs don't break down!—and you can keep it up for more years. Oh, we're practical—we're practical!" St. George repeated, going to the table and taking up all mechanically the bundle of proofs. But, pulling off the wrapper, he had a change of attention that appealed afresh to our hero. He lost himself a moment, examining the sheets of his new book, while the younger man's eyes wandered over the room again.

"Lord, what good things I should do if I had such a charming place as this to do them in!" Paul reflected. The outer world, the world of accident and ugliness, was so successfully excluded, and within the rich protecting square, beneath the patronising sky, the dream-figures, the summoned company, could hold their particular revel. It was a fond prevision of Overt's rather than an observation on actual data, for which occasions had been too few, that the Master thus more closely viewed would have the quality, the charming gift, of flashing out, all surprisingly, in personal intercourse and at moments of suspended or perhaps even of diminished expectation. A happy relation with him would be a thing proceeding by jumps, not by traceable stages.

"Do you read them—really?" he asked, laying down the proofs on Paul's inquiring of him how soon the work would be published. And when the young man answered, "Oh, yes, always," he was moved to mirth again by something he caught in his manner of saying that. "You go to see your grandmother on her birthday—and very proper it is, especially as she won't last for ever. She has lost every faculty and every sense; she neither sees, nor hears, nor speaks; but all customary pieties and kindly habits are respectable. Only you're strong if you *do* read 'em! *I* couldn't, my dear fellow. You *are* strong, I know; and that's just a part of what I wanted to say to you. You're very strong indeed. I've been going into your other things—they've interested me immensely. Some one ought to have told me about them before—some one I could believe. But whom can one believe? You're wonderfully on the right road—it's awfully decent work. Now do you mean to keep it up?—that's what I want to ask you."

"Do I mean to do others?" Paul asked, looking up from his sofa at his erect inquisitor and feeling partly like a happy little boy when the schoolmaster is gay, and partly like some pilgrim of old who might have consulted a world-famous oracle. St. George's own performance had been infirm, but as an adviser he would be infallible.

"Others—others? Ah, the number won't matter; one other would do, if it were really a further step—a throb of the same effort. What I mean is, have you it in your heart to go in for some sort of decent perfection?"

"Ah, decency, ah, perfection—!" the young man sincerely sighed. "I talked of them the other Sunday with Miss Fancourt."

It produced on the Master's part a laugh of odd acrimony. "Yes, they'll 'talk' of them as much as you like! But they'll do little to help one to them. There's no obligation of course; only you strike me as capable," he went on. "You must have thought it all over. I can't believe you're without a plan. That's the sensation you give me, and it's so rare that it really stirs one up—it makes you remarkable. If you haven't a plan, if you *don't* mean to keep it up, surely you're within your rights; it's nobody's business, no one can force you, and not more than two or three people will notice you don't go straight. The others—*all* the rest, every blest soul in England, will think you do—will think you *are* keeping it up: upon my honour they will! I shall be one of the two or three who know better. Now the question is whether you can do it for two or three. Is that the stuff you're made of?"

It locked his guest a minute as in closed throbbing arms. "I could do it for one, if you were the one."

"Don't say that; I don't deserve it; it scorches me," he protested with eyes suddenly grave and glowing. "The 'one' is of course one's self, one's conscience, one's idea, the singleness of one's aim. I think of that pure spirit as a man thinks of a woman he has in some detested hour of his youth loved and forsaken. She haunts him with reproachful eyes, she lives for ever before him. As an artist, you know, I've married for money." Paul stared and even blushed a little, confounded by this avowal; whereupon his host, observing the expression of his face, dropped a quick laugh and pursued: "You don't follow my figure. I'm not speaking of my dear wife, who had a small fortune—which, however, was not my bribe. I fell in love with her, as many other people have done. I refer to the mercenary muse whom I led to the altar of literature. Don't, my boy, put your nose into *that* yoke. The awful jade will lead you a life!"

Our hero watched him, wondering and deeply touched. "Haven't you been happy!"

"Happy? It's a kind of hell."

"There are things I should like to ask you," Paul said after a pause.

"Ask me anything in all the world. I'd turn myself inside out to save you."

"To 'save' me?" he quavered.

"To make you stick to it—to make you see it through. As I said to you the other night at Summersoft, let my example be vivid to you."

"Why, your books are not so bad as that," said Paul, fairly laughing and feeling that if ever a fellow had breathed the air of art—!

"So bad as what?"

"Your talent's so great that it's in everything you do, in what's less good as well as in what's best. You've some forty volumes to show for it—forty volumes of wonderful life, of rare observation, of magnificent ability."

"I'm very clever, of course I know that"—but it was a thing, in fine, this author made nothing of. "Lord, what rot they'd all be if I hadn't been! I'm a successful charlatan," he went on—"I've been able to pass off my system. But do you know what it is? It's carton-pierre."

"Carton-pierre?" Paul was struck, and gaped.

"Lincrusta-Walton!"

"Ah, don't say such things—you make me bleed!" the younger man protested. "I see you in a beautiful fortunate home, living in comfort and honour."

"Do you call it honour?"—his host took him up with an intonation that often comes back to him. "That's what I want you to go in for. I mean the real thing. This is brummagem."

"Brummagem?" Paul ejaculated while his eyes wandered, by a movement natural at the moment, over the luxurious room.

"Ah, they make it so well today—it's wonderfully deceptive!"

Our friend thrilled with the interest and perhaps even more with the pity of it. Yet he wasn't afraid to seem to patronise when he could still so far envy. "Is it deceptive that I find you living with every appearance of domestic felicity—blest with a devoted, accomplished wife, with children whose acquaintance I haven't yet had the pleasure of making, but who must be delightful young people, from what I know of their parents?"

St. George smiled as for the candour of his question. "It's all excellent, my dear fellow—heaven forbid I should deny it. I've made a great deal of money; my wife has known how to take care of it, to use it without wasting it, to put a good bit of it by, to make it fructify. I've got a loaf on the shelf; I've got everything in fact but the great thing."

"The great thing?" Paul kept echoing.

"The sense of having done the best—the sense which is the real life of the artist and the absence of which is his death, of having drawn from his intellectual instrument the finest music that nature had hidden in it, of having played it as it should be played. He either does that or he doesn't—and if he doesn't he isn't worth speaking of. Therefore, precisely, those who really know *don't* speak of him. He may still hear a great chatter, but what he hears most is the incorruptible silence of Fame. I've squared her, you may say, for my little hour—but what's my little hour? Don't imagine for a moment," the Master pursued, "that I'm such a cad as to have brought you down here to abuse or to complain of my wife to you. She's a woman of distinguished qualities, to whom my obligations are immense; so that, if you please, we'll say nothing about her. My boys—my children are all boys—are straight and strong, thank God, and have no poverty of growth about them, no penury of needs. I receive periodically the most satisfactory attestation from Harrow, from Oxford, from Sandhurst—oh, we've done the best for them!—of their eminence as living thriving consuming organisms."

"It must be delightful to feel that the son of one's loins is at Sandhurst," Paul remarked enthusiastically.

"It is—it's charming. Oh, I'm a patriot!"

The young man then could but have the greater tribute of questions to pay. "Then what did you mean—the other night at Summersoft—by saying that children are a curse?"

"My dear youth, on what basis are we talking?" and St. George dropped upon the sofa at a short distance from him. Sitting a little sideways he leaned back against the opposite arm with his hands raised and interlocked behind his head. "On the supposition that a certain perfection's possible and even desirable—isn't it so? Well, all I say is that one's children interfere with perfection. One's wife interferes. Marriage interferes."

"You think, then, the artist shouldn't marry?"

"He does so at his peril—he does so at his cost."

"Not even when his wife's in sympathy with his work?"

"She never is—she can't be! Women haven't a conception of such things."

"Surely they on occasion work themselves," Paul objected.

"Yes, very badly indeed. Oh, of course, often, they think they understand, they think they sympathise. Then it is they're most dangerous. Their idea is that you shall do a great lot and get a great lot of money. Their great nobleness and virtue, their exemplary conscientiousness as British females, is in keeping you up to that. My wife makes all my bargains with my publishers for me, and has done so for twenty years. She does it consummately well—that's why I'm really pretty well off. Aren't you the father of their innocent babes, and will you withhold from them their natural sustenance? You asked me the other night if they're not an immense incentive. Of course they are—there's no doubt of that!"

Paul turned it over: it took, from eyes he had never felt open so wide, so much looking at. "For myself I've an idea I need incentives."

"Ah, well, then, *n'en parlons plus!*" his companion handsomely smiled.

"*You* are an incentive, I maintain," the young man went on. "You don't affect me in the way you'd apparently like to. Your great success is what I see—the pomp of Ennismore Gardens!"

"Success?"—St. George's eyes had a cold fine light. "Do you call it success to be spoken of as you'd speak of me if you were sitting here with another artist—a young man intelligent and sincere like yourself? Do you call it success to make you blush—as you *would* blush!—if some foreign critic (some fellow, of course I mean, who should know what he was talking about and should have shown you he did, as foreign critics like to show it) were to say to you: 'He's the one, in this country, whom they consider the most perfect, isn't he?' Is it success to be the occasion of a young Englishman's having to stammer as you would have to stammer at such a moment for old England? No, no; success is to have made people wriggle to another tune. Do try it!"

Paul continued all gravely to glow. "Try what?"

"Try to do some really good work."

"Oh, I want to, heaven knows!"

"Well, you can't do it without sacrifices—don't believe that for a moment," the Master said. "I've made none. I've had everything. In other words, I've missed everything."

"You've had the full rich masculine human general life, with all the responsibilities and duties and burdens and sorrows and joys —all the domestic and social initiations and complications. They

must be immensely suggestive, immensely amusing," Paul anxiously
submitted.

"Amusing?"

"For a strong man—yes."

"They've given me subjects without number, if that's what you
mean; but they've taken away at the same time the power to use
them. I've touched a thousand things, but which one of them have
I turned into gold? The artist has to do only with that—he knows
nothing of any baser metal. I've led the life of the world, with my
wife and my progeny; the clumsy conventional expensive material-
ised vulgarised brutalised life of London. We've got everything
handsome, even a carriage—we're perfect Philistines and prosperous
hospitable eminent people. But, my dear fellow, don't try to stultify
yourself and pretend you don't know what we *haven't* got. It's bigger
than all the rest. Between artists—come!" the Master wound up.
"You know as well as you sit there that you'd put a pistol ball into
your brain if you had written my books!"

It struck his listener that the tremendous talk promised by him at
Summersoft had indeed come off, and with a promptitude, a fulness, with which the latter's young imagination had scarcely reck-
oned. His impression fairly shook him and he throbbed with the
excitement of such deep soundings and such strange confidences. He
throbbed indeed with the conflict of his feelings—bewilderment and
recognition and alarm, enjoyment and protest and assent, all com-
mingled with tenderness (and a kind of shame in the participation)
for the sores and bruises exhibited by so fine a creature, and with
a sense of the tragic secret nursed under his trappings. The idea of
his, Paul Overt's, becoming the occasion of such an act of humility
made him flush and pant, at the same time that his consciousness
was in certain directions too much alive not to swallow—and not
intensely to taste—every offered spoonful of the revelation. It had
been his odd fortune to blow upon the deep waters, to make them
surge and break in waves of strange eloquence. But how couldn't he
give out a passionate contradiction of his host's last extravagance,
how couldn't he enumerate to him the parts of his work he loved,
the splendid things he had found in it, beyond the compass of any
other writer of the day? St. George listened a while, courteously;
then he said, laying his hand on his visitor's: "That's all very well;
and if your idea's to do nothing better, there's no reason you shouldn't

have as many good things as I—as many human and material ap-
pendages, as many sons or daughters, a wife with as many gowns,
a house with as many servants, a stable with as many horses, a heart
with as many aches." The Master got up when he had spoken thus
—he stood a moment—near the sofa, looking down on his agitated
pupil. "Are you possessed of any property?" it occurred to him to ask.
    "None to speak of."
    "Oh, well then there's no reason why you shouldn't make a goodish
income—if you set about it the right way. Study *me* for that—study
me well. You may really have horses."
    Paul sat there some minutes without speaking. He looked straight
before him—he turned over many things. His friend had wandered
away, taking up a parcel of letters from the table where the roll of
proofs had lain. "What was the book Mrs. St. George made you
burn—the one she didn't like?" our young man brought out.
    "The book she made me burn—how did you know that?" The
Master looked up from his letters quite without the facial convulsion
the pupil had feared.
    "I heard her speak of it at Summersoft."
    "Ah, yes—she's proud of it. I don't know—it was rather good."
    "What was it about?"
    "Let me see." And he seemed to make an effort to remember. "Oh,
yes—it was about myself." Paul gave an irrepressible groan for the
disappearance of such a production, and the elder man went on:
"Oh, but *you* should write it—*you* should do me." And he pulled
up—from the restless motion that had come upon him; his fine
smile a generous glare. "There's a subject, my boy: no end of stuff
in it!"
    Again Paul was silent, but it was all tormenting. "Are there no
women who really understand—who can take part in a sacrifice?"
    "How can they take part? They themselves are the sacrifice. They're
the idol and the altar and the flame."
    "Isn't there even *one* who sees further?" Paul continued.
    For a moment St. George made no answer; after which, having
torn up his letters, he came back to the point all ironic. "Of course
I know the one you mean. But not even Miss Fancourt."
    "I thought you admired her so much."
    "It's impossible to admire her more. Are you in love with her?"
St. George asked.
    "Yes," Paul Overt presently said.

"Well, then, give it up."

Paul stared. "Give up my 'love'?"

"Bless me, no. Your idea." And then as our hero but still gazed: "The one you talked with her about. The idea of a decent perfection."

"She'd help it—she'd help it!" the young man cried.

"For about a year—the first year, yes. After that she'd be as a millstone round its neck."

Paul frankly wondered. "Why, she has a passion for the real thing, for good work—for everything you and I care for most."

"'You and I' is charming, my dear fellow!" his friend laughed. "She has it indeed, but she'd have a still greater passion for her children—and very proper too. She'd insist on everything's being made comfortable, advantageous, propitious for them. That isn't the artist's business."

"The artist—the artist! Isn't he a man all the same?"

St. George had a grand grimace. "I mostly think not. You know as well as I what he has to do: the concentration, the finish, the independence he must strive for from the moment he begins to wish his work really decent. Ah, my young friend, his relation to women, and especially to the one he's most intimately concerned with, is at the mercy of the damning fact that whereas he can in the nature of things have but one standard, they have about fifty. That's what makes them so superior," St. George amusingly added. "Fancy an artist with a change of standards as you'd have a change of shirts or of dinner plates. To do it—to do it and make it divine—is the only thing he has to think about. 'Is it done or not?' is his only question. Not 'Is it done as well as a proper solicitude for my dear little family will allow?' He has nothing to do with the relative—he has only to do with the absolute; and a dear little family may represent a dozen relatives."

"Then you don't allow him the common passions and affections of men?" Paul asked.

"Hasn't he a passion, an affection, which includes all the rest? Besides, let him have all the passions he likes—if he only keeps his independence. He must be able to be poor."

Paul slowly got up. "Why, then, did you advise me to make up to her?"

St. George laid a hand on his shoulder. "Because she'd make a splendid wife! And I hadn't read you then."

The young man had a strained smile. "I wish you had left me alone!"

"I didn't know that that wasn't good enough for you," his host returned.

"What a false position, what a condemnation of the artist, that he's a mere disfranchised monk and can produce his effect only by giving up personal happiness. What an arraignment of art!" Paul went on with a trembling voice.

"Ah, you don't imagine by chance that I'm defending art? 'Arraignment'—I should think so! Happy the societies in which it hasn't made its appearance, for from the moment it comes they have a consuming ache, they have an incurable corruption, in their breast. Most assuredly is the artist in a false position! But I thought we were taking him for granted. Pardon me," St. George continued: " 'Ginistrella' made me!"

Paul stood looking at the floor—one o'clock struck, in the stillness, from a neighbouring church-tower. "Do you think she'd ever look at me?" he put to his friend at last.

"Miss Fancourt—as a suitor? Why shouldn't I think it? That's why I've tried to favour you—I've had a little chance or two of bettering your opportunity."

"Forgive my asking you, but do you mean by keeping away yourself?" Paul said with a blush.

"I'm an old idiot—my place isn't there," St. George stated gravely.

"I'm nothing yet, I've no fortune; and there must be so many others," his companion pursued.

The Master took this considerably in, but made little of it. "You're a gentleman and a man of genius. I think you might do something."

"But if I must give that up—the genius?"

"Lots of people, you know, think I've kept mine," St. George wonderfully grinned.

"You've a genius for mystification!" Paul declared, but grasping his hand gratefully in attenuation of this judgement.

"Poor, dear boy, I do worry you! But try, try, all the same. I think your chances are good and you'll win a great prize."

Paul held fast the other's hand a minute; he looked into the strange deep face. "No, I *am* an artist—I can't help it!"

"Ah, show it then!" St. George pleadingly broke out. "Let me see before I die the thing I most want, the thing I yearn for; a life in which the passion—ours—is really intense. If you can be rare don't fail of it! Think what it is—how it counts—how it lives!"

They had moved to the door and he had closed both his hands over his companion's. Here they paused again and our hero breathed deep. "I want to live!"

"In what sense?"

"In the greatest."

"Well, then, stick to it—see it through."

"With your sympathy—your help?"

"Count on that—you'll be a great figure to me. Count on my highest appreciation, my devotion. You'll give me satisfaction—if that has any weight with you!" After which, as Paul appeared still to waver, his host added: "Do you remember what you said to me at Summersoft?"

"Something infatuated, no doubt!"

" 'I'll do anything in the world you tell me.' You said that."

"And you hold me to it?"

"Ah, what am I?" the Master expressively sighed.

"Lord, what things I shall have to do!" Paul almost moaned as he departed.

VI

"It goes on too much abroad—hang abroad!" These or something like them had been the Master's remarkable words in relation to the action of "Ginistrella"; and yet, though they had made a sharp impression on the author of that work, like almost all spoken words from the same source, he a week after the conversation I have noted left England for a long absence and full of brave intentions. It is not a perversion of the truth to pronounce that encounter the direct cause of his departure. If the oral utterance of the eminent writer had the privilege of moving him deeply it was especially on his turning it over at leisure, hours and days later, that it appeared to yield him its full meaning and exhibit its extreme importance. He spent the summer in Switzerland and, having in September begun a new task, determined not to cross the Alps till he should have made a good start. To this end he returned to a quiet corner he knew well, on the edge of the Lake of Geneva and within sight of the towers of Chillon: a region and a view for which he had an affection that sprang from

old associations and was capable of mysterious revivals and refresh-
ments. Here he lingered late, till the snow was on the nearer hills,
almost down to the limit to which he could climb when his stint,
on the shortening afternoons, was performed. The autumn was fine,
the lake was blue, and his book took form and direction. These
felicities, for the time, embroidered his life, which he suffered to
cover him with its mantle. At the end of six weeks he felt he had
learnt St. George's lesson by heart, had tested and proved its doctrine.
Nevertheless he did a very inconsistent thing: before crossing the
Alps he wrote to Marian Fancourt. He was aware of the perversity
of this act, and it was only as a luxury, an amusement, the reward
of a strenuous autumn, that he justified it. She had asked of him no
such favour when, shortly before he left London, three days after
their dinner in Ennismore Gardens, he went to take leave of her. It
was true she had had no ground—he hadn't named his intention of
absence. He had kept his counsel for want of due assurance: it was
that particular visit that was, the next thing, to settle the matter. He
had paid the visit to see how much he really cared for her, and
quick departure, without so much as an explicit farewell, was the
sequel to this inquiry, the answer to which had created within him
a deep yearning. When he wrote her from Clarens he noted that
he owed her an explanation (more than three months after!) for
not having told her what he was doing.

She replied now briefly but promptly, and gave him a striking
piece of news: that of the death, a week before, of Mrs. St. George.
This exemplary woman had succumbed, in the country, to a violent
attack of inflammation of the lungs—he would remember that for
a long time she had been delicate. Miss Fancourt added that she
believed her husband was overwhelmed by the blow; he would miss
her too terribly—she had been everything in life to him. Paul Overt,
on this, immediately wrote to St. George. He would from the day of
their parting have been glad to remain in communication with him,
but had hitherto lacked the right excuse for troubling so busy a man.
Their long nocturnal talk came back to him in every detail, but this
was no bar to an expression of proper sympathy with the head of
the profession, for hadn't that very talk made it clear that the late
accomplished lady was the influence that ruled his life? What catastrophe could be more cruel than the extinction of such an influence?
This was to be exactly the tone taken by St. George in answering his
young friend upwards of a month later. He made no allusion of

course to their important discussion. He spoke of his wife as frankly and generously as if he had quite forgotten that occasion, and the feeling of deep bereavement was visible in his words. "She took everything off my hands—off my mind. She carried on our life with the greatest art, the rarest devotion, and I was free, as few men can have been, to drive my pen, to shut myself up with my trade. This was a rare service—the highest she could have rendered me. Would I could have acknowledged it more fitly!"

A certain bewilderment, for our hero, disengaged itself from these remarks: they struck him as a contradiction, a retraction, strange on the part of a man who hadn't the excuse of witlessness. He had certainly not expected his correspondent to rejoice in the death of his wife, and it was perfectly in order that the rupture of a tie of more than twenty years should have left him sore. But if she had been so clear a blessing what in the name of consistency had the dear man meant by turning *him* upside down that night—by dosing him to that degree, at the most sensitive hour of his life, with the doctrine of renunciation? If Mrs. St. George was an irreparable loss, then her husband's inspired advice had been a bad joke and renunciation was a mistake. Overt was on the point of rushing back to London to show that, for his part, he was perfectly willing to consider it so, and he went so far as to take the manuscript of the first chapters of his new book out of his table-drawer and insert it into a pocket of his portmanteau. This led to his catching a glimpse of certain pages he hadn't looked at for months, and that accident, in turn, to his being struck with the high promise they revealed—a rare result of such retrospections, which it was his habit to avoid as much as possible: they usually brought home to him that the glow of composition might be a purely subjective and misleading emotion. On this occasion a certain belief in himself disengaged itself whimsically from the serried erasures of his first draft, making him think it best after all to pursue his present trial to the end. If he could write so well under the rigour of privation it might be a mistake to change the conditions before that spell had spent itself. He would go back to London of course, but he would go back only when he should have finished his book. This was the vow he privately made, restoring his manuscript to the table-drawer. It may be added that it took him a long time to finish his book, for the subject was as difficult as it was fine, and he was literally embarrassed by the fulness of his notes. Something within him warned him he must make it supremely good

—otherwise he should lack, as regards his private behaviour, a handsome excuse. He had a horror of this deficiency and found himself as firm as need be on the question of the lamp and the file. He crossed the Alps at last and spent the winter, the spring, the ensuing summer, in Italy, where still, at the end of a twelvemonth, his task was unachieved. "Stick to it—see it through": this general injunction of St. George's was good also for the particular case. He applied it to the utmost, with the result that when in its slow order the summer had come round again he felt he had given all that was in him. This time he put his papers into his portmanteau, with the address of his publisher attached, and took his way northward.

He had been absent from London for two years; two years which, seeming to count as more, had made such a difference in his own life—through the production of a novel far stronger, he believed, than "Ginistrella"—that he turned out into Piccadilly, the morning after his arrival, with a vague expectation of changes, of finding great things had happened. But there were few transformations in Piccadilly—only three or four big red houses where there had been low black ones—and the brightness of the end of June peeped through the rusty railings of the Green Park and glittered in the varnish of the rolling carriages as he had seen it in other, more cursory Junes. It was a greeting he appreciated; it seemed friendly and pointed, added to the exhilaration of his finished book, of his having his own country and the huge oppressive amusing city that suggested everything, that contained everything, under his hand again. "Stay at home and do things here—do subjects we can measure," St. George had said; and now it struck him he should ask nothing better than to stay at home for ever. Late in the afternoon he took his way to Manchester Square, looking out for a number he hadn't forgotten. Miss Fancourt, however, was not at home, so that he turned rather dejectedly from the door. His movement brought him face to face with a gentleman just approaching it and recognised on another glance as Miss Fancourt's father. Paul saluted this personage, and the General returned the greeting with his customary good manner—a manner so good, however, that you could never tell whether it meant he placed you. The disappointed caller felt the impulse to address him; then, hesitating, became both aware of having no particular remark to make, and convinced that though the old soldier remembered him he remembered him wrong. He therefore went his way without computing the irresistible effect his own evident recognition would have on the General, who never neglected a chance to gossip. Our young man's face was expressive, and observation seldom let it pass. He hadn't taken ten steps before he heard himself called after with a friendly semi-articulate "Er—I beg your pardon!" He turned round and the General, smiling at him from the porch, said: "Won't you come in? I won't leave you the advantage of me!" Paul declined to come in, and then felt regret, for Miss Fancourt, so late in the afternoon, might return at any moment. But her father gave him no second chance; he appeared mainly to wish not to have struck him as ungracious. A further look at the visitor had recalled something, enough at least to enable him to say: "You've come back, you've come back?" Paul was on the point of replying that he had come back the night before, but he suppressed, the next instant, this strong light on the immediacy of his visit and, giving merely a general assent, alluded to the young lady he deplored not having found. He had come late in the hope she would be in. "I'll tell her—I'll tell her," said the old man; and then he added quickly, gallantly: "You'll be giving us something new? It's a long time, isn't it?" Now he remembered him right.

"Rather long. I'm very slow," Paul explained. "I met you at Summersoft a long time ago."

"Oh, yes—with Henry St. George. I remember very well. Before his poor wife—" General Fancourt paused a moment, smiling a little less. "I daresay you know."

"About Mrs. St. George's death? Certainly—I heard at the time."

"Oh, no, I mean—I mean he's to be married."

"Ah, I've not heard that!" But just as Paul was about to add "To whom?" the General crossed his intention.

"When did you come back? I know you've been away—by my daughter. She was very sorry. You ought to give her something new."

"I came back last night," said our young man, to whom something had occurred which made his speech for the moment a little thick.

"Ah, most kind of you to come so soon. Couldn't you turn up at dinner?"

"At dinner?" Paul just mechanically repeated, not liking to ask whom St. George was going to marry, but thinking only of that.

"There are several people, I believe. Certainly St. George. Or afterwards if you like better. I believe my daughter expects—" He appeared to notice something in the visitor's raised face (on his steps he stood higher) which led him to interrupt himself, and the interruption gave him a momentary sense of awkwardness, from which he sought a quick issue. "Perhaps, then, you haven't heard she's to be married."

Paul gaped again. "To be married?"

"To Mr. St. George—it has just been settled. Odd marriage, isn't it?" Our listener uttered no opinion on this point: he only continued to stare. "But I daresay it will do—she's so awfully literary!" said the General.

Paul had turned very red. "Oh, it's a surprise—very interesting, very charming! I'm afraid I can't dine—so many thanks!"

"Well, you must come to the wedding!" cried the General. "Oh, I remember that day at Summersoft. He's a great man, you know."

"Charming—charming!" Paul stammered for retreat. He shook hands with the General and got off. His face was red and he had the sense of its growing more and more crimson. All the evening at home—he went straight to his rooms and remained there dinnerless —his cheek burned at intervals as if it had been smitten. He didn't understand what had happened to him, what trick had been played him, what treachery practised. "None, none," he said to himself. "I've nothing to do with it. I'm out of it—it's none of my business." But that bewildered murmur was followed again and again by the incongruous ejaculation: "Was it a plan—was it a plan?" Sometimes he cried to himself, breathless, "Have I been duped, sold, swindled?" If at all, he was an absurd, an abject victim. It was as if he hadn't lost her till now. He had renounced her, yes; but that was another affair—that was a closed but not a locked door. Now he seemed to see the door quite slammed in his face. Did he expect her to wait— was she to give him his time like that: two years at a stretch? He didn't know what he had expected—he only knew what he hadn't. It wasn't this—it wasn't this. Mystification bitterness and wrath rose and boiled in him when he thought of the deference, the devotion, the credulity with which he had listened to St. George. The evening wore on and the light was long; but even when it had darkened he remained without a lamp. He had flung himself on the sofa, where he lay through the hours with his eyes either closed or gazing at the gloom, in the attitude of a man teaching himself to bear something, to bear having been made a fool of. He had made it too easy—that idea passed over him like a hot wave. Suddenly, as he heard eleven o'clock strike, he jumped up, remembering what General Fancourt had said about his coming after dinner. He'd go—he'd see her at least; perhaps he should see what it meant. He felt as if some of the elements of a hard sum had been given him and the others were wanting: he couldn't do his sum till he had got all his figures.

He dressed and drove quickly, so that by half-past eleven he was at Manchester Square. There were a good many carriages at the door —a party was going on; a circumstance which at the last gave him a slight relief, for now he would rather see her in a crowd. People passed him on the staircase; they were going away, going "on" with the hunted herdlike movement of London society at night. But sundry groups remained in the drawing-room, and it was some minutes, as she didn't hear him announced, before he discovered and spoke to her. In this short interval he had seen St. George talking to a lady before the fireplace; but he at once looked away, feeling unready for an encounter, and therefore couldn't be sure the author of "Shadowmere" noticed him. At all events he didn't come over; though Miss Fancourt did as soon as she saw him—she almost rushed at him, smiling rustling radiant beautiful. He had forgotten what her head, what her face offered to the sight; she was in white, there were gold figures on her dress and her hair was a casque of gold. He saw in a single moment that she was happy, happy with an aggressive splendour. But she wouldn't speak to him of that, she would speak only of himself.

"I'm so delighted; my father told me. How kind of you to come!" She struck him as so fresh and brave, while his eyes moved over her, that he said to himself irresistibly: "Why to him, why not to youth, to strength, to ambition, to a future? Why, in her rich young force, to failure, to abdication, to superannuation?" In his thought at that sharp moment he blasphemed even against all that had been left of his faith in the peccable master. "I'm so sorry I missed you," she went on. "My father told me. How charming of you to have come so soon!"

"Does that surprise you?" Paul Overt asked.

"The first day? No, from you—nothing that's nice." She was interrupted by a lady who bade her good-night, and he seemed to read that it cost her nothing to speak to him in that tone; it was her old liberal lavish way, with a certain added amplitude that time had brought; and if this manner began to operate on the spot, at such a juncture in her history, perhaps in the other days too it had meant just as little or as much—a mere mechanical charity, with the difference now that she was satisfied, ready to give but in want of nothing. Oh, she was satisfied—and why shouldn't she be? Why shouldn't she have been surprised at his coming the first day—for all the good she had ever got from him? As the lady continued to hold her attention Paul turned from her with a strange irritation in his complicated artistic soul and a sort of disinterested disappointment. She was so happy that it was almost stupid—a disproof of the extraordinary intelligence he had formerly found in her. Didn't she know how bad St. George could be, hadn't she recognised the awful thinness—? If she didn't she was nothing, and if she did why such an insolence of serenity? This question expired as our young man's eyes settled at last on the genius who had advised him in a great crisis. St. George was still before the chimney-piece, but now he was alone—fixed, waiting, as if he meant to stop after every one—and he met the clouded gaze of the young friend so troubled as to the degree of his right (the right his resentment would have enjoyed) to regard himself as a victim. Somehow the ravage of the question was checked by the Master's radiance. It was as fine in its way as Marian Fancourt's, it denoted the happy human being; but also it represented to Paul Overt that the author of "Shadowmere" had now definitely ceased to count—ceased to count as a writer. As he smiled a welcome across the place he was almost *banal*, was almost smug. Paul fancied that for a moment he hesitated to make a movement, as if, for all the world, he *had* his bad conscience; then they had already met in the middle of the room and had shaken hands—expressively, cordially on St. George's part. With which they had passed back together to where the elder man had been standing, while St. George said: "I hope you're never going away again. I've been dining here; the General told me." He was handsome, he was young, he looked as if he had still a great fund of life. He bent the friendliest, most unconfessing eyes on his disciple of a couple of years before; asked him about everything, his health, his plans, his late occupations, the new book. "When will it be out—soon, soon, I hope? Splendid, eh? That's right; you're a comfort, you're a luxury! I've read you all over again these last six months." Paul waited to see if he'd tell him what the General had told him in the afternoon and what Miss Fancourt, verbally at least, of course hadn't. But as it didn't come out he at last put the question, "Is it true, the great news I hear—that you're to be married?"

"Ah, you *have* heard it, then?"

"Didn't the General tell you?" Paul asked.

The Master's face was wonderful. "Tell me what?"

"That he mentioned it to me this afternoon?"

"My dear fellow, I don't remember. We've been in the midst of people. I'm sorry, in the case, that I lose the pleasure, myself, of announcing to you a fact that touches me so nearly. It *is* a fact, strange as it may appear. It has only just become one. Isn't it ridiculous?" St. George made this speech without confusion, but on the other hand, so far as our friend could judge, without latent impudence. It struck his interlocutor that, to talk so comfortably and coolly, he must simply have forgotten what had passed between them. His next words, however, showed he hadn't, and they produced, as an appeal to Paul's own memory, an effect which would have been ludicrous if it hadn't been cruel. "Do you recall the talk we had at my house that night, into which Miss Fancourt's name entered? I've often thought of it since."

"Yes; no wonder you said what you did"—Paul was careful to meet his eyes.

"In the light of the present occasion? Ah, but there was no light then. How could I have foreseen this hour?"

"Didn't you think it probable?"

"Upon my honour, no," said Henry St. George. "Certainly I owe you that assurance. Think how my situation has changed."

"I see—I see," our young man murmured.

His companion went on as if, now that the subject had been broached, he was, as a person of imagination and tact, quite ready to give every satisfaction—being both by his genius and his method so able to enter into everything another might feel. "But it's not only that; for honestly, at my age, I never dreamed—a widower with big boys and with so little else! It has turned out differently from anything one could have dreamed, and I'm fortunate beyond all measure. She has been so free, and yet she consents. Better than any one else perhaps—for I remember how you liked her before you went away, and how she liked you—you can intelligently congratulate me."

"She has been so free!" Those words made a great impression on Paul Overt, and he almost writhed under that irony in them as to which it so little mattered whether it was designed or casual. Of course she had been free, and appreciably perhaps by his own act; for wasn't the Master's allusion to her having liked him a part of the irony too? "I thought that by your theory you disapproved of a writer's marrying."

"Surely—surely. But you don't call me a writer?"

"You ought to be ashamed," said Paul.

"Ashamed of marrying again?"

"I won't say that—but ashamed of your reasons."

The elder man beautifully smiled. "You must let me judge of them, my good friend."

"Yes; why not? For you judged wonderfully of mine."

The tone of these words appeared suddenly, for St. George, to suggest the unsuspected. He stared as if divining a bitterness. "Don't you think I've been straight?"

"You might have told me at the time perhaps."

"My dear fellow, when I say I couldn't pierce futurity—!"

"I mean afterwards."

·The Master wondered. "After my wife's death?"

"When this idea came to you."

"Ah, never, never! I wanted to save you, rare and precious as you are."

Poor Overt looked hard at him. "Are you marrying Miss Fancourt to save me?"

"Not absolutely, but it adds to the pleasure. I shall be the making of you." St. George smiled. "I was greatly struck, after our talk, with the brave, devoted way you quitted the country, and still more perhaps with your force of character in remaining abroad. You're very strong—you're wonderfully strong."

Paul tried to sound his shining eyes; the strange thing was that he seemed sincere—not a mocking fiend. He turned away, and as he did so heard the Master say something about his giving them all the proof, being the joy of his old age. He faced him again, taking another look. "Do you mean to say you've stopped writing?"

"My dear fellow, of course I have. It's too late. Didn't I tell you?"

"I can't believe it!"

"Of course you can't—with your own talent! No, no; for the rest of my life I shall only read *you*."

"Does she know that—Miss Fancourt?"

"She will—she will." Did he mean this, our young man wondered, as a covert intimation that the assistance he should derive from that young lady's fortune, moderate as it was, would make the difference of putting it in his power to cease to work ungratefully an exhausted vein? Somehow, standing there in the ripeness of his successful manhood, he didn't suggest that any of his veins were exhausted. "Don't

you remember the moral I offered myself to you that night as pointing?" St. George continued. "Consider at any rate the warning I
am at present."

This was too much—he *was* the mocking fiend. Paul turned from
him with a mere nod for good-night and the sense in a sore heart
that he might come back to him and his easy grace, his fine way
of arranging things, some time in the far future, but he couldn't
fraternise with him now. It was necessary to his soreness to believe
for the hour in the intensity of his grievance—all the more cruel for
its not being a legal one. It was doubtless in the attitude of hugging
this wrong that he descended the stairs without taking leave of Miss
Fancourt, who hadn't been in view at the moment he quitted the
room. He was glad to get out into the honest dusky unsophisticating
night, to move fast, to take his way home on foot. He walked a long
time, going astray, paying no attention. He was thinking of too many
other things. His steps recovered their direction, however, and at
the end of an hour he found himself before his door in the small
inexpensive empty street. He lingered, questioning himself still before going in, with nothing around and above him but moonless
blackness, a bad lamp or two, and a few far-away dim stars. To these
last faint features he raised his eyes; he had been saying to himself
that he should have been "sold" indeed, diabolically sold, if now,
on his new foundation, at the end of a year, St. George were to put
forth something of his prime quality—something of the type of
"Shadowmere" and finer than his finest. Greatly as he admired his
talent Paul literally hoped such an incident wouldn't occur; it seemed
to him just then that he shouldn't be able to bear it. His late adviser's
words were still in his ears—"You're very strong, wonderfully
strong." Was he really? Certainly he would have to be, and it might a
little serve for revenge. *Is* he? the reader may ask in turn, if his
interest has followed the perplexed young man so far. The best
answer to that perhaps is that he's doing his best, but that it's too
soon to say. When the new book came out in the autumn Mr. and
Mrs. St. George found it really magnificent. The former still has
published nothing, but Paul doesn't even yet feel safe. I may say for
him, however, that if this event were to occur he would really be the
very first to appreciate it: which is perhaps a proof that the Master
was essentially right and that nature had dedicated him to intellectual, not to personal passion.

Greville Fane

*C*OMING in to dress for dinner I found a telegram: "Mrs. Stormer dying; can you give us half a column for to-morrow evening? Let her down easily, but not too easily." I was late; I was in a hurry; I had very little time to think; but at a venture I despatched a reply: "Will do what I can." It was not till I had dressed and was rolling away to dinner that, in the hansom, I bethought myself of the difficulty of the condition attached. The difficulty was not of course in letting her down easily but in qualifying that indulgence. "So I simply won't qualify it," I said. I didn't admire but liked her, and had known her so long that I almost felt heartless in sitting down at such an hour to a feast of indifference. I must have seemed abstracted, for the early years of my acquaintance with her came back to me. I spoke of her to the lady I had taken down, but the lady I had taken down had never heard of Greville Fane. I tried my other neighbour, who pronounced her books "too vile." I had never thought them very good, but I should let her down more easily than that.

I came away early, for the express purpose of driving to ask about her. The journey took time, for she lived in the northwest district, in the neighbourhood of Primrose Hill. My apprehension that I should be too late was justified in a fuller sense than I had attached to it—I had only feared that the house would be shut up. There were lights in the windows, and the temperate tinkle of my bell brought a servant immediately to the door; but poor Mrs. Stormer had passed into a state in which the resonance of no earthly knocker was to be feared. A lady hovering behind the servant came forward into the hall when she heard my voice. I recognised Lady Luard, but she had mistaken me for the doctor.

"Pardon my appearing at such an hour," I said; "it was the first possible moment after I heard."

"It's all over," Lady Luard replied. "Dearest mamma!"

She stood there under the lamp with her eyes on me; she was

very tall, very stiff, very cold, and always looked as if these things, and some others beside, in her dress, in her manner and even in her name, were an implication that she was very admirable. I had never been able to follow the argument, but that's a detail. I expressed briefly and frankly what I felt, while the little mottled maidservant flattened herself against the wall of the narrow passage and tried to look detached without looking indifferent. It was not a moment to make a visit, and I was on the point of retreating when Lady Luard arrested me with a queer casual drawling "Would you—a—would you perhaps be *writing* something?" I felt for the instant like an infamous interviewer, which I wasn't. But I pleaded guilty to this intention, on which she returned: "I'm so very glad—but I think my brother would like to see you." I detested her brother, but it wasn't an occasion to act this out; so I suffered myself to be inducted, to my surprise, into a small back room which I immediately recognised as the scene, during the later years, of Mrs. Stormer's imperturbable industry. Her table was there, the battered and blotted accessory to innumerable literary lapses, with its contracted space for the arms (she wrote only from the elbow down) and the confusion of scrappy scribbled sheets which had already become literary remains. Leolin was also there, smoking a cigarette before the fire and looking impudent even in his grief, sincere as it well might have been.

To meet him, to greet him, I had to make a sharp effort; for the air he wore to me as he stood before me was quite that of his mother's murderer. She lay silent for ever upstairs—as dead as an unsuccessful book, and his swaggering erectness was a kind of symbol of his having killed her. I wondered if he had already, with his sister, been calculating what they could get for the poor papers on the table; but I hadn't long to wait to learn, since in reply to the few words of sympathy I addressed him he puffed out: "It's miserable, miserable, yes; but she has left three books complete." His words had the oddest effect; they converted the cramped little room into a seat of trade and made the "book" wonderfully feasible. He would certainly get all that could be got for the three. Lady Luard explained to me that her husband had been with them, but had had to go down to the House. To her brother she mentioned that I was going to write something, and to me again made it clear that she hoped I would "do mamma justice." She added that she didn't think this had ever been done. She said to her brother: "Don't you think there are some things he ought thoroughly to understand?" and on his instantly exclaiming

"Oh thoroughly, thoroughly!" went on rather austerely: "I mean about mamma's birth."

"Yes and her connexions," Leolin added.

I professed every willingness, and for five minutes I listened; but it would be too much to say I clearly understood. I don't even now, but it's not important. My vision was of other matters than those they put before me, and while they desired there should be no mistake about their ancestors I became keener and keener about themselves. I got away as soon as possible and walked home through the great dusky empty London—the best of all conditions for thought. By the time I reached my door my little article was practically composed—ready to be transferred on the morrow from the polished plate of fancy. I believe it attracted some notice, was thought "graceful" and was said to be by some one else. I had to be pointed without being lively, and it took some doing. But what I said was much less interesting than what I thought—especially during the half-hour I spent in my armchair by the fire, smoking the cigar I always light before going to bed. I went to sleep there, I believe; but I continued to moralise about Greville Fane. I'm reluctant to lose that retrospect altogether, and this is a dim little memory of it, a document not to "serve." The dear woman had written a hundred stories, but none so curious as her own.

When first I knew her she had published half a dozen fictions, and I believe I had also perpetrated a novel. She was more than a dozen years my elder, but a person who always acknowledged her comparative state. It wasn't so very long ago, but in London, amid the big waves of the present, even a near horizon gets hidden. I met her at some dinner and took her down, rather flattered at offering my arm to a celebrity. She didn't look like one, with her matronly mild inanimate face, but I supposed her greatness would come out in her conversation. I gave it all the opportunities I could, but was nevertheless not disappointed when I found her only a dull kind woman. This was why I liked her—she rested me so from literature. To myself literature was an irritation, a torment; but Greville Fane slumbered in the intellectual part of it even as a cat on a hearthrug or a Creole in a hammock. She wasn't a woman of genius, but her faculty was so special, so much a gift out of hand, that I've often wondered why she fell below that distinction.) This was doubtless because the transaction, in her case, had remained incomplete; genius always pays for the gift, feels the debt, and she was placidly unconscious of a call. She could invent stories by the yard, but couldn't write a page of English. She went down to her grave without suspecting that though she had contributed volumes to the diversion of her contemporaries she hadn't contributed a sentence to the language. This hadn't prevented bushels of criticism from being heaped on her head; she was worth a couple of columns any day to the weekly papers, in which it was shown that her pictures of life were dreadful but her style superior. She asked me to come and see her and I complied. She lived then in Montpelier Square; which helped me to see how dissociated her imagination was from her character.

An industrious widow, devoted to her daily stint, to meeting the butcher and baker and making a home for her son and daughter, from the moment she took her pen in her hand she became a creature of passion. She thought the English novel deplorably wanting in that element, and the task she had cut out for herself was to supply the deficiency. Passion in high life was the general formula of this work, for her imagination was at home only in the most exalted circles. She adored in truth the aristocracy, and they constituted for her the romance of the world or, what is more to the point, the prime material of fiction. Their beauty and luxury, their loves and revenges, their temptations and surrenders, their immoralities and diamonds were as familiar to her as the blots on her writing-table. She was not a belated producer of the old fashionable novel, but, with a cleverness and a modernness of her own, had freshened up the fly-blown tinsel. She turned off plots by the hundred and—so far as her flying quill could convey her—was perpetually going abroad. Her types, her illustrations, her tone were nothing if not cosmopolitan. She recognised nothing less provincial than European society, and her fine folk knew each other and made love to each other from Doncaster to Bucharest. She had an idea that she resembled Balzac, and her favourite historical characters were Lucien de Rubempré and the Vidame de Pamiers. I must add that when I once asked her who the latter personage was she was unable to tell me. She was very brave and healthy and cheerful, very abundant and innocent and wicked. She was expert and vulgar and snobbish, and never so intensely British as when she was particularly foreign.

This combination of qualities had brought her early success, and I remember having heard with wonder and envy of what she "got," in those days, for a novel. The revelation gave me a pang: it was such a proof that, practising a totally different style, I should never

make my fortune. And yet when, as I knew her better she told me
her real tariff and I saw how rumour had quadrupled it, I liked her
enough to be sorry. After a while I discovered too that if she got less
it was not that *I* was to get any more. My failure never had what
Mrs. Stormer would have called the banality of being relative—it
was always admirably absolute. She lived at ease however in those
days—ease is exactly the word, though she produced three novels a
year. She scorned me when I spoke of difficulty—it was the only
thing that made her angry. If I hinted at the grand licking into shape
that a work of art required she thought it a pretension and a *pose*.
She never recognised the "torment of form"; the furthest she went
was to introduce into one of her books (in satire her hand was
heavy) a young poet who was always talking about it. I couldn't
quite understand her irritation on this score, for she had nothing at
stake in the matter. She had a shrewd perception that form, in prose
at least, never recommended any one to the public we were condemned to address; according to which she lost nothing (her private
humiliation not counted) by having none to show. She made no pretence of producing works of art, but had comfortable tea-drinking
hours in which she freely confessed herself a common pastrycook,
dealing in such tarts and puddings as would bring customers to the
shop. She put in plenty of sugar and of cochineal, or whatever it is
that gives these articles a rich and attractive colour. She had a calm
independence of observation and opportunity which constituted an
inexpugnable strength and would enable her to go on indefinitely.
It's only real success that wanes, it's only solid things that melt.
Greville Fane's ignorance of life was a resource still more unfailing
than the most approved receipt. On her saying once that the day
would come when she should have written herself out I answered:
"Ah you open straight into fairyland, and the fairies love you and
they never change. Fairyland's always there; it always was from the
beginning of time and always will be to the end. They've given you
the key and you can always open the door. With me it's different; I
try, in my clumsy way, to be in some direct relation to life." "Oh
bother your direct relation to life!" she used to reply, for she was
always annoyed by the phrase—which wouldn't in the least prevent
her using it as a note of elegance. With no more prejudices than an
old sausage-mill, she would give forth again with patient punctuality
any poor verbal scrap that had been dropped into her. I cheered her
with saying that the dark day, at the end, would be for the 'likes'

of *me;* since, proceeding in our small way by experience and study
—priggish wel—we depended not on a revelation but on a little
tiresome process. Attention depended on occasion, and where should
we be when occasion failed?

One day she told me that as the novelist's life was so delightful
and, during the good years at least, such a comfortable support—she
had these staggering optimisms—she meant to train up her boy to
follow it. She took the ingenious view that it was a profession like
another and that therefore everything was to be gained by beginning
young and serving an apprenticeship. Moreover the education would
be less expensive than any other special course, inasmuch as she could
herself administer it. She didn't profess to keep a school, but she
could at least teach her own child. It wasn't that she had such a gift,
but—she confessed to me as if she were afraid I should laugh at her
—that *he* had. I didn't laugh at her for that, because I thought the
boy sharp—I had seen him sundry times. He was well-grown and
good-looking and unabashed, and both he and his sister made me
wonder about their defunct papa, concerning whom the little I knew
was that he had been a country vicar and brother to a small squire.
I explained them to myself by suppositions and imputations possibly
unjust to the departed; so little were they—superficially at least—the
children of their mother. There used to be on an easel in her drawing-
room an enlarged photograph of her husband, done by some horrible
posthumous "process" and draped, as to its florid frame, with a silken
scarf which testified to the candour of Greville Fane's bad taste. It
made him look like an unsuccessful tragedian, but it wasn't a thing
to trust. He may have been a successful comedian. Of the two children the girl was the elder, and struck me in all her younger years
as singularly colourless. She was only long, very long, like an unde-
cipherable letter. It wasn't till Mrs. Stormer came back from a pro-
tracted residence abroad that Ethel (which was this young lady's
name) began to produce the effect, large and stiff and afterwards
eminent in her, of a certain kind of resolution, something as public
and important as if a meeting and a chairman had passed it. She
gave one to understand she meant to do all she could for herself.
She was long-necked and near-sighted and striking, and I thought I
had never seen sweet seventeen in a form so hard and high and dry.
She was cold and affected and ambitious, and she carried an eyeglass
with a long handle, which she put up whenever she wanted not to
see. She had come out, as the phrase is, immensely; and yet I felt as if

she were surrounded with a spiked iron railing. What she meant to do for herself was to marry, and it was the only thing, I think, that she meant to do for any one else; yet who would be inspired to clamber over that bristling barrier? What flower of tenderness or of intimacy would such an adventurer conceive as his reward?)

This was for Sir Baldwin Luard to say; but he naturally never confided me the secret. He was a joyless jokeless young man, with the air of having other secrets as well, and a determination to get on politically that was indicated by his never having been known to commit himself—as regards any proposition whatever—beyond an unchallengeable "Oh!" His wife and he must have conversed mainly in prim ejaculations, but they understood sufficiently that they were kindred spirits. I remember being angry with Greville Fane when she announced these nuptials to me as magnificent; I remember asking her what splendour there was in the union of the daughter of a woman of genius with an irredeemable mediocrity. "Oh he has immense ability," she said; but she blushed for the maternal fib. What she meant was that though Sir Baldwin's estates were not vast—he had a dreary house in South Kensington and a still drearier "Hall" somewhere in Essex, which was let—the connexion was a "smarter" one than a child of hers could have aspired to form. In spite of the social bravery of her novels she took a very humble and dingy view of herself, so that of all her productions "my daughter Lady Luard" was quite the one she was proudest of. That personage thought our authoress vulgar and was distressed and perplexed by the frequent freedoms of her pen, but had a complicated attitude for this indirect connexion with literature. So far as it was lucrative her ladyship approved of it and could compound with the inferiority of the pursuit by practical justice to some of its advantages. I had reason to know—my reason was simply that poor Mrs. Stormer told me—how she suffered the inky fingers to press an occasional banknote into her palm. On the other hand she deplored the "peculiar style" to which Greville Fane had devoted herself, and wondered where a spectator with the advantage of so ladylike a daughter could have picked up such views about the best society. "She might know better, with Leolin and me," Lady Luard had been heard to remark; but it appeared that some of Greville Fane's superstitions were incurable. She didn't live in Lady Luard's society, and the best wasn't good enough for her—she must improve on it so prodigiously.

I could see this necessity increase in her during the years she spent abroad, when I had glimpses of her in the shifting sojourns that lay in the path of my annual ramble. She betook herself from Germany to Switzerland and from Switzerland to Italy; she favoured cheap places and set up her desk in the smaller capitals. I took a look at her whenever I could, and I always asked how Leolin was getting on. She gave me beautiful accounts of him, and, occasion favouring, the boy was produced for my advantage. I had entered from the first into the joke of his career—I pretended to regard him as a consecrated child. It had been a joke for Mrs. Stormer at first, but the youth himself had been shrewd enough to make the matter serious. If his parent accepted the principle that the intending novelist can't begin too early to see life, Leolin wasn't interested in hanging back from the application of it. He was eager to qualify himself and took to cigarettes at ten on the highest literary grounds. His fond mother gazed at him with extravagant envy and, like Desdemona, wished heaven had made *her* such a man. She explained to me more than once that in her profession she had found her sex a dreadful drawback. She loved the story of Madame George Sand's early rebellion against this hindrance, and believed that if she had worn trousers she could have written as well as that lady. Leolin had for the career at least the qualification of trousers, and as he grew older he recognised its importance by laying in ever so many pair. He grew up thus in gorgeous apparel, which was his way of interpreting his mother's system. Whenever I met her, accordingly, I found her still under the impression that she was carrying this system out and that the sacrifices made him were bearing heavy fruit. She was giving him experience, she was giving him impressions, she was putting a *gagne-pain* into his hand. It was another name for spoiling him with the best conscience in the world. The queerest pictures come back to me of this period of the good lady's life and of the extraordinarily virtuous muddled bewildering tenor of it. She had an idea she was seeing foreign manners as well as her petticoats would allow; but in reality she wasn't seeing anything, least of all, fortunately, how much she was laughed at. She drove her whimsical pen at Dresden and at Florence—she produced in all places and at all times the same romantic and ridiculous fictions. She carried about her box of properties, tumbling out promptly the familiar tarnished old puppets. She believed in them when others couldn't, and as they were like nothing that was to be seen under the sun it was impossible to prove by comparison that they were wrong. You can't compare birds and

fishes; you could only feel that, as Greville Fane's characters had the
fine plumage of the former species, human beings must be of the
latter.

It would have been droll if it hadn't been so exemplary to see her
tracing the loves of the duchesses beside the innocent cribs of her
children. The immoral and the maternal lived together, in her dili-
gent days, on the most comfortable terms, and she stopped curling
the moustaches of her Guardsmen to pat the heads of her babes. She
was haunted by solemn spinsters who came to tea from Continental
pensions, and by unsophisticated Americans who told her she was
just loved in *their* country. "I had rather be just paid there," she
usually replied; for this tribute of transatlantic opinion was the only
thing that galled her. The Americans went away thinking her coarse;
though as the author of so many beautiful love-stories she was dis-
appointing to most of these pilgrims, who hadn't expected to find a
shy stout ruddy lady in a cap like a crumbled pyramid. She wrote
about the affections and the impossibility of controlling them, but
she talked of the price of pension and the convenience of an English
chemist. She devoted much thought and many thousands of francs
to the education of her daughter, who spent three years at a very
superior school at Dresden, receiving wonderful instruction in sci-
ences, arts and tongues, and who, taking a different line from Leolin,
was to be brought up wholly as a *femme du monde.* The girl was
musical and philological; she went in for several languages and
learned enough about them to be inspired with a great contempt for
her mother's artless accents. Greville Fane's French and Italian were
droll; the imitative faculty had been denied her, and she had an un-
equalled gift, especially pen in hand, of squeezing big mistakes into
small opportunities. She knew it but didn't care; correctness was the
virtue in the world that, like her heroes and heroines, she valued least.
Ethel, who had noted in her pages some remarkable lapses, undertook at one time to revise her proofs; but I remember her telling me
a year after the girl had left school that this function had been very
briefly exercised. "She can't read me," said Mrs. Stormer; "I offend
her taste. She tells me that at Dresden—at school—I was never allowed." The good lady seemed surprised at this, having the best
conscience in the world about her lucubrations. She had never meant
to fly in the face of anything, and considered that she grovelled before the Rhadamanthus of the English literary tribunal, the celebrated and awful Young Person. I assured her, as a joke, that she was

frightfully indecent—she had in fact that element of truth as little as any other—my purpose being solely to prevent her guessing that her daughter had dropped her not because she was immoral but because she was vulgar. I used to figure her children closeted together and putting it to each other with a gaze of dismay: "Why should she *be* so—and so *fearfully* so—when she has the advantage of our society? Shouldn't *we* have taught her better?" Then I imagined their recognising with a blush and a shrug that she was unteachable, irreformable. Indeed she was, poor lady, but it's never fair to read by the light of taste things essentially not written in it. Greville Fane kept through all her riot of absurdity a witless confidence that should have been as safe from criticism as a stutter or a squint.

She didn't make her son ashamed of the profession to which he was destined, however; she only made him ashamed of the way she herself exercised it. But he bore his humiliation much better than his sister, being ready to assume he should one day restore the balance. A canny and far-seeing youth, with appetites and aspirations, he hadn't a scruple in his composition. His mother's theory of the happy knack he could pick up deprived him of the wholesome discipline required to prevent young idlers from becoming cads. He enjoyed on foreign soil a casual tutor and the common snatch or two of a Swiss school, but addressed himself to no consecutive study nor to any prospect of a university or a degree. It may be imagined with what zeal, as the years went on, he entered into the pleasantry of there being no manual so important to him as the massive book of life. It was an expensive volume to peruse, but Mrs. Stormer was willing to lay out a sum in what she would have called her *premier frais*. Ethel disapproved—she found this education irregular for an English gentleman. Her voice was for Eton and Oxford or for any public school—she would have resigned herself to one of the scrubbier—with the army to follow. But Leolin never was afraid of his sister, and they visibly disliked, though they sometimes agreed to assist, each other. They could combine to work the oracle—to keep their mother at her desk.

When she reappeared in England, telling me she had "secured" all the Continent could give her, Leolin was a broad-shouldered red-faced young man with an immense wardrobe and an extraordinary assurance of manner. She was fondly, quite aggressively certain she had taken the right course with him, and addicted to boasting of all he knew and had seen. He was now quite ready to embark on the family profession, to commence author, as they used to say, and a little while later she told me he had started. He had written something tremendously clever which was coming out in the "Cheapside." I believe it came out; I had no time to look for it; I never heard anything about it. I took for granted that if this contribution had passed through his mother's hands it would virtually rather illustrate *her* fine facility, and it was interesting to consider the poor lady's future in the light of her having to write her son's novels as well as her own. This wasn't the way she looked at it herself—she took the charming ground that he'd help her to write hers. She used to assure me he supplied passages of the greatest value to these last—all sorts of telling technical things, happy touches about hunting and yachting and cigars and wine, about City slang and the way men talk at clubs—that she couldn't be expected to get very straight. It was all so much practice for him and so much alleviation for herself. I was unable to identify such pages, for I had long since ceased to "keep up" with Greville Fane; but I could quite believe at least that the wine-question had been put by Leolin's good offices on a better footing, for the dear woman used to mix her drinks—she was perpetually serving the most splendid suppers—in the queerest fashion. I could see him quite ripe to embrace regularly that care. It occurred to me indeed, when she settled in England again, that she might by a shrewd use of both her children be able to rejuvenate her style. Ethel had come back to wreak her native, her social yearning, and if she couldn't take her mother into company would at least go into it herself. Silently, stiffly, almost grimly, this young lady reared her head, clenched her long teeth, squared her lean elbows and found her way up the staircases she had marked. The only communication she ever made, the only effusion of confidence with which she ever honoured me, was when she said "I don't want to know the people mamma knows, I mean to know others." I took due note of the remark, for I wasn't one of the "others." I couldn't trace therefore the steps and stages of her climb; I could only admire it at a distance and congratulate her mother in due course on the results. The results, the gradual, the final, the wonderful, were that Ethel went to "big" parties and got people to take her. Some of them were people she had met abroad, and others people the people she had met abroad had met. They ministered alike to Miss Ethel's convenience, and I wondered how she extracted so many favours without the expenditure a smile. Her smile was the dimmest thing in nature, diluted, u sweetened, inexpensive lemonade, and she had arrived precociously at social wisdom, recognising that if she was neither pretty enough nor rich enough nor clever enough, she could at least, in her muscular youth, be rude enough. Therefore, so placed to give her parent tips, to let her know what really occurred in the mansions of the great, to supply her with local colour, with *data* to work from, she promoted the driving of the well-worn quill, over the brave old battered blotting book, to a still lustier measure and precisely at the moment when most was to depend on this labour. But if she became a great critic it appeared that the labourer herself was constitutionally inapt for the lesson. It was late in the day for Greville Fane to learn, and I heard nothing of her having developed a new manner. She was to have had only one manner, as Leolin would have said, from start to finish.

She was weary and spent at last, but confided to me that she couldn't afford to pause. She continued to speak of her son's work as the great hope of their future—she had saved no money—though the young man wore to my sense an air more and more professional if you like, but less and less literary. There was at the end of a couple of years something rare in the impudence of his playing of his part in the comedy. When I wondered how she could play hers it was to feel afresh the fatuity of her fondness, which was proof, I believed—I indeed saw to the end—against any interference of reason. She loved the young impostor with a simple blind benighted love, and of all the heroes of romance who had passed before her eyes he was by far the brightest. He was at any rate the most real—she could touch him, pay for him, suffer for him, worship him. He made her think of her princes and dukes, and when she wished to fix these figures in her mind's eye she thought of her boy. She had often told me she was herself carried away by her creations, and she was certainly carried away by Leolin. He vivified—by what romantically might have been at least—the whole question of youth and passion. She held, not unjustly, that the sincere novelist should feel the whole flood of life; she acknowledged with regret that she hadn't had time to feel it herself, and the lapse in her history was in a manner made up by the sight of its rush through this magnificent young man. She exhorted him, I suppose, to encourage the rush; she wrung her own flaccid little sponge into the torrent. What passed between them in her pedagogic hours was naturally a blank to me, but I gathered that she mainly impressed on him that the great thing was to live, because that gave you material. He asked nothing better; he collected material, and the recipe served as a universal pretext. You had only to look at him to see that, with his rings and breastpins, his cross-barred jackets, his early *embonpoint*, his eyes that looked like imitation jewels, his various indications of a dense full-blown temperament, his idea of life was singularly vulgar; but he was so far auspicious as that his response to his mother's expectations was in a high degree practical. If she had imposed a profession on him from his tenderest years it was exactly a profession that he followed. The two were not quite the same, inasmuch as the one he had adopted was simply to live at her expense; but at least she couldn't say he hadn't taken a line. If she insisted on believing in him he offered himself to the sacrifice. My impression is that her secret dream was that he should have a *liaison* with a countess, and he persuaded her without difficulty that he had one. I don't know what countesses are capable of, but I've a clear notion of what Leolin was.

He didn't persuade his sister, who despised him—she wished to work her mother in her own way; so that I asked myself why the girl's judgement of him didn't make me like her better. It was because it didn't save her after all from the mute agreement with him to go halves. There were moments when I couldn't help looking hard into his atrocious young eyes, challenging him to confess his fantastic fraud and give it up. Not a little tacit conversation passed between us in this way, but he had always the best of the business. If I said: "Oh come now, with *me* you needn't keep it up; plead guilty and I'll let you off," he wore the most ingenuous, the most candid expression, in the depths of which I could read: "Ah yes, I know it exasperates you—that's just why I do it." He took the line of earnest inquiry, talked about Balzac and Flaubert, asked me if I thought Dickens *did* exaggerate and Thackeray *ought* to be called a pessimist. Once he came to see me, at his mother's suggestion he declared, on purpose to ask me how far, in my opinion, in the English novel, one really might venture to "go." He wasn't resigned to the usual pruderies, the worship of childish twaddle; he suffered already from too much bread and butter. He struck out the brilliant idea that nobody knew how far we might go, since nobody had ever tried. Did I think *he* might safely try—would it injure his mother if he did? He would rather disgrace himself by his timidities than injure his mother, but certainly some one ought to try. Wouldn't *I* try—couldn't I be prevailed upon to look at it as a duty? Surely the ultimate point ought to be fixed—he was worried, haunted by the question. He patronised me unblushingly, made me feel a foolish amateur, a helpless novice, inquired into my habits of work and conveyed to me that I was utterly *vieux jeu* and hadn't had the advantage of an early training. I hadn't been brought up from the egg, I knew nothing of life —didn't go at it on *his system.* He had dipped into French feuilletons and picked up plenty of phrases, and he made a much better show in talk than his poor mother, who never had time to read anything and could only be showy with her pen. If I didn't kick him downstairs it was because he would have landed on her at the bottom.

When she went to live at Primrose Hill I called there and found her wasted and wan. It had visibly dropped, the elation caused the year before by Ethel's marriage; the foam on the cup had subsided and there was bitterness in the draught. She had had to take a cheaper house—and now had to work still harder to pay even for that. Sir Baldwin was obliged to be close; his charges were fearful, and the dream of her living with her daughter—a vision she had never mentioned to me—must be renounced. "I'd have helped them with things, and could have lived perfectly in one room," she said; "I'd have paid for everything, and—after all—I'm some one, ain't I? But I don't fit in, and Ethel tells me there are tiresome people she *must* receive. I can help them from here, no doubt, better than from there. She told me once, you know, what she thinks of my picture of life. 'Mamma, your picture of life's preposterous!' No doubt it is, but she's vexed with me for letting my prices go down; and I had to write three novels to pay for all her marriage cost me. I did it very well —I mean the outfit and the wedding; but that's why I'm here. At any rate she doesn't want a dingy old woman at Blicket. I should give the place an atmosphere of literary prestige, but literary prestige is only the eminence of nobodies. Besides, she knows what to think of my glory—she knows I'm glorious only at Peckham and Hackney. She doesn't want her friends to ask if I've never known nice people. She can't tell them I've never been in society. She tried to teach me better once, but I couldn't catch on. It would seem too as if Peckham and Hackney had had enough of me; for (don't tell any one) I've had to take less for my last than I ever took for anything." I asked her how little this had been, not from curiosity, but in order to upbraid her, more disinterestedly than Lady Luard had done, for such concessions. She answered "I'm ashamed to tell you" and then began to cry.

I had never seen her break down and I was proportionately moved;
she sobbed like a frightened child over the extinction of her vogue
and the exhaustion of her vein. Her little workroom seemed indeed
a barren place to grow flowers for the market, and I wondered in
the after years (for she continued to produce and publish) by what
desperate and heroic process she dragged them out of the soil. I remember asking her on that occasion what had become of Leolin and
how much longer she intended to allow him to amuse himself at her
cost. She retorted with spirit, wiping her eyes, that he was down at
Brighton hard at work—he was in the midst of a novel—and that
he *felt* life so, in all its misery and mystery, that it was cruel to speak
of such experiences as a pleasure. "He goes beneath the surface," she
said, "and he *forces* himself to look at things from which he'd rather
turn away. Do you call that amusing yourself? You should see his face
sometimes! And he does it for me as much as for himself. He tells
me everything—he comes home to me with his *trouvailles*. We're
artists together, and to the artist all things are pure. I've often heard
you say so yourself." The novel Leolin was engaged in at Brighton
never saw the light, but a friend of mine and of Mrs. Stormer's who
was staying there happened to mention to me later that he had seen
the young apprentice to fiction driving, in a dog-cart, a young lady
with a very pink face. When I suggested that she was perhaps a
woman of title with whom he was conscientiously flirting my informant replied: "She is indeed, but do you know what her title
is?" He pronounced it—it was familiar and descriptive—but I won't
reproduce it here. I don't know whether Leolin mentioned it to his
mother: she would have needed all the purity of the artist to forgive
him. I hated so to come across him that in the very last years I went
rarely to see her, though I knew she had come pretty well to the
end of her rope. I didn't want her to tell me she had fairly to give
her books away; I didn't want to see her old and abandoned and
derided; I didn't want, in a word, to see her terribly cry. She still,
however, kept it up amazingly, and every few months, at my club, I
saw three new volumes, in green, in crimson, in blue, on the book-
table that groaned with light literature. Once I met her at the Acad-
emy soirée, where you meet people you thought were dead, and she
vouchsafed the information, as if she owed it to me in candour, that
Leolin had been obliged to recognise the insuperable difficulties of
the question of *form*—he was so fastidious; but that she had now
arrived at a definite understanding with him (it was such a comfort!)

that *she* would do the form if he would bring home the substance. That was now his employ—he foraged for her in the great world at a salary. "He's my 'devil,' don't you see? as if I were a great lawyer: he gets up the case and I argue it." She mentioned further that in addition to his salary he was paid by the piece: he got so much for a striking character, so much for a pretty name, so much for a plot, so much for an incident, and had so much promised him if he would invent a new crime.

"He *has* invented one," I said, "and he's paid every day of his life."

"What is it?" she asked, looking hard at the picture of the year, "Baby's Tub," near which we happened to be standing.

I hesitated a moment. "I myself will write a little story about it, and then you'll see."

But she never saw; she had never seen anything, and she passed away with her fine blindness unimpaired. Her son published every scrap of scribbled paper that could be extracted from her table-drawers, and his sister quarrelled with him mortally about the proceeds, which showed her only to have wanted a pretext, for they can't have been great. I don't know what Leolin lives on unless on a queer lady many years older than himself, whom he lately married. The last time I met him he said to me with his infuriating smile: "Don't you think we can go a little further still—just a little?" *He* really—with me at least—goes too far.

The Real Thing

*W*HEN the porter's wife who used to answer the house-bell, announced "A gentleman and a lady, sir," I had, as I often had in those days—the wish being father to the thought—an immediate vision of sitters. Sitters my visitors in this case proved to be; but not in the sense I should have preferred. There was nothing at first however to indicate that they mightn't have come for a portrait. The gentleman, a man of fifty, very high and very straight, with a moustache slightly grizzled and a dark grey walking-coat admirably fitted, both of which I noted professionally—I don't mean as a barber or yet as a tailor—would have struck me as a celebrity if celebrities often were striking. It was a truth of which I had for some time been conscious that a figure with a good deal of frontage was, as one might say, almost never a public institution. A glance at the lady helped to remind me of this paradoxical law: she also looked too distinguished to be a "personality." Moreover one would scarcely come across two variations together.

Neither of the pair immediately spoke—they only prolonged the preliminary gaze suggesting that each wished to give the other a chance. They were visibly shy; they stood there letting me take them in—which, as I afterwards perceived, was the most practical thing they could have done. In this way their embarrassment served their cause. I had seen people painfully reluctant to mention that they desired anything so gross as to be represented on canvas; but the scruples of my new friends appeared almost insurmountable. Yet the gentleman might have said "I should like a portrait of my wife," and the lady might have said "I should like a portrait of my husband." Perhaps they weren't husband and wife—this naturally would make the matter more delicate. Perhaps they wished to be done together—in which case they ought to have brought a third person to break the news.

"We come from Mr. Rivet," the lady finally said with a dim smile that had the effect of a moist sponge passed over a "sunk" piece of painting, as well as of a vague allusion to vanished beauty. She was as tall and straight, in her degree, as her companion, and with ten years less to carry. She looked as sad as a woman could look whose face was not charged with expression; that is her tinted oval mask showed waste as an exposed surface shows friction. The hand of time had played over her freely, but to an effect of elimination. She was slim and stiff, and so well-dressed, in dark blue cloth, with lappets and pockets and buttons, that it was clear she employed the same tailor as her husband. The couple had an indefinable air of prosperous thrift—they evidently got a good deal of luxury for their money. If I was to be one of their luxuries, it would behoove me to consider my terms.

"Ah, Claude Rivet recommended me?" I echoed; and I added that it was very kind of him, though I could reflect that, as he only painted landscape, this wasn't a sacrifice.

The lady looked very hard at the gentleman, and the gentleman looked round the room. Then, staring at the door a moment and stroking his moustache, he rested his pleasant eyes on me with the remark: "He said you were the right one."

"I try to be, when people want to sit."

"Yes, we should like to," said the lady anxiously.

"Do you mean together?"

My visitors exchanged a glance. "If you could do anything with *me* I suppose it would be double," the gentleman stammered.

"Oh, yes, there's naturally a higher charge for two figures than for one."

"We should like to make it pay," the husband confessed.

"That's very good of you," I returned, appreciating so unwonted a sympathy—for I supposed he meant pay the artist.

A sense of strangeness seemed to dawn on the lady. "We mean for the illustrations—Mr. Rivet said you might put one in."

"Put in—an illustration?" I was equally confused.

"Sketch her off, you know," said the gentleman, colouring.

It was only then that I understood the service Claude Rivet had rendered me; he had told them how I worked in black and white, for magazines, for storybooks, for sketches of contemporary life, and consequently had copious employment for models. These things were true, but it was not less true—I may confess it now; whether because the aspiration was to lead to everything or to nothing I leave the reader to guess—that I couldn't get the honours, to say nothing of the emoluments, of a great painter of portraits out of my head. My "illustrations" were my pot-boilers; I looked to a different branch of art—far and away the most interesting it had always seemed to me—to perpetuate my fame. There was no shame in looking to it also to make my fortune; but that fortune was by so much further from being made from the moment my visitors wished to be "done" for something. I was disappointed; for in the pictorial sense I had immediately seen them. I had seized their type—I had already settled what I would do with it. Something that wouldn't absolutely have pleased them, I afterwards reflected.

"Ah, you're—you're—a—?" I began as soon as I had mastered my surprise. I couldn't bring out the dingy word "models": it seemed so little to fit the case.

"We haven't had much practice," said the lady.

"We've got to *do* something, and we've thought that an artist in your line might perhaps make something of us," her husband threw off. He further mentioned that they didn't know many artists and that they had gone first, on the off chance—he painted views of course, but sometimes put in figures; perhaps I remembered—to Mr. Rivet, whom they had met a few years before at a place in Norfolk where he was sketching.

"We used to sketch a little ourselves," the lady hinted.

"It's very awkward, but we absolutely *must* do something," her husband went on.

"Of course we're not so *very* young," she admitted with a wan smile.

With the remark that I might as well know something more about them the husband had handed me a card extracted from a neat new pocket-book—their appurtenances were all of the freshest—and inscribed with the words "Major Monarch." Impressive as these words were they didn't carry my knowledge much further; but my visitor presently added: "I've left the army and we've had the misfortune to lose our money. In fact our means are dreadfully small."

"It's awfully trying—a regular strain," said Mrs. Monarch.

They evidently wished to be discreet—to take care not to swagger because they were gentlefolk. I felt them willing to recognise this as something of a drawback, at the same time that I guessed at an underlying sense—their consolation in adversity—that they *had* their points. They certainly had; but these advantages struck me as preponderantly social; such, for instance, as would help to make a drawing-room look well. However, a drawing-room was always, or ought to be, a picture.

In consequence of his wife's allusion to their age Major Monarch observed: "Naturally it's more for the figure that we thought of going in. We can still hold ourselves up." On the instant I saw that the figure was indeed their strong point. His "naturally" didn't sound vain, but it lighted up the question. "*She* has the best one," he continued, nodding at his wife with a pleasant after-dinner absence of circumlocution. I could only reply, as if we were in fact sitting over our wine, that this didn't prevent his own from being very good; which led him in turn to make answer: "We thought that if you ever have to do people like us we might be something like it. *She* particularly—for a lady in a book, you know."

I was so amused by them that, to get more of it, I did my best to take their point of view; and though it was an embarrassment to find myself appraising physically, as if they were animals on hire or useful blacks, a pair whom I should have expected to meet only in one of the relations in which criticism is tacit, I looked at Mrs. Monarch judicially enough to be able to exclaim after a moment with conviction: "Oh, yes, a lady in a book!" She was singularly like a bad illustration.

"We'll stand up, if you like," said the Major; and he raised himself before me with a really grand air.

I could take his measure at a glance—he was six feet two and a perfect gentleman. It would have paid any club in process of formation and in want of a stamp to engage him at a salary to stand in the principal window. What struck me at once was that in coming to me they had rather missed their vocation; they could surely have been turned to better account for advertising purposes. I couldn't of course see the thing in detail, but I could see them make somebody's fortune—I don't mean their own. There was something in them for a waistcoat-maker, an hotel-keeper or a soap-vendor. I could imagine "We always use it" pinned on their bosoms with the greatest effect; I had a vision of the brilliancy with which they would launch a table d'hôte.

Mrs. Monarch sat still, not from pride but from shyness, and presently her husband said to her: "Get up, my dear, and show how smart you are." She obeyed, but she had no need to get up to show it. She walked to the end of the studio and then came back blushing, her fluttered eyes on the partner of her appeal. I was reminded of an incident I had accidentally had a glimpse of in Paris—being with a friend there, a dramatist about to produce a play, when an actress came to him to ask to be entrusted with a part. She went through her paces before him, walked up and down as Mrs. Monarch was doing. Mrs. Monarch did it quite as well, but I abstained from applauding. It was very odd to see such people apply for such poor pay. She looked as if she had ten thousand a year. Her husband had used the word that described her: she was in the London current jargon essentially and typically "smart." Her figure was, in the same order of ideas, conspicuously and irreproachably "good." For a woman of her age her waist was surprisingly small; her elbow moreover had the orthodox crook. She held her head at the conventional angle, but why did she come to *me?* She ought to have tried on jackets at a big shop. I feared my visitors were not only destitute but "artistic"—which would be a great complication. When she sat down again I thanked her, observing that what a draughtsman most valued in his model was the faculty of keeping quiet.

"Oh, *she* can keep quiet," said Major Monarch. Then he added jocosely: "I've always kept her quiet."

"I'm not a nasty fidget, am I?" It was going to wring tears from me, I felt, the way she hid her head, ostrich-like, in the other broad bosom.

The owner of this expanse addressed his answer to me. "Perhaps it isn't out of place to mention—because we ought to be quite businesslike, oughtn't we?—that when I married her she was known as the Beautiful Statue."

"Oh dear!" said Mrs. Monarch ruefully.

"Of course I should want a certain amount of expression," I rejoined.

"Of *course!*"—and I had never heard such unanimity.

"And then I suppose you know that you'll get awfully tired."

"Oh, we *never* get tired!" they eagerly cried.

"Have you had any kind of practice?"

They hesitated—they looked at each other. "We've been photographed—*immensely*," said Mrs. Monarch.

"She means the fellows have asked us themselves," added the Major.

"I see—because you're so good-looking."

"I don't know what they thought, but they were always after us."

"We always got our photographs for nothing," sm
arch.

"We might have brought some, my dear," her husbano

"I'm not sure we have any left. We've given quantities a
explained to me.

"With our autographs and that sort of thing," said the Major.

"Are they to be got in the shops?" I inquired as a harmless pleasantry.

"Oh, yes, *hers*—they used to be."

"Not now," said Mrs. Monarch with her eyes on the floor.

II

I could fancy the "sort of thing" they put on the presentation
copies of their photographs, and I was sure they wrote a beautiful
hand. It was odd how quickly I was sure of everything that concerned them. If they were now so poor as to have to earn shillings
and pence they could never have had much of a margin. Their good
looks had been their capital, and they had good-naturedly made the
most of the career that this resource marked out for them. It was in
their faces, the blankness, the deep intellectual repose of the twenty
years of country-house visiting that had given them pleasant intonations. I could see the sunny drawing-rooms, sprinkled with periodicals she didn't read, in which Mrs. Monarch had continuously sat;
I could see the wet shrubberies in which she had walked, equipped
to admiration for either exercise. I could see the rich covers the
Major had helped to shoot and the wonderful garments in which,
late at night, he repaired to the smoking-room to talk about them.
I could imagine their leggings and waterproofs, their knowing tweeds
and rugs, their rolls of sticks and cases of tackle and neat umbrellas;
and I could evoke the exact appearance of their servants and the
compact variety of their luggage on platforms of country stations.

They gave small tips, but they were liked; they didn't do anything
themselves, but they were welcome. They looked so well everywhere;
they gratified the general relish for stature, complexion and "form."
They knew it without fatuity or vulgarity, and they respected themselves in consequence. They weren't superficial; they were thorough
and kept themselves up—it had been their line. People with such a
taste for activity had to have some line. I could feel how even in a

dull house they could have been counted on for the joy of life. At present something had happened—it didn't matter what, their little income had grown less, it had grown least—and they had to do something for pocket-money. Their friends could like them, I made out, without liking to support them. There was something about them that represented credit—their clothes, their manners, their type; but if credit is a large empty pocket in which an occasional chink reverberates, the chink at least must be audible. What they wanted of me was help to make it so. Fortunately they had no children—I soon divined that. They would also perhaps wish our relations to be kept secret: this was why it was "for the figure"—the reproduction of the face would betray them.

I liked them—I felt, quite as their friends must have done—they were so simple; and I had no objection to them if they would suit. But somehow with all their perfections I didn't easily believe in them. After all they were amateurs, and the ruling passion of my life was the detestation of the amateur. Combined with this was another perversity—an innate preference for the represented subject over the real one: the defect of the real one was so apt to be a lack of representation. I liked things that appeared; then one was sure. Whether they *were* or not was a subordinate and almost always a profitless question. There were other considerations, the first of which was that I already had two or three recruits in use, notably a young person with big feet, in alpaca, from Kilburn, who for a couple of years had come to me regularly for my illustrations and with whom I was still—perhaps ignobly—satisfied. I frankly explained to my visitors how the case stood, but they had taken more precautions than I supposed. They had reasoned out their opportunity, for Claude Rivet had told them of the projected *édition de luxe* of one of the writers of our day—the rarest of the novelists—who, long neglected by the multitudinous vulgar and dearly prized by the attentive (need I mention Philip Vincent?), had had the happy fortune of seeing, late in life, the dawn and then the full light of a higher criticism; an estimate in which on the part of the public there was something really of expiation. The edition preparing, planned by a publisher of taste, was practically an act of high reparation; the woodcuts with which it was to be enriched were the homage of English art to one of the most independent representatives of English letters. Major and Mrs. Monarch confessed to me they had hoped I might be able to work *them* into my branch of the enterprise. They knew I was to do the first of the books, *Rutland Ramsay*, but I had to make clear to them that my participation in the rest of the affair—this first book was to be a test—must depend on the satisfaction I should give. If this should be limited my employers would drop me with scarce common forms. It was therefore a crisis for me, and naturally I was making special preparations, looking about for new people, should they be necessary, and securing the best types. I admitted however that I should like to settle down to two or three good models who would do for everything.

"Should we have often to—a—put on special clothes?" Mrs. Monarch timidly demanded.

"Dear, yes—that's half the business."

"And should we be expected to supply our own costumes?"

"Oh, no; I've got a lot of things. A painter's models put on—or put off—anything he likes."

"And you mean—a—the same?"

"The same?"

Mrs. Monarch looked at her husband again.

"Oh, she was just wondering," he explained, "if the costumes are in *general* use." I had to confess that they were, and I mentioned further that some of them—I had a lot of genuine greasy last-century things—had served their time, a hundred years ago, on living world-stained men and women; on figures not perhaps so far removed, in that vanished world, from *their* type, the Monarchs', *quoi!* of a breeched and bewigged age. "We'll put on anything that *fits*," said the Major.

"Oh, I arrange that—they fit in the pictures."

"I'm afraid I should do better for the modern books. I'd come as you like," said Mrs. Monarch.

"She has got a lot of clothes at home: they might do for contemporary life," her husband continued.

"Oh, I can fancy scenes in which you'd be quite natural." And indeed I could see the slipshod rearrangements of stale properties—the stories I tried to produce pictures for without the exasperation of reading them—whose sandy tracts the good lady might help to people. But I had to return to the fact that for this sort of work—the daily mechanical grind—I was already equipped: the people I was working with were fully adequate.

"We only thought we might be more like *some* characters," said Mrs. Monarch mildly, getting up.

Her husband also rose; he stood looking at me with a dim wistfulness that was touching in so fine a man. "Wouldn't it be rather a pull sometimes to have—a—to have—?" He hung fire; he wanted me to help him by phrasing what he meant. But I couldn't—I didn't know. So he brought it out awkwardly: "The *real* thing; a gentleman, you know, or a lady." I was quite ready to give a general assent —I admitted that there was a great deal in that. This encouraged Major Monarch to say, following up his appeal with an unacted gulp: "It's awfully hard—we've tried everything." The gulp was communicative; it proved too much for his wife. Before I knew it Mrs. Monarch had dropped again upon a divan and burst into tears. Her husband sat down beside her, holding one of her hands; whereupon she quickly dried her eyes with the other, while I felt embarrassed as she looked up at me. "There isn't a confounded job I haven't applied for—waited for—prayed for. You can fancy we'd be pretty bad first. Secretaryships and that sort of thing? You might as well ask for a peerage. I'd be *anything*—I'm strong; a messenger or a coal-heaver. I'd put on a gold-laced cap and open carriage-doors in front of the haberdasher's; I'd hang about a station to carry portmanteaus; I'd be a postman. But they won't *look* at you; there are thousands as good as yourself already on the ground. *Gentlemen*, poor beggars, who've drunk their wine, who've kept their hunters!"

I was as reassuring as I knew how to be, and my visitors were presently on their feet again while, for the experiment, we agreed on an hour. We were discussing it when the door opened and Miss Churm came in with a wet umbrella. Miss Churm had to take the omnibus to Maida Vale and then walk half a mile. She looked a trifle blowsy and slightly splashed. I scarcely ever saw her come in without thinking afresh how odd it was that, being so little in herself, she should yet be so much in others. She was a meagre little Miss Churm, but was such an ample heroine of romance. She was only a freckled cockney, but she could represent everything, from a fine lady to a shepherdess; she had the faculty as she might have had a fine voice or long hair. She couldn't spell and she loved beer, but she had two or three "points," and practice, and a knack, and mother-wit, and a whimsical sensibility, and a love of the theatre, and seven sisters, and not an ounce of respect, especially for the *h*. The first thing my visitors saw was that her umbrella was wet, and in their spotless perfection they visibly winced at it. The rain had come on since their arrival.

"I'm all in a soak; there *was* a mess of people in the 'bus. I wish you lived near a stytion," said Miss Churm. I requested her to get ready as quickly as possible, and she passed into the room in which she always changed her dress. But before going out she asked me what she was to get into this time.

"It's the Russian princess, don't you know?" I answered; "the one with the 'golden eyes,' in black velvet, for the long thing in the *Cheapside.*"

"Golden eyes? I *say!*" cried Miss Churm, while my companions watched her with intensity as she withdrew. She always arranged herself, when she was late, before I could turn round; and I kept my visitors a little on purpose, so that they might get an idea, from seeing her, what would be expected of themselves. I mentioned that she was quite my notion of an excellent model—she was really very clever.

"Do you think she looks like a Russian princess?" Major Monarch asked with lurking alarm.

"When I make her, yes."

"Oh, if you have to *make* her—!" he reasoned, not without point.

"That's the most you can ask. There are so many who are not makeable."

"Well, now, *here's* a lady"—and with a persuasive smile he passed his arm into his wife's—"who's already made!"

"Oh, I'm not a Russian princess," Mrs. Monarch protested a little coldly. I could see she had known some and didn't like them. There at once was a complication of a kind I never had to fear with Miss Churm.

This young lady came back in black velvet—the gown was rather rusty and very low on her lean shoulders—and with a Japanese fan in her red hands. I reminded her that in the scene I was doing she had to look over someone's head. "I forget whose it is; but it doesn't matter. Just look over a head."

"I'd rather look over a stove," said Miss Churm; and she took her station near the fire. She fell into position, settled herself into a tall attitude, gave a certain backward inclination to her head and a certain forward droop to her fan, and looked, at least to my prejudiced sense, distinguished and charming, foreign and dangerous. We left her looking so while I went downstairs with Major and Mrs. Monarch.

"I believe I could come about as near it as that," said Mrs. Monarch.

"Oh, you think she's shabby, but you must allow for the alchemy of art."

However, they went off with an evident increase of comfort founded on their demonstrable advantage in being the real thing) I could fancy them shuddering over Miss Churm. She was very droll about them when I went back, for I told her what they wanted.

"Well, if *she* can sit I'll tyke to bookkeeping," said my model.

"She's very ladylike," I replied as an innocent form of aggravation.

"So much the worse for *you*. That means she can't turn round."

"She'll do for the fashionable novels."

"Oh, yes, she'll *do* for them!" my model humorously declared. "Ain't they bad enough without her?" I had often sociably denounced them to Miss Churm.

III

It was for the elucidation of a mystery in one of these works that I first tried Mrs. Monarch. Her husband came with her, to be useful if necessary—it was sufficiently clear that as a general thing he would prefer to come with her. At first I wondered if this were for "propriety's" sake—if he were going to be jealous and meddling. The idea was too tiresome, and if it had been confirmed it would speedily have brought our acquaintance to a close. But I soon saw there was nothing in it and that if he accompanied Mrs. Monarch it was—in addition to the chance of being wanted—simply because he had nothing else to do. When they were separate his occupation was gone, and they never *had* been separate. I judged rightly that in their awkward situation their close union was their main comfort and that this union had no weak spot. It was a real marriage, an encouragement to the hesitating, a nut for pessimists to crack. Their address was humble—I remember afterwards thinking it had been the only thing about them that was really professional—and I could fancy the lamentable lodgings in which the Major would have been left alone. He could sit there more or less grimly with his wife—he couldn't sit there anyhow without her.)

He had too much tact to try and make himself agreeable when he couldn't be useful; so when I was too absorbed in my work to talk he simply sat and waited. But I liked to hear him talk—it made my work, when not interrupting it, less mechanical, less special. To listen to him was to combine the excitement of going out with the economy of staying at home. There was only one hindrance—that I seemed not to know any of the people this brilliant couple had known. I think he wondered extremely, during the term of our intercourse, whom the deuce I *did* know. He hadn't a stray sixpence of an idea to fumble for, so we didn't spin it very fine; we confined ourselves to questions of leather and even of liquor—saddlers and breeches-makers and how to get excellent claret cheap—and matters like "good trains" and the habits of small game. His lore on these last subjects was astonishing—he managed to interweave the station-master with the ornithologist. When he couldn't talk about greater things he could talk cheerfully about small, and since I couldn't accompany him into reminiscences of the fashionable world he could lower the conversation without a visible effort to my level.

So earnest a desire to please was touching in a man who could so easily have knocked one down. He looked after the fire and had an opinion on the draught of the stove without my asking him, and I could see that he thought many of my arrangements not half knowing. I remember telling him that if I were only rich I'd offer him a salary to come and teach me how to live. Sometimes he gave a random sigh of which the essence might have been: "Give me even such a bare old barrack as *this*, and I'd do something with it!" When I wanted to use him he came alone; which was an illustration of the superior courage of women.' His wife could bear her solitary second floor, and she was in general more discreet; showing by various small reserves that she was alive to the propriety of keeping our relations markedly professional—not letting them slide into sociability. She wished it to remain clear that she and the Major were employed, not cultivated, and if she approved of me as a superior, who could be kept in his place, she never thought me quite good enough for an equal.

She sat with great intensity, giving the whole of her mind to it, and was capable of remaining for an hour almost as motionless as before a photographer's lens. I could see she had been photographed often, but somehow the very habit that made her good for that purpose unfitted her for mine. At first I was extremely pleased with her ladylike air, and it was a satisfaction, on coming to follow her lines, to see how good they were and how far they could lead the pencil. But after a little skirmishing I began to find her too insurmountably stiff; do what I would with it my drawing looked like a photograph or a copy of a photograph. Her figure had no variety of expression

—she herself had no sense of variety. You may say that this was my business and was only a question of placing her. Yet I placed her in every conceivable position and she managed to obliterate their differences. She was always a lady certainly, and into the bargain was always the same lady. She was the real thing, but always the same thing. There were moments when I rather writhed under the serenity of her confidence that she *was* the real thing. All her dealings with me and all her husband's were an implication that this was lucky for *me*. Meanwhile I found myself trying to invent types that approached her own, instead of making her own transform itself—in the clever way that was not impossible for instance to poor Miss Churm. Arrange as I would and take the precautions I would, she always came out, in my pictures, too tall—landing me in the dilemma of having represented a fascinating woman as seven feet high, which (out of respect perhaps to my own very much scantier inches) was far from my idea of such a personage.

The case was worse with the Major—nothing I could do would keep *him* down, so that he became useful only for representation of brawny giants. I adored variety and range, I cherished human accidents, the illustrative note; I wanted to characterise closely, and the thing in the world I most hated was the danger of being ridden by a type. I had quarrelled with some of my friends about it; I had parted company with them for maintaining that one *had* to be, and that if the type was beautiful—witness Raphael and Leonardo—the servitude was only a gain. I was neither Leonardo nor Raphael—I might only be a presumptuous young modern searcher; but I held that everything was to be sacrificed sooner than character. When they claimed that the obsessional form could easily *be* character I retorted, perhaps superficially, "Whose?" It couldn't be everybody's—it might end in being nobody's.

After I had drawn Mrs. Monarch a dozen times I felt surer even than before that the value of such a model as Miss Churm resided precisely in the fact that she had no positive stamp, combined of course with the other fact that what she did have was a curious and inexplicable talent for imitation. Her usual appearance was like a curtain which she could draw up at request for a capital performance. This performance was simply suggestive; but it was a word to the wise—it was vivid and pretty. Sometimes even I thought it, though she was plain herself, too insipidly pretty; I made it a reproach to her that the figures drawn from her were monotonously (*bêtement*,

as we used to say) graceful. Nothing made her more angry: it was
so much her pride to feel she could sit for characters that had nothing in common with each other. She would accuse me at such moments of taking away her "reputytion."

It suffered a certain shrinkage, this queer quantity, from the repeated visits of my new friends. Miss Churm was greatly in demand,
never in want of employment, so I had no scruple in putting her
off occasionally, to try them more at my ease. It was certainly amusing at first to do the real thing—it was amusing to do Major Monarch's trousers. They were the real thing, even if he did come out
colossal. It was amusing to do his wife's back hair—it was so mathe-
matically neat—and the particular "smart" tension of her tight stays.
She lent herself especially to positions in which the face was somewhat averted or blurred; she abounded in ladylike back views and
profils perdus. When she stood erect she took naturally one of the
attitudes in which court painters represent queens and princesses;
so that I found myself wondering whether, to draw out this accom-
plishment, I couldn't get the editor of the Cheapside to publish a
really royal romance, "A Tale of Buckingham Palace." Sometimes,
however, the real thing and the make-believe came into contact:
by which I mean that Miss Churm, keeping an appointment or coming to make one on days when I had much work in hand, encountered
her invidious rivals. The encounter was not on their part, for they
noticed her no more than if she had been the housemaid; not from
intentional loftiness, but simply because as yet, professionally, they
didn't know how to fraternise, as I could imagine they would have
liked—or at least that the Major would. They couldn't talk about
the omnibus—they always walked; and they didn't know what else
to try—she wasn't interested in good trains or cheap claret. Besides,
they must have felt—in the air—that she was amused at them, secretly
derisive of their ever knowing how. She wasn't a person to conceal
the limits of her faith if she had had a chance to show them. On
the other hand Mrs. Monarch didn't think her tidy; for why else
did she take pains to say to me—it was going out of the way, for Mrs.
Monarch—that she didn't like dirty women?

One day when my young lady happened to be present with my
other sitters—she even dropped in, when it was convenient, for a
chat—I asked her to be so good as to lend a hand in getting tea,
a service with which she was familiar and which was one of a class
that, living as I did in a small way, with slender domestic resources,

I often appealed to my models to render. They liked to lay hands on my property, to break the sitting, and sometimes the china—it made them feel Bohemian. The next time I saw Miss Churm after this incident she surprised me greatly by making a scene about it—she accused me of having wished to humiliate her. She hadn't resented the outrage at the time, but had seemed obliging and amused, enjoying the comedy of asking Mrs. Monarch, who sat vague and silent, whether she would have cream and sugar, and putting an exaggerated simper into the question. She had tried intonations—as if she too wished to pass for the real thing—till I was afraid my other visitors would take offence.

Oh, they were determined not to do this, and their touching patience was the measure of their great need. They would sit by the hour, uncomplaining, till I was ready to use them; they would come back on the chance of being wanted and would walk away cheerfully if it failed. I used to go to the door with them to see in what magnificent order they retreated. I tried to find other employment for them—I introduced them to several artists. But they didn't "take," for reasons I could appreciate, and I became rather anxiously aware that after such disappointments they fell back upon me with a heavier weight. They did me the honour to think me most *their* form. They weren't romantic enough for the painters, and in those days there were few serious workers in black-and-white. Besides, they had an eye to the great job I had mentioned to them—they had secretly set their hearts on supplying the right essence for my pictorial vindication of our fine novelist. They knew that for this undertaking I should want no costume effects, none of the frippery of past ages—that it was a case in which everything would be contemporary and satirical and presumably genteel. If I could work them into it their future would be assured, for the labour would of course be long and the occupation steady.

One day Mrs. Monarch came without her husband—she explained his absence by his having had to go to the City. While she sat there in her usual relaxed majesty there came at the door a knock which I immediately recognised as the subdued appeal of a model out of work. It was followed by the entrance of a young man whom I at once saw to be a foreigner and who proved in fact an Italian acquainted with no English word but my name, which he uttered in a way that made it seem to include all others. I hadn't then visited his country, nor was I proficient in his tongue; but as he was not

so meanly constituted—what Italian is?—as to depend only on that
member for expression he conveyed to me, in familiar but graceful
mimicry, that he was in search of exactly the employment in which
the lady before me was engaged. I was not struck with him at first,
and while I continued to draw I dropped few signs of interest or
encouragement. He stood his ground, however—not importunately,
but with a dumb dog-like fidelity in his eyes that amounted to innocent impudence, the manner of a devoted servant—he might have
been in the house for years—unjustly suspected. Suddenly it struck
me that this very attitude and expression made a picture; whereupon
I told him to sit down and wait till I should be free. There was
another picture in the way he obeyed me, and I observed as I worked
that there were others still in the way he looked wonderingly, with
his head thrown back, about the high studio. He might have been
crossing himself in Saint Peter's. Before I finished I said to myself,
"The fellow's a bankrupt orange-monger, but a treasure."

When Mrs. Monarch withdrew he passed across the room like a
flash to open the door for her, standing there with the rapt, pure
gaze of the young Dante spellbound by the young Beatrice. As I
never insisted, in such situations, on the blankness of the British
domestic, I reflected that he had the making of a servant—and I
needed one, but couldn't pay him to be only that—as well as of a
model; in short I resolved to adopt my bright adventurer if he would
agree to officiate in the double capacity. He jumped at my offer, and
in the event my rashness—for I had really known nothing about
him—wasn't brought home to me. He proved a sympathetic though
a desultory ministrant, and had in a wonderful degree the *sentiment
de la pose*. It was uncultivated, instinctive, a part of the happy instinct that had guided him to my door and helped him to spell out
my name on the card nailed to it. He had had no other introduction to me than a guess, from the shape of my high north window,
seen outside, that my place was a studio and that as a studio it would
contain an artist. He had wandered to England in search of fortune,
like other itinerants, and had embarked, with a partner and a small
green handcart, on the sale of penny ices. The ices had melted away
and the partner had dissolved in their train. My young man wore
tight yellow trousers with reddish stripes and his name was Oronte.
He was sallow but fair, and when I put him into some old clothes
of my own he looked like an Englishman. He was as good as Miss
Churm, who could look, when requested, like an Italian.

IV

I thought Mrs. Monarch's face slightly convulsed when, on her coming back with her husband, she found Oronte installed. It was strange to have to recognise in a scrap of a lazzarone a competitor to her magnificent Major. It was she who scented danger first, for the Major was anecdotically unconscious. But Oronte gave us tea, with a hundred eager confusions—he had never been concerned in so queer a process—and I think she thought better of me for having at last an "establishment." They saw a couple of drawings that I had made of the establishment, and Mrs. Monarch hinted that it never would have struck her he had sat for them. "Now the drawings you make from *us*, they look exactly like us," she reminded me, smiling in triumph; and I recognised that this was indeed just their defect. When I drew the Monarchs I couldn't anyhow get away from them—get into the character I wanted to represent; and I hadn't the least desire my model should be discoverable in my picture. Miss Churm never was, and Mrs. Monarch thought I hid her, very properly, because she was vulgar; whereas if she was lost it was only as the dead who go to heaven are lost—in the gain of an angel the more.

By this time I had got a certain start with "Rutland Ramsay," the first novel in the great projected series; that is, I had produced a dozen drawings, several with the help of the Major and his wife, and I had sent them in for approval. My understanding with the publishers, as I have already hinted, had been that I was to be left to do my work, in this particular case, as I liked, with the whole book committed to me; but my connexion with the rest of the series was only contingent. There were moments when, frankly, it *was* a comfort to have the real thing under one's hand; for there were characters in "Rutland Ramsay" that were very much like it. There were people presumably as erect as the Major and women of as good a fashion as Mrs. Monarch. There was a great deal of country-house life—treated, it is true, in a fine fanciful ironical generalised way —and there was a considerable implication of knickerbockers and kilts. There were certain things I had to settle at the outset; such things for instance as the exact appearance of the hero and the particular bloom and figure of the heroine. The author of course gave me a lead, but there was a margain for interpretation. I took

the Monarchs into my confidence, I told them frankly what I was
about, I mentioned my embarrassments and alternatives. "Oh, take
him!" Mrs. Monarch murmured sweetly, looking at her husband;
and "What could you want better than my wife?" the Major inquired
with the comfortable candour that now prevailed between us.

I wasn't obliged to answer these remarks—I was only obliged to
place my sitters. I wasn't easy in mind, and I postponed a little
timidly perhaps the solving of my question. The book was a large
canvas, the other figures were numerous, and I worked off at first
some of the episodes in which the hero and the heroine were not
concerned. When once I had set *them* up I should have to stick
to them—I couldn't make my young man seven feet high in one
place and five feet nine in another. I inclined on the whole to the
latter measurement, though the Major more than once reminded
me that *he* looked about as young as any one. It was indeed quite
possible to arrange him, for the figure, so that it would have been
difficult to detect his age. After the spontaneous Oronte had been
with me a month, and after I had given him to understand several
times over that his native exuberance would presently constitute
an insurmountable barrier to our further intercourse, I waked to a
sense of his heroic capacity. He was only five feet seven, but the
remaining inches were latent. I tried him almost secretly at first, for
I was really rather afraid of the judgement my other models would
pass on such a choice. If they regarded Miss Churm as little better
than a snare what would they think of the representation of a person so little the real thing as an Italian street-vendor of a protagonist
formed by a public school?

If I went a little in fear of them it wasn't because they bullied me,
because they had got an oppressive foothold, but because in their
really pathetic decorum and mysteriously permanent newness they
counted on me so intensely. I was therefore very glad when Jack
Hawley came home: he was always of such good counsel. He painted
badly himself, but there was no one like him for putting his finger
on the place. He had been absent from England for a year; he had
been somewhere—I don't remember where—to get a fresh eye. I
was in a good deal of dread of any such organ, but we were old
friends; he had been away for months and a sense of emptiness was
creeping into my life. I hadn't dodged a missile for a year.

He came back with a fresh eye, but with the same old black velvet
blouse, and the first evening he spent in my studio we smoked

cigarettes till the small hours. He had done no work himself, he
had only got the eye; so the field was clear for the production of my
little things. He wanted to see what I had produced for the *Cheapside,* but he was disappointed in the exhibition. That at least seemed
the meaning of two or three comprehensive groans which, as he
lounged on my big divan, his leg folded under him, looking at my
latest drawings, issued from his lips with the smoke of the cigarette.

"What's the matter with you?" I asked.

"What's the matter with *you?*"

"Nothing save that I'm mystified."

"You are indeed. You're quite off the hinge. What's the meaning
of this new fad?" And he tossed me, with visible irreverence, a drawing in which I happened to have depicted both my elegant models.
I asked if he didn't think it good, and he replied that it struck him
as execrable, given the sort of thing I had always represented myself to him as wishing to arrive at; but I let that pass—I was so
anxious to see exactly what he meant. The two figures in the picture
looked colossal, but I supposed this was *not* what he meant, inasmuch as, for aught he knew to the contrary, I might have been trying for some such effect. I maintained that I was working exactly
in the same way as when he last had done me the honour to tell me
I might do something some day. "Well, there's a screw loose somewhere," he answered; "wait a bit and I'll discover it." I depended
upon him to do so: where else was the fresh eye? But he produced
at last nothing more luminous than "I don't know—I don't like your
types." This was lame for a critic who had never consented to
discuss with me anything but the question of execution, the direction
of strokes and the mystery of values.

"In the drawings you've been looking at I think my types are
very handsome."

"Oh, they won't do!"

"I've been working with new models."

"I see you have. *They* won't do."

"Are you very sure of that?"

"Absolutely—they're stupid."

"You mean *I* am—for I ought to get round that."

"You *can't*—with such people. Who are they?"

I told him, so far as was necessary, and he concluded heartlessly:
"Ce sont des gens qu'il faut mettre à la porte."

"You've never seen them; they're awfully good"—I flew to their defence.

"Not seen them? Why all this recent work of yours drops to pieces with them. It's all I want to see of them."

"No one else has said anything against it—the *Cheapside* people are pleased."

"Every one else is an ass, and the *Cheapside* people the biggest asses of all. Come, don't pretend at this time of day to have pretty illusions about the public, especially about publishers and editors. It's not for *such* animals you work—it's for those who know, *coloro che sanno;* so keep straight for *me* if you can't keep straight for yourself. There was a certain sort of thing you used to try for—and a very good thing it was. But this twaddle isn't *in* it." When I talked with Hawley later about "Rutland Ramsay" and its possible successors he declared that I must get back into my boat again or I should go to the bottom. His voice in short was the voice of warning.

I noted the warning, but I didn't turn my friends out of doors. They bored me a good deal; but the very fact that they bored me admonished me not to sacrifice them—if there was anything to be done with them—simply to irritation. As I look back at this phase they seem to me to have pervaded my life not a little. I have a vision of them as most of the time in my studio, seated against the wall on an old velvet bench to be out of the way, and resembling the while a pair of patient courtiers in a royal ante-chamber. I'm convinced that during the coldest weeks of the winter they held their ground because it saved them fire. Their newness was losing its gloss, and it was impossible not to feel them objects of charity. Whenever Miss Churm arrived they went away, and after I was fairly launched in "Rutland Ramsay" Miss Churm arrived pretty often. They managed to express to me tacitly that they supposed I wanted her for the low life of the book, and I let them suppose it, since they had attempted to study the work—it was lying about the studio—without discovering that it dealt only with the highest circles. They had dipped into the most brilliant of our novelists without deciphering many passages. I still took an hour from them, now and again, in spite of Jack Hawley's warning: it would be time enough to dismiss them, if dismissal should be necessary, when the rigour of the season was over. Hawley had made their acquaintance—he had met them at my fireside—and thought them a ridiculous pair. Learning that he was a painter they tried to approach him, to show him too that they were the real thing; but he looked at them, across the big room, as if they were miles away: they were a compendium of everything he most objected to in the social system of his country. Such people as that, all convention and patent-leather, with ejaculations that stopped conversation, had no business in a studio. A studio was a place to learn to see, and how could you see through a pair of feather-beds?

The main inconvenience I suffered at their hands was that at first I was shy of letting it break upon them that my artful little servant had begun to sit to me for "Rutland Ramsay." They knew I had been odd enough—they were prepared by this time to allow oddity to artists—to pick a foreign vagabond out of the streets when I might have had a person with whiskers and credentials; but it was some time before they learned how high I rated his accomplishments. They found him in an attitude more than once, but they never doubted I was doing him as an organ-grinder. There were several things they never guessed, and one of them was that for a striking scene in the novel, in which a footman briefly figured, it occurred to me to make use of Major Monarch as the menial. I kept putting this off, I didn't like to ask him to don the livery—besides the difficulty of finding a livery to fit him. At last, one day late in the winter, when I was at work on the despised Oronte, who caught one's idea on the wing, and was in the glow of feeling myself go very straight, they came in, the Major and his wife, with their society laugh about nothing (there was less and less to laugh at); came in like country-callers— they always reminded me of that—who have walked across the park after church and are presently persuaded to stay to luncheon. Luncheon was over, but they could stay to tea—I knew they wanted it. The fit was on me, however, and I couldn't let my ardour cool and my work wait, with the fading daylight, while my model prepared it. So I asked Mrs. Monarch if she would mind laying it out—a request which for an instant brought all the blood to her face. Her eyes were on her husband's for a second, and some mute telegraphy passed between them. Their folly was over the next instant; his cheerful shrewdness put an end to it. So far from pitying their wounded pride, I must add, I was moved to give it as complete a lesson as I could. They bustled about together and got out the cups and saucers and made the kettle boil. I know they felt as if they were waiting on my servant, and when the tea was prepared I said: "He'll have a cup, please—he's tired." Mrs. Monarch brought him one where he stood, and he took it from her as if he had been a gentleman at a party squeezing a crush-hat with an elbow.

Then it came over me that she had made a great effort for me—made it with a kind of nobleness—and that I owed her a compensation. Each time I saw her after this I wondered what the compensation could be. I couldn't go on doing the wrong thing to oblige them. Oh, it *was* the wrong thing, the stamp of the work for which they sat—Hawley was not the only person to say it now. I sent in a large number of the drawings I had made for "Rutland Ramsay," and I received a warning that was more to the point than Hawley's. The artistic adviser of the house for which I was working was of opinion that many of my illustrations were not what had been looked for. Most of these illustrations were the subjects in which the Monarchs had figured. Without going into the question of what *had* been looked for, I had to face the fact that at this rate I shouldn't get the other books to do. I hurled myself in despair on Miss Churm—I put her through all her paces. I not only adopted Oronte publicly as my hero, but one morning when the Major looked in to see if I didn't require him to finish a *Cheapside* figure for which he had begun to sit the week before, I told him I had changed my mind—I'd do the drawing from my man. At this my visitor turned pale and stood looking at me. "Is *he* your idea of an English gentleman?" he asked.

I was disappointed, I was nervous, I wanted to get on with my work; so I replied with irritation: "Oh my dear Major—I can't be ruined for *you!*"

It was a horrid speech, but he stood another moment—after which, without a word, he quitted the studio. I drew a long breath, for I said to myself that I shouldn't see him again. I hadn't told him definitely that I was in danger of having my work rejected, but I was vexed at his not having felt the catastrophe in the air, read with me the moral of our fruitless collaboration, the lesson that in the deceptive atmosphere of art even the highest respectability may fail of being plastic.

I didn't owe my friends money, but I did see them again. They reappeared together three days later, and, given all the other facts, there was something tragic in that one. It was a clear proof they could find nothing else in life to do. They had threshed the matter out in a dismal conference—they had digested the bad news that they were not in for the series. If they weren't useful to me even for the *Cheapside,* their function seemed difficult to determine, and I could only judge at first that they had come, forgivingly, decorously, to take a last leave. This made me rejoice in secret that I had little leisure for a scene; for I had placed both my other models in position together and I was pegging away at a drawing from which I hoped to derive glory. It had been suggested by the passage in which Rutland Ramsay, drawing up a chair to Artemisia's piano-stool, says extraordinary things to her while she ostensibly fingers out a difficult piece of music. I had done Miss Churm at the piano before—it was an attitude in which she knew how to take on an absolutely poetic grace. I wished the two figures to "compose" together with intensity, and my little Italian had entered perfectly into my conception. The pair were vividly before me, the piano had been pulled out; it was a charming show of blended youth and murmured love, which I had only to catch and keep. My visitors stood and looked at it, and I was friendly to them over my shoulder.

They made no response, but I was used to silent company and went on with my work, only a little disconcerted—even though exhilarated by the sense that *this* was at least the ideal thing—at not having got rid of them after all. Presently I heard Mrs. Monarch's sweet voice beside or rather above me: "I wish her hair were a little better done." I looked up and she was staring with a strange fixedness at Miss Churm, whose back was turned to her. "Do you mind my just touching it?" she went on—a question which made me spring up for an instant as with the instinctive fear that she might do the young lady a harm. But she quieted me with a glance I shall never forget—I confess I should like to have been able to paint *that*—and went for a moment to my model. She spoke to her softly, laying a hand on her shoulder and bending over her; and as the girl, understanding, gratefully assented, she disposed her rough curls, with a few quick passes, in such a way as to make Miss Churm's head twice as charming. It was one of the most heroic personal services I've ever seen rendered. Then Mrs. Monarch turned away with a low sigh and, looking about her as if for something to do, stooped to the floor with a noble humility and picked up a dirty rag that had dropped out of my paint-box.

The Major meanwhile had also been looking for something to do, and, wandering to the other end of the studio, saw before him my breakfast-things neglected, unremoved. "I say, can't I be useful *here?*" he called out to me with an irrepressible quaver. I assented with a laugh that I fear was awkward, and for the next ten minutes, while I worked, I heard the light clatter of china and the tinkle of spoons and glass. Mrs. Monarch assisted her husband—they washed up my crockery, they put it away. They wandered off into my little scullery, and I afterwards found that they had cleaned my knives and that my slender stock of plate had an unprecedented surface. When it came over me, the latent eloquence of what they were doing, I confess that my drawing was blurred for a moment—the picture swam. They had accepted their failure, but they couldn't accept their fate. They had bowed their heads in bewilderment to the perverse and cruel law in virtue of which the real thing could be so much less precious than the unreal; but they didn't want to starve. If my servants were my models, then my models might be my servants. They would reverse the parts—the others would sit for the ladies and gentlemen and *they* would do the work. They would still be in the studio—it was an intense dumb appeal to me not to turn them out. "Take us on," they wanted to say—"we'll do *anything*."

My pencil dropped from my hand; my sitting was spoiled and I got rid of my sitters, who were also evidently rather mystified and awestruck. Then, alone with the Major and his wife I had a most uncomfortable moment. He put their prayer into a single sentence: "I say, you know—just let *us* do for you, can't you?" I couldn't—it was dreadful to see them emptying my slops; but I pretended I could, to oblige them, for about a week. Then I gave them a sum of money to go away, and I never saw them again. I obtained the remaining books, but my friend Hawley repeats that Major and Mrs. Monarch did me a permanent harm, got me into false ways. If it be true I'm content to have paid the price—for the memory.

The Middle Years

THE April day was soft and bright, and poor Dencombe, happy
in the conceit of reasserted strength, stood in the garden of the
hotel, comparing, with a deliberation in which however there was
still something of languor, the attractions of easy strolls. He liked
the feeling of the south so far as you could have it in the north, he
liked the sandy cliffs and the clustered pines, he liked even the colourless sea. "Bournemouth as a health-resort" had sounded like a mere
advertisement, but he was thankful now for the commonest con-
veniences. The sociable country postman, passing through the garden, had just given him a small parcel which he took out with him,
leaving the hotel to the right and creeping to a bench he had already
haunted, a safe recess in the cliff. It looked to the south, to the tinted
walls of the Island, and was protected behind by the sloping shoulder
of the down. He was tired enough when he reached it, and for a
moment was disappointed; he was better of course, but better, after
all, than what? He should never again, as at one or two great moments of the past, be better than himself. The infinite of life was
gone, and what remained of the dose a small glass scored like a
thermometer by the apothecary. He sat and stared at the sea, which
appeared all surface and twinkle, far shallower than the spirit of
man. It was the abyss of human illusion that was the real, the tide-
less deep. He held his packet, which had come by book-post, un-
opened on his knee, liking, in the lapse of so many joys—his illness
had made him feel his age—to know it was there, but taking for
granted there could be no complete renewal of the pleasure, dear to
young experience, of seeing one's self "just out." Dencombe, who
had a reputation, had come out too often and knew too well in advance how he should look.

His postponement associated itself vaguely, after a little, with a
group of three persons, two ladies and a young man, whom, beneath
him, straggling and seemingly silent, he could see move slowly together along the sands. The gentleman had his head bent over a

book and was occasionally brought to a stop by the charm of this volume, which, as Dencombe could perceive even at a distance, had a cover alluringly red. Then his companions, going a little further, waited for him to come up, poking their parasols into the beach, looking around them at the sea and sky and clearly sensible of the beauty of the day. To these things the young man with the book was still more clearly indifferent; lingering, credulous, absorbed, he was an object of envy to an observer from whose connexion with literature all such artlessness had faded. One of the ladies was large and mature; the other had the spareness of comparative youth and of a social situation possibly inferior. The large lady carried back Dencombe's imagination to the age of crinoline; she wore a hat of the shape of a mushroom, decorated with a blue veil, and had the air, in her aggressive amplitude, of clinging to a vanished fashion or even a lost cause. Presently her companion produced from under the folds of a mantle a limp portable chair which she stiffened out and of which the large lady took possession. This act, and something in the movement of either party, at once characterised the performers —they performed for Dencombe's recreation—as opulent matron and humble dependent. Where, moreover, was the virtue of an approved novelist if one couldn't establish a relation between such figures? the clever theory for instance that the young man was the son of the opulent matron and that the humble dependent, the daughter of a clergyman or an officer, nourished a secret passion for him. Was that not visible from the way she stole behind her protectress to look back at him?—back to where he had let himself come to a full stop when his mother sat down to rest. His book was a novel, it had the catchpenny binding; so that while the romance of life stood neglected at his side he lost himself in that of the circulating library. He moved mechanically to where the sand was softer and ended by plumping down in it to finish his chapter at his ease. The humble dependent, discouraged by his remoteness, wandered with a martyred droop of the head in another direction, and the exorbitant lady, watching the waves, offered a confused resemblance to a flying-machine that had broken down.

When his drama began to fail Dencombe remembered that he had after all another pastime. Though such promptitude on the part of the publisher was rare he was already able to draw from its wrapper his "latest," perhaps his last. The cover of "The Middle Years" was duly meretricious, the smell of the fresh pages the very odour of sanctity; but for the moment he went no further—he had become conscious of a strange alienation. He had forgotten what his book was about. Had the assault of his old ailment, which he had so fallaciously come to Bournemouth to ward off, interposed utter blankness as to what had preceded it? He had finished the revision of proof before quitting London, but his subsequent fortnight in bed had passed the sponge over colour. He couldn't have chanted to himself a single sentence, couldn't have turned with curiosity or confidence to any particular page. His subject had already gone from him, leaving scarce a superstition behind. He uttered a low moan as he breathed the chill of this dark void, so desperately it seemed to represent the completion of a sinister process. The tears filled his mild eyes; something precious had passed away. This was the pang that had been sharpest during the last few years—the sense of ebbing time, of shrinking opportunity; and now he felt not so much that his last chance was going as that it was gone indeed. He had done all he should ever do, and yet hadn't done what he wanted. This was the laceration—that practically his career was over: it was as violent as a grip at his throat. He rose from his seat nervously—a creature hunted by a dread; then he fell back in his weakness and nervously opened his book. It was a single volume; he preferred single volumes and aimed at a rare compression. He began to read and, little by little, in this occupation, was pacified and reassured. Everything came back to him, but came back with a wonder, came back above all with a high and magnificent beauty. He read his own prose, he turned his own leaves, and had as he sat there with the spring sunshine on the page an emotion peculiar and intense. His career was over, no doubt, but it was over, when all was said, with *that*.

He had forgotten during his illness the work of the previous year; but what he had chiefly forgotten was that it was extraordinarily good. He dived once more into his story and was drawn down, as by a siren's hand, to where, in the dim underworld of fiction, the great glazed tank of art, strange silent subjects float. He recognised his motive and surrendered to his talent. Never probably had that talent, such as it was, been so fine. His difficulties were still there, but what was also there, to his perception, though probably, alas! to nobody's else, was the art that in most cases had surmounted them. In his surprised enjoyment of this ability he had a glimpse of a possible reprieve. Surely its force wasn't spent—there was life and service in it yet. It hadn't come to him easily, it had been backward and roundabout. It was the child of time, the nursling of delay; he had struggled and suffered for it, making sacrifices not to be counted, and now that it was really mature was it to cease to yield, to confess itself brutally beaten? There was an infinite charm for Dencombe in feeling as he had never felt before that diligence *vincit omnia*. The result produced in his little book was somehow a result beyond his conscious intention: it was as if he had planted his genius, had trusted his method, and they had grown up and flowered with this sweetness. If the achievement had been real, however, the process had been painful enough. What he saw so intensely to-day, what he felt as a nail driven in, was that only now, at the very last, had he come into possession. His development had been abnormally slow, almost grotesquely gradual. He had been hindered and retarded by experience, he had for long periods only groped his way. It had taken too much of his life to produce too little of his art. The art had come, but it had come after everything else. At such a rate a first existence was too short—long enough only to collect material; so that to fructify, to use the material, one should have a second age, an extension. This extension was what poor Dencombe sighed for. As he turned the last leaves of his volume he murmured "Ah for another go, ah for a better chance!"

The three persons drawing his attention to the sands had vanished and then reappeared; they had now wandered up a path, an artificial and easy ascent, which led to the top of the cliff. Dencombe's bench was halfway down, on a sheltered ledge, and the large lady, a massive heterogeneous person with bold black eyes and kind red cheeks, now took a few moments to rest. She wore dirty gauntlets and immense diamond ear-rings; at first she looked vulgar, but she contradicted this announcement in an agreeable off-hand tone. While her companions stood waiting for her she spread her skirts on the end of Dencombe's seat. The young man had gold spectacles, through which, with his finger still in his red-covered book, he glanced at the volume, bound in the same shade of the same colour, lying on the lap of the original occupant of the bench. After an instant Dencombe felt him struck with a resemblance; he had recognised the gilt stamp on the crimson cloth, was reading "The Middle Years" and now noted that somebody else had kept pace with him. The stranger was startled, possibly even a little ruffled, to find himself not the only person favoured with an early copy. The eyes of the two proprietors met a moment, and Dencombe borrowed amusement from the ex-

Dencombe just debated. If the young man had begun to abuse him he would have confessed on the spot to his identity, but there was no harm in drawing out any impulse to praise. He drew it out with such success that in a few moments his new acquaintance, seated by his side, was confessing candidly that the works of the author of the volumes before them were the only ones he could read a second time. He had come the day before from London, where a friend of his, a journalist, had lent him his copy of the last, the copy sent to the office of the journal and already the subject of a "notice" which, as was pretended there—but one had to allow for "swagger" —it had taken a full quarter of an hour to prepare. He intimated that he was ashamed for his friend, and in the case of a work demanding and repaying study, of such inferior manners; and, with his fresh appreciation and his so irregular wish to express it, he speedily became for poor Dencombe a remarkable, a delightful apparition. Chance had brought the weary man of letters face to face with the greatest admirer in the new generation of whom it was supposable he might boast. The admirer in truth was mystifying, so rare a case was it to find a bristling young doctor—he looked like a German physiologist—enamoured of literary form. It was an accident, but happier than most accidents, so that Dencombe, exhilarated as well as confounded, spent half an hour in making his visitor talk while he kept himself quiet. He explained his premature possession of "The Middle Years" by an allusion to the friendship of the publisher, who, knowing he was at Bournemouth for his health, had paid him this graceful attention. He allowed he had been ill, for Doctor Hugh would infallibly have guessed it; he even went so far as to wonder if he mightn't look for some hygienic "tip" from a personage combining so bright an enthusiasm with a presumable knowledge of the remedies now in vogue. It would shake his faith a little perhaps to have to take a doctor seriously who could take *him* so seriously, but he enjoyed this gushing modern youth and felt with an acute pang that there would still be work to do in a world in which such odd combinations were presented. It wasn't true, what he had tried for renunciation's sake to believe, that all the combinations were exhausted. They weren't by any means—they were infinite: the exhaustion was in the miserable artist.

Doctor Hugh, an ardent physiologist, was saturated with the spirit of the age—in other words he had just taken his degree; but he was independent and various, he talked like a man who would have preferred to love literature best. He would fain have made fine phrases, but nature had denied him the trick. Some of the finest in "The Middle Years" had struck him inordinately, and he took the liberty of reading them to Dencombe in support of his plea. He grew vivid, in the balmy air, to his companion, for whose deep refreshment he seemed to have been sent; and was particularly ingenuous in describing how recently he had become acquainted, and how instantly infatuated, with the only man who had put flesh between the ribs of an art that was starving on superstitions. He hadn't yet written to him—he was deterred by a strain of respect. Dencombe at this moment rejoiced more inwardly than ever that he had never answered the photographers. His visitor's attitude promised him a luxury of intercourse, though he was sure a due freedom for Doctor Hugh would depend not a little on the Countess. He learned without delay what type of Countess was involved, mastering as well the nature of the tie that united the curious trio. The large lady, an Englishwoman by birth and the daughter of a celebrated baritone, whose taste *minus* his talent she had inherited, was the widow of a French nobleman and mistress of all that remained of the handsome fortune, the fruit of her father's earnings, that had constituted her dower. Miss Vernham, an odd creature but an accomplished pianist, was attached to her person at a salary. The Countess was generous, independent, eccentric; she travelled with her minstrel and her medical man. Ignorant and passionate she had nevertheless moments in which she was almost irresistible. Dencombe saw her sit for her portrait in Doctor Hugh's free sketch, and felt the picture of his young friend's relation to her frame itself in his mind. This young friend, for a representative of the new psychology, was himself easily hypnotised, and if he became abnormally communicative it was only a sign of his real subjection. Dencombe did accordingly what he wanted with him, even without being known as Dencombe.

Taken ill on a journey in Switzerland the Countess had picked him up at an hotel, and the accident of his happening to please her had made her offer him, with her imperious liberality, terms that couldn't fail to dazzle a practitioner without patients and whose resources had been drained dry by his studies. It wasn't the way he would have proposed to spend his time, but it was time that would pass quickly, and meanwhile she was wonderfully kind. She exacted perpetual attention, but it was impossible not to like her. He gave details about his queer patient, a "type" if there ever was one, who had in connexion with her flushed obesity, and in addition to the morbid strain of a violent and aimless will, a grave organic disorder; but he came back to his loved novelist, whom he was so good as to pronounce more essentially a poet than many of those who went in for verse, with a zeal excited, as all his indiscretion had been excited, by the happy chance of Dencombe's sympathy and the coincidence of their occupation. Dencombe had confessed to a slight personal acquaintance with the author of "The Middle Years," but had not felt himself as ready as he could have wished when his companion, who had never yet encountered a being so privileged, began to be eager for particulars. He even divined in Doctor Hugh's eye at that moment a glimmer of suspicion. But the young man was too inflamed to be shrewd and repeatedly caught up the book to exclaim: "Did you notice this?" or "Weren't you immensely struck with that?" "There's a beautiful passage toward the end," he broke out; and again he laid his hand on the volume. As he turned the pages he came upon something else, while Dencombe saw him suddenly change colour. He had taken up as it lay on the bench Dencombe's copy instead of his own, and his neighbour at once guessed the reason of his start. Doctor Hugh looked grave an instant; then he said: "I see you've been altering the text!" Dencombe was a passionate corrector, a fingerer of style; the last thing he ever arrived at was a form final for himself. His ideal would have been to publish secretly, and then, on the published text, treat himself to the terrified revise, sacrificing always a first edition and beginning for posterity and even for the collectors, poor dears, with a second. This morning, in "The Middle Years," his pencil had pricked a dozen lights. He was amused at the effect of the young man's reproach; for an instant it made him change colour. He stammered at any rate ambiguously, then through a blur of ebbing consciousness saw Doctor Hugh's mystified eyes. He only had time to feel he was about to be ill again—that emotion, excitement, fatigue, the heat of the sun, the solicitation of the air, had combined to play him a trick, before, stretching out a hand to his visitor with a plaintive cry, he lost his senses altogether.

Later he knew he had fainted and that Doctor Hugh had got him home in a Bath-chair, the conductor of which, prowling within hail for custom, had happened to remember seeing him in the garden of the hotel. He had recovered his perception on the way, and had, in bed that afternoon, a vague recollection of Doctor Hugh's young face, as they went together, bent over him in a comforting laugh and expressive of something more than a suspicion of his identity. That identity was ineffaceable now, and all the more that he was rueful and sore. He had been rash, been stupid, had gone out too soon, stayed out too long. He oughtn't to have exposed himself to strangers, he ought to have taken his servant. He felt as if he had fallen into a hole too deep to descry any little patch of heaven. He was confused about the time that had passed—he pieced the fragments together. He had seen his doctor, the real one, the one who had treated him from the first and who had again been very kind. His servant was in and out on tiptoe, looking very wise after the fact. He said more than once something about the sharp young gentleman. The rest was vagueness in so far as it wasn't despair. The vagueness, however, justified itself by dreams, dozing anxieties from which he finally emerged to the consciousness of a dark room and a shaded candle.

"You'll be all right again—I know all about you now," said a voice near him that he felt to be young. Then his meeting with Doctor Hugh came back. He was too discouraged to joke about it yet, but made out after a little that the interest was intense for his visitor. "Of course I can't attend you professionally—you've got your own man, with whom I've talked and who's excellent," Doctor Hugh went on. "But you must let me come to see you as a good friend. I've just looked in before going to bed. You're doing beautifully, but it's a good job I was with you on the cliff. I shall come in early to-morrow. I want to do something for you. I want to do everything. You've done a tremendous lot for me." The young man held his hand, hanging over him, and poor Dencombe, weakly aware of this living pressure, simply lay there and accepted his devotion. He couldn't do anything less—he needed help too much.

The idea of the help he needed was very present to him that night, which he spent in a lucid stillness, an intensity of thought that constituted a reaction from his hours of stupor. He was lost, he was lost—he was lost if he couldn't be saved. He wasn't afraid of suffering, of death, wasn't even in love with life; but he had had a deep demonstration of desire. It came over him in the long quiet hours that only with "The Middle Years" had he taken his flight; only on that day, visited by soundless processions, had he recognised his kingdom. He had had a revelation of his range. What he dreaded was the idea that his reputation should stand on the unfinished. It wasn't with his past but with his future that it should properly be concerned. Illness and age rose before him like spectres with pitiless eyes! how was he to bribe such fates to give him the second chance? He had had the one chance that all men have—he had had the chance of life. He went to sleep again very late, and when he awoke Doctor Hugh was sitting at hand. There was already by this time something beautifully familiar in him.

"Don't think I've turned out your physician," he said: "I'm acting with his consent. He has been here and seen you. Somehow he seems to trust me. I told him how we happened to come together yesterday, and he recognises that I've a peculiar right."

Dencombe felt his own face pressing. "How have you squared the Countess?"

The young man blushed a little, but turned it off. "Oh never mind the Countess!"

"You told me she was very exacting."

Doctor Hugh had a wait. "So she is."

"And Miss Vernham's an *intrigante*."

"How do you know that?"

"I know everything. One *has* to, to write decently!"

"I think she's mad," said limpid Doctor Hugh.

"Well, don't quarrel with the Countess—she's a present help to you."

"I don't quarrel," Doctor Hugh returned. "But I don't get on with silly women." Presently he added: "You seem very much alone."

"That often happens at my age. I've outlived, I've lost by the way."

Doctor Hugh faltered; then surmounting a soft scruple: "Whom have you lost?"

"Every one."

"Ah no," the young man breathed, laying a hand on his arm.

"I once had a wife—I once had a son. My wife died when my child was born, and my boy, at school, was carried off by typhoid."

"I wish I'd been there!" cried Doctor Hugh.

"Well—if you're here!" Dencombe answered with a smile that, in spite of dimness, showed how he valued being sure of his companion's whereabouts.

"You talk strangely of your age. You're not old."

"Hypocrite—so early!"

"I speak physiologically."

"That's the way I've been speaking for the last five years, and it's exactly what I've been saying to myself. It isn't till we *are* old that we begin to tell ourselves we're not."

"Yet I know I myself am young," Doctor Hugh returned.

"Not so well as I!" laughed his patient, whose visitor indeed would have established the truth in question by the honesty with which he changed the point of view, remarking that it must be one of the charms of age—at any rate in the case of high distinction—to feel that one has laboured and achieved. Doctor Hugh employed the common phrase about earning one's rest, and it made poor Dencombe for an instant almost angry. He recovered himself, however, to explain, lucidly enough, that if, ungraciously, he knew nothing of such a balm, it was doubtless because he had wasted inestimable years. He had followed literature from the first, but he had taken a lifetime to get abreast of her. Only to-day at last had he begun to see, so that all he had hitherto shown was a movement without a direction. He had ripened too late and was so clumsily constituted that he had had to teach himself by mistakes.

"I prefer your flowers then to other people's fruit, and your mistakes to other people's successes," said gallant Doctor Hugh. "It's for your mistakes I admire you."

"You're happy—you don't know," Dencombe answered.

Looking at his watch the young man had got up; he named the hour of the afternoon at which he would return. Dencombe warned him against committing himself too deeply, and expressed again all his dread of making him neglect the Countess—perhaps incur her displeasure.

"I want to be like you—I want to learn by mistakes!" Doctor Hugh laughed.

"Take care you don't make too grave a one! But do come back," Dencombe added with the glimmer of a new idea.

"You should have had more vanity!" His friend spoke as if he knew the exact amount required to make a man of letters normal.

"No, no—I only should have had more time. I want another go."

"Another go?"

"I want an extension."

"An extension?" Again Doctor Hugh repeated Dencombe's words, with which he seemed to have been struck.

"Don't you know?—I want to what they call 'live.' "

The young man, for good-bye, had taken his hand, which closed with a certain force. They looked at each other hard. "You *will* live," said Doctor Hugh.

"Don't be superficial. It's too serious!"

"You *shall* live!" Dencombe's visitor declared, turning pale.

"Ah that's better!" And as he retired the invalid, with a troubled laugh, sank gratefully back.

All that day and all the following night he wondered if it mightn't be arranged. His doctor came again, his servant was attentive, but it was to his confident young friend that he felt himself mentally appeal. His collapse on the cliff was plausibly explained and his liberation, on a better basis, promised for the morrow; meanwhile, however, the intensity of his meditations kept him tranquil and made him indifferent. The idea that occupied him was none the less absorbing because it was a morbid fancy. Here was a clever son of the age, ingenious and ardent, who happened to have set him up for connoisseurs to worship. This servant of his altar had all the new learning in science and all the old reverence in faith; wouldn't he therefore put his knowledge at the disposal of his sympathy, his craft at the disposal of his love? Couldn't he be trusted to invent a remedy for a poor artist to whose art he had paid a tribute? If he couldn't the alternative was hard: Dencombe would have to surrender to silence unvindicated and undivined. The rest of the day and all the next he toyed in secret with this sweet futility. Who would work the miracle for him but the young man who could combine such lucidity with such passion? He thought of the fairy-tales of science and charmed himself into forgetting that he looked for a magic that was not of this world. Doctor Hugh was an apparition, and that placed him above the law. He came and went while his patient, who now sat up, followed him with supplicating eyes. The interest of knowing the great author had made the young man begin "The Middle Years" afresh and would help him to find a richer sense between its covers. Dencombe had told him what he "tried for"; with all his intelligence, on a first perusal, Doctor Hugh had failed to guess it. The baffled celebrity wondered then who in the world *would* guess it: he was amused once more at the diffused massive weight that could be thrown into the missing of an intention. Yet he wouldn't rail at the general mind to-day—consoling as that ever had been: the revelation of his own slowness had seemed to make all stupidity sacred.

Doctor Hugh, after a little, was visibly worried, confessing, on inquiry, to a source of embarrassment at home. "Stick to the Countess —don't mind me," Dencombe said repeatedly; for his companion was frank enough about the large lady's attitude. She was so jealous that she had fallen ill—she resented such a breach of allegiance.

She paid so much for his fidelity that she must have it all: she refused
him the right to other sympathies, charged him with scheming to
make her die alone, for it was needless to point out how little Miss
Vernham was a resource in trouble. When Doctor Hugh mentioned
that the Countess would already have left Bournemouth if he hadn't
kept her in bed, poor Dencombe held his arm tighter and said with
decision: "Take her straight away." They had gone out together,
walking back to the sheltered nook in which, the other day, they
had met. The young man, who had given his companion a personal
support, declared with emphasis that his conscience was clear—he
could ride two horses at once. Didn't he dream for his future of a
time when he should have to ride five hundred? Longing equally for
virtue, Dencombe replied that in that golden age no patient would
pretend to have contracted with him for his whole attention. On the
part of the Countess wasn't such an avidity lawful? Doctor Hugh
denied it, said there was no contract, but only a free understanding,
and that a sordid servitude was impossible to a generous spirit; he
liked moreover to talk about art, and that was the subject on which,
this time, as they sat together on the sunny bench, he tried most to
engage the author of "The Middle Years." Dencombe, soaring again
a little on the weak wings of convalescence and still haunted by that
happy notion of an organised rescue, found another strain of eloquence to plead the cause of a certain splendid "last manner," the
very citadel, as it would prove, of his reputation, the stronghold
into which his real treasure would be gathered. While his listener
gave up the morning and the great still sea ostensibly waited he
had a wondrous explanatory hour. Even for himself he was inspired
as he told what his treasure would consist of; the precious metals
he would dig from the mine, the jewels rare, strings of pearls, he
would hang between the columns of his temple. He was wondrous
for himself, so thick his convictions crowded, but still more wondrous for Doctor Hugh, who assured him none the less that the very
pages he had just published were already encrusted with gems. This
admirer, however, panted for the combinations to come and, before the face of the beautiful day, renewed to Dencombe his guarantee that his profession would hold itself responsible for such a life.
Then he suddenly clapped his hand upon his watch-pocket and asked
leave to absent himself for half an hour. Dencombe waited there for
his return, but was at last recalled to the actual by the fall of a
shadow across the ground. The shadow darkened into that of Miss

Vernham, the young lady in attendance on the Countess; whom
Dencombe, recognising her, perceived so clearly to have come to
speak to him that he rose from his bench to acknowledge the civility.
Miss Vernham indeed proved not particularly civil; she looked
strangely agitated, and her type was now unmistakable.

"Excuse me if I do ask," she said, "whether it's too much to hope
that you may be induced to leave Doctor Hugh alone." Then before
our poor friend, greatly disconcerted, could protest: "You ought to
be informed that you stand in his light—that you may do him a terrible injury."

"Do you mean by causing the Countess to dispense with his services?"

"By causing her to disinherit him." Dencombe stared at this, and
Miss Vernham pursued, in the gratification of seeing she could produce an impression: "It has depended on himself to come into something very handsome. He has had a grand prospect, but I think you've
succeeded in spoiling it."

"Not intentionally, I assure you. Is there no hope the accident may
be repaired?" Dencombe asked.

"She was ready to do anything for him. She takes great fancies, she
lets herself go—it's her way. She has no relations, she's free to dispose
of her money, and she's very ill," said Miss Vernham for a climax.

"I'm very sorry to hear it," Dencombe stammered.

"Wouldn't it be possible for you to leave Bournemouth? That's
what I've come to see about."

He sank to his bench. "I'm very ill myself, but I'll try!"

Miss Vernham still stood there with her colourless eyes and the
brutality of her good conscience. "Before it's too late, please!" she
said; and with this she turned her back, in order, quickly, as if it had
been a business to which she could spare but a precious moment, to
pass out of his sight.

Oh yes, after this Dencombe was certainly very ill. Miss Vernham
had upset him with her rough fierce news; it was the sharpest shock
to him to discover what was at stake for a penniless young man of
fine parts. He sat trembling on his bench, staring at the waste of
waters, feeling sick with the directness of the blow. He was indeed
too weak, too unsteady, too alarmed; but he would make the effort
to get away, for he couldn't accept the guilt of interference and his
honour was really involved. He would hobble home, at any rate, and

then think what was to be done. He made his way back to the hotel
and, as he went, had a characteristic vision of Miss Vernham's great
motive. The Countess hated women of course—Dencombe was lucid
about that; so the hungry pianist had no personal hopes and could
only console herself with the bold conception of helping Doctor
Hugh in order to marry him after he should get his money or else
induce him to recognise her claim for compensation and buy her
off. If she had befriended him at a fruitful crisis he would really,
as a man of delicacy—and she knew what to think of that point—
have to reckon with her.

At the hotel Dencombe's servant insisted on his going back to bed.
The invalid had talked about catching a train and had begun with
orders to pack; after which his racked nerves had yielded to a sense
of sickness. He consented to see his physician, who immediately was
sent for, but he wished it to be understood that his door was irrev-
ocably closed to Doctor Hugh. He had his plan, which was so fine
that he rejoiced in it after getting back to bed. Doctor Hugh, suddenly finding himself snubbed without mercy, would, in natural
disgust and to the joy of Miss Vernham, renew his allegiance to the
Countess. When his physician arrived Dencombe learned that he
was feverish and that this was very wrong: he was to cultivate calm-
ness and try, if possible, not to think. For the rest of the day he
wooed stupidity; but there was an ache that kept him sentient, the
probable sacrifice of his "extension," the limit of his course. His
medical adviser was anything but pleased; his successive relapses
were ominous. He charged this personage to put out a strong hand
and take Doctor Hugh off his mind—it would contribute so much
to his being quiet. The agitating name, in his room, was not mentioned again, but his security was a smothered fear, and it was not
confirmed by the receipt, at ten o'clock that evening, of a telegram
which his servant opened and read him and to which, with an address in London, the signature of Miss Vernham was attached. "Be-
seech you to use all influence to make our friend join us here in the
morning. Countess much the worse for dreadful journey, but everything may still be saved." The two ladies had gathered themselves
up and had been capable in the afternoon of a spiteful revolution.
They had started for the capital, and if the elder one, as Miss Vernham had announced, was very ill, she had wished to make it clear
that she was proportionately reckless. Poor Dencombe, who was not

reckless and who only desired that everything should indeed be "saved," sent this missive straight off to the young man's lodging and had on the morrow the pleasure of knowing that he had quitted Bournemouth by an early train.

Two days later he pressed in with a copy of a literary journal in his hand. He had returned because he was anxious and for the pleasure of flourishing the great review of "The Middle Years." Here at least was something adequate—it rose to the occasion; it was an acclamation, a reparation, a critical attempt to place the author in the niche he had fairly won. Dencombe accepted and submitted; he made neither objection nor inquiry, for old complications had returned and he had had two dismal days. He was convinced not only that he should never again leave his bed, so that his young friend might pardonably remain, but that the demand he should make on the patience of beholders would be of the most moderate. Doctor Hugh had been to town, and he tried to find in his eyes some confession that the Countess was pacified and his legacy clinched; but all he could see there was the light of his juvenile joy in two or three of the phrases of the newspaper. Dencombe couldn't read them, but when his visitor had insisted on repeating them more than once he was able to shake an unintoxicated head. "Ah no—but they would have been true of what I *could* have done!"

"What people 'could have done' is mainly what they've in fact done," Doctor Hugh contended.

"Mainly, yes; but I've been an idiot!" Dencombe said.

Doctor Hugh did remain; the end was coming fast. Two days later his patient observed to him, by way of the feeblest of jokes, that there would now be no question whatever of a second chance. At this the young man stared; then he exclaimed: "Why it has come to pass—it has come to pass! The second chance has been the public's—the chance to find the point of view, to pick up the pearl!"

"Oh the pearl!" poor Dencombe uneasily sighed. A smile as cold as a winter sunset flickered on his drawn lips as he added: "The pearl is the unwritten—the pearl is the unalloyed, the *rest*, the lost!"

From that hour he was less and less present, heedless to all appearance of what went on round him. His disease was definitely mortal, of an action as relentless, after the short arrest that had enabled him to fall in with Doctor Hugh, as a leak in a great ship. Sinking steadily, though this visitor, a man of rare resources, now cordially approved by his physician/showed endless art in guarding him from pain, poor Dencombe kept no reckoning of favour or neglect, betrayed no symptom of regret or speculation. Yet toward the last he gave a sign of having noticed how for two days Doctor Hugh hadn't been in his room, a sign that consisted of his suddenly opening his eyes to put a question. Had he spent those days with the Countess?

"The Countess is dead," said Doctor Hugh. "I knew that in a particular contingency she wouldn't resist. I went to her grave."

Dencombe's eyes opened wider. "She left you 'something handsome'?"

The young man gave a laugh almost too light for a chamber of woe. "Never a penny. She roundly cursed me."

"Cursed you?" Dencombe wailed.

"For giving her up. I gave her up for *you*. I had to choose," his companion explained.

"You chose to let a fortune go?"

"I chose to accept, whatever they might be, the consequences of my infatuation," smiled Doctor Hugh. Then as a larger pleasantry: "The fortune be hanged! It's your own fault if I can't get your things out of my head."

The immediate tribute to his humour was a long bewildered moan; after which, for many hours, many days, Dencombe lay motionless and absent. A response so absolute, such a glimpse of a definite result and such a sense of credit, worked together in his mind and, producing a strange commotion, slowly altered and transfigured his despair. The sense of cold submersion left him—he seemed to float without an effort. The incident was extraordinary as evidence, and it shed an intenser light. At last he signed to Doctor Hugh to listen and, when he was down on his knees by the pillow, brought him very near. "You've made me think it all a delusion."

"Not your glory, my dear friend," stammered the young man.

"Not my glory—what there is of it! It *is* glory—to have been tested, to have had our little quality and cast our little spell. The thing is to have made somebody care. You happen to be crazy of course, but that doesn't affect the law."

"You're a great success!" said Doctor Hugh, putting into his young voice the ring of a marriage-bell.

Dencombe lay taking this in; then he gathered strength to speak once more. "A second chance—*that's* the delusion. There never was to be but one. We work in the dark—we do what we can—we give what we have. Our doubt is our passion and our passion is our task. The rest is the madness of art."

"If you've doubted, if you've despaired, you've always 'done' it," his visitor subtly argued.

"We've done something or other," Dencombe conceded.

"Something or other is everything. It's the feasible. It's *you!*"

"Comforter!" poor Dencombe ironically sighed.

"But it's true," insisted his friend.

"It's true. It's frustration that doesn't count."

"Frustration's only life," said Doctor Hugh.

"Yes, it's what passes." Poor Dencombe was barely audible, but he had marked with the words the virtual end of his first and only chance.

The Death of the Lion

I HAD simply, I suppose, a change of heart, and it must have begun when I received my manuscript back from Mr. Pinhorn. Mr. Pinhorn was my "chief," as he was called in the office: he had accepted the high mission of bringing the paper up. This was a weekly periodical, which had been supposed to be almost past redemption when he took hold of it. It was Mr. Deedy who had let the thing down so dreadfully: he was never mentioned in the office now save in connexion with that misdemeanour. Young as I was I had been in a manner taken over from Mr. Deedy, who had been owner as well as editor; forming part of a promiscuous lot, mainly plant and office-furniture, which poor Mrs. Deedy, in her bereavement and depression, parted with at a rough valuation. I could account for my continuity but on the supposition that I had been cheap. I rather resented the practice of fathering all flatness on my late protector, who was in his unhonoured grave; but as I had my way to make I found matter enough for complacency in being on a "staff." At the same time I was aware of my exposure to suspicion as a product of the old lowering system. This made me feel I was doubly bound to have ideas, and had doubtless been at the bottom of my proposing to Mr. Pinhorn that I should lay my lean hands on Neil Paraday. I remember how he looked at me—quite, to begin with, as if he had never heard of this celebrity, who indeed at that moment was by no means in the centre of the heavens; and even when I had knowingly explained he expressed but little confidence in the demand for any such stuff. When I had reminded him that the great principle on which we were supposed to work was just to create the demand we required, he considered a moment and then returned: "I see—you want to write him up."

"Call it that if you like."

"And what's your inducement?"

"Bless my soul—my admiration!"

Mr. Pinhorn pursed up his mouth. "Is there much to be done with him?"

"Whatever there is we should have it all to ourselves, for he hasn't been touched."

This argument was effective and Mr. Pinhorn responded. "Very well, touch him." Then he added: "But where can you do it?"

"Under the fifth rib!"

Mr. Pinhorn stared. "Where's that?"

"You want me to go down and see him?" I asked when I had enjoyed his visible search for the obscure suburb I seemed to have named.

"I don't 'want' anything—the proposal's your own. But you must remember that that's the way we do things *now*," said Mr. Pinhorn with another dig at Mr. Deedy.

Unregenerate as I was I could read the queer implications of this speech. The present owner's superior virtue as well as his deeper craft spoke in his reference to the late editor as one of that baser sort who deal in false representations. Mr. Deedy would as soon have sent me to call on Neil Paraday as he would have published a "holiday-number"; but such scruples presented themselves as mere ignoble thrift to his successor, whose own sincerity took the form of ringing door-bells and whose definition of genius was the art of finding people at home. It was as if Mr. Deedy had published reports without his young men's having, as Pinhorn would have said, really been there. I was unregenerate, as I have hinted, and couldn't be concerned to straighten out the journalistic morals of my chief, feeling them indeed to be an abyss over the edge of which it was better not to peer. Really to be there this time, moreover, was a vision that made the idea of writing something subtle about Neil Paraday only the more inspiring. I would be as considerate as even Mr. Deedy could have wished, and yet I should be as present as only Mr. Pinhorn could conceive. My allusion to the sequestered manner in which Mr. Paraday lived—it had formed part of my explanation, though I knew of it only by hearsay—was, I could divine, very much what had made Mr. Pinhorn nibble. It struck him as inconsistent with the success of his paper that any one should be so sequestered as that. And then wasn't an immediate exposure of everything just what the public wanted? Mr. Pinhorn effectually called me to order by reminding me of the promptness with which I had met Miss Braby at Liverpool on her return from her fiasco in the States. Hadn't we published, while its freshness and flavour were unimpaired, Miss Braby's own version of that great international episode? I felt somewhat uneasy at this lumping of the actress and the author, and I confess that after having enlisted Mr. Pinhorn's sympathies I procrastinated a little. I had succeeded better than I wished, and I had, as it happened, work nearer at hand. A few days later I called on Lord Crouchley and carried off in triumph the most unintelligible statement that had yet appeared of his lordship's reasons for his change of front. I thus set in motion in the daily papers columns of virtuous verbiage. The following week I ran down to Brighton for a chat, as Mr. Pinhorn called it, with Mrs. Bounder, who gave me, on the subject of her divorce, many curious particulars that had not been articulated in court. If ever an article flowed from the primal fount it was that article on Mrs. Bounder. By this time, however, I became aware that Neil Paraday's new book was on the point of appearing and that its approach had been the ground of my original appeal to Mr. Pinhorn, who was now annoyed with me for having lost so many days. He bundled me off—we would at least not lose another. I've always thought his sudden alertness a remarkable example of the journalistic instinct) Nothing had occurred, since I first spoke to him, to create a visible urgency, and no enlightenment could possibly have reached him. It was a pure case of professional *flair*—he had smelt the coming glory as an animal smells his distant prey.

II

I may as well say at once that this little record pretends in no degree to be a picture either of my introduction to Mr. Paraday or of certain proximate steps and stages. The scheme of my narrative allows no space for these things, and in any case a prohibitory sentiment would hang about my recollection of so rare an hour. These meagre notes are essentially private, so that if they see the light the insidious forces that, as my story itself shows, make at present for publicity will simply have overmastered my precautions. The curtain fell lately enough on the lamentable drama. My memory of the day I alighted at Mr. Paraday's door is a fresh memory of kindness, hospitality, compassion, and of the wonderful illuminating talk in which the welcome was conveyed. Some voice of the air had taught me the right moment, the moment of his life at which an act of unexpected young allegiance might come home to him. He had recently recovered from a long grave illness. I had gone to the neighbouring inn for the night, but I spent the evening in his company, and he insisted the next day on my sleeping under his roof. I hadn't an indefinite leave: Mr. Pinhorn supposed us to put our victims through on the gallop. It was later, in the office, that the rude motions of the jig were set to music. I fortified myself, however, as my training had taught me to do, by the conviction that nothing could be more advantageous for my article than to be written in the very atmosphere. I said nothing to Mr. Paraday about it, but in the morning, after my removal from the inn, while he was occupied in his study, as he had notified me he should need to be, I committed to paper the main heads of my impression. Then thinking to commend myself to Mr. Pinhorn by my celerity, I walked out and posted my little packet before luncheon. Once my paper was written I was free to stay on, and if it was calculated to divert attention from my levity in so doing I could reflect with satisfaction that I had never been so clever. I don't mean to deny of course that I was aware it was much too good for Mr. Pinhorn; but I was equally conscious that Mr. Pinhorn had the supreme shrewdness of recognising from time to time the cases in which an article was not too bad only because it was too good. There was nothing he loved so much as to print on the right occasion a thing he hated. I had begun my visit to the great man on a Monday, and on the Wednesday his book came out. A copy of it arrived by the first post, and he let me go out into the garden with it immediately after breakfast. I read it from beginning to end that day, and in the evening he asked me to remain with him the rest of the week and over the Sunday.

That night my manuscript came back from Mr. Pinhorn, accompanied with a letter the gist of which was the desire to know what I meant by trying to fob off on him such stuff. That was the meaning of the question, if not exactly its form, and it made my mistake immense to me. Such as this mistake was I could now only look it in the face and accept it. I knew where I had failed, but it was exactly where I couldn't have succeeded. I had been sent down to be personal and then in point of fact hadn't been personal at all: what I had dispatched to London was just a little finicking feverish study of my author's talent. Anything less relevant to Mr. Pinhorn's purpose couldn't well be imagined, and he was visibly angry at my having (at his expense, with a second-class ticket) approached the subject of our enterprise only to stand off so helplessly. For myself, I knew but too well what had happened, and how a miracle—as pretty as some

old miracle of legend—had been wrought on the spot to save me.
There had been a big brush of wings, the flash of an opaline robe,
and then, with a great cool stir of the air, the sense of an angel's having swooped down and caught me to his bosom. He held me only
till the danger was over, and it all took place in a minute. With my
manuscript back on my hands I understood the phenomenon better, and the reflexions I made on it are what I meant, at the beginning
of this anecdote, by my change of heart. Mr. Pinhorn's note was not
only a rebuke decidedly stern, but an invitation immediately to send
him—it was the case to say so—the genuine article, the revealing and
reverberating sketch to the promise of which, and of which alone, I
owed my squandered privilege. A week or two later I recast my
peccant paper and, giving it a particular application to Mr. Paraday's
new book, obtained for it the hospitality of another journal, where,
I must admit, Mr. Pinhorn was so far vindicated as that it attracted
not the least attention.

III

I was frankly, at the end of three days, a very prejudiced critic, so
that one morning when, in the garden, my great man had offered
to read me something I quite held my breath as I listened. It was the
written scheme of another book—something put aside long ago, before his illness, but that he had lately taken out again to reconsider.
He had been turning it round when I came down on him, and it
had grown magnificently under this second hand. Loose liberal confident, it might have passed for a great gossiping eloquent letter—
the overflow into talk of an artist's amorous plan. The theme I
thought singularly rich, quite the strongest he had yet treated; and
this familiar statement of it, full too of fine maturities, was really, in
summarised splendour, a mine of gold, a precious independent work.
I remember rather profanely wondering whether the ultimate production could possibly keep at the pitch. His reading of the fond
epistle, at any rate, made me feel as if I were, for the advantage of
posterity, in close correspondence with him—were the distinguished
person to whom it had been affectionately addressed. It was a high
distinction simply to be told such things. The idea he now communicated had all the freshness, the flushed fairness, of the conception untouched and untried: it was Venus rising from the sea and
before the airs had blown upon her. I had never been so throbbingly

present at such an unveiling. But when he had tossed the last bright word after the others, as I had seen cashiers in banks, weighing mounds of coin, drop a final sovereign into the tray, I knew a sudden prudent alarm.

"My dear master, how, after all, are you going to do it? It's infinitely noble, but what time it will take, what patience and independence, what assured, what perfect conditions! Oh for a lone isle in a tepid sea!"

"Isn't this practically a lone isle, and aren't you, as an encircling medium, tepid enough?" he asked, alluding with a laugh to the wonder of my young admiration and the narrow limits of his little provincial home. "Time isn't what I've lacked hitherto: the question hasn't been to find it, but to use it. Of course my illness made, while it lasted, a great hole—but I dare say there would have been a hole at any rate. The earth we tread has more pockets than a billiard-table. The great thing is now to keep on my feet."

"That's exactly what I mean."

Neil Paraday looked at me with eyes—such pleasant eyes as he had—in which, as I now recall their expression, I seem to have seen a dim imagination of his fate. He was fifty years old, and his illness had been cruel, his convalescence slow. "It isn't as if I weren't all right."

"Oh if you weren't all right I wouldn't look at you!" I tenderly said.

We had both got up, quickened as by this clearer air, and he had lighted a cigarette. I had taken a fresh one, which with an intenser smile, by way of answer to my exclamation, he applied to the flame of his match. "If I weren't better I shouldn't have thought of *that!*" He flourished his script in his hand.

"I don't want to be discouraging, but that's not true," I returned. "I'm sure that during the months you lay here in pain you had visitations sublime. You thought of a thousand things. You think of more and more all the while. That's what makes you, if you'll pardon my familiarity, so respectable. At a time when so many people are spent you come into your second wind. But, thank God, all the same, you're better! Thank God too you're not, as you were telling me yesterday, 'successful.' If *you* weren't a failure what would be the use of trying? That's my one reserve on the subject of your recovery—that it makes you 'score,' as the newspapers say. It looks well in the newspapers, and almost anything that does that's hor-

rible. 'We are happy to announce that Mr. Paraday, the celebrated
author, is again in the enjoyment of excellent health.' Somehow I
shouldn't like to see it."

"You won't see it; I'm not in the least celebrated—my obscurity
protects me. But couldn't you bear even to see I was dying or dead?"
my host inquired.

"Dead—*passe encore; there's nothing so safe*. One never knows
what a living artist may do—one has mourned so many. However,
one must make the worst of it. You must be as dead as you can."

"Don't I meet that condition in having just published a book?"

"Adequately, let us hope; for the book's verily a masterpiece."

At this moment the parlour-maid appeared in the door that
opened from the garden: Paraday lived at no great cost, and the frisk
of petticoats, with a timorous "Sherry, sir?" was about his modest
mahogany. He allowed half his income to his wife, from whom he
had succeeded in separating without redundancy of legend. I had
a general faith in his having behaved well, and I had once, in London, taken Mrs. Paraday down to dinner. He now turned to speak
to the maid, who offered him, on a tray, some card or note, while,
agitated, excited, I wandered to the end of the precinct. The idea
of his security became supremely dear to me, and I asked myself if
I were the same young man who had come down a few days before
to scatter him to the four winds. When I retraced my steps he had
gone into the house, and the woman—the second London post had
come in—had placed my letters and a newspaper on a bench. I sat
down there to the letters, which were a brief business, and then,
without heeding the address, took the paper from its envelope. It
was the journal of highest renown, *The Empire* of that morning. It
regularly came to Paraday, but I remembered that neither of us had
yet looked at the copy already delivered. This one had a great mark
on the "editorial" page, and, crumpling the wrapper, I saw it to be
directed to my host and stamped with the name of his publishers. I
instantly divined that *The Empire* had spoken of him, and I've not
forgotten the odd little shock of the circumstance. It checked all
eagerness and made me drop the paper a moment. As I sat there conscious of a palpitation I think I had a vision of what was to be. I
had also a vision of the letter I would presently address to Mr. Pinhorn, breaking, as it were, with Mr. Pinhorn. Of course, however,
the next minute the voice of *The Empire* was in my ears.

The article wasn't, I thanked heaven, a review; it was a "leader," the last of three, presenting Neil Paraday to the human race. His new book, the fifth from his hand, had been but a day or two out, and *The Empire*, already aware of it, fired, as if on the birth of a prince, a salute of a whole column. The guns had been booming these three hours in the house without our suspecting them. The big blundering newspaper had discovered him, and now he was proclaimed and anointed and crowned. His place was assigned him as publicly as if a fat usher with a wand had pointed to the topmost chair; he was to pass up and still up, higher and higher, between the watching faces and the envious sounds—away up to the dais and the throne. The article was "epoch-making," a landmark in his life: he had taken rank at a bound, waked up a national glory. A national glory was needed, and it was an immense convenience he was there. What all this meant rolled over me, and I fear I grew a little faint— it meant so much more than I could say "yea" to on the spot. In a flash, somehow, all was different; the tremendous wave I speak of had swept something away. It had knocked down, I suppose, my little customary altar, my twinkling tapers and my flowers, and had reared itself into the likeness of a temple vast and bare. When Neil Paraday should come out of the house he would come out a contemporary. That was what had happened: the poor man was to be squeezed into his horrible age. I felt as if he had been overtaken on the crest of the hill and brought back to the city. A little more and he would have dipped down the short cut to posterity and escaped.

IV

When he came out it was exactly as if he had been in custody, for beside him walked a stout man with a big black beard, who, save that he wore spectacles, might have been a policeman, and in whom at a second glance I recognised the highest contemporary enterprise.

"This is Mr. Morrow," said Paraday, looking, I thought, rather white: "he wants to publish heaven knows what about me."

I winced as I remembered that this was exactly what I myself had wanted. "Already?" I cried with a sort of sense that my friend had fled to me for protection.

Mr. Morrow glared, agreeably, through his glasses: they suggested the electric headlights of some monstrous modern ship, and I felt as if Paraday and I were tossing terrified under his bows. I saw his momentum was irresistible. "I was confident that I should be the first in the field. A great interest is naturally felt in Mr. Paraday's surroundings," he heavily observed.

"I hadn't the least idea of it," said Paraday, as if he had been told he had been snoring.

"I find he hasn't read the article in *The Empire*," Mr. Morrow remarked to me. "That's so very interesting—it's something to start with," he smiled. He had begun to pull off his gloves, which were violently new, and to look encouragingly round the little garden. As a "surrounding" I felt how I myself had already been taken in; I was a little fish in the stomach of a bigger one. "I represent," our visitor continued, "a syndicate of influential journals, no less than thirty-seven, whose public—whose publics, I may say—are in peculiar sympathy with Mr. Paraday's line of thought. They would greatly appreciate any expression of his views on the subject of the art he so nobly exemplifies. In addition to my connexion with the syndicate just mentioned I hold a particular commission from *The Tatler*, whose most prominent department, 'Smatter and Chatter'—I dare say you've often enjoyed it—attracts such attention. I was honoured only last week, as a representative of *The Tatler*, with the confidence of Guy Walsingham, the brilliant author of 'Obsessions.' She pronounced herself thoroughly pleased with my sketch of her method; she went so far as to say that I had made her genius more comprehensible even to herself."

Neil Paraday had dropped on the garden-bench and sat there at once detached and confounded; he looked hard at a bare spot in the lawn, as if with an anxiety that had suddenly made him grave. His movement had been interpreted by his visitor as an invitation to sink sympathetically into a wicker chair that stood hard by, and while Mr. Morrow so settled himself I felt he had taken official possession and that there was no undoing it. One had heard of unfortunate people's having "a man in the house," and this was just what *we* had. There was a silence of a moment, during which we seemed to acknowledge in the only way that was possible the presence of universal fate; the sunny stillness took no pity, and my thought, as I was sure Paraday's was doing, performed within the minute a great distant revolution. I saw just how emphatic I should make my rejoinder to Mr. Pinhorn, and that having come, like Mr. Morrow, to betray, I must remain as long as possible to save. Not because I had brought my mind back, but because our visitor's last words were in my ear, I presently inquired with gloomy irrelevance if Guy Walsingham were a woman.

"Oh yes, a mere pseudonym—rather pretty, isn't it?—and convenient, you know, for a lady who goes in for the larger latitude. 'Obsessions, by Miss So-and-so,' would look a little odd, but men are more naturally indelicate. Have you peeped into 'Obsessions'?" Mr. Morrow continued sociably to our companion.

Paraday, still absent, remote, made no answer, as if he hadn't heard the question: a form of intercourse that appeared to suit the cheerful Mr. Morrow as well as any other. Imperturbably bland, he was a man of resources—he only needed to be on the spot. He had pocketed the whole poor place while Paraday and I were woolgathering, and I could imagine that he had already got his "heads." His system, at any rate, was justified by the inevitability with which I replied, to save my friend the trouble: "Dear no—he hasn't read it. He doesn't read such things!" I unwarily added.

"Things that are *too* far over the fence, eh?" I was indeed a godsend to Mr. Morrow. It was the psychological moment; it determined the appearance of his note-book, which, however, he at first kept slightly behind him, even as the dentist approaching his victim keeps the horrible forceps. "Mr. Paraday holds with the good old proprieties—I see!" And thinking of the thirty-seven influential journals, I found myself, as I found poor Paraday, helplessly assisting at the promulgation of this ineptitude. "There's no point on which distinguished views are so acceptable as on this question—raised perhaps more strikingly than ever by Guy Walsingham—of the permissibility of the larger latitude. I've an appointment, precisely in connexion with it, next week, with Dora Forbes, author of 'The Other Way Round,' which everybody's talking about. Has Mr. Paraday glanced at 'The Other Way Round'?" Mr. Morrow now frankly appealed to me. I took on myself to repudiate the supposition, while our companion, still silent, got up nervously and walked away. His visitor paid no heed to his withdrawal, but opened out the note-book with a more fatherly pat. "Dora Forbes, I gather, takes the ground, the same as Guy Walsingham's, that the larger latitude has simply got to come. He holds that it has got to be squarely faced. Of course his sex makes him a less prejudiced witness. But an authoritative word from Mr. Paraday—from the point of view of *his* sex, you know —would go right round the globe. He takes the line that we *haven't* got to face it?"

I was bewildered: it sounded somehow as if there were three sexes.
My interlocutor's pencil was poised, my private responsibility great.
I simply sat staring, none the less, and only found presence of mind
to say: "Is this Miss Forbes a gentleman?"

Mr. Morrow had a subtle smile. "It wouldn't be 'Miss'—there's a
wife!"

"I mean is she a man?"

"The wife?"—Mr. Morrow was for a moment as confused as myself. But when I explained that I alluded to Dora Forbes in person
he informed me, with visible amusement at my being so out of it,
that this was the "pen-name" of an indubitable male—he had a big
red moustache. "He goes in for the slight mystification because the
ladies are such popular favourites. A great deal of interest is felt
in his acting on that idea—which *is* clever, isn't it?—and there's
every prospect of its being widely imitated." Our host at this moment
joined us again, and Mr. Morrow remarked invitingly that he should
be happy to make a note of any observation the movement in question, the bid for success under a lady's name, might suggest to Mr.
Paraday. But the poor man, without catching the allusion, excused
himself, pleading that, though greatly honoured by his visitor's interest, he suddenly felt unwell and should have to take leave of him
—have to go and lie down and keep quiet. His young friend might be
trusted to answer for him, but he hoped Mr. Morrow didn't expect
great things even of his young friend. His young friend, at this moment, looked at Neil Paraday with an anxious eye, greatly wondering if he were doomed to be ill again; but Paraday's own kind face
met his question reassuringly, seemed to say in a glance intelligible
enough: "Oh I'm not ill, but I'm scared; get him out of the house as
quietly as possible." Getting newspaper-men out of the house was
odd business for an emissary of Mr. Pinhorn, and I was so exhilarated
by the idea of it that I called after him as he left us: "Read the article
in *The Empire* and you'll soon be all right!"

<h2 style="text-align:center">V</h2>

"Delicious my having come down to tell him of it!" Mr. Morrow
ejaculated. "My cab was at the door twenty minutes after *The Empire*
had been laid on my breakfast-table. Now what have you got for
me?" he continued, dropping again into his chair, from which, however, he the next moment eagerly rose. "I was shown into the

drawing-room, but there must be more to see—his study, his literary sanctum, the little things he has about, or other domestic objects and features. He wouldn't be lying down on his study-table? There's a great interest always felt in the scene of an author's labours. Sometimes we're favoured with very delightful peeps. Dora Forbes showed me all his table-drawers, and almost jammed my hand into one into which I made a dash! I don't ask that of you, but if we could talk things over right there where he sits I feel as if I should get the key-note."

I had no wish whatever to be rude to Mr. Morrow, I was much too initiated not to tend to more diplomacy; but I had a quick inspiration, and I entertained an insurmountable, an almost superstitious objection to his crossing the threshold of my friend's little lonely shabby consecrated workshop. "No, no—we shan't get at his life that way," I said. "The way to get at his life is to— But wait a moment!" I broke off and went quickly into the house, whence I in three minutes reappeared before Mr. Morrow with the two volumes of Paraday's new book. "His life's here," I went on, "and I'm so full of this admirable thing that I can't talk of anything else. The artist's life's his work, and this is the place to observe him. What he has to tell us he tells us with *this* perfection. My dear sir, the best interviewer's the best reader."

Mr. Morrow good-humouredly protested. "Do you mean to say that no other source of information should be open to us?"

"None other till this particular one—by far the most copious—has been quite exhausted. Have you exhausted it, my dear sir? Had you exhausted it when you came down here? It seems to me in our time almost wholly neglected, and something should surely be done to restore its ruined credit. It's the course to which the artist himself at every step, and with such pathetic confidence, refers us. This last book of Mr. Paraday's is full of revelations."

"Revelations?" panted Mr. Morrow, whom I had forced again into his chair.

"The only kind that count. It tells you with a perfection that seems to me quite final all the author thinks, for instance, about the advent of the 'larger latitude.' "

"Where does it do that?" asked Mr. Morrow, who had picked up the second volume and was insincerely thumbing it.

"Everywhere—in the whole treatment of his case. Extract the opinion, disengage the answer—those are the real acts of homage."

Mr. Morrow, after a minute, tossed the book away. "Ah but you mustn't take me for a reviewer."

"Heaven forbid I should take you for anything so dreadful! You came down to perform a little act of sympathy, and so, I may confide to you, did I. Let us perform our little act together. These pages overflow with the testimony we want: let us read them and taste them and interpret them. You'll of course have perceived for yourself that one scarcely does read Neil Paraday till one reads him aloud; he gives out to the ear an extraordinary full tone, and it's only when you expose it confidently to that test that you really get near his style. Take up your book again and let me listen, while you pay it out, to that wonderful fifteenth chapter. If you feel you can't do it justice, compose yourself to attention while I produce for you—I think I can!—this scarcely less admirable ninth."

Mr. Morrow gave me a straight look which was as hard as a blow between the eyes; he had turned rather red, and a question had formed itself in his mind which reached my sense as distinctly as if he had uttered it: "What sort of a damned fool are *you?*" Then he got up, gathering together his hat and gloves, buttoning his coat, projecting hungrily all over the place the big transparency of his mask. It seemed to flare over Fleet Street and somehow made the actual spot distressingly humble: there was so little for it to feed on unless he counted the blisters of our stucco or saw his way to do something with the roses. Even the poor roses were common kinds. Presently his eyes fell on the manuscript from which Paraday had been reading to me and which still lay on the bench. As my own followed them I saw it looked promising, looked pregnant, as if it gently throbbed with the life the reader had given it. Mr. Morrow indulged in a nod at it and a vague thrust of his umbrella. "What's that?"

"Oh it's a plan—a secret."

"A secret!" There was an instant's silence, and then Mr. Morrow made another movement. I may have been mistaken, but it affected me as the translated impulse of the desire to lay hands on the manuscript, and this led me to indulge in a quick anticipatory grab which may very well have seemed ungraceful, or even impertinent, and which at any rate left Mr. Paraday's two admirers very erect, glaring at each other while one of them held a bundle of papers well behind him. An instant later Mr. Morrow quitted me abruptly, as if he had really carried something off with him. To reassure myself, watching his broad back recede, I only grasped my manuscript the

tighter. He went to the back door of the house, the one he had come
out from, but on trying the handle he appeared to find it fastened.
So he passed round into the front garden, and by listening intently
enough I could presently hear the outer gate close behind him with
a bang. I thought again of the thirty-seven influential journals and
wondered what would be his revenge. I hasten to add that he was
magnanimous: which was just the most dreadful thing he could
have been. *The Tatler* published a charming chatty familiar account
of Mr. Paraday's "Home-life," and on the wings of the thirty-seven
influential journals it went, to use Mr. Morrow's own expression,
right round the globe.

VI

A week later, early in May, my glorified friend came up to town,
where, it may be veraciously recorded, he was the king of the beasts of
the year. No advancement was ever more rapid, no exaltation more
complete, no bewilderment more teachable. His book sold but mod-
erately, though the article in *The Empire* had done unwonted won-
ders for it; but he circulated in person to a measure that the libraries
might well have envied. His formula had been found—he was a
"revelation." His momentary terror had been real, just as mine had
been—the overclouding of his passionate desire to be left to finish
his work. He was far from unsociable, but he had the finest conception of being let alone that I've ever met. For the time, none the less,
he took his profit where it seemed most to crowd on him, having in
his pocket the portable sophistries about the nature of the artist's
task. Observation too was a kind of work and experience a kind of
success; London dinners were all material and London ladies were
fruitful toil. "No one has the faintest conception of what I'm trying
for," he said to me, "and not many have read three pages that I've
written; but I must dine with them first—they'll find out why when
they've time." It was rather rude justice perhaps; but the fatigue had
the merit of being a new sort, while the phantasmagoric town was
probably after all less of a battlefield than the haunted study. He
once told me that he had had no personal life to speak of since his
fortieth year, but had had more than was good for him before. London closed the parenthesis and exhibited him in relations; one of
the most inevitable of these being that in which he found himself
to Mrs. Weeks Wimbush, wife of the boundless brewer and pro-

prietress of the universal menagerie. In this establishment, as everybody knows, on occasions when the crush is great, the animals rub shoulders freely with the spectators and the lions sit down for whole evenings with the lambs.

It had been ominously clear to me from the first that in Neil Paraday this lady, who, as all the world agreed, was tremendous fun, considered that she had secured a prime attraction, a creature of almost heraldic oddity. Nothing could exceed her enthusiasm over her capture, and nothing could exceed the confused apprehensions it excited in me. I had an instinctive fear of her which I tried without effect to conceal from her victim, but which I let her notice with perfect impunity. Paraday heeded it, but she never did, for her conscience was that of a romping child. She was a blind violent force to which I could attach no more idea of responsibility than to the creaking of a sign in the wind. It was difficult to say what she conduced to but circulation. She was constructed of steel and leather, and all I asked of her for our tractable friend was not to do him to death. He had consented for a time to be of india-rubber, but my thoughts were fixed on the day he should resume his shape or at least get back into his box. It was evidently all right, but I should be glad when it was well over. I had a special fear —the impression was ineffaceable of the hour when, after Mr. Morrow's departure, I had found him on the sofa in his study. That pretext of indisposition had not in the least been meant as a snub to the envoy of *The Tatler*—he had gone to lie down in very truth. He had felt a pang of his old pain, the result of the agitation wrought in him by this forcing open of a new period. His old programme, his old ideal even had to be changed. Say what one would, success was a complication and recognition had to be reciprocal. The monastic life, the pious illumination of the missal in the convent-cell were things of the gathered past. It didn't engender despair, but at least it required adjustment. Before I left him on that occasion we had passed a bargain, my part of which was that I should make it my business to take care of him. Let whoever would represent the interest in his presence (I must have had a mystical prevision of Mrs. Weeks Wimbush) I should represent the interest in his work—or otherwise expressed in his absence. These two interests were in their essence opposed; and I doubt, as youth is fleeting, if I shall ever again know the intensity of joy with which I felt that in so good a cause I was willing to make myself odious.

One day in Sloane Street I found myself questioning **Paraday's** landlord, who had come to the door in answer to my knock. Two vehicles, a barouche and a smart hansom, were drawn up before the house.

"In the drawing-room, sir? Mrs. Weeks Wimbush."

"And in the dining-room?"

"A young lady, sir—waiting: I think a foreigner."

It was three o'clock, and on days when Paraday didn't lunch out he attached a value to these appropriated hours. On which days, however, didn't the dear man lunch out? Mrs. Wimbush, at such a crisis, would have rushed round immediately after her own repast. I went into the dining-room first, postponing the pleasure of seeing how, upstairs, the lady of the barouche would, on my arrival, point the moral of my sweet solicitude. No one took such an interest as herself in his doing only what was good for him, and she was always on the spot to see that he did it. She made appointments with him to discuss the best means of economising his time and protecting his privacy. She further made his health her special business, and had so much sympathy with my own zeal for it that she was the author of pleasing fictions on the subject of what my devotion had led me to give up. I gave up nothing (I don't count Mr. Pinhorn) because I had nothing, and all I had as yet achieved was to find myself also in the menagerie. I had dashed in to save my friend, but I had only got domesticated and wedged; so that I could do little more for him than exchange with him over people's heads looks of intense but futile intelligence.

VII

The young lady in the dining-room had a brave face, black hair, blue eyes, and in her lap a big volume. "I've come for his autograph," she said when I had explained to her that I was under bonds to see people for him when he was occupied. "I've been waiting half an hour, but I'm prepared to wait all day." I don't know whether it was this that told me she was American, for the propensity to wait all day is not in general characteristic of her race. I was enlightened probably not so much by the spirit of the utterance as by some quality of its sound. At any rate I saw she had an individual patience and a lovely frock, together with an expression that played among her pretty features like a breeze among flowers. Putting her

book on the table she showed me a massive album, showily bound
and full of autographs of price. The collection of faded notes, of
still more faded "thoughts," of quotations, platitudes, signatures,
represented a formidable purpose.

I could only disclose my dread of it. "Most people apply to Mr.
Paraday by letter, you know."

"Yes, but he doesn't answer. I've written three times."

"Very true," I reflected; "the sort of letter you mean goes straight
into the fire."

"How do you know the sort I mean?" My interlocutress had
blushed and smiled, and in a moment she added: "I don't believe
he gets many like them!"

"I'm sure they're beautiful, but he burns without reading." I
didn't add that I had convinced him he ought to.

"Isn't he then in danger of burning things of importance?"

"He would perhaps be so if distinguished men hadn't an infallible
nose for nonsense."

She looked at me a moment—her face was sweet and gay. "Do *you*
burn without reading too?"—in answer to which I assured her that
if she'd trust me with her repository I'd see that Mr. Paraday should
write his name in it.

She considered a little. "That's very well, but it wouldn't make
me see him."

"Do you want very much to see him?" It seemed ungracious to
catechise so charming a creature, but somehow I had never yet taken
my duty to the great author so seriously.

"Enough to have come from America for the purpose."

I stared. "All alone?"

"I don't see that that's exactly your business, but if it will make
me more seductive I'll confess that I'm quite by myself. I had to
come alone or not come at all."

She was interesting; I could imagine she had lost parents, natural
protectors—could conceive even she had inherited money. I was at
a pass of my own fortunes when keeping hansoms at doors seemed to
me pure swagger. As a trick of this bold and sensitive girl, however,
it became romantic—a part of the general romance of her freedom,
her errand, her innocence. The confidence of young Americans was
notorious, and I speedily arrived at a conviction that no impulse
could have been more generous than the impulse that had operated
here. I foresaw at that moment that it would make her my peculiar

charge, just as circumstances had made Neil Paraday. She would
be another person to look after, so that one's honour would be concerned in guiding her straight. These things became clearer to me
later on; at the instant I had scepticism enough to observe to her, as
I turned the pages of her volume, that her net had all the same caught
many a big fish. She appeared to have had fruitful access to the great
ones of the earth; there were people moreover whose signatures she
had presumably secured without a personal interview. She couldn't
have worried George Washington and Friedrich Schiller and Han-
nah More. She met this argument, to my surprise, by throwing up
the album without a pang. It wasn't even her own; she was responsible for none of its treasures. It belonged to a girl-friend in America,
a young lady in a western city. This young lady had insisted on her
bringing it, to pick up more autographs: she thought they might
like to see, in Europe, in what company they would be. The "girl-
friend," the western city, the immortal names, the curious errand,
the idyllic faith, all made a story as strange to me, and as beguiling,
as some tale in the Arabian Nights. Thus it was that my informant
had encumbered herself with the ponderous tome; but she hastened
to assure me that this was the first time she had brought it out.
For her visit to Mr. Paraday it had simply been a pretext. She
didn't really care a straw that he should write his name; what she
did want was to look straight into his face.

I demurred a little. "And why do you require to do that?"

"Because I just love him!" Before I could recover from the agitating effect of this crystal ring my companion had continued: "Hasn't
there ever been any face that *you've* wanted to look into?"

How could I tell her so soon how much I appreciated the opportunity of looking into hers? I could only assent in general to the
proposition that there were certainly for every one such yearnings,
and even such faces; and I felt the crisis demand all my lucidity, all
my wisdom. "Oh yes, I'm a student of physiognomy. Do you mean,"
I pursued, "that you've a passion for Mr. Paraday's books?"

"They've been everything to me and a little more beside—I know
them by heart. They've completely taken hold of me. There's no
author about whom I'm in such a state as I'm in about Neil Paraday."

"Permit me to remark then," I presently returned, "that you're
one of the right sort."

"One of the enthusiasts? Of course I am!"

"Oh there are enthusiasts who are quite of the wrong. I mean you're one of those to whom an appeal can be made."

"An appeal?" Her face lighted as if with the chance of some great sacrifice.

If she was ready for one it was only waiting for her, and in a moment I mentioned it. "Give up this crude purpose of seeing him. Go away without it. That will be far better."

She looked mystified, then turned visibly pale. "Why, hasn't he any personal charm?" The girl was terrible and laughable in her bright directness.

"Ah that dreadful word 'personal'!" I wailed; "we're dying of it, for you women bring it out with murderous effect. When you meet with a genius as fine as this idol of ours let him off the dreary duty of being a personality as well. Know him only by what's best in him and spare him for the same sweet sake."

My young lady continued to look at me in confusion and mistrust, and the result of her reflexion on what I had just said was to make her suddenly break out: "Look here, sir—what's the matter with him?"

"The matter with him is that if he doesn't look out people will eat a great hole in his life."

She turned it over. "He hasn't any disfigurement?"

"Nothing to speak of!"

"Do you mean that social engagements interfere with his occupation?"

"That but feebly expresses it."

"So that he can't give himself up to his beautiful imagination?"

"He's beset, badgered, bothered—he's pulled to pieces on the pretext of being applauded. People expect him to give them his time, his golden time, who wouldn't themselves give five shillings for one of his books."

"Five? I'd give five thousand!"

"Give your sympathy—give your forbearance. Two thirds of those who approach him only do it to advertise themselves."

"Why it's too bad!" the girl exclaimed with the face of an angel. "It's the first time I was ever called crude!" she laughed.

I followed up my advantage. "There's a lady with him now who's a terrible complication, and who yet hasn't read, I'm sure, ten pages he ever wrote."

My visitor's wide eyes grew tenderer. "Then how does she talk—?"

"Without ceasing. I only mention her as a single case. Do you want to know how to show a superlative consideration? Simply avoid him."

"Avoid him?" she despairingly breathed.

"Don't force him to have to take account of you; admire him in silence, cultivate him at a distance and secretly appropriate his message. Do you want to know," I continued, warming to my idea, "how to perform an act of homage really sublime?" Then as she hung on my words: "Succeed in never seeing him at all!"

"Never at all?"—she suppressed a shriek for it.

"The more you get into his writings the less you'll want to, and you'll be immensely sustained by the thought of the good you're doing him."

She looked at me without resentment or spite, and at the truth I had put before her with candour, credulity, pity. I was afterwards happy to remember that she must have gathered from my face the liveliness of my interest in herself. "I think I see what you mean."

"Oh I express it badly, but I should be delighted if you'd let me come to see you—to explain it better."

She made no response to this, and her thoughtful eyes fell on the big album, on which she presently laid her hands as if to take it away. "I did use to say out West that they might write a little less for autographs—to all the great poets, you know—and study the thoughts and style a little more."

"What do they care for the thoughts and style? They didn't even understand you. I'm not sure," I added, "that I do myself, and I dare say that you by no means make me out."

She had got up to go, and though I wanted her to succeed in not seeing Neil Paraday I wanted her also, inconsequently, to remain in the house. I was at any rate far from desiring to hustle her off. As Mrs. Weeks Wimbush, upstairs, was still saving our friend in her own way, I asked my young lady to let me briefly relate, in illustration of my point, the little incident of my having gone down into the country for a profane purpose and been converted on the spot to holiness. Sinking again into her chair to listen she showed a deep interest in the anecdote. Then thinking it over gravely she returned with her odd intonation: "Yes, but you do see him!" I had to admit that this was the case; and I wasn't so prepared with an effective attenuation as I could have wished. She eased the situation off, however, by the charming quaintness with which she finally said: "Well, I wouldn't want him to be lonely!" This time she rose in earnest, but

I persuaded her to let me keep the album to show Mr. Paraday. I
assured her I'd bring it back to her myself. "Well, you'll find my
address somewhere in it on a paper!" she sighed all resignedly at the
door.

VIII

I blush to confess it, but I invited Mr. Paraday that very day to
transcribe into the album one of his most characteristic passages.
I told him how I had got rid of the strange girl who had brought it
—her ominous name was Miss Hurter and she lived at an hotel;
quite agreeing with him moreover as to the wisdom of getting rid
with equal promptitude of the book itself. This was why I carried
it to Albemarle Street no later than on the morrow. I failed to find
her at home, but she wrote to me and I went again: she wanted so
much to hear more about Neil Paraday. I returned repeatedly, I may
briefly declare, to supply her with this information. She had been
immensely taken, the more she thought of it, with that idea of mine
about the act of homage: it had ended by filling her with a generous
rapture. She positively desired to do something sublime for him,
though indeed I could see that, as this particular flight was difficult,
she appreciated the fact that my visits kept her up. I had it on my
conscience to keep her up; I neglected nothing that would contribute
to it, and her conception of our cherished author's independence became at last as fine as his very own. "Read him, read him—*that* will
be an education in decency," I constantly repeated; while, seeking
him in his works even as God in nature, she represented herself as
convinced that, according to my assurance, this was the system that
had, as she expressed it, weaned her. We read him together when I
could find time, and the generous creature's sacrifice was fed by our
communion. There were twenty selfish women about whom I told
her and who stirred her to a beautiful rage. Immediately after my
first visit her sister, Mrs. Milsom, came over from Paris, and the two
ladies began to present, as they called it, their letters. I thanked our
stars that none had been presented to Mr. Paraday. They received invitations and dined out, and some of these occasions enabled Fanny
Hurter to perform, for consistency's sake, touching feats of submission. Nothing indeed would now have induced her even to look at
the object of her admiration. Once, hearing his name announced
at a party, she instantly left the room by another door and then

straightway quitted the house. At another time when I was at the opera with them—Mrs. Milsom had invited me to their box—I attempted to point Mr. Paraday out to her in the stalls. On this she asked her sister to change places with her and, while that lady devoured the great man through a powerful glass, presented, all the rest of the evening, her inspired back to the house. To torment her tenderly I pressed the glass upon her, telling her how wonderfully near it brought our friend's handsome head. By way of answer she simply looked at me in charged silence, letting me see that tears had gathered in her eyes. These tears, I may remark, produced an effect on me of which the end is not yet. There was a moment when I felt it my duty to mention them to Neil Paraday, but I was deterred by the reflexion that there were questions more relevant to his happiness.

These questions indeed, by the end of the season, were reduced to a single one—the question of reconstituting so far as might be possible the conditions under which he had produced his best work. Such conditions could never all come back, for there was a new one that took up too much place; but some perhaps were not beyond recall. I wanted above all things to see him sit down to the subject he had, on my making his acquaintance, read me that admirable sketch of. Something told me there was no security but in his doing so before the new factor, as we used to say at Mr. Pinhorn's, should render the problem incalculable. It only half-reassured me that the sketch itself was so copious and so eloquent that even at the worst there would be the making of a small but complete book, a tiny volume which, for the faithful, might well become an object of adoration. There would even not be wanting critics to declare, I foresaw, that the plan was a thing to be more thankful for than the structure to have been reared on it. My impatience for the structure, none the less, grew and grew with the interruptions. He had on coming up to town begun to sit for his portrait to a young painter, Mr. Rumble, whose little game, as we also used to say at Mr. Pinhorn's, was to be the first to perch on the shoulders of renown. Mr. Rumble's studio was a circus in which the man of the hour, and still more the woman, leaped through the hoops of his showy frames almost as electrically as they burst into telegrams and "specials." He pranced into the exhibitions on their back; he was the reporter on canvas, the Vandyke up to date, and there was one roaring year in which Mrs. Bounder and Miss Braby, Guy Walsingham and Dora Forbes proclaimed in chorus from the same pictured walls that no one had yet got ahead of him.

Paraday had been promptly caught and saddled, accepting with characteristic good humour his confidential hint that to figure in his show was not so much a consequence as a cause of immortality. From Mrs. Wimbush to the last "representative" who called to ascertain his twelve favourite dishes, it was the same ingenuous assumption that he would rejoice in the repercussion. There were moments when I fancied I might have had more patience with them if they hadn't been so fatally benevolent. I hated at all events Mr. Rumble's picture, and had my bottled resentment ready when, later on, I found my distracted friend had been stuffed by Mrs. Wimbush into the mouth of another cannon. A young artist in whom she was intensely interested, and who had no connexion with Mr. Rumble, was to show how far *he* could make him go. Poor Paraday, in return, was naturally to write something somewhere about the young artist. She played her victims against each other with admirable ingenuity, and her establishment was a huge machine in which the tiniest and the biggest wheels went round to the same treadle. I had a scene with her in which I tried to express that the function of such a man was to exercise his genius—not to serve as a hoarding for pictorial posters. The people I was perhaps angriest with were the editors of magazines who had introduced what they called new features, so aware were they that the newest feature of all would be to make him grind their axes by contributing his views on vital topics and taking part in the periodical prattle about the future of fiction. I made sure that before I should have done with him there would scarcely be a current form of words left me to be sick of; but meanwhile I could make surer still of my animosity to bustling ladies for whom he drew the water that irrigated their social flower-beds.

I had a battle with Mrs. Wimbush over the artist she protected, and another over the question of a certain week, at the end of July, that Mr. Paraday appeared to have contracted to spend with her in the country. I protested against this visit; I intimated that he was too unwell for hospitality without a *nuance,* for caresses without imagination; I begged he might rather take the time in some restorative way. A sultry air of promises, of ponderous parties, hung over his August, and he would greatly profit by the interval of rest. He hadn't told me he was ill again—that he had had a warning; but I hadn't needed this, for I found his reticence his worst symptom. The only thing he said to me was that he believed a comfortable attack of something or other would set him up: it would put out of the question everything but the exemptions he prized. I'm afraid I shall have presented him as a martyr in a very small cause if I fail to explain that he surrendered himself much more liberally than I surrendered him. He filled his lungs, for the most part, with the comedy of his queer fate: the tragedy was in the spectacles through which I chose to look. He was conscious of inconvenience, and above all of a great renouncement; but how could he have heard a mere dirge in the bells of his accession? The sagacity and the jealousy were mine, and his the impressions and the harvest. Of course, as regards Mrs. Wimbush, I was worsted in my encounters, for wasn't the state of his health the very reason for his coming to her at Prestidge? Wasn't it precisely at Prestidge that he was to be coddled, and wasn't the dear Princess coming to help her to coddle him? The dear Princess, now on a visit to England, was of a famous foreign house, and, in her gilded cage, with her retinue of keepers and feeders, was the most expensive specimen in the good lady's collection. I don't think her august presence had had to do with Paraday's consenting to go, but it's not impossible he had operated as a bait to the illustrious stranger. The party had been made up for him, Mrs. Wimbush averred, and every one was counting on it, the dear Princess most of all. If he was well enough he was to read them something absolutely fresh, and it was on that particular prospect the Princess had set her heart. She was so fond of genius in *any* walk of life, and was so used to it and understood it so well: she was the greatest of Mr. Paraday's admirers, she devoured everything he wrote. And then he read like an angel. Mrs. Wimbush reminded me that he had again and again given her, Mrs. Wimbush, the privilege of listening to him.

I looked at her a moment. "What has he read to you?" I crudely inquired.

For a moment too she met my eyes, and for the fraction of a moment she hesitated and coloured. "Oh all sorts of things!"

I wondered if this were an imperfect recollection or only a perfect fib, and she quite understood my unuttered comment on her measure of such things. But if she could forget Neil Paraday's beauties she could of course forget my rudeness, and three days later she invited me, by telegraph, to join the party at Prestidge. This time she might indeed have had a story about what I had given up to be near the master. I addressed from that fine residence several com-

munications to a young lady in London, a young lady whom, I confess, I quitted with reluctance and whom the reminder of what she
herself could give up was required to make me quit at all. It adds to
the gratitude I owe her on other grounds that she kindly allows me
to transcribe from my letters a few of the passages in which that
hateful sojourn is candidly commemorated.

IX

"I suppose I ought to enjoy the joke of what's going on here," I
wrote, "but somehow it doesn't amuse me. Pessimism on the contrary possesses me and cynicism deeply engages. I positively feel my
own flesh sore from the brass nails in Neil Paraday's social harness.
The house is full of people who like him, as they mention, awfully,
and with whom his talent for talking nonsense has prodigious success. I delight in his nonsense myself; why is it therefore that I grudge
these happy folk their artless satisfaction? Mystery of the human
heart—abyss of the critical spirit! Mrs. Wimbush thinks she can answer that question, and as my want of gaiety has at last worn out
her patience she has given me a glimpse of her shrewd guess. I'm
made restless by the selfishness of the insincere friend—I want to
monopolise Paraday in order that he may push me on. To be intimate with him's a feather in my cap; it gives me an importance that
I couldn't naturally pretend to, and I seek to deprive him of social
refreshment because I fear that meeting more disinterested people
may enlighten him as to my real motive. All the disinterested people
here are his particular admirers and have been carefully selected as
such. There's supposed to be a copy of his last book in the house,
and in the hall I come upon ladies, in attitudes, bending gracefully
over the first volume. I discreetly avert my eyes, and when I next
look round the precarious joy has been superseded by the book of
life. There's a sociable circle or a confidential couple, and the re-
linquished volume lies open on its face and as dropped under extreme coercion. Somebody else presently finds it and transfers it,
with its air of momentary desolation, to another piece of furniture.
Every one's asking every one about it all day, and every one's telling
every one where they put it last. I'm sure it's rather smudgy about
the twentieth page. I've a strong impression too that the second volume is lost—has been packed in the bag of some departing guest;

and yet everybody has the impression that somebody else has read to the end. You see therefore that the beautiful book plays a great part in our existence. Why should I take the occasion of such distinguished honours to say that I begin to see deeper into Gustave Flaubert's doleful refrain about the hatred of literature? I refer you again to the perverse constitution of man.

"The Princess is a massive lady with the organisation of an athlete and the confusion of tongues of a *valet de place*. She contrives to commit herself extraordinarily little in a great many languages, and is entertained and conversed with in detachments and relays, like an institution which goes on from generation to generation or a big building contracted for under a forfeit. She can't have a personal taste any more than, when her husband succeeds, she can have a personal crown, and her opinion on any matter is rusty and heavy and plain—made, in the night of ages, to last and be transmitted. I feel as if I ought to "tip" some *custode* for my glimpse of it. She has been told everything in the world and has never perceived anything, and the echoes of her education respond awfully to the rash footfall—I mean the casual remark—in the cold Valhalla of her memory. Mrs. Wimbush delights in her wit and says there's nothing so charming as to hear Mr. Paraday draw it out. He's perpetually detailed for this job, and he tells me it has a peculiarly exhausting effect. Every one's beginning—at the end of two days—to sidle obsequiously away from her, and Mrs. Wimbush pushes him again and again into the breach. None of the uses I have yet seen him put to infuriate me quite so much. He looks very fagged and has at last confessed to me that his condition makes him uneasy—has even promised me he'll go straight home instead of returning to his final engagements in town. Last night I had some talk with him about going to-day, cutting his visit short; so sure am I that he'll be better as soon as he's shut up in his lighthouse. He told me that this is what he would like to do; reminding me, however, that the first lesson of his greatness has been precisely that he can't do what he likes. Mrs. Wimbush would never forgive him if he should leave her before the Princess has received the last hand. When I hint that a violent rupture with our hostess would be the best thing in the world for him he gives me to understand that if his reason assents to the proposition his courage hangs woefully back. He makes no secret of being mortally afraid of her, and when I ask what harm she can do him that she hasn't already done he simply repeats: 'I'm afraid, I'm afraid! Don't

inquire too closely,' he said last night; 'only believe that I feel a sort
of terror. It's strange, when she's so kind! At any rate, I'd as soon
overturn that piece of priceless Sèvres as tell her I must go before
my date.' It sounds dreadfully weak, but he has some reason, and he
pays for his imagination, which puts him (I should hate it) in the
place of others and makes him feel, even against himself, their
feelings, their appetites, their motives. It's indeed inveterately against
himself that he makes his imagination act. What a pity he has such
a lot of it! He's too beastly intelligent.) Besides, the famous reading's still to come off, and it has been postponed a day to allow Guy
Walsingham to arrive. It appears this eminent lady's staying at a
house a few miles off, which means of course that Mrs. Wimbush has
forcibly annexed her. She's too come over in a day or two—Mrs.
Wimbush wants her to hear Mr. Paraday.

"To-day's wet and cold, and several of the company, at the invitation of the Duke, have driven over to luncheon at Bigwood. I saw
poor Paraday wedge himself, by command, into the little supple-
mentary seat of a brougham in which the Princess and our hostess
were already ensconced. If the front glass isn't open on his dear old
back perhaps he'll survive. Bigwood, I believe, is very grand and
frigid, all marble and precedence, and I wish him well out of the
adventure. I can't tell you how much more and more *your* attitude
to him, in the midst of all this, shines out by contrast. I never will-
ingly talk to these people about him, but see what a comfort I find it
to scribble to you! I appreciate it—it keeps me warm; there are no
fires in the house. Mrs. Wimbush goes by the calendar, the temperature goes by the weather, the weather goes by God knows what, and
the Princess is easily heated. I've nothing but my acrimony to warm
me, and have been out under an umbrella to restore my circulation.
Coming in an hour ago I found Lady Augusta Minch rummaging
about the hall. When I asked her what she was looking for she said
she had mislaid something that Mr. Paraday had lent her. I ascer-
tained in a moment that the article in question is a manuscript, and
I've a foreboding that it's the noble morsel he read me six weeks
ago. When I expressed my surprise that he should have bandied
about anything so precious (I happen to know it's his only copy—
in the most beautiful hand in all the world) Lady Augusta confessed
to me that she hadn't had it from himself, but from Mrs. Wimbush,
who had wished to give her a glimpse of it as a salve for her not being
able to stay and hear it read.

" 'Is that the piece he's to read,' I asked, 'when Guy Walsingham arrives?''

" 'It's not for Guy Walsingham they're waiting now, it's for Dora Forbes,' Lady Augusta said. 'She's coming, I believe, early to-morrow. Meanwhile Mrs. Wimbush has found out about *him*, and is actively wiring to him. She says he also must hear him.'

" 'You bewilder me a little,' I replied; 'in the age we live in one gets lost among the genders and the pronouns. The clear thing is that Mrs. Wimbush doesn't guard such a treasure so jealously as she might.'

" 'Poor dear, she has the Princess to guard! Mr. Paraday lent her the manuscript to look over.'

" 'She spoke, you mean, as if it were the morning paper?'

"Lady Augusta stared—my irony was lost on her. 'She didn't have time, so she gave me a chance first; because unfortunately I go to-morrow to Bigwood.'

" 'And your chance has only proved a chance to lose it?'

" 'I haven't lost it. I remember now—it was very stupid of me to have forgotten. I told my maid to give it to Lord Dorimont—or at least to his man.'

" 'And Lord Dorimont went away directly after luncheon.'

" 'Of course he gave it back to my maid—or else his man did,' said Lady Augusta. 'I dare say it's all right.'

"The conscience of these people is like a summer sea. They haven't time to 'look over' a priceless composition; they've only time to kick it about the house. I suggested that the 'man,' fired with a noble emulation, had perhaps kept the work for his own perusal; and her ladyship wanted to know whether, if the thing shouldn't reappear for the grand occasion appointed by our hostess, the author wouldn't have something else to read that would do just as well. Their questions are too delightful! I declared to Lady Augusta briefly that nothing in the world can ever do so well as the thing that does best; and at this she looked a little disconcerted. But I added that if the manuscript had gone astray our little circle would have the less of an effort of attention to make. The piece in question was very long— it would keep them three hours.

" 'Three hours! Oh the Princess will get up!' said Lady Augusta.

" 'I thought she was Mr. Paraday's greatest admirer.'

" 'I dare say she is—she's so awfully clever. But what's the use of being a Princess—'

" 'If you can't dissemble your love?' I asked as Lady Augusta was vague. She said at any rate that she'd question her maid; and I'm hoping that when I go down to dinner I shall find the manuscript has been recovered."

X

"It has *not* been recovered," I wrote early the next day, "and I'm moreover much troubled about our friend. He came back from Bigwood with a chill and, being allowed to have a fire in his room, lay down a while before dinner. I tried to send him to bed and indeed thought I had put him in the way of it; but after I had gone to dress Mrs. Wimbush came up to see him, with the inevitable result that when I returned I found him under arms and flushed and feverish, though decorated with the rare flower she had brought him for his button-hole. He came down to dinner, but Lady Augusta Minch was very shy of him. To-day he's in great pain, and the advent of *ces dames*—I mean of Guy Walsingham and Dora Forbes—doesn't at all console me. It does Mrs. Wimbush, however, for she has consented to his remaining in bed so that he may be all right to-morrow for the listening circle. Guy Walsingham's already on the scene, and the doctor for Paraday also arrived early. I haven't yet seen the author of 'Obsessions,' but of course I've had a moment by myself with the Doctor. I tried to get him to say that our invalid must go straight home—I mean to-morrow or next day; but he quite refuses to talk about the future. Absolute quiet and warmth and the regular administration of an important remedy are the points he mainly insists on. He returns this afternoon, and I'm to go back to see the patient at one o'clock, when he next takes his medicine. It consoles me a little that he certainly won't be able to read—an exertion he was already more than unfit for. Lady Augusta went off after breakfast, assuring me her first care would be to follow up the lost manuscript. I can see she thinks me a shocking busybody and doesn't understand my alarm, but she'll do what she can, for she's a good-natured woman. 'So are they all honourable men.' That was precisely what made her give the thing to Lord Dorimont and made Lord Dorimont bag it. What use *he* has for it God only knows. I've the worst forebodings, but somehow I'm strangely without passion—desperately calm. As I consider the unconscious, the well-meaning ravages of our appreciative circle I bow my head in submission to some great natural, some universal accident; I'm rendered almost indifferent, in fact quite gay (ha-ha!) by the sense of immitigable fate. Lady Augusta promises me to trace the precious object and let me have it through the post by the time Paraday's well enough to play his part with it. The last evidence is that her maid did give it to his lordship's valet. One would suppose it some thrilling number of *The Family Budget*. Mrs. Wimbush, who's aware of the accident, is much less agitated by it than she would doubtless be were she not for the hour inevitably engrossed with Guy Walsingham."

Later in the day I informed my correspondent, for whom indeed I kept a loose diary of the situation, that I had made the acquaintance of this celebrity and that she was a pretty little girl who wore her hair in what used to be called a crop. She looked so juvenile and so innocent that if, as Mr. Morrow had announced, she was resigned to the larger latitude, her superiority to prejudice must have come to her early. I spent most of the day hovering about Neil Paraday's room, but it was communicated to me from below that Guy Walsingham, at Prestidge, was a success. Toward evening I became conscious somehow that her superiority was contagious, and by the time the company separated for the night I was sure the larger latitude had been generally accepted. I thought of Dora Forbes and felt that he had no time to lose. Before dinner I received a telegram from Lady Augusta Minch. "Lord Dorimont thinks he must have left bundle in train—inquire." How could I inquire—if I was to take the word as a command? I was too worried and now too alarmed about Neil Paraday. The Doctor came back, and it was an immense satisfaction to me to be sure he was wise and interested. He was proud of being called to so distinguished a patient, but he admitted to me that night that my friend was gravely ill. It was really a relapse, a recrudescence of his old malady. There could be no question of moving him: we must at any rate see first, on the spot, what turn his condition would take. Meanwhile, on the morrow, he was to have a nurse. On the morrow the dear man was easier, and my spirits rose to such cheerfulness that I could almost laugh over Lady Augusta's second telegram: "Lord Dorimont's servant been to station—nothing found. Push inquiries." I did laugh, I'm sure, as I remembered this to be the mystic scroll I had scarcely allowed poor Mr. Morrow to point his umbrella at. Fool that I had been: the thirty-seven influential journals wouldn't have destroyed it, they'd only have printed it. Of course I said nothing to Paraday.

When the nurse arrived she turned me out of the room, on which I went downstairs. I should premise that at breakfast the news that our brilliant friend was doing well excited universal complacency, and the Princess graciously remarked that he was only to be commiserated for missing the society of Miss Collop. Mrs. Wimbush, whose social gift never shone brighter than in the dry decorum with which she accepted this fizzle in her fireworks, mentioned to me that Guy Walsingham had made a very favourable impression on her Imperial Highness. Indeed I think every one did so, and that, like the money-market or the national honour, her Imperial Highness was constitutionally sensitive. There was a certain gladness, a perceptible bustle in the air, however, which I thought slightly anomalous in a house where a great author lay critically ill. "*Le roy est mort—vive le roy*": I was reminded that another great author had already stepped into his shoes. When I came down again after the nurse had taken possession I found a strange gentleman hanging about the hall and pacing to and fro by the closed door of the drawing-room. This personage was florid and bald; he had a big red moustache and wore showy knickerbockers—characteristics all that fitted to my conception of the identity of Dora Forbes. In a moment I saw what had happened: the author of "The Other Way Round" had just alighted at the portals of Prestidge, but had suffered a scruple to restrain him from penetrating further. I recognised his scruple when, pausing to listen at his gesture of caution, I heard a shrill voice lifted in a sort of rhythmic uncanny chant. The famous reading had begun, only it was the author of "Obsessions" who now furnished the sacrifice. The new visitor whispered to me that he judged something was going on he oughtn't to interrupt.

"Miss Collop arrived last night," I smiled, "and the Princess has a thirst for the *inédit*."

Dora Forbes raised his bushy brows. "Miss Collop?"

"Guy Walsingham, your distinguished *confrère*—or shall I say your formidable rival?"

"Oh!" growled Dora Forbes. Then he added: "Shall I spoil it if I go in?"

"I should think nothing could spoil it!" I ambiguously laughed.

Dora Forbes evidently felt the dilemma; he gave an irritated crook to his moustache. "*Shall* I go in?" he presently asked.

We looked at each other hard a moment; then I expressed something bitter that was in me, expressed it in an infernal "Do!" After this I got out into the air, but not so fast as not to hear, when the door of the drawing-room opened, the disconcerted drop of Miss Collop's public manner: she must have been in the midst of the larger latitude. Producing with extreme rapidity, Guy Walsingham has just published a work in which amiable people who are not initiated have been pained to see the genius of a sister-novelist held up to unmistakable ridicule; so fresh an exhibition does it seem to them of the dreadful way men have always treated women. Dora Forbes, it's true, at the present hour, is immensely pushed by Mrs. Wimbush and has sat for his portrait to the young artists she protects, sat for it not only in oils but in monumental alabaster.

What happened at Prestidge later in the day is of course contemporary history. If the interruption I had whimsically sanctioned was almost a scandal, what is to be said of that general scatter of the company which, under the Doctor's rule, began to take place in the evening? His rule was soothing to behold, small comfort as I was to have at the end. He decreed in the interest of his patient an absolutely soundless house and a consequent break-up of the party. Little country practitioner as he was, he literally packed off the Princess. She departed as promptly as if a revolution had broken out, and Guy Walsingham emigrated with her. I was kindly permitted to remain, and this was not denied even to Mrs. Wimbush. The privilege was withheld indeed from Dora Forbes; so Mrs. Wimbush kept her latest capture temporarily concealed. This was so little, however, her usual way of dealing with her eminent friends that a couple of days of it exhausted her patience and she went up to town with him in great publicity. The sudden turn for the worst her afflicted guest had, after a brief improvement, taken on the third night raised an obstacle to her seeing him before her retreat; a fortunate circumstance doubtless, for she was fundamentally disappointed in him. This was not the kind of performance for which she had invited him to Prestidge, let alone invited the Princess. I must add that none of the generous acts marking her patronage of intellectual and other merit have done so much for her reputation as her lending Neil Paraday the most beautiful of her numerous homes to die in. He took advantage to the utmost of the singular favour. Day by day I saw him sink, and I roamed alone about the empty terraces and gardens. His wife never came near him, but I scarcely noticed it: as I paced there with rage in my heart I was too full of another wrong. In the event of his death it would fall to me perhaps to bring out in some charming form, with notes, with the tenderest editorial care, that precious heritage of his written project. But where *was* that precious heritage, and were both the author and the book to have been snatched from us? Lady Augusta wrote me she had done all she could and that poor Lord Dorimont, who had really been worried to death, was extremely sorry. I couldn't have the matter out with Mrs. Wimbush, for I didn't want to be taunted by her with desiring to aggrandise myself by a public connexion with Mr. Paraday's sweepings. She had signified her willingness to meet the expense of all advertising, as indeed she was always ready to do. The last night of the horrible series, the night before he died, I put my ear closer to his pillow.

"That thing I read you that morning, you know."

"In your garden that dreadful day? Yes!"

"Won't it do as it is?"

"It would have been a glorious book."

"It *is* a glorious book," Neil Paraday murmured. "Print it as it stands—beautifully."

"Beautifully!" I passionately promised.

It may be imagined whether, now that he's gone, the promise seems to me less sacred. I'm convinced that if such pages had appeared in his lifetime the Abbey would hold him to-day. I've kept the advertising in my own hands, but the manuscript has not been recovered. It's impossible, and at any rate intolerable, to suppose it can have been wantonly destroyed. Perhaps some hazard of a blind hand, some brutal fatal ignorance has lighted kitchen-fires with it. Every stupid and hideous accident haunts my meditations. My undiscourageable search for the lost treasure would make a long chapter. Fortunately I've a devoted associate in the person of a young lady who has every day a fresh indignation and a fresh idea, and who maintains with intensity that the prize will still turn up. Sometimes I believe her, but I've quite ceased to believe myself. The only thing for us at all events is to go on seeking and hoping together, and we should be closely united by this firm tie even were we not at present by another.

The Next Time

MRS. HIGHMORE'S errand this morning was odd enough to deserve commemoration: she came to ask me to write a notice of her great forthcoming work. Her great works have come forth so frequently without my assistance that I was sufficiently entitled on this occasion to open my eyes; but what really made me stare was the ground on which her request reposed, and what prompts a note of the matter is the train of memory lighted by that explanation. Poor Ray Limbert, while we talked, seemed to sit there between us: she reminded me that my acquaintance with him had begun, eighteen years ago, with her having come in, precisely as she came to-day before luncheon, to bespeak my charity for him. If she didn't know then how little my charity was worth she's at least enlightened now, and this is just what makes the drollery of her visit. As I hold up the torch to the dusky years—by which I mean as I cipher up with a pen that stumbles and stops the figured column of my reminiscences—I see that Limbert's public hour, or at least my small apprehension of it, is rounded by those two occasions. It was *finis*, with a little moralising flourish, that Mrs. Highmore seemed to trace to-day at the bottom of the page. "One of the most voluminous writers of the time," she has often repeated this sign; but never, I daresay, in spite of her professional command of appropriate emotion, with an equal sense of that mystery and that sadness of things which to people of imagination generally hover over the close of human histories. This romance at any rate is bracketed by her early and her late appeal; and when its melancholy protrusions had caught the declining light again from my half-hour's talk with her I took a private vow to recover while that light still lingers something of the delicate flush, to pick out with a brief patience the perplexing lesson.

It was wonderful to see how for herself Mrs. Highmore had already done so: she wouldn't have hesitated to announce to me what was the matter with Ralph Limbert, or at all events to give me a glimpse of the high admonition she had read in his career. There could have been no better proof of the vividness of this parable, which we were really in our pleasant sympathy quite at one about, than that Mrs. Highmore, of all hardened sinners, should have been converted. It wasn't indeed news to me: she impressed on me that for the last ten years she had wanted to do something artistic, something as to which she was prepared not to care a rap whether or no it should sell. She brought home to me further that it had been mainly seeing what her brother-in-law did and how he did it that had wedded her to this perversity. As *he* didn't sell, dear soul, and as several persons, of whom I was one, thought highly of that, the fancy had taken her —taken her even quite early in her prolific course—of reaching, if only once, the same heroic eminence. She yearned to be, like Limbert, but of course only once, an exquisite failure. There was something a failure was, a failure in the market, that a success somehow wasn't. A success was as prosaic as a good dinner: there was nothing more to be said about it than that you had had it. Who but vulgar people, in such a case, made gloating remarks about the courses? It was often by such vulgar people that a success was attested. It made, if you came to look at it, nothing but money; that is, it made so much that any other result showed small in comparison. A failure now could make—oh, with the aid of immense talent of course, for there were failures and failures—such a reputation! She did me the honour—she had often done it—to intimate that what she meant by reputation was seeing *me* toss a flower. If it took a failure to catch a failure I was by my own admission well qualified to place the laurel. It was because she had made so much money and Mr. Highmore had taken such care of it that she could treat herself to an hour of pure glory. She perfectly remembered that as often as I had heard her heave that sigh I had been prompt with my declaration that a book sold might easily be as glorious as a book unsold. Of course she knew this, but she knew also that it was the age of trash triumphant and that she had never heard me speak of anything that had "done well" exactly as she had sometimes heard me speak of something that hadn't—with just two or three words of respect which, when I used them, seemed to convey more than they commonly stood for, seemed to hush the discussion up a little, as for the very beauty of the secret.

I may declare in regard to these allusions that, whatever I then thought of myself as a holder of the scales, I had never scrupled to laugh out at the humour of Mrs. Highmore's pursuit of quality at any price. It had never rescued her even for a day from the hard doom of popularity, and though I never gave her my word for it there was no reason at all why it should. The public *would* have her, as her husband used roguishly to remark; not indeed that, making her bargains, standing up to her publishers, and even in his higher flights to her reviewers, he ever had a glimpse of her attempted conspiracy against her genius, or rather, as I may say, against mine. It wasn't that when she tried to be what she called subtle (for wasn't Limbert subtle, and wasn't I?); her fond consumers, bless them, didn't suspect the trick nor show what they thought of it: they straightway rose on the contrary to the morsel she had hoped to hold too high, and, making but a big cheerful bite of it, wagged their great collective tail artlessly for more. It was not given to her not to please, not granted even to her best refinements to affright. I had always respected the mystery of those humiliations, but I was fully aware this morning that they were practically the reason why she had come to me. Therefore when she said with the flush of a bold joke in her kind coarse face, "What I feel is, you know, that *you* could settle me if you only would," I knew quite well what she meant. She meant that of old it had always appeared to be the fine blade (as some one had hyperbolically called it) of my particular opinion that snapped the silken thread by which Limbert's chance in the market was wont to hang. She meant that my favour was compromising, that my praise indeed was fatal. I had cultivated the queer habit of seeing nothing in certain celebrities, of seeing overmuch in an occasional nobody, and of judging from a point of view that, say what I would for it (and I had a monstrous deal to say), mostly remained perverse and obscure. Mine was in short the love that killed, for my subtlety, unlike Mrs. Highmore's, produced no tremor of the public tail. She hadn't forgotten how, toward the end, when his case was worst, Limbert would absolutely come to me with an odd shy pathos in his eyes and say: "My dear fellow, I think I've done it this time, if you'll only keep quiet." If my keeping quiet in those days was to help him to appear to have hit the usual taste, for the want of which he was starving, so now my breaking-out was to help Mrs. Highmore to appear to have hit the unusual.

The moral of all this was that I had frightened the public too much for our late friend, but that as she was not starving this was exactly what her grosser reputation required. And then, she good-naturedly and delicately intimated, there would always be, if further reasons were wanting, the price of my clever little article. I think

she gave that hint with a flattering impression—spoiled child of the
booksellers as she is—that the offered fee for my clever little articles
is heavy. Whatever it is, at any rate, she had evidently reflected that
poor Limbert's anxiety for his own profit used to involve my sacrificing mine. Any inconvenience that my obliging her might entail
would not in fine be pecuniary. Her appeal, her motive, her fantastic
thirst for quality and her ingenious theory of my influence struck
me all as excellent comedy, and when I consented at hazard to oblige
her she left me the sheets of her new novel. I could plead no inconvenience and have been looking them over; but I'm frankly ap-
palled at what she expects of me. What's she thinking of, poor dear,
and what has put it into her head that the muse of "quality" has
ever sat with her for so much as three minutes? Why does she suppose that she has been "artistic"? She hasn't been anything whatever,
I surmise, that she hasn't inveterately been. What does she imagine
she has left out? What does she conceive she has put in? She has
neither left out nor put in anything. I shall have to write her an
embarrassed note. The book doesn't exist and there's nothing in life
to say about it. How can there be anything but the same old faithful rush for it?

I

This rush had already begun when, early in the seventies, in the
interest of her prospective brother-in-law, she approached me on
the singular ground of the unencouraged sentiment I had entertained
for her sister. Pretty pink Maud had cast me out, but I appear to
have passed in the flurried little circle for a magnanimous youth.
Pretty pink Maud, so lovely then, before her troubles, that dusky
Jane was gratefully conscious of all she made up for, Maud Stannace, very literary too, very languishing and extremely bullied by
her mother, had yielded, invidiously as it might have struck me, to
Ray Limbert's suit, which Mrs. Stannace wasn't the woman to
stomach. Mrs. Stannace was seldom the woman to do anything:
she had been shocked at the way her children, with the grubby taint
of their father's blood—he had published pale Remains or flat Con-
versations of _his_ father—breathed the alien air of authorship. If not
the daughter, nor even the niece, she was, if I'm not mistaken, the
second cousin of a hundred earls and a great stickler for relationship, so that she had other views for her brilliant child, especially

after her quiet one—such had been her original discreet forecast of the producer of eighty volumes—became the second wife of an ex-army-surgeon, already the father of four children. Mrs. Stannace had too manifestly dreamed it would be given to pretty pink Maud to detach some one of the noble hundred, who wouldn't be missed, from the cluster. It was because she cared only for cousins that I unlearnt the way to her house, which she had once reminded me was one of the few paths of gentility I could hope to tread. Ralph Limbert, who belonged to nobody and had done nothing—nothing even at Cambridge—had only the uncanny spell he had cast on her younger daughter to recommend him; but if her younger daughter had a spark of filial feeling she wouldn't commit the indecency of deserting for his sake a deeply dependent and intensely aggravated mother.

These things I learned from Jane Highmore, who, as if her books had been babies—they remained her only ones—had waited till after marriage to show what she could do, and now bade fair to surround her satisfied spouse (he took, for some mysterious reason, a part of the credit) with a little family, in sets of triplets, which properly handled would be the support of his declining years. The young couple, neither of whom had a penny, were now virtually engaged: the thing was subject to Ralph's putting his hand on some regular employment. People more enamoured couldn't be conceived, and Mrs. Highmore, honest woman, who had moreover a professional sense for a love story, was eager to take them under her wing. What was wanted was a decent opening for Limbert, which it had occurred to her I might assist her to find, though indeed I had not yet found any such matter for myself. But it was well known that I was too particular, whereas poor Ralph, with the easy manners of genius, was ready to accept almost anything to which a salary, even a small one, was attached. If he could only for instance get a place on a newspaper, the rest of his maintenance would come freely enough. It was true that his two novels, one of which she had brought to leave with me, had passed unperceived, and that to her, Mrs. Highmore personally, they didn't irresistibly appeal; but she could all the same assure me that I should have only to spend ten minutes with him—and our encounter must speedily take place—to receive an impression of latent power.

Our encounter took place soon after I had read the volumes Mrs. Highmore had left with me, in which I recognised an intention of a

sort that I had then pretty well given up the hope of meeting. I daresay that without knowing it I had been looking out rather hungrily
for an altar of sacrifice: however that may be, I submitted when I
came across Ralph Limbert to one of the rarest emotions of my
literary life, the sense of an activity in which I could critically rest.
The rest was deep and salutary, and has not been disturbed to this
hour. It has been a long large surrender, the luxury of dropped
discriminations. He couldn't trouble me, whatever he did, for I
practically enjoyed him as much when he was worse as when he was
better. It was a case, I suppose, of natural prearrangement, in which,
I hasten to add, I keep excellent company. We're a numerous band,
partakers of the same repose, who sit together in the shade of the
tree, by the plash of the fountain, with the glare of the desert round
us and no great vice that I know of but the habit perhaps of esti-
mating people a little too much by what they think of a certain style.
If it had been laid upon these few pages, none the less, to be the
history of an enthusiasm, I shouldn't have undertaken them: they're
concerned with Ralph Limbert in relations to which I was a stranger
or in which I participated but by sympathy. I used to talk about his
work, but I seldom talk now: the brotherhood of the faith have become, like the Trappists, a silent order. If to the day of his death,
after mortal disenchantments, the impression he first produced always evoked the word "ingenuous," those to whom his face was
familiar can easily imagine what it must have been when it still had
the light of youth. I had never seen a man of genius show so for
passive, a man of experience so off his guard. At the time I made his
acquaintance this freshness was all unbrushed. His foot had begun
to stumble, but he was full of big intentions and of sweet Maud Stannace. Black-haired and pale, deceptively languid, he had the eyes
of a clever child and the voice of a bronze bell. He saw more even-
than I had done in the girl he was engaged to; as time went on I became conscious that we had both, properly enough, seen rather more
than there was. Our odd situation, that of the three of us, became
perfectly possible from the moment I recognised how much more
patience he had with her than I should have had. I was happy at
not having to supply this quantity, and she, on her side, found
pleasure in being able to be impertinent to me without incurring
the reproach of the bad wife.

Limbert's novels appeared to have brought him no money: they
had only brought him, so far as I could then make out, tributes that

took up his time. These indeed brought him from several quarters some other things, and on my part at the end of three months *The Blackport Beacon*. I don't to-day remember how I obtained for him the London correspondence of the great northern organ, unless it was through somebody's having obtained it for myself. I seem to recall that I got rid of it in Limbert's interest, urging on the editor that he was much the better man. The better man was naturally the man who had pledged himself at the altar to provide for a charming woman. We were neither of us good, as the event proved, but he had the braver badness. *The Blackport Beacon* rejoiced in two London correspondents—one a supposed haunter of political circles, the other a votary of questions sketchily classified as literary. They were both expected to be lively, and what was held out to each was that it was honourably open to him to be livelier than the other. I recollect the political correspondent of that period and how the problem offered to Ray Limbert was to try to be livelier than Pat Moyle. He had not yet seemed to me so candid as when he undertook this exploit, which brought matters to a head with Mrs. Stannace, inasmuch as her opposition to the marriage now logically fell to the ground. It's all tears and laughter as I look back upon that admirable time, in which nothing was so romantic as our intense vision of the real. No fool's paradise ever rustled such a cradle-song. It was anything but Bohemia—it was the very temple of Mrs. Grundy. We knew we were too critical, and that made us sublimely indulgent; we believed we did our duty or wanted to, and that made us free to dream. But we dreamed over the multiplication table; we were nothing if not practical. Oh, the long smokes and sudden happy thoughts, the knowing hints and banished scruples! The great thing was for Limbert to bring out his next book, which was just what his delightful engagement with the *Beacon* would give him leisure and liberty to do. The kind of work, all human and elastic and suggestive, was capital experience: in picking up things for his bi-weekly letter he would pick up life as well, he would pick up literature. The new publications, the new pictures, the new people—there would be nothing too novel for us and nobody too sacred. We introduced everything and everybody into Mrs. Stannace's drawing-room, of which I again became a familiar.

Mrs. Stannace, it was true, thought herself in strange company; she didn't particularly mind the new books, though some of them seemed queer enough, but to the new people she had decided objections. It was notorious, however, that poor Lady Robeck secretly wrote for one of the papers, and the thing had certainly, in its glance at the doings of the great world, a side that might be made attractive. But we were going to make every side attractive, and we had everything to say about the sort of thing a paper like the *Beacon* would want. To give it what it would want and to give it nothing else was not doubtless an inspiring but was a perfectly respectable task, especially for a man with an appealing bride and a contentious mother-in-law. I thought Limbert's first letters as charming as the type allowed, though I won't deny that in spite of my sense of the importance of concessions I was just a trifle disconcerted at the way he had caught the tone. The tone was of course to be caught, but need it have been caught so in the act? The creature was even cleverer, as Maud Stannace said, than she had ventured to hope. Verily it was a good thing to have a dose of the wisdom of the serpent. If it had to be journalism—well, it *was* journalism. If he had to be "chatty"—well, he *was* chatty. Now and then he made a hit that—it was stupid of me—brought the blood to my face. I hated him to be so personal; but still, if it would make his fortune—! It wouldn't of course directly, but the book would, practically and in the sense to which our pure ideas of fortune were confined; and these things were all for the book. The daily balm meanwhile was in what one knew of the book—there were exquisite things to know; in the quiet monthly checks from Blackport and in the deeper rose of Maud's little preparations, which were as dainty, on their tiny scale, as if she had been a humming-bird building a nest. When at the end of three months her betrothed had fairly settled down to his correspondence—in which Mrs. Highmore was the only person, so far as we could discover, disappointed, even she moreover being in this particular tortuous and possibly jealous; when the situation had assumed such a comfortable shape it was quite time to prepare. I published at that moment my first volume, mere faded ink to-day, a little collection of literary impressions, odds and ends of criticism contributed to a journal less remunerative but also less chatty than the *Beacon*, small ironies and ecstasies, great phrases and mistakes; and the very week it came out poor Limbert devoted half of one of his letters to it, with the happy sense this time of gratifying both himself and me as well as the Blackport breakfast-tables. I remember his saying it wasn't literature, the stuff, superficial stuff, he had to write about me; but what did that matter if it came back, as we

knew, to the making for literature in the roundabout way? I had
sold the thing, I recall, for ten pounds, and with the money I bought
in Vigo Street a quaint piece of old silver for Maud Stannace, which
I carried her with my own hand as a wedding-gift. In her mother's
small drawing-room, a faded bower of photography fenced in and
bedimmed by folding screens out of which sallow persons of fashion
with dashing signatures looked at you from retouched eyes and
little windows of plush, I was left to wait long enough to feel in
the air of the house a hushed vibration of disaster. When our young
lady came in she was very pale and *her* eyes too had been retouched.

"Something horrid has happened," I at once said; and having
really all along but half believed in her mother's meagre permission, I risked with an unguarded groan the introduction of Mrs.
Stannace's name.

"Yes, she had made a dreadful scene; she insists on our putting it
off again. We're very unhappy: poor Ray has been turned off." Her
tears recommenced to flow.

I had such a good conscience that I stared. "Turned off what?"

"Why, his paper of course. The *Beacon* has given him what he
calls the sack. They don't like his letters—they're not the style of
thing they want."

My blankness could only deepen. "Then what style of thing, in
God's name, *do* they want?"

"Something more chatty."

"More?" I cried, aghast.

"More gossipy, more personal. They want 'journalism.' They want
tremendous trash."

"Why, that's just what his letters have *been!*" I broke out.

This was strong, and I caught myself up, but the girl offered me
the pardon of a beautiful wan smile. "So Ray himself declares. He
says he has stooped so low."

"Very well—he must stoop lower. He *must* keep the place."

"He can't!" poor Maud wailed. "He says he has tried all he knows,
has been abject, has gone on all fours, has crawled like a worm; and
that if they don't like that—"

"He accepts his dismissal?" I interposed in dismay.

She gave a tragic shrug. "What other course is open to him? He
wrote to them that such work as he has done is the very worst he
can do for the money."

"Therefore," I pressed with a flash of hope, "they'll offer him more for worse?"

"No, indeed," she answered, "they haven't even offered him to go on at a reduction. He isn't funny enough."

I reflected a moment. "But surely such a thing as his notice of my book—!"

"It was your wretched book that was the last straw! He should have treated it superficially."

"Well, if he didn't—!" I began. Then I checked myself. "*Je vous porte malheur.*"

She didn't deny this; she only went on: "What on earth is he to do?"

"He's to do better than the monkeys! He's to write!"

"But what on earth are we to marry on?"

I considered once more. "You're to marry on 'The Major Key.' "

II

"The Major Key" was the new novel, and the great thing accordingly was to finish it; a consummation for which three months of the *Beacon* had in some degree prepared the way. The action of that journal was indeed a shock, but I didn't know then the worst, didn't know that in addition to being a shock it was also a symptom. It was the first hint of the difficulty to which poor Limbert was eventually to succumb. His state was the happier, of a truth, for his not immediately seeing all it meant. Difficulty was the law of life, but one could thank heaven it was quite abnormally present in that awful connection. There was the difficulty that inspired, the difficulty of "The Major Key" to wit, which it was after all base to sacrifice to the turning of somersaults for pennies. These convictions my friend beguiled his fresh wait by blandly entertaining: not indeed, I think, that the failure of his attempt to be chatty didn't leave him slightly humiliated. If it was bad enough to have grinned through a horse-collar, it was very bad indeed to have grinned in vain. Well, he would try no more grinning or at least no more horse-collars. The only success worth one's powder was success in the line of one's idiosyncrasy. Consistency was in itself distinction, and what was talent but the art of being completely whatever it was that one happened to be? One's things were characteristic or they were nothing. I look back rather fondly on our having exchanged in those days these admirable remarks and many others; on our having been very happy too, in spite of postponements and obscurities, in spite also of such occasional hauntings as could spring from our lurid glimpse of the fact that even twaddle cunningly calculated was far above people's heads. It was easy to wave away spectres by the reflexion that all one had to do was not to write for people; it was certainly not for people that Limbert wrote while he hammered at "The Major Key." The taint of literature was fatal only in a certain kind of air, which was precisely the kind against which we had now closed our window. Mrs. Stannace rose from her crumpled cushions as soon as she had obtained an adjournment, and Maud looked pale and proud, quite victorious and superior, at her having obtained nothing more. Maud behaved well, I thought, to her mother, and well indeed, for a girl who had mainly been taught to be flowerlike, to every one. What she gave Ray Limbert her fine abundant needs made him then and ever pay for; but the gift was liberal, almost wonderful—an assertion I made even while remembering to how many clever women, early and late, his work has been dear. It was not only that the woman he was to marry was in love with him, but that—this was the strangeness—she had really seen almost better than any one what he could do. The greatest strangeness was that she didn't want him to do something different. This boundless belief was indeed the main way of her devotion; and as an act of faith it naturally asked for miracles. She was a rare wife for a poet, if she was not perhaps the best to have been picked out for a poor man.

Well, we were to have the miracles at all events and we were in a perfect state of mind to receive them. There were more of us every day, and we thought highly even of our friend's odd jobs and pot-boilers. The *Beacon* had had no successor, but he found some quiet corners and stray chances. Perpetually poking the fire and looking out of the window, he was certainly not a monster of facility, but he was, thanks perhaps to a certain method in that madness, a monster of certainty. It wasn't every one, however, who knew him for this: many editors printed him but once. He was getting a small reputation as a man it was well to have the first time; he created obscure apprehensions as to what might happen the second. He was good for making an impression, but no one seemed exactly to know what the impression was good for when made. The reason was simply that they had not seen yet "The Major Key," that fiery-hearted rose as to which we watched in private the formation of petal after petal and flame after flame. Nothing mattered but this, for it had already

elicited a splendid bid, much talked about in Mrs. Highmore's drawing-room, where at this point my reminiscences grow particularly
thick. *Her* roses bloomed all the year and her sociability increased
with her row of prizes. We had an idea that we "met every one" there
—so we naturally thought when we met each other. Between our
hostess and Ray Limbert flourished the happiest relation, the only
cloud on which was that her husband eyed him rather askance. When
he was called clever, this personage wanted to know what he had to
"show"; and it was certain that he showed nothing that could compare with Jane Highmore. Mr. Highmore took his stand on accomplished work and, turning up his coat-tails, warmed his rear with a
good conscience at the neat bookcase in which the generations of
triplets were chronologically arranged. The harmony between his
companions rested on the fact that, as I have already hinted, each
would have liked so much to be the other. Limbert couldn't but
have a feeling about a woman who, in addition to being the best
creature and her sister's backer, would have made, could she have
condescended, such a success with the *Beacon*. On the other hand
Mrs. Highmore used freely to say: "Do you know, he'll do exactly
the thing that *I* want to do? I shall never do it myself, but he'll do
it instead. Yes, he'll do *my* thing, and I shall hate him for it—the
wretch." Hating him was her pleasant humour, for the wretch was
personally to her taste.

She prevailed on her own publisher to promise to take "The Major
Key" and to engage to pay a considerable sum down, as the phrase is,
on the presumption of its attracting attention. This was good news
for the evening's end at Mrs. Highmore's when there were only four
or five left and cigarettes ran low; but there was better to come,
and I have never forgotten how, as it was I who had the good fortune
to bring it, I kept it back on one of those occasions, for the sake of
my effect, till only the right people remained. The right people were
now more and more numerous, but this was a revelation addressed
only to a choice residuum—a residuum including of course Limbert
himself, with whom I haggled for another cigarette before I announced that as a consequence of an interview I had had with him
that afternoon, and of a subtle argument I had brought to bear,
Mrs. Highmore's pearl of publishers had agreed to put forth the
new book as a serial. He was to "run" it in his magazine and he
was to pay ever so much more for the privilege. I produced a fine gasp
which presently found a more articulate relief, but poor Limbert's

voice failed him once for all—he knew he was to walk away with me—and it was some one else who asked me what my subtle argument had been. I forget what florid description I then gave of it: to-day I've no reason not to confess that it had resided in the simple plea that the book was exquisite. I had said: "Come, my dear friend, be original; just risk it for that!" My dear friend seemed to rise to the chance, and I followed up my advantage, permitting him honestly no illusion as to the nature of the thing. He clutched interrogatively at two or three attenuations, but I dashed them aside, leaving him face to face with the formidable truth. It was just a pure gem: was he the man not to flinch? His danger appeared to have acted on him as the anaconda acts on the rabbit; fascinated and paralysed, he had been engulfed in the long pink throat. When a week before, at my request, Limbert had left with me for a day the complete manuscript, beautifully copied out by Maud Stannace, I had flushed with indignation at its having to be said of the author of such pages that he hadn't the common means to marry. I had taken the field in a great glow to repair this scandal, and it was therefore quite directly my fault if three months later, when "The Major Key" began to run, Mrs. Stannace was driven to the wall. She had made a condition of a fixed income, and at last a fixed income was achieved.

She had to recognise it, and after much prostration among the photographs she recognised it to the extent of accepting some of the convenience of it in the form of a project for a common household, to the expenses of which each party should proportionately contribute. Jane Highmore made a great point of her not being left alone, but Mrs. Stannace herself determined the proportion, which on Limbert's side at least and in spite of many other fluctuations was never altered. His income had been "fixed" with a vengeance: having painfully stooped to the comprehension of it Mrs. Stannace rested on this effort to the end and asked no further question on the subject. "The Major Key" in other words ran ever so long, and before it was half out Limbert and Maud had been married and the common household set up. These first months were probably the happiest in the family annals, with wedding-bells and budding laurels, the quiet assured course of the book and the friendly familiar note, round the corner, of Mrs. Highmore's big guns. They gave Ralph time to block in another picture as well as to let me know after a while that he had the happy prospect of becoming a father. We had at times some dispute as to whether "The Major Key" was making an impression, but our difference could only be futile so long as we were not agreed as to what an impression consisted of. Several persons wrote to the author and several others asked to be introduced to him: wasn't that an impression? One of the lively "weeklies," snapping at the deadly "monthlies," said the whole thing was "grossly inartistic"—wasn't *that?* It was somewhere else proclaimed "a wonderfully subtle character-study"—wasn't that too? The strongest effect doubtless was produced on the publisher when, in its lemon-coloured volumes, like a little dish of three custards, the book was at last served cold: he never got his money back and so far as I know has never got it back to this day. "The Major Key" was rather a great performance than a great success. It converted readers into friends and friends into lovers; it placed the author, as the phrase is—placed him all too definitely; but it shrank to obscurity in the account of sales eventually rendered. It was in short an exquisite thing, but it was scarcely a thing to have published and certainly not a thing to have married on. I heard all about the matter, for my intervention had much exposed me. Mrs. Highmore was emphatic as to the second volume's having given her ideas, and the ideas are probably to be found in some of her works, to the circulation of which they have even perhaps contributed. This was not absolutely yet the very thing she wanted to do—though on the way to it. So much, she informed me, she particularly perceived in the light of a critical study that I put forth in a little magazine; a thing the publisher in his advertisements quoted from profusely, and as to which there sprang up some absurd story that Limbert himself had written it. I remember that on my asking some one why such an idiotic thing had been said my interlocutor replied: "Oh because, you know, it's just the way he *would* have written!" My spirit sank a little perhaps as I reflected that with such analogies in our manner there might prove to be some in our fate.

It was during the next four or five years that our eyes were open to what, unless something could be done, that fate, at least on Limbert's part, might be. The thing to be done was of course to write the book, the book that would make the difference, really justify the burden he had accepted and consummately express his power. For the works that followed upon "The Major Key" he had inevitably to accept conditions the reverse of brilliant, at a time too when the strain upon his resources had begun to show sharpness. With three babies in due course, an ailing wife and a complication still greater than these, it became highly important that a man should do only his best. Whatever Limbert did was his best; so at least each time I thought and so I unfailingly said somewhere, though it was not my saying it, heaven knows, that made the desired difference. Every one else indeed said it, and there was among multiplied worries always the comfort that his position was quite assured. The two books that followed "The Major Key" did more than anything else to assure it, and Jane Highmore was always crying out: "You stand alone, dear Ray; you stand absolutely alone!" Dear Ray used to leave me in no doubt of how he felt the truth of this in feebly attempted discussions with his bookseller. His sister-in-law gave him good advice into the bargain; she was a repository of knowing hints, of esoteric learning. These things were doubtless not the less valuable to him for bearing wholly on the question of how a reputation might be with a little gumption, as Mrs. Highmore said, "worked." Save when she occasionally bore testimony to her desire to do, as Limbert did, something some day for her own very self, I never heard her speak of the literary motive as if it were distinguishable from the pecuniary. She cocked up his hat, she pricked up his prudence for him, reminding him that as one seemed to take one's self so the silly world was ready to take one. It was a fatal mistake to be too candid even with those who were all right—not to look and to talk prosperous, not at least to pretend one had beautiful sales. To listen to her you would have thought the profession of letters a wonderful game of bluff. Wherever one's idea began it ended somehow in inspired paragraphs in the newspapers. "*I* pretend, I assure you, that you're going off like wildfire—I can at least do that for you!" she often declared, prevented as she was from doing much else by Mr. Highmore's insurmountable objection to *their* taking Mrs. Stannace.

I couldn't help regarding the presence of this latter lady in Limbert's life as the major complication: whatever he attempted it appeared given to him to achieve as best he could in the mere margin of the space in which she swung her petticoats. I may err in the belief that she practically lived on him, for though it was not in him to follow adequately Mrs. Highmore's counsel there were exasperated confessions he never made, scant domestic curtains he rattled on their rings. I may exaggerate in the retrospect his apparent anxieties, for these after all were the years when his talent was freshest and when as a writer he most laid down his line. It wasn't of Mrs. Stannace nor even as time went on of Mrs. Limbert that we

mainly talked when I got at longer intervals a smokier hour in the
little grey den from which we could step out, as we used to say, to
the lawn. The lawn was the back-garden, and Limbert's study was
behind the dining-room, with folding doors not impervious to the
clatter of the children's tea. We sometimes took refuge from it in
the depths—a bush and a half deep—of the shrubbery, where was a
bench that gave us while we gossiped a view of Mrs. Stannace's tiara-
like headdress nodding at an upper window. Within doors and without Limbert's life was overhung by an awful region that figured in
his conversation, comprehensively and with unpremeditated art, as
Upstairs. It was Upstairs that the thunder gathered, that Mrs. Stannace kept her accounts and her state, that Mrs. Limbert had her
babies and her headaches, that the bells for ever jangled at the maids,
that everything imperative in short took place—everything that he
had somehow, pen in hand, to meet, to deal with and dispose of,
in the little room on the garden-level. I don't think he liked to go
Upstairs, but no special burst of confidence was needed to make
me feel that a terrible deal of service went. It was the habit of the
ladies of the Stannace family to be extremely waited on, and I've
never been in a house where three maids and a nursery governess
gave such an impression of a retinue. "Oh, they're so deucedly, so
hereditarily fine!"—I remember how that dropped from him in some
worried hour. Well, it was because Maud was so universally fine that
we had both been in love with her. It was not an air, moreover, for
the plaintive note: no private inconvenience could long outweigh
for him the great happiness of these years—the happiness that sat
with us when we talked and that made it always amusing to talk,
the sense of his being on the heels of success, coming closer and
closer, touching it at last, knowing that he should touch it again
and hold it fast and hold it high. Of course when we said success
we didn't mean exactly what Mrs. Highmore for instance meant.
He used to quote at me as a definition something from a nameless
page of my own, some stray dictum to the effect that the man of his
craft had achieved it when of a beautiful subject his expression was
complete. Well, wasn't Limbert's in all conscience complete?

III

It was bang upon this completeness all the same that the turn
arrived, the turn I can't say of his fortune—for what was that?—

but of his confidence, of his spirits and, what was more to the point, of his system. The whole occasion on which the first symptom flared out is before me as I write. I had met them both at dinner: they were diners who had reached the penultimate stage—the stage which in theory is a rigid selection and in practice a wan submission. It was late in the season and stronger spirits than theirs were broken; the night was close and the air of the banquet such as to restrict conversation to the refusal of dishes and consumption to the sniffing of a flower. It struck me all the more that Mrs. Limbert was flying her flag. As vivid as a page of her husband's prose, she had one of those flickers of freshness that are the miracle of her sex and one of those expensive dresses that are the miracle of ours. She had also a neat brougham in which she had offered to rescue an old lady from the possibilities of a queer cab-horse; so that when she had rolled away with her charge I proposed a walk home with her husband, whom I had overtaken on the doorstep. Before I had gone far with him he told me he had news for me—he had accepted, of all people and of all things, an "editorial position." It had come to pass that very day, from one hour to another, without time for appeals or ponderations: Mr. Bousefield, the proprietor of a "high-class monthly," making, as they said, a sudden change, had dropped on him heavily out of the blue. It was all right—there was a salary and an idea, and both of them, as such things went, rather high. We took our way slowly through the vacant streets, and in the explanations and revelations that as we lingered under lampposts I drew from him I found with an apprehension that I tried to gulp down a foretaste of the bitter end. He told me more than he had ever told me yet. He couldn't balance accounts—that was the trouble: his expenses were too rising a tide. It was imperative he should at last make money, and now he must work only for that. The need this last year had gathered the force of a crusher: it had rolled over him and laid him on his back. He had his scheme; this time he knew what he was about; on some good occasion, with leisure to talk it over, he would tell me the blest whole. His editorship would help him, and for the rest he must help himself. If he couldn't they would have to do something fundamental —change their life altogether, give up London, move into the country, take a house at thirty pounds a year, send their children to the Board-school. I saw he was excited, and he admitted he was: he had waked out of a trance. He had been on the wrong tack; he had piled

mistake on mistake. It was the vision of his remedy that now excited
him: ineffably, grotesquely simple, it had yet come to him only
within a day or two. No, he wouldn't tell me what it was; he would
give me the night to guess, and if I shouldn't guess it would be because I was as big an ass as himself. However, a lone man might be
an ass: he had room in his life for his ears. Ray had a burden that
demanded a back: the back must therefore now be properly insti-
tuted. As to the editorship, it was simply heaven-sent, being not at
all another case of *The Blackport Beacon* but a case of the very opposite. The proprietor, the great Mr. Bousefield, had approached him
precisely because his name, which was to be on the cover, *didn't*
represent the chatty. The whole thing was to be—oh, on fiddling
little lines of course—a protest against the chatty. Bousefield wanted
him to be himself; it was for himself Bousefield had picked him out.
Wasn't it beautiful and brave of Bousefield? He wanted literature,
he saw the great reaction coming, the way the cat was going to jump.
"Where will you get literature?" I woefully asked; to which he replied with a laugh that what he had to get was not literature but
only what Bousefield would take for it.
  In that single phrase I without more ado discovered his famous
remedy. What was before him for the future was not to do his work
but to do what somebody else would take for it. I had the question
out with him on the next opportunity, and of all the lively discussions into which we had been destined to drift it lingers in my mind
as the liveliest. This was not, I hasten to add, because I disputed his
conclusions: it was an effect of the very force with which, when I had
fathomed his wretched premises, I took them to my soul. It was very
well to talk with Jane Highmore about his standing alone: the
eminent relief of this position had brought him to the verge of ruin.
Several persons admired his books—nothing was less contestable;
but they appeared to have a mortal objection to acquiring them by
subscription or by purchase: they begged or borrowed or stole, they
delegated one of the party perhaps to commit the volumes to memory
and repeat them, like the bards of old, to listening multitudes. Some
ingenious theory was required at any rate to account for the inexorable limits of his circulation. It wasn't a thing for five people to live
on; therefore either the objects circulated must change their nature
or the organisms to be nourished must. The former change was perhaps the easier to consider first. Limbert considered it with sovereign

ingenuity from that time on, and the ingenuity, greater even than any I had yet had occasion to admire in him, made the whole next stage of his career rich in curiosity and suspense.

"I've been butting my skull against a wall," he had said in those hours of confidence; "and, to be as sublime a blockhead, if you'll allow me the word, you, my dear fellow, have kept sounding the charge. We've sat prating here of 'success,' heaven help us, like chanting monks in a cloister, hugging the sweet delusion that it lies somewhere in the work itself, in the expression, as you said, of one's subject or the intensification, as somebody else somewhere says, of one's note. One has been going on in short as if the only thing to do were to accept the law of one's talent, and thinking that if certain consequences didn't follow it was only because one wasn't logical enough. My disaster has served me right—I mean for using that ignoble word at all. It's a mere distributor's, a mere hawker's word. What is 'success' anyhow? When a book's right it's right—shame to it surely if it isn't. When it sells it sells—it brings money like potatoes or beer. If there's dishonour one way and inconvenience the other, it certainly is comfortable, but it as certainly isn't glorious, to have escaped them. People of delicacy don't brag either about their probity or about their luck. Success be hanged!—I want to sell. It's a question of life and death. I must study the way. I've studied too much the other way—I know the other way now, every inch of it. I must cultivate the market—it's a science like another. I must go in for an infernal cunning. It will be very amusing, I foresee that; I shall lead a dashing life and drive a roaring trade. I haven't been obvious—I must be obvious. I haven't been popular—I must be popular. It's another art—or perhaps it isn't an art at all. It's something else; one must find out what it is. Is it something awfully queer?—you blush!—something barely decent? All the greater incentive to curiosity! Curiosity's an immense motive; we shall have tremendous sport. 'They all do it'—doesn't somebody sing at a music hall?—it's only a question of how. Of course I've everything to unlearn; but what's life, as Jane Highmore says, but a lesson? I must get all I can, all she can give me, from Jane. She can't explain herself much; she's all intuition; her processes are obscure; it's the spirit that swoops down and catches her up. But I must study her reverently in her works. Yes, you've defied me before, but now my loins are girded: I declare I'll read one of them—I really will; I'll put it through if I perish!"

I won't pretend he made all these remarks at once; but there wasn't one that he didn't make at one time or another, for suggestion and occasion were plentiful enough, his life being now given up altogether to his new necessity. It wasn't a question of his having or not having, as they say, my intellectual sympathy: the brute force of the pressure left no room for judgement; it made all emotion a mere recourse to the spyglass. I watched him as I should have watched a long race or a long chase, irresistibly siding with him, yet much occupied with the calculation of odds. I confess indeed that my heart, for the endless stretch he covered so fast, was often in my throat. I saw him peg away over the sun-dappled plain, I saw him double and wind and gain and lose; and all the while I secretly entertained a conviction. I wanted him to feed his many mouths, but at the bottom of all things was my sense that if he should succeed in doing so in this particular way I should think less well of him. Now I had an absolute terror of that. Meanwhile so far as I could I backed him up, I helped him: all the more that I had warned him immensely at first, smiled with a compassion it was very good of him not to have found exasperating over the complacency of his assumption that a man could escape from himself. Ray Limbert at all events would certainly never escape; but one could make believe for him, make believe very hard—an undertaking in which at first Mr. Bousefield was visibly a blessing. Ralph was delightful on the business of this being at last my chance too—my chance, so miraculously vouchsafed, to appear with a certain luxuriance. He didn't care how often he printed me, for wasn't it exactly in my direction Mr. Bousefield held the cat was going to jump? This was the least he could do for me. I might write on anything I liked—on anything at least but Mr. Limbert's second manner. He didn't wish attention strikingly called to his second manner; it was to operate insidiously; people were to be left to believe they had discovered it long ago. "Ralph Limbert? Why, when did we ever live without him?"—that's what he wanted them to say. Besides, they hated manners—let sleeping dogs lie. His understanding with Mr. Bousefield—on which he had had not at all to insist; it was the excellent man who insisted—was that he should run one of his beautiful stories in the magazine. As to the beauty of his story, however, Limbert was going to be less admirably straight than as to the beauty of everything else. That was another reason why I mustn't write about his new line: Mr. Bousefield was not to be too definitely warned that such a periodical was exposed to prostitution. By the time he should find it out for himself the public—*le gros*

public—would have bitten, and then perhaps he would be concil-
iated and forgive. Everything else would be literary in short, and
above all *I* would be; only Ralph Limbert wouldn't—he'd chuck up
the whole thing sooner. He'd be vulgar, he'd be vile, he'd be abject:
he'd be elaborately what he hadn't been before.

I duly noticed that he had more trouble in making "everything
else" literary than he had at first allowed for; but this was largely
counteracted by the ease with which he was able to obtain that his
mark shouldn't be overshot. He had taken well to heart the old
lesson of the *Beacon;* he remembered that he was after all there to
keep his contributors down much rather than to keep them up. I
thought at times that he kept them down a trifle too far, but he assured me that I needn't be nervous: he had his limit—his limit was
inexorable. He would reserve pure vulgarity for his serial, over
which he was sweating blood and water; elsewhere it should be qualified by the prime qualification, the mediocrity that attaches, that
endears. Bousefield, he allowed, was proud, was difficult: nothing
was really good enough for him but the middling good; he himself,
however, was prepared for adverse comment, resolute for his noble
course. Hadn't Limbert, moreover, in the event of a charge of laxity
from headquarters the great strength of being able to point to my
contributions? Therefore I must let myself go, I must abound in
my peculiar sense, I must be a resource in case of accidents. Limbert's
vision of accidents hovered mainly over the sudden awakening of
Mr. Bousefield to the stuff that in the department of fiction his
editor was palming off. He would then have to confess in all humility that this was not what the old boy wanted, but I should be all
the more there as a salutary specimen. I would cross the scent with
something showily impossible, splendidly unpopular—I must be
sure to have something on hand. I always had plenty on hand—
poor Limbert needn't have worried: the magazine was forearmed
each month by my care with a retort to any possible accusation of
trifling with Mr. Bousefield's standard. He had admitted to Limbert,
after much consideration indeed, that he was prepared to be perfectly human; but he had added that he was not prepared for an
abuse of this admission. The thing in the world I think I least felt
myself was an abuse, even though—as I had never mentioned to my
friendly editor—I too had my project for a bigger reverberation. I
daresay I trusted mine more than I trusted Limbert's; at all events
the golden mean in which, for the special case, he saw his salvation

as an editor was something I should be most sure of were I to exhibit
it myself. I exhibited it month after month in the form of a monstrous levity, only praying heaven that my editor might now not tell
me, as he had so often told me, that my result was awfully good.
I knew what that would signify—it would signify, sketchily speaking,
disaster. What he did tell me heartily was that it was just what his
game required: his new line had brought with it an earnest assumption—earnest save when we privately laughed about it—of the locu-
tions proper to real bold enterprise. If I tried to keep him in the
dark even as he kept Mr. Bousefield, there was nothing to show that
I wasn't tolerably successful: each case therefore presented a promising analogy for the other. He never noticed my descent, and it
was accordingly possible Mr. Bousefield would never notice his. But
would nobody notice it at all?—that was a question that added a
prospective zest to one's possession of a critical sense. So much depended upon it that I was rather relieved than otherwise not to know
the answer too soon. I waited in fact a year—the trial year for which
Limbert had cannily engaged with Mr. Bousefield; the year as to
which, through the same sharpened shrewdness, it had been conveyed in the agreement between them that Mr. Bousefield wasn't to
intermeddle. It had been Limbert's general prayer that we would
during this period let him quite alone. His terror of my direct rays
was a droll dreadful force that always operated: he explained it by
the fact that I understood him too well, expressed too much of his
intention, saved him too little from himself. The less he was saved
the more he didn't sell: I positively interpreted, and that was simply
fatal.

I held my breath accordingly; I did more—I closed my eyes, I
guarded my treacherous ears. He induced several of us to do that—
of such devotions we were capable—so that, not even glancing at the
thing from month to month and having nothing but his shamed
anxious silence to go by, I participated only vaguely in the little hum
that surrounded his act of sacrifice. It was blown about the town
that the public would be surprised; it was hinted, it was printed,
that he was making a desperate bid. His new work was spoken of as
"more calculated for general acceptance." These tidings produced
in some quarters much reprobation, and nowhere more, I think,
than on the part of certain persons who had never read a word of
him, or assuredly had never spent a shilling on him, and who hung
for hours over the other attractions of the newspaper that announced

his abasement. So much asperity cheered me a little—seemed to signify that he might really be doing something. On the other hand,
I had a distinct alarm; some one sent me for some alien reason an
American journal—containing frankly more than that source of
affliction—in which was quoted a passage from our friend's last in-
stalment. The passage—I couldn't for my life help reading it—was
simply superb. Ah, he *would* have to move to the country if that was
the worst he could do! It gave me a pang to see how little after all he
had improved since the days of his competition with Pat Moyle.
There was nothing in the passage quoted in the American paper
that Pat would for a moment have owned.

During the last weeks, as the opportunity of reading the complete thing drew near, one's suspense was barely endurable, and I
shall never forget the July evening on which I put it to rout. Coming
home to dinner I found the two volumes on my table, and I sat up
with them half the night, dazed, bewildered, rubbing my eyes, wondering at the monstrous joke. *Was* it a monstrous joke, his second
manner—was *this* the new line, the desperate bit, the scheme for
more general acceptance and the remedy for material failure? Had
he made a fool of all his following, or had he most injuriously made a
still bigger fool of himself? Obvious?—where the deuce was it obvious? Popular?—how on earth could it be popular? The thing was
charming with all his charm and powerful with all his power: it was
an unscrupulous, an unsparing, a shameless merciless masterpiece.
It was, no doubt, like the old letters to the *Beacon*, the worst he could
do: but the perversity of the effort, even though heroic, had been
frustrated by the purity of the gift. Under what illusion had he laboured, with what wavering treacherous compass had he steered? His
honour was inviolable, his measurements were all wrong. I was
thrilled with the whole impression and with all that came crowding
in its train. It was too grand a collapse—it was too hideous a triumph; I exulted almost with tears—I lamented with a strange delight. Indeed as the short night waned and, threshing about in my
emotion, I fidgeted to my high-perched window for a glimpse of the
summer dawn, I became at last aware that I was staring at it out of
eyes that had compassionately and admiringly filled. The eastern sky,
over the London house-tops, had a wonderful tragic crimson. That
was the colour of his magnificent mistake.

IV

If something less had depended on my impression, I daresay I should have communicated it as soon as I had swallowed my breakfast; but the case was so embarrassing that I spent the first half of the day in reconsidering it, dipping into the book again, almost feverishly turning its leaves and trying to extract from them, for my friend's benefit, some symptom of reassurance, some ground for felicitation. This rash challenge had consequences merely dreadful; the wretched volumes, imperturbable and impeccable, with their shyer secrets and their second line of defence, were like a beautiful woman more denuded or a great symphony on a new hearing. There was something quite sinister in the way they stood up to me. I couldn't, however, be dumb—that was to give the wrong tinge to my disappointment; so that later in the afternoon, taking my courage in both hands, I approached with a vain tortuosity poor Limbert's door. A smart victoria waited before it, in which, from the bottom of the street, I saw that a lady who had apparently just issued from the house was settling herself. I recognised Jane Highmore and instantly paused till she should drive down to me. She soon met me halfway and directly she saw me stopped her carriage in agitation. This was a relief—it postponed a moment the sight of that pale fine face of our friend's fronting me for the right verdict. I gathered from the flushed eagerness with which Mrs. Highmore asked me if I had heard the news that a verdict of some sort had already been rendered.

"What news?—about the book?"

"About that horrid magazine. They're shockingly upset. He has lost his position—he has had a fearful flare-up with Mr. Bousefield."

I stood there blank, but not unaware in my blankness of how history repeats itself. There came to me across the years Maud's announcement of their ejection from the *Beacon,* and dimly, confusedly, the same explanation was in the air. This time, however, I had been on my guard; I had had my suspicion. "He has made it too flippant?"— I found breath after an instant to inquire.

Mrs. Highmore's vacuity exceeded my own. "Too 'flippant'? He has made it too oracular; Mr. Bousefield says he has killed it." Then perceiving my stupefaction: "Don't you know what has happened?" she pursued; "isn't it because in his trouble, poor love, he has sent for you that you've come? You've heard nothing at all? Then you had better know before you see them. Get in here with me—I'll take

you a turn and tell you." We were close to the Park, the Regent's,
and when with extreme alacrity I had placed myself beside her and
the carriage had begun to enter it she went on: "It was what I feared,
you know. It reeked with culture. He keyed it up too high."

I felt myself sinking in the general collapse. "What are you talking
about?"

"Why, about that beastly magazine. They're all on the streets. I
shall have to take mamma."

I pulled myself together. "What on earth, then, did Bousefield
want? He said he wanted intellectual power."

"Yes, but Ray overdid it."

"Why, Bousefield said it was a thing he *couldn't* overdo."

"Well, Ray managed: he took Mr. Bousefield too literally. It
appears the thing has been doing dreadfully, but the proprietor
couldn't say anything, because he had covenanted to leave the editor
quite free. He describes himself as having stood there in a fever and
seen his ship go down. A day or two ago the year was up, so he could
at last break out. Maud says he did break out quite fearfully—he
came to the house and let poor Ray have it. Ray gave it him back—
he reminded him of his own idea of the way the cat was going to
jump."

I gasped with dismay. "Has Bousefield abandoned that idea? *Isn't*
the cat going to jump?"

Mrs. Highmore hesitated. "It appears she doesn't seem in a hurry.
Ray at any rate has jumped too far ahead of her. He should have
temporised a little, Mr. Bousefield says; but I'm beginning to think,
you know," said my companion, "that Ray *can't* temporise." Fresh
from my emotion of the previous twenty-four hours I was scarcely
in a position to disagree with her. "He published too much pure
thought."

"Pure thought?" I cried. "Why, it struck me so often—certainly in
a due proportion of cases—as pure drivel!"

"Oh, you're more keyed up than he! Mr. Bousefield says that of
course he wanted things that were suggestive and clever, things that
he could point to with pride. But he contends that Ray didn't allow
for human weakness. He gave everything in too stiff doses."

Sensibly, I fear, to my neighbour, I winced at her words—I felt a
prick that made me meditate. Then I said: "Is that, by chance, the
way he gave *me?*" Mrs. Highmore remained silent so long that I had
somehow the sense of a fresh pang; and after a minute, turning in

my seat, I laid my hand on her arm, fixed my eyes on her face, and pursued pressingly: "Do you suppose it to be to my 'Occasional Remarks' that Mr. Bousefield refers?"

At last she met my look. "Can you bear to hear it?"

"I think I can bear anything now."

"Well then, it was really what I wanted to give you an inkling of. It's largely over you that they've quarrelled. Mr. Bousefield wants him to chuck you."

I grabbed her arm again. "And our friend *won't?*"

"He seems to cling to you. Mr. Bousefield says no magazine can afford you."

I gave a laugh that agitated the very coachman. "Why, my dear lady, has he any idea of my price?"

"It isn't your price—he says you're dear at any price: you do so much to sink the ship. Your 'Remarks' are called 'Occasional,' but nothing could be more deadly regular; you're there month after month and you're never anywhere else. And you supply no public want."

"I supply the most delicious irony."

"So Ray appears to have declared. Mr. Bousefield says that's not in the least a public want. No one can make out what you're talking about and no one would care if he could. I'm only quoting *him,* mind."

"Quote, quote—if Ray holds out. I think I must leave you now, please: I must rush back to express to him what I feel."

"I'll drive you to his door. That isn't all," said Mrs. Highmore. And on the way, when the carriage had turned, she communicated the rest. "Mr. Bousefield really arrived with an ultimatum: it had the form of something or other by Minnie Meadows."

"Minnie Meadows?" I was stupefied.

"The new lady humourist every one seems talking about. It's the first of a series of screaming sketches for which poor Ray was to find a place."

"Is *that* Mr. Bousefield's idea of literature?"

"No, but he says it's the public's, and you've got to take *some* account of the public. *Aux grands maux les grands remèdes.* They had a tremendous lot of ground to make up, and no one would make it up like Minnie. She would be the best concession they could make to human weakness; she would strike at least this note of showing that it wasn't going to be quite all—well, all *you.* Now Ray draws the line at Minnie; he won't stoop to Minnie; he declines to touch, to look at Minnie. When Mr. Bousefield—rather imperiously, I believe—made Minnie a *sine qua non* of his retention of his post he said something rather violent, told him to go to some unmentionable place and take Minnie with him. That of course put the fat on the fire. They had really a considerable scene."

"So had he with the *Beacon* man," I musingly replied. "Poor dear, he seems born for considerable scenes! It's on Minnie, then, they've really split?" Mrs. Highmore exhaled her despair in a sound which I took for assent, and when we had rolled a little further I rather inconsequently and to her visible surprise broke out of my reverie. "It will never do in the world—he *must* stoop to Minnie!"

"It's too late—and what I've told you still isn't all. Mr. Bousefield raises another objection."

"What other, pray?"

"Can't you guess?"

I wondered. "No more of Ray's fiction?"

"Not a line. That's something else no magazine can stand. Now that his novel has run its course Mr. Bousefield's distinctly disappointed."

I fairly bounded in my place. "Then it may do?"

Mrs. Highmore looked bewildered. "Why so, if he finds it too dull?"

"Dull? Ralph Limbert? He's as fine as the spray of a lawn irrigator."

"It comes to the same thing, when your lawn's as coarse as a turnip field. Mr. Bousefield had counted on something that *would* do, something that would have a wider acceptance. Ray says he wants gutter-pipes and slop-buckets." I collapsed again; my flicker of elation dropped to a throb of quieter comfort; and after a moment's silence I asked my neighbour if she had herself read the work our friend had just put forth. "No," she returned, "I gave him my word at the beginning, on his urgent request, that I wouldn't."

"Not even as a book?"

"He begged me never to look at it at all. He said he was trying a low experiment. Of course I knew what he meant and I entreated him to let me just for curiosity take a peep. But he was firm, he declared he couldn't bear the thought that a woman like me should see him in the depths."

"He's only, thank God, in the depths of distress," I answered. "His experiment's·nothing worse than a failure."

· "Then Bousefield *is* right—his circulation won't budge?"

"It won't move one, as they say in Fleet Street. The book has extraordinary beauty."

"Poor duck—after trying so hard!" Jane Highmore sighed with real tenderness. "What *will*, then, become of them?"

I was silent an instant. "You must take your mother."

She was silent too. "I must speak of it to Cecil!" she presently said. Cecil is Mr. Highmore, who then entertained, I knew, strong views on the inadjustability of circumstances in general to the idiosyncrasies of Mrs. Stannace. He held it supremely happy that in an important relation she should have met her match. Her match was Ray Limbert—not much of a writer but a practical man. "The dear things still think, you know," my companion continued, "that the book will be the beginning of their fortune. Their illusion, if you're right, will be rudely dispelled."

"That's what makes me dread to face them. I've just spent with his volumes an unforgettable night. His illusion has lasted because so many of us have been pledged till this moment to turn our faces the other way. We haven't known the truth and have therefore had nothing to say. Now that we do know it indeed we have practically quite as little. I hang back from the threshold. How can I follow up with a burst of enthusiasm such a catastrophe as Mr. Bousefield's visit?"

As I turned uneasily about, my neighbour more comfortably snuggled. "Well, I'm glad, then, I haven't read him and have nothing unpleasant to say!" We had come back to Limbert's door, and I made the coachman stop short of it. "But he'll try again, with that determination of his: he'll build his hopes on the next time."

"On what else has he built them from the very first? It's never the present for him that bears the fruit; that's always postponed and for somebody else: there has always to be another try. I admit that his idea of a 'new line' has made him try harder than ever. It makes no difference," I brooded, still timorously lingering; "his achievement of his necessity, his hope of a market, will continue to attach itself to the future. But the next time will disappoint him as each last time has done—and then the next and the next and the next!"

I found myself seeing it all with a clearness almost inspired: it evidently cast a chill on Mrs. Highmore. "Then what on earth will become of him?" she plaintively repeated.

"I don't think I particularly care what may become of *him*," I returned with a conscious reckless increase of my exaltation; "I feel it almost enough to be concerned with what may become of one's enjoyment of him. I don't know in short what will become of his circulation; I'm only quite at my ease as to what will become of his work. It will simply keep all its quality. He'll try again for the common with what he'll believe to be a still more infernal cunning, and again the common will fatally elude him, for his infernal cunning will have been only his genius in an ineffectual disguise." We sat drawn up by the pavement, facing poor Limbert's future as I saw it. It relieved me in a manner to know the worst, and I prophesied with an assurance which as I look back upon it strikes me as rather remarkable. "*Que voulez-vous?*" I went on; "you can't make a sow's ear of a silk purse! It's grievous indeed if you like—there are people who can't be vulgar for trying. *He* can't—it wouldn't come off, I promise you, even once. It takes more than trying—it comes by grace. It happens not to be given to Limbert to fall. He belongs to the heights—he breathes there, he lives there, and it's accordingly to the heights I must ascend," I said as I took leave of my conductress, "to carry him this wretched news from where *we* move!"

V

A few months were sufficient to show how right I had been about his circulation. It didn't move one, as I had said; it stopped short in the same place, fell off in a sheer descent, like some precipice gaped up at by tourists. The public, in other words, drew the line for him as sharply as he had drawn it for Minnie Meadows. Minnie has skipped with a flouncing caper over his line, however; whereas the mark traced by a lustier cudgel has been a barrier insurmountable to Limbert. Those next times I had spoken of to Jane Highmore, I see them simplified by retrocession. Again and again he made his desperate bid—again and again he tried to. His rupture with Mr. Bousefield caused him in professional circles, I fear, to be thought impracticable, and I'm perfectly aware, to speak candidly, that no sordid advantage ever accrued to him from such public patronage of my performances as he had occasionally been in a position to offer. I reflect for my comfort that any injury I may have done him by untimely

application of a faculty of analysis which could point to no con-
verts gained by honourable exercise was at least equalled by the injury he did himself. More than once, as I have hinted, I held my
tongue at his request, but my frequent plea that such favours weren't
politic never found him, when in other connexions there was an
opportunity to give me a lift, anything but indifferent to the danger
of the association. He let them have me, in a word, whenever he
could; sometimes in periodicals in which he had credit, sometimes
only at dinner. He talked about me when he couldn't get me in, but
it was always part of the bargain that I shouldn't make him a topic.
"How can I successfully serve you if you do?" he used to ask: he was
more afraid than I thought he ought to have been of the charge of tit
for tat. I didn't care, for I never could distinguish tat from tit; but, as
I've intimated, I dropped into silence really more than anything else
because there was a certain fascinated observation of his course which
was quite testimony enough and to which in this huddled conclusion
of it he practically reduced me.

I see it all foreshortened, his wonderful remainder—see it from
the end backward, with the direction widening toward me as if on
a level with the eye. The migration to the country promised him at
first great things—smaller expenses, larger leisure, conditions emi-
nently conducive on each occasion to the possible triumph of the
next time. Mrs. Stannace, who altogether disapproved of it, gave as
one of her reasons that her son-in-law, living mainly in a village on
the edge of a goose-green, would be deprived of that contact with the
great world which was indispensable to the painter of manners. She
had the showiest arguments for keeping him in touch, as she called
it, with good society; wishing to know with some force where, from
the moment he ceased to represent it from observation, the novelist
could be said to be. In London fortunately a clever man was just a
clever man; there were charming houses in which a person of Ray's
undoubted ability, even though without the knack of making the
best use of it, could always be sure of a quiet corner for watching
decorously the social kaleidoscope. But the kaleidoscope of the goose-
green, what in the world was that, and what such delusive thrift as
drives about the land (with a fearful account for flys from the inn)
to leave cards on the country magnates? This solicitude for Limbert's subject matter was the specious colour with which, deeply determined not to affront mere tolerance in a cottage, Mrs. Stannace
overlaid her indisposition to place herself under the heel of Cecil

Highmore. She knew that he ruled Upstairs as well as down, and she clung to the fable of the association of interests in the north of London. The Highmores had a better address, they lived now in Stanhope Gardens; but Cecil was fearfully artful—he wouldn't hear of an association of interests nor treat with his mother-in-law save as a visitor. She didn't like false positions; but on the other hand she didn't like the sacrifice of everything she was accustomed to. Her universe at all events was a universe of card-leavings and charming houses, and it was fortunate that she couldn't, Upstairs, catch the sound of the doom to which, in his little grey den, describing to me his diplomacy, Limbert consigned alike the country magnates and the opportunities of London. Despoiled of every guarantee she went to Stanhope Gardens like a mere maidservant, with restrictions on her very luggage, while during the year that followed this upheaval Limbert, strolling with me on the goose-green, to which I often ran down, played extravagantly over the theme that with what he was now going in for it was a positive comfort not to have the social kaleidoscope. With a cold-blooded trick in view, what had life or manners or the best society or flys from the inn to say to the question? It was as good a place as another to play his new game. He had found a quieter corner than any corner of the great world, and a damp old house at tenpence a year, which, beside leaving him all his margin to educate his children, would allow of the supreme luxury of his frankly presenting himself as a poor man. This was a convenience that *ces dames,* as he called them, had never yet fully permitted him.

It rankled in me at first to see his reward so meagre, his conquest so mean; but the simplification effected had a charm that I finally felt: it was a forcing-house for the three or four other fine miscarriages to which his scheme was evidently condemned. I limited him to three or four, having had my sharp impression, in spite of the perpetual broad joke of the thing, that a spring had really broken in him on the occasion of that deeply disconcerting sequel to the episode of his editorship. He never lost his sense of the grotesque want, in the difference made, of adequate relation to the effort that had been the intensest of his life. He had carried from that moment a charge of shot, and it slowly worked its way to a vital part. As he met his embarrassments each year with his punctual false remedy, I wondered periodically where he found the energy to return to the attack. He did it every time with a rage more blanched, but it was clear to me that the tension must finally snap the cord. We got again and again the irrepressible work of art, but what did *he* get, poor man, who wanted something so different? There were likewise odder questions than this in the matter, phenomena more curious and mysteries more puzzling, which often for sympathy, if not for illumination, I intimately discussed with Mrs. Limbert. She had her burdens, dear lady; after the removal from London and a considerable interval she twice again became a mother. Mrs. Stannace too, in a more restricted sense, exhibited afresh, in relation to the home she had abandoned, the same exemplary character. In her poverty of guarantees at Stanhope Gardens there had been least of all, it appeared, a proviso that she shouldn't resentfully revert again from Goneril to Regan. She came down to the goose-green like Lear himself, with fewer knights, or at least baronets, and the joint household was at last patched up. It fell to pieces and was put together on various occasions before Ray Limbert died. He was ridden to the end by the superstition that he had broken up Mrs. Stannace's original home on pretences that had proved hollow, and that if he hadn't given Maud what she might have had he could at least give her back her mother. I was always sure that a sense of the compensations he owed was half the motive of the dogged pride with which he tried to wake up the libraries. I believed Mrs. Stannace still had money, though she pretended that, called upon at every turn to retrieve deficits, she had long since poured it into the general fund. This conviction haunted me; I suspected her of secret hoards, and I said to myself that she couldn't be so infamous as not some day on her deathbed to leave everything to her less opulent daughter. My compassion for the Limberts led me to hover perhaps indiscreetly round that closing scene, to dream of some happy time when such an accession of means would make up a little for their present penury.

This, however, was crude comfort, as in the first place I had nothing definite to go by and in the second I held it for more and more indicated that Ray wouldn't outlive her. I never ventured to sound him as to what in this particular he hoped or feared, for after the crisis marked by his leaving London I had new scruples about suffering him to be reminded of where he fell short. The poor man was in truth humiliated, and there were things as to which that kept us both silent. In proportion as he tried more fiercely for the market the old plaintive arithmetic, fertile in jokes, dropped from our conversation. We joked immensely still about the process, but our treatment of the results became sparing and superficial. He talked as much as ever, with monstrous arts and borrowed hints, of the traps he kept setting, but we all agreed to take merely for granted that the animal was caught. This propriety had really dawned upon me the day that, after Mr. Bousefield's visit, Mrs. Highmore put me down at his door. Mr. Bousefield at that juncture had been served up to me anew, but after we had disposed of him we came to the book, which I was obliged to confess I had already rushed through. It was from this moment—the moment at which my terrible impression of it had blinked out at his anxious query—that the image of his scared face was to abide with me. I couldn't attenuate then—the cat was out of the bag; but later, each of the next times, I did, I acknowledge, attenuate. We all did religiously, so far as was possible; we cast ingenious ambiguities over the strong places, the beauties that betrayed him most, and found ourselves in the queer position of admirers banded to mislead a confiding artist. If we stifled our cheers, however, if we dissimulated our joy, our fond hypocrisy accomplished little, for Limbert's finger was on a pulse that told a plainer story. It was a satisfaction to have secured a greater freedom with his wife, who at last, much to her honour, entered into the conspiracy and whose sense of responsibility was flattered by the frequency of our united appeal to her for some answer to the marvellous riddle. We had all turned it over till we were tired of it, threshing out the question of why the note he strained every chord to pitch for common ears should invariably insist on addressing itself to the angels. Being, as it were, ourselves the angels, we had only a limited quarrel in each case with the event; but its inconsequent character, given the forces set in motion, was peculiarly baffling. It was like an interminable sum that wouldn't come straight; nobody had the time to handle so many figures. Limbert gathered, to make his pudding, dry bones and dead husks; how, then, was one to formulate the law that made the dish prove a feast? What was the cerebral treachery that defied his own vigilance? There was some obscure interference of taste, some obsession of the exquisite. All one could say was that genius was a fatal disturber or that the unhappy man had no effectual *flair*. When he went abroad to gather garlic he came home with heliotrope.

I hasten to add that if Mrs. Limbert was not directly illuminating she was yet rich in anecdote and example, having found a refuge from mystification exactly where the rest of us had found it, in a

more devoted embrace and the sense of a finer glory. Her disappointments and eventually her privations had been many, her discipline
severe; but she had ended by accepting the long grind of life and
was now quite willing to take her turn at the mill. She was essentially
one of us—she always understood. Touching and admirable at the
last, when through the unmistakable change in Limbert's health her
troubles were thickest, was the spectacle of the particular pride that
she wouldn't have exchanged for prosperity. She had said to me
once—only once, in a gloomy hour of London days when things were
not going at all—that one really had to think him a very great man,
since if one didn't one would be rather ashamed of him. She had
distinctly felt it at first—and in a very tender place—that almost
every one passed him on the road; but I believe that in these final
years she would almost have been ashamed of him if he had suddenly gone into editions. It's certain indeed that her complacency
was not subjected to that shock. She would have liked the money
immensely, but she would have missed something she had taught
herself to regard as rather rare. There's another remark I remember
her making, a remark to the effect that of course if she could have
chosen she would have liked him to be Shakespeare or Scott, but
that failing this she was very glad he wasn't—well, she named the
two gentlemen, but I won't. I daresay she sometimes laughed out to
escape an alternative. She contributed passionately to the capture of
the second manner, foraging for him further afield than he could
conveniently go, gleaming in the barest stubble, picking up shreds
to build the nest and in particular, in the study of the great secret of
how, as we always said, they all did it, laying waste of the circulating
libraries. If Limbert had a weakness he rather broke down in his
reading. It was fortunately not till after the appearance of "The Hidden Heart" that he broke down in everything else. He had had rheu-
matic fever in the spring, when the book was but half-finished, and
this ordeal had in addition to interrupting his work enfeebled his
powers of resistance and greatly reduced his vitality. He recovered
from the fever and was able to take up the book again, but the organ
of life was pronounced ominously weak and it was enjoined upon
him with some sharpness that he should lend himself to no worries.
It might have struck me as on the cards that his worries would now
be surmountable, for when he began to mend he expressed to me
a conviction almost contagious that he had never yet made so adroit
a bid as in the idea of "The Hidden Heart." It is grimly droll to re-

flect that this superb little composition, the shortest of his novels but perhaps the loveliest, was planned from the first as an "adventure story" on approved lines. It was the way they all did the adventure story that he had tried dauntlessly to emulate. I wonder how many readers ever divined to which of their book-shelves "The Hidden Heart" was so exclusively addressed. High medical advice early in the summer had been quite viciously clear as to the inconvenience that might ensue to him should he neglect to spend the winter in Egypt. He was not a man to neglect anything; but Egypt seemed to us all then as unattainable as a second edition. He finished "The Hidden Heart" with the energy of apprehension and desire, for if the book should happen to do what "books of that class," as the publisher said, sometimes did, he might well have a fund to draw on. As soon as I read the fine, deep thing I knew, as I had known in each case before, exactly how well it would do. Poor Limbert in this long business always figured to me an undiscourageable parent to whom only girls kept being born. A bouncing boy, a son and heir, was devoutly prayed for and almanacks and old wives consulted; but the spell was inveterate, incurable, and "The Hidden Heart" proved, so to speak, but another female child. When the winter arrived accordingly Egypt was out of the question. Jane Highmore, to my knowledge, wanted to lend him money, and there were even greater devotees who did their best to induce him to lean on them. There was so marked a "movement" among his friends that a very considerable sum would have been at his disposal; but his stiffness was invincible: it had its root, I think, in his sense, on his own side, of sacrifices already made. He had sacrificed honour and pride, and he had sacrificed them precisely to the question of money. He would evidently, should he be able to go on, have to continue to sacrifice them, but it must be all in the way to which he had now, as he considered, hardened himself. He had spent years in plotting for favour, and since on favour he must live it could only be as a bargain and a price.

He got through the early part of the season better than we feared, and I went down in great elation to spend Christmas on the goose-green. He told me late on Christmas Eve, after our simple domestic revels had sunk to rest and we sat together by the fire, how he had been visited the night before in wakeful hours by the finest fancy for a really good thing that he had ever felt descend in the darkness. "It's just the vision of a situation that contains, upon my honour, everything," he said, "and I wonder I've never thought of it before."

He didn't describe it further, contrary to his common practice, and I only knew later, by Mrs. Limbert, that he had begun "Derogation" and was completely full of his subject. It was, however, a subject he wasn't to live to treat. The work went on for a couple of months in quiet mystery, without revelations even to his wife. He hadn't invited her to help him get up his case—she hadn't taken the field with him as on his previous campaigns. We only knew he was at it again, but that less even than ever had been said about the impression to be made on the market. I saw him in February and thought him sufficiently at ease. The great thing was that he was immensely interested and was pleased with the omens. I got a strange stirring sense that he had not consulted the usual ones and indeed that he had floated away into a grand indifference, into a reckless consciousness of art. The voice of the market had suddenly grown faint and far: he had come back at the last, as people so often do, to one of the moods, the sincerities of his prime. Was he really, with a blurred sense of the urgent, doing something now only for himself? We wondered and waited—we felt he was a little confused. What had happened, I was afterwards satisfied, was that he had quite forgotten whether he generally sold or not. He had merely waked up one morning again in the country of the blue and had stayed there with a good conscience and a great idea. He stayed till death knocked at the gate, for the pen dropped from his hand only at the moment when, from sudden failure of the heart, his eyes, as he sank back in his chair, closed for ever. "Derogation" is a splendid fragment; it evidently would have been one of his highest successes. I am not prepared to say it would have waked up the libraries.

The Figure in the Carpet

I HAD done a few things and earned a few pence—I had perhaps even had time to begin to think I was finer than was perceived by the patronising; but when I take the little measure of my course (a fidgety habit, for it's none of the longest yet) I count my real start from the evening George Corvick, breathless and worried, came in to ask me a service. He had done more things than I, and earned more pence, though there were chances for cleverness I thought he sometimes missed. I could only, however, that evening declare to him that he never missed one for kindness. There was almost rapture in hearing it proposed to me to prepare for *The Middle*, the organ of our lucubrations, so called from the position in the week of its day of appearance, an article for which he had made himself responsible and of which, tied up with a stout string, he laid on my table the subject. I pounced upon my opportunity—that is on the first volume of it—and paid scant attention to my friend's explanation of his appeal. What explanation could be more to the point than my obvious fitness for the task? I had written on Hugh Vereker, but never a word in *The Middle*, where my dealings were mainly with the ladies and the minor poets. This was his new novel, an advance copy, and whatever much or little it should do for his reputation I was clear on the spot as to what it should do for mine. Moreover if I always read him as soon as I could get hold of him I had a particular reason for wishing to read him now: I had accepted an invitation to Bridges for the following Sunday, and it had been mentioned in Lady Jane's note that Mr. Vereker was to be there. I was young enough for a flutter at meeting a man of his renown, and innocent enough to believe the occasion would demand the display of an acquaintance with his "last."

Corvick, who had promised a review of it, had not even had time to read it; he had gone to pieces in consequence of news requiring —as on precipitate reflexion he judged—that he should catch the night-mail to Paris. He had had a telegram from Gwendolen Erme in answer to his letter offering to fly to her aid. I knew already about Gwendolen Erme; I had never seen her, but I had my ideas, which were mainly to the effect that Corvick would marry her if her mother would only die. That lady seemed now in a fair way to oblige him; after some dreadful mistake about a climate or a "cure" she had suddenly collapsed on the return from abroad. Her daughter, unsupported and alarmed, desiring to make a rush for home but hesitating at the risk, had accepted our friend's assistance, and it was my secret belief that at sight of him Mrs. Erme would pull round. His own belief was scarcely to be called secret; it discernibly at any rate differed from mine. He had showed me Gwendolen's photograph with the remark that she wasn't pretty but was awfully interesting; she had published at the age of nineteen a novel in three volumes, "Deep Down," about which, in *The Middle,* he had been really splendid. He appreciated my present eagerness and undertook that the periodical in question should do no less; then at the last, with his hand on the door, he said to me: "Of course you'll be all right, you know." Seeing I was a trifle vague he added: "I mean you won't be silly."

"Silly—about Vereker! Why what do I ever find him but awfully clever?"

"Well, what's that but silly? What on earth does 'awfully clever' mean? For God's sake try to get *at* him. Don't let him suffer by our arrangement. Speak of him, you know, if you can, as *I* should have spoken of him."

I wondered an instant. "You mean as far and away the biggest of the lot—that sort of thing?"

Corvick almost groaned. "Oh you know, I don't put them back to back that way; it's the infancy of art! But he gives me a pleasure so rare; the sense of"—he mused a little—"something or other."

I wondered again. "The sense, pray, of what?"

"My dear man, that's just what I want *you* to say!"

Even before he had banged the door I had begun, book in hand, to prepare myself to say it. I sat up with Vereker half the night; Corvick couldn't have done more than that. He was awfully clever—I stuck to that, but he wasn't a bit the biggest of the lot. I didn't allude to the lot, however; I flattered myself that I emerged on this occasion from the infancy of art. "It's all right," they declared vividly at the office; and when the number appeared I felt there was a basis on which I could meet the great man. It gave me confidence for a day or two

—then that confidence dropped. I had fancied him reading it with relish, but if Corvick wasn't satisfied how could Vereker himself be? I reflected indeed that the heat of the admirer was sometimes grosser even than the appetite of the scribe. Corvick at all events wrote me from Paris a little ill-humouredly. Mrs. Erme was pulling round, and I hadn't at all said what Vereker gave him the sense of.

II

The effect of my visit to Bridges was to turn me out for more profundity. Hugh Vereker, as I saw him there, was of a contact so void of angles that I blushed for the poverty of imagination involved in my small precautions. If he was in spirits it wasn't because he had read my review; in fact on the Sunday morning I felt sure he hadn't read it, though *The Middle* had been out three days and bloomed, I assured myself, in the stiff garden of periodicals which gave one of the ormolu tables the air of a stand at a station. The impression he made on me personally was such that I wished him to read it, and I corrected to this end with a surreptitious hand what might be wanting in the careless conspicuity of the sheet. I'm afraid I even watched the result of my manœuvre, but up to luncheon I watched in vain.

When afterwards, in the course of our gregarious walk, I found myself for half an hour, not perhaps without another manœuvre, at the great man's side, the result of his affability was a still livelier desire that he shouldn't remain in ignorance of the peculiar justice I had done him. It wasn't that he seemed to thirst for justice; on the contrary I hadn't yet caught in his talk the faintest grunt of a grudge —a note for which my young experience had already given me an ear. Of late he had had more recognition, and it was pleasant, as we used to say in *The Middle,* to see how it drew him out. He wasn't of course popular, but I judged one of the sources of his good humour to be precisely that his success was independent of that. He had none the less become in a manner the fashion; the critics at least had put on a spurt and caught up with him. We had found out at last how clever he was, and he had had to make the best of the loss of his mystery. I was strongly tempted, as I walked beside him, to let him know how much of that unveiling was my act; and there was a moment when I probably should have done so had not one of the ladies of our party, snatching a place at his other elbow, just then

appealed to him in a spirit comparatively selfish. It was very discouraging: I almost felt the liberty had been taken with myself.

I had had on my tongue's end, for my own part, a phrase or two
about the right word at the right time; but later on I was glad not
to have spoken, for when on our return we clustered at tea I perceived Lady Jane, who had not been out with us, brandishing *The
Middle* with her longest arm. She had taken it up at her leisure;
she was delighted with what she had found, and I saw that, as a mistake in a man may often be a felicity in a woman, she would practically do for me what I hadn't been able to do for myself. "Some
sweet little truths that needed to be spoken," I heard her declare,
thrusting the paper at rather a bewildered couple by the fireplace.
She grabbed it away from them again on the reappearance of Hugh
Vereker, who after our walk had been upstairs to change something.
"I know you don't in general look at this kind of thing, but it's an
occasion really for doing so. You *haven't* seen it? Then you must.
The man has actually got *at* you, at what *I* always feel, you know."
Lady Jane threw into her eyes a look evidently intended to give an
idea of what she always felt; but she added that she couldn't have
expressed it. The man in the paper expressed it in a striking manner. "Just see there, and there, where I've dashed it, how he brings
it out." She had literally marked for him the brightest patches of
my prose, and if I was a little amused Vereker himself may well have
been. He showed how much he was when before us all Lady Jane
wanted to read something aloud. I liked at any rate the way he de-
feated her purpose by jerking the paper affectionately out of her
clutch. He'd take it upstairs with him and look at it on going to
dress. He did this half an hour later—I saw it in his hand when he
repaired to his room. That was the moment at which, thinking to
give her pleasure, I mentioned to Lady Jane that I was the author
of the review. I did give her pleasure, I judged, but perhaps not quite
so much as I had expected. If the author was "only me" the thing
didn't seem quite so remarkable. Hadn't I had the effect rather of
diminishing the lustre of the article than of adding to my own? Her
ladyship was subject to the most extraordinary drops. It didn't matter; the only effect I cared about was the one it would have on
Vereker up there by his bedroom fire.

At dinner I watched for the signs of this impression, tried to fancy
some happier light in his eyes; but to my disappointment Lady Jane
gave me no chance to make sure. I had hoped she'd call triumphantly

down the table, publicly demand if she hadn't been right. The party was large—there were people from outside as well, but I had never seen a table long enough to deprive Lady Jane of a triumph. I was just reflecting in truth that this interminable board would deprive *me* of one when the guest next me, dear woman—she was Miss Poyle, the vicar's sister, a robust unmodulated person—had the happy inspiration and the unusual courage to address herself across it to Vereker, who was opposite, but not directly, so that when he replied they were both leaning forward. She inquired, artless body, what he thought of Lady Jane's "panegyric," which she had read—not connecting it however with her right-hand neighbour; and while I strained my ear for his reply I heard him, to my stupefaction, call back gaily, his mouth full of bread: "Oh it's all right—the usual twaddle!"

I had caught Vereker's glance as he spoke, but Miss Poyle's surprise was a fortunate cover for my own. "You mean he doesn't do you justice?" said the excellent woman.

Vereker laughed out, and I was happy to be able to do the same. "It's a charming article," he tossed us.

Miss Poyle thrust her chin half across the cloth. "Oh you're so deep!" she drove home.

"As deep as the ocean! All I pretend is that the author doesn't see—" But a dish was at this point passed over his shoulder, and we had to wait while he helped himself.

"Doesn't see what?" my neighbour continued.

"Doesn't see anything."

"Dear me—how very stupid!"

"Not a bit," Vereker laughed again. "Nobody does."

The lady on his further side appealed to him and Miss Poyle sank back to myself. "Nobody sees anything!" she cheerfully announced; to which I replied that I had often thought so too, but had somehow taken the thought for a proof on my own part of a tremendous eye. I didn't tell her the article was mine; and I observed that Lady Jane, occupied at the end of the table, had not caught Vereker's words.

I rather avoided him after dinner, for I confess he struck me as cruelly conceited, and the revelation was a pain. "The usual twaddle"—my acute little study! That one's admiration should have had a reserve or two could gall him to that point? I had thought him placid, and he was placid enough; such a surface was the hard polished glass that encased the bauble of his vanity. I was really ruffled, and the only comfort was that if nobody saw anything George Corvick was quite as much out of it as I. This comfort however was not sufficient, after the ladies had dispersed, to carry me in the proper manner—I mean in a spotted jacket and humming an air—into the smoking-room. I took my way in some dejection to bed; but in the passage I encountered Mr. Vereker, who had been up once more to change, coming out of his room. *He* was humming an air and had on a spotted jacket, and as soon as he saw me his gaiety gave a start.

"My dear young man," he exclaimed, "I'm so glad to lay hands on you! I'm afraid I most unwittingly wounded you by those words of mine at dinner to Miss Poyle. I learned but half an hour ago from Lady Jane that you're the author of the little notice in *The Middle*."

I protested that no bones were broken; but he moved with me to my own door, his hand, on my shoulder, kindly feeling for a fracture; and on hearing that I had come up to bed he asked leave to cross my threshold and just tell me in three words what his qualification of my remarks had represented. It was plain he really feared I was hurt, and the sense of his solicitude suddenly made all the difference to me. My cheap review fluttered off into space, and the best things I had said in it became flat enough beside the brilliancy of his being there. I can see him there still, on my rug, in the firelight and his spotted jacket, his fine clear face all bright with the desire to be tender to my youth. I don't know what he had at first meant to say, but I think the sight of my relief touched him, excited him, brought up words to his lips from far within. It was so these words presently conveyed to me something that, as I afterwards knew, he had never uttered to any one. I've always done justice to the generous impulse that made him speak; it was simply compunction for a snub unconsciously administered to a man of letters in a position inferior to his own, a man of letters moreover in the very act of praising him. To make the thing right he talked to me exactly as an equal and on the ground of what we both loved best. The hour, the place, the unexpectedness deepened the impression: he couldn't have done anything more intensely effective.

III

"I don't quite know how to explain it to you," he said, "but it was the very fact that your notice of my book had a spice of intelligence, it was just your exceptional sharpness, that produced the feeling—a

very old story with me, I beg you to believe—under the momentary
influence of which I used in speaking to that good lady the words
you so naturally resent. I don't read the things in the newspapers
unless they're thrust upon me as that one was—it's always one's best
friend who does it! But I used to read them sometimes—ten years
ago. I dare say they were in general rather stupider then; at any rate
it always struck me they missed my little point with a perfection
exactly as admirable when they patted me on the back as when they
kicked me in the shins. Whenever since I've happened to have a
glimpse of them they were still blazing away—still missing it, I mean,
deliciously. You miss it, my dear fellow, with inimitable assurance;
the fact of your being awfully clever and your article's being awfully
nice doesn't make a hair's breadth of difference. It's quite with you
rising young men," Vereker laughed, "that I feel most what a failure
I am!"

I listened with keen interest; it grew keener as he talked. "You a
failure—heavens! What then may your 'little point' happen to be?"

"Have I got to *tell* you, after all these years and labours?" There
was something in the friendly reproach of this—jocosely exaggerated
—that made me, as an ardent young seeker for truth, blush to the
roots of my hair. I'm as much in the dark as ever, though I've grown
used in a sense to my obtuseness; at that moment, however, Vereker's
happy accent made me appear to myself, and probably to him, a rare
dunce. I was on the point of exclaiming "Ah yes, don't tell me: for
my honour, for that of the craft, don't!" when he went on in a manner that showed he had read my thought and had his own idea of
the probability of our some day redeeming ourselves. By my little
point I mean—what shall I call it?—the particular thing I've written
my books most *for*. Isn't there for every writer a particular thing of
that sort, the thing that most makes him apply himself, the thing
without the effort to achieve which he wouldn't write at all, the very
passion of his passion, the part of the business in which, for him,
the flame of art burns most intensely? Well, it's *that!*"

I considered a moment—that is I followed at a respectful distance,
rather gasping. I was fascinated—easily, you'll say; but I wasn't going
after all to be put off my guard. "Your description's certainly beautiful, but it doesn't make what you describe very distinct."

"I promise you it would be distinct if it should dawn on you at all."
I saw that the charm of our topic overflowed for my companion into
an emotion as lively as my own. "At any rate," he went on, "I can

speak for myself: there's an idea in my work without which I wouldn't have given a straw for the whole job. It's the finest fullest intention of the lot, and the application of it has been, I think, a triumph of patience, of ingenuity. I ought to leave that to somebody else to say; but that nobody does say it is precisely what we're talking about. It stretches, this little trick of mine, from book to book, and everything else, comparatively, plays over the surface of it. The order, the form, the texture of my books will perhaps someday constitute for the initiated a complete representation of it. So it's naturally the thing for the critic to look for. It strikes me," my visitor added, smiling, "even as the thing for the critic to find."

This seemed a responsibility indeed. "You call it a little trick?"

"That's only my little modesty. It's really an exquisite scheme."

"And you hold that you've carried the scheme out?"

"The way I've carried it out is the thing in life I think a bit well of myself for."

I had a pause. "Don't you think you ought—just a trifle—to assist the critic?"

"Assist him? What else have I done with every stroke of my pen? I've shouted my intention in his great blank face!" At this, laughing out again, Vereker laid his hand on my shoulder to show the allusion wasn't to my personal appearance.

"But you talk about the initiated. There must therefore, you see, be initiation."

"What else in heaven's name is criticism supposed to be?" I'm afraid I coloured at this too; but I took refuge in repeating that his account of his silver lining was poor in something or other that a plain man knows things by. "That's only because you've never had a glimpse of it," he returned. "If you had had one the element in question would soon have become practically all you'd see. To me it's exactly as palpable as the marble of this chimney. Besides, the critic just isn't a plain man: if he were, pray, what would he be doing in his neighbour's garden? You're anything but a plain man yourself, and the very raison d'être of you all is that you're little demons of subtlety. If my great affair's a secret, that's only because it's a secret in spite of itself—the amazing event has made it one. I not only never took the smallest precaution to keep it so, but never dreamed of any such accident. If I had I shouldn't in advance have had the heart to go on. As it was, I only became aware little by little, and meanwhile I had done my work."

"And now you quite like it?" I risked.

"My work?"

"Your secret. It's the same thing."

"Your guessing that," Vereker replied, "is a proof that you're as clever as I say!" I was encouraged by this to remark that he would clearly be pained to part with it, and he confessed that it was indeed with him now the great amusement of life. "I live almost to see if it will ever be detected." He looked at me for a jesting challenge; something far within his eyes seemed to peep out. "But I needn't worry—it won't!"

"You fire me as I've never been fired," I declared; "you make me determined to do or die." Then I asked: "Is it a kind of esoteric message?"

His countenance fell at this—he put out his hand as if to bid me good-night. "Ah my dear fellow, it can't be described in cheap journalese!"

I knew of course he'd be awfully fastidious, but our talk had made me feel how much his nerves were exposed. I was unsatisfied—I kept hold of his hand. "I won't make use of the expression then," I said, "in the article in which I shall eventually announce my discovery, though I dare say I shall have hard work to do without it. But meanwhile, just to hasten that difficult birth, can't you give a fellow a clue?" I felt much more at my ease.

"My whole lucid effort gives him the clue—every page and line and letter. The thing's as concrete there as a bird in a cage, a bait on a hook, a piece of cheese in a mouse-trap. It's stuck into every volume as your foot is stuck into your shoe. It governs every line, it chooses every word, it dots every i, it places every comma."

I scratched my head. "Is it something in the style or something in the thought? An element of form or an element of feeling?"

He indulgently shook my hand again, and I felt my questions to be crude and my distinctions pitiful. "Good-night, my dear boy—don't bother about it. After all, you do like a fellow."

"And a little intelligence might spoil it?" I still detained him.

He hesitated. "Well, you've got a heart in your body. Is that an element of form or an element of feeling? What I contend that nobody has ever mentioned in my work is the organ of life."

"I see—it's some idea about life, some sort of philosophy. Unless it be," I added with the eagerness of a thought perhaps still happier, "some kind of game you're up to with your style, something you're after in the language. Perhaps it's a preference for the letter P!" I ventured profanely to break out. "Papa, potatoes, prunes—that sort of thing?" He was suitably indulgent: he only said I hadn't got the right letter. But his amusement was over; I could see he was bored. There was nevertheless something else I had absolutely to learn. "Should you be able, pen in hand, to state it clearly yourself —to name it, phrase it, formulate it?"

"Oh," he almost passionately sighed, "if I were only, pen in hand, one of you chaps!"

"That would be a great chance for you of course. But why should you despise us chaps for not doing what you can't do yourself?"

"Can't do?" He opened his eyes. "Haven't I done it in twenty volumes? I do it in my way," he continued. "Go you and do it in yours."

"Ours is so devilish difficult," I weakly observed.

"So's mine! We each choose our own. There's no compulsion. You won't come down and smoke?"

"No. I want to think this thing out."

"You'll tell me then in the morning that you've laid me bare?"

"I'll see what I can do; I'll sleep on it. But just one word more," I added. We had left the room—I walked again with him a few steps along the passage. "This extraordinary 'general intention,' as you call it—for that's the most vivid description I can induce you to make of it—is then, generally, a sort of buried treasure?"

His face lighted. "Yes, call it that, though it's perhaps not for me to do so."

"Nonsense!" I laughed. "You know you're hugely proud of it."

"Well, I didn't propose to tell you so; but it is the joy of my soul!"

"You mean it's a beauty so rare, so great?"

He waited a little again. "The loveliest thing in the world!" We had stopped, and on these words he left me; but at the end of the corridor, while I looked after him rather yearningly, he turned and caught sight of my puzzled face. It made him earnestly, indeed I thought quite anxiously, shake his head and wave his finger. "Give it up—give it up!"

This wasn't a challenge—it was fatherly advice. If I had had one of his books at hand I'd have repeated my recent act of faith—I'd have spent half the night with him. At three o'clock in the morning, not sleeping, remembering moreover how indispensable he was to Lady Jane, I stole down to the library with a candle. There wasn't, so far as I could discover, a line of his writing in the house.

IV

Returning to town I feverishly collected them all; I picked out each in its order and held it up to the light. This gave me a maddening month, in the course of which several things took place. One of these, the last, I may as well immediately mention, was that I acted on Vereker's advice: I renounced my ridiculous attempt. I could really make nothing of the business; it proved a dead loss. After all I had always, as he had himself noted, liked him; and what now occurred was simply that my new intelligence and vain preoccupation damaged my liking. I not only failed to run a general intention to earth, I found myself missing the subordinate intentions I had formerly enjoyed. His books didn't even remain the charming things they had been for me; the exasperation of my search put me out of conceit of them. Instead of being a pleasure the more they became a resource the less; for from the moment I was unable to follow up the author's hint I of course felt it a point of honour not to make use professionally of my knowledge of them. I had no knowledge—nobody had any. It was humiliating, but I could bear it—they only annoyed me now. At last they even bored me, and I accounted for my confusion—perversely, I allow—by the idea that Vereker had made a fool of me. The buried treasure was a bad joke, the general intention a monstrous *pose.*

The great point of it all is, however, that I told George Corvick what had befallen me and that my information had an immense effect on him. He had at last come back, but so, unfortunately, had Mrs. Erme, and there was as yet, I could see, no question of his nuptials. He was immensely stirred up by the anecdote I had brought from Bridges; it fell in so completely with the sense he had had from the first that there was more in Vereker than met the eye. When I remarked that the eye seemed what the printed page had been expressly invented to meet he immediately accused me of being spiteful because I had been foiled. Our commerce had always that pleasant latitude. The thing Vereker had mentioned to me was exactly the thing he, Corvick, had wanted me to speak of in my review. On my suggesting at last that with the assistance I had now given him he would doubtless be prepared to speak of it himself he admitted freely that before doing this there was more he must understand. What he would have said, had he reviewed the new book, was that there was evidently in the writer's inmost art something to be understood. I hadn't so much as hinted at that: no wonder the writer hadn't been flattered! I asked Corvick what he really considered he meant by his own supersubtlety, and, unmistakably kindled, he replied: "It isn't for the vulgar—it isn't for the vulgar!" He had hold of the tail of something: he would pull hard, pull it right out. He pumped me dry on Vereker's strange confidence and, pronouncing me the luckiest of mortals, mentioned half-a-dozen questions he wished to goodness I had had the gumption to put. Yet on the other hand he didn't want to be told too much—it would spoil the fun of seeing what would come. The failure of *my* fun was at the moment of our meeting not complete, but I saw it ahead, and Corvick saw that I saw it. I, on my side, saw likewise that one of the first things he would do would be to rush off with my story to Gwendolen.

On the very day after my talk with him I was surprised by the receipt of a note from Hugh Vereker, to whom our encounter at Bridges had been recalled, as he mentioned, by his falling, in a magazine, on some article to which my signature was attached. "I read it with great pleasure," he wrote, "and remembered under its influence our lively conversation by your bedroom fire. The consequence of this has been that I begin to measure the temerity of my having saddled you with a knowledge that you may find something of a burden. Now that the fit's over I can't imagine how I came to be moved so much beyond my wont. I had never before mentioned, no matter in what state of expansion, the fact of my little secret, and I shall never speak of that mystery again. I was accidentally so much more explicit with you than it had ever entered into my game to be, that I find this game—I mean the pleasure of playing it—suffers considerably. In short, if you can understand it, I've rather spoiled my sport. I really don't want to give anybody what I believe you clever young men call the tip. That's of course a selfish solicitude, and I name it to you for what it may be worth to you. If you're disposed to humour me don't repeat my revelation. Think me demented—it's your right; but don't tell anybody why."

The sequel to this communication was that as early on the morrow as I dared I drove straight to Mr. Vereker's door. He occupied in those years one of the honest old houses in Kensington Square. He received me immediately, and as soon as I came in I saw I hadn't lost my power to minister to his mirth. He laughed out at sight of my face, which doubtless expressed my perturbation. I had been indiscreet—my compunction was great. "I *have* told somebody," I panted, "and I'm sure that person will by this time have told somebody else! It's a woman, into the bargain."

"The person you've told?"

"No, the other person. I'm quite sure he must have told her."

"For all the good it will do her—or do *me!* A woman will never find out."

"No, but she'll talk all over the place: she'll do just what you don't want."

Vereker thought a moment, but wasn't so disconcerted as I had feared: he felt that if the harm was done it only served him right. "It doesn't matter—don't worry."

"I'll do my best, I promise you, that your talk with me shall go no further."

"Very good; do what you can."

"In the meantime," I pursued, "George Corvick's possession of the tip may, on his part, really lead to something."

"That will be a brave day."

I told him about Corvick's cleverness, his admiration, the intensity of his interest in my anecdote; and without making too much of the divergence of our respective estimates mentioned that my friend was already of opinion that he saw much further into a certain affair than most people. He was quite as fired as I had been at Bridges. He was moreover in love with the young lady: perhaps the two together would puzzle something out.

Vereker seemed struck with this. "Do you mean they're to be married?"

"I dare say that's what it will come to."

"That may help them," he conceded, "but we must give them time!"

I spoke of my own renewed assault and confessed my difficulties; whereupon he repeated his former advice: "Give it up, give it up!" He evidently didn't think me intellectually equipped for the adventure. I stayed half an hour, and he was most good-natured, but I couldn't help pronouncing him a man of unstable moods. He had been free with me in a mood, he had repented in a mood, and now in a mood he had turned indifferent. This general levity helped me to believe that, so far as the subject of the tip went, there wasn't much in it. I contrived however to make him answer a few more questions about it, though he did so with visible impatience. For himself, beyond doubt, the thing we were all so blank about was vividly there. It was something, I guessed, in the primal plan; something like a complex figure in a Persian carpet. He highly approved of this image when I used it, and he used another himself. "It's the very string," he said, "that my pearls are strung on!" The reason of his note to me had been that he really didn't want to give us a grain of succour—our density was a thing too perfect in its way to touch. He had formed the habit of depending on it, and if the spell was to break it must break by some force of its own. He comes back to me from that last occasion—for I was never to speak to him again—as a man with some safe preserve for sport. I wondered as I walked away where he had got *his* tip.

V

When I spoke to George Corvick of the caution I had received he made me feel that any doubt of his delicacy would be almost an insult. He had instantly told Gwendolen, but Gwendolen's ardent response was in itself a pledge of discretion. The question would now absorb them and would offer them a pastime too precious to be shared with the crowd. They appeared to have caught instinctively at Vereker's high idea of enjoyment. Their intellectual pride, however, was not such as to make them indifferent to any further light I might throw on the affair they had in hand. They were indeed of the "artistic temperament," and I was freshly struck with my colleague's power to excite himself over a question of art. He'd call it letters, he'd call it life, but it was all one thing. In what he said I now seemed to understand that he spoke equally for Gwendolen, to whom, as soon as Mrs. Erme was sufficiently better to allow her a little leisure, he made a point of introducing me. I remember our going together one Sunday in August to a huddled house in Chelsea, and my renewed envy of Corvick's possession of a friend who had some light to mingle with his own. He could say things to her that I could never say to him. She had indeed no sense of humour and, with her pretty way of holding her head on one side, was one of those persons whom you want, as the phrase is, to shake, but who have learnt Hungarian by themselves. She conversed perhaps in Hungarian with Corvick; she had remarkably little English for his friend. Corvick afterwards told me that I had chilled her by my apparent indisposition to oblige them with the detail of what Vereker had said to me. I allowed that I felt I had given thought enough to that indication: hadn't I even made up my mind that it was vain and would lead nowhere? The importance they attached to it was irritating and quite envenomed my doubts.

That statement looks unamiable, and what probably happened was that I felt humiliated at seeing other persons deeply beguiled by an experiment that had brought me only chagrin. I was out in the cold while, by the evening fire, under the lamp, they followed the chase for which I myself had sounded the horn. They did as I had done, only more deliberately and sociably—they went over their author from the beginning. There was no hurry, Corvick said—the future was before them and the fascination could only grow; they would take him page by page, as they would take one of the classics, inhale him in slow draughts and let him sink all the way in. They would scarce have got so wound up, I think, if they hadn't been in love: poor Vereker's inner meaning gave them endless occasion to put and to keep their young heads together. None the less it represented the kind of problem for which Corvick had a special aptitude, drew out the particular pointed patience of which, had he lived, he would have given more striking and, it is to be hoped, more fruitful examples. He at least was, in Vereker's words, a little demon of subtlety. We had begun by disputing, but I soon saw that without my stirring a finger his infatuation would have its bad hours. He would bound off on false scents as I had done—he would clap his hands over new lights and see them blown out by the wind of the turned page. He was like nothing, I told him, but the maniacs who embrace some bedlamitical theory of the cryptic character of Shakespeare. To this he replied that if we had had Shakespeare's own word for his being cryptic he would at once have accepted it. The case there was altogether different—we had nothing but the word of Mr. Snooks. I returned that I was stupefied to see him attach such importance even to the word of Mr. Vereker. He wanted thereupon to know if I treated Mr. Vereker's word as a lie. I wasn't perhaps prepared, in my unhappy rebound, to go so far as that, but I insisted that till the contrary was proved I should view it as too fond an imagination. I didn't, I confess, say—I didn't at that time quite know

—all I felt. Deep down, as Miss Erme would have said, I was uneasy, I was expectant. At the core of my disconcerted state—for my wonted curiosity lived in its ashes—was the sharpness of a sense that Corvick would at last probably come out somewhere. He made, in defence of his credulity, a great point of the fact that from of old, in his study of this genius, he had caught whiffs and hints of he didn't know what, faint wandering notes of a hidden music. That was just the rarity, that was the charm: it fitted so perfectly into what I reported.

If I returned on several occasions to the little house in Chelsea I dare say it was as much for news of Vereker as for news of Miss Erme's ailing parent. The hours spent there by Corvick were present to my fancy as those of a chessplayer bent with a silent scowl, all the lamplit winter, over his board and his moves. As my imagination filled it out the picture held me fast. On the other side of the table was a ghostlier form, the faint figure of an antagonist good-humouredly but a little wearily secure—an antagonist who leaned back in his chair with his hands in his pockets and a smile on his fine clear face. Close to Corvick, behind him, was a girl who had begun to strike me as pale and wasted and even, on more familiar view, as rather handsome, and who rested on his shoulder and hung on his moves. He would take up a chessman and hold it poised a while over one of the little squares, and then would put it back in its place with a long sigh of disappointment. The young lady, at this, would slightly but uneasily shift her position and look across, very hard, very long, very strangely, at their dim participant. I had asked them at an early stage of the business if it mightn't contribute to their success to have some closer communication with him. The special circumstances would surely be held to have given me a right to introduce them. Corvick immediately replied that he had no wish to approach the altar before he had prepared the sacrifice. He quite agreed with our friend both as to the delight and as to the honour of the chase—he would bring down the animal with his own rifle. When I asked him if Miss Erme were as keen a shot he said after thinking: "No, I'm ashamed to say she wants to set a trap. She'd give anything to see him; she says she requires another tip. She's really quite morbid about it. But she must play fair—she shan't see him!" he emphatically added. I wondered if they hadn't even quarrelled a little on the subject—a suspicion not corrected by the way he more than once exclaimed to me: "She's quite incredibly literary, you know—quite fantastically!" I remember his saying of her that she felt in italics and thought in capitals. "Oh when I've run him to earth," he also said, "then, you know, I shall knock at his door. Rather—I beg you to believe. I'll have it from his own lips: 'Right you are, my boy; you've done it this time!' He shall crown me victor—with the critical laurel."

Meanwhile he really avoided the chances London life might have given him of meeting the distinguished novelist; a danger, however, that disappeared with Vereker's leaving England for an indefinite absence, as the newspapers announced—going to the south for motives connected with the health of his wife, which had long kept her in retirement. A year—more than a year—had elapsed since the incident at Bridges, but I had had no further sight of him. I think I was at bottom rather ashamed—I hated to remind him that, though I had irremediably missed his point, a reputation for acuteness was rapidly overtaking me. This scruple led me a dance; kept me out of Lady Jane's house, made me even decline, when in spite of my bad manners she was a second time so good as to make me a sign, an invitation to her beautiful seat. I once became aware of her under Vereker's escort at a concert, and was sure I was seen by them, but I slipped out without being caught. I felt, as on that occasion I splashed along in the rain, that I couldn't have done anything else; and yet I remember saying to myself that it was hard, was even cruel. Not only had I lost the books, but I had lost the man himself: they and their author had been alike spoiled for me. I knew too which was the loss I most regretted. I had taken to the man still more than I had ever taken to the books.

VI

Six months after our friend had left England George Corvick, who made his living by his pen, contracted for a piece of work which imposed on him an absence of some length and a journey of some difficulty, and his undertaking of which was much of a surprise to me. His brother-in-law had become editor of a great provincial paper, and the great provincial paper, in a fine flight of fancy, had conceived the idea of sending a "special commissioner" to India. Special commissioners had begun, in the "metropolitan press," to be the fashion, and the journal in question must have felt it had passed too long for a mere country cousin. Corvick had no hand, I knew, for the big brush of the correspondent, but that was his brother-in-law's affair, and the fact that a particular task was not in his line was apt to be with himself exactly a reason for accepting it. He was prepared to out-Herod the metropolitan press; he took solemn precautions against priggishness, he exquisitely outraged taste. Nobody ever knew it—that offended principle was all his own. In addition to his expenses he was to be conveniently paid, and I found myself able to help him, for the usual fat book, to a plausible arrangement with the usual fat publisher. I naturally inferred that his obvious desire to make a little money was not unconnected with the prospect of a union with Gwendolen Erme. I was aware that her mother's opposition was largely addressed to his want of means and of lucrative abilities, but it so happened that, on my saying the last time I saw him something that bore on the question of his separation from our young lady, he brought out with an emphasis that startled me: "Ah I'm not a bit engaged to her, you know!"

"Not overtly," I answered, "because her mother doesn't like you. But I've always taken for granted a private understanding."

"Well, there *was* one. But there isn't now." That was all he said save something about Mrs. Erme's having got on her feet again in the most extraordinary way—a remark pointing, as I supposed, the moral that private understandings were of little use when the doctor didn't share them. What I took the liberty of more closely inferring was that the girl might in some way have estranged him. Well, if he had taken the turn of jealousy, for instance, it could scarcely be jealousy of me. In that case—over and above the absurdity of it—he wouldn't have gone away just to leave us together. For some time before his going we had indulged in no allusion to the buried treasure, and from his silence, which my reserve simply emulated, I had drawn a sharp conclusion. His courage had dropped, his ardour had gone the way of mine—this appearance at least he left me to scan. More than that he couldn't do; he couldn't face the triumph with which I might have greeted an explicit admission. He needn't have been afraid, poor dear, for I had by this time lost all need to triumph. In fact I considered I showed magnanimity in not reproaching him with his collapse, for the sense of his having thrown up the game made me feel more than ever how much I at last depended on him. If Corvick had broken down I should never know; no one would be of any use if *he* wasn't. It wasn't a bit true I had ceased to care for knowledge; little by little my curiosity not only had begun to ache again, but had become the familiar torment of my days and my nights. There are doubtless people to whom torments of such an order appear hardly more natural than the contortions of disease; but I don't after all know why I should in this connexion so much as mention them. For the few persons, at any rate, abnormal or not, with whom my anecdote is concerned, literature was a game of skill, and skill meant courage, and courage meant honour, and honour meant passion, meant life. The stake on the table was a special substance and our roulette the revolving mind, but we sat round the green board as intently as the grim gamblers at Monte Carlo. Gwendolen Erme, for that matter, with her white face and her fixed eyes, was of the very type of the lean ladies one had met in the temples of chance. I recognised in Corvick's absence that she made this analogy vivid. It was extravagant, I admit, the way she lived for the art of the pen. Her passion visibly preyed on her, and in her presence I felt almost tepid. I got hold of "Deep Down" again: it was a desert in which she had lost herself, but in which too she had dug a wonderful hole in the sand—a cavity out of which Corvick had still more remarkably pulled her.

Early in March I had a telegram from her, in consequence of which I repaired immediately to Chelsea, where the first thing she said to me was: "He has got it, he has got it!"

She was moved, as I could see, to such depths that she must mean the great thing. "Vereker's idea?"

"His general intention. George has cabled from Bombay."

She had the missive open there; it was emphatic though concise. "Eureka. Immense." That was all—he had saved the cost of the signature. I shared her emotion, but I was disappointed. "He doesn't say what it is."

"How could he—in a telegram? He'll write it."

"But how does he know?"

"Know it's the real thing? Oh I'm sure that when you see it you do know. Vera incessu patuit dea!"

"It's you, Miss Erme, who are a 'dear' for bringing me such news!" —I went all lengths in my high spirits. "But fancy finding our goddess in the temple of Vishnu! How strange of George to have been able to go into the thing again in the midst of such different and such powerful solicitations!"

"He hasn't gone into it, I know; it's the thing itself, let severely alone for six months, that has simply sprung out at him like a tigress out of the jungle. He didn't take a book with him—on purpose; indeed he wouldn't have needed to—he knows every page, as I do, by heart. They all worked in him together, and some day somewhere, when he wasn't thinking, they fell, in all their superb intricacy, into the one right combination. The figure in the carpet came out. That's the way he knew it would come and the real reason —you didn't in the least understand, but I suppose I may tell you now—why he went and why I consented to his going. We knew the change would do it—that the difference of thought, of scene, would give the needed touch, the magic shake. We had perfectly, we had admirably calculated. The elements were all in his mind, and in the *secousse* of a new and intense experience they just struck light." She positively struck light herself—she was literally, facially luminous. I stammered something about unconscious cerebration, and she continued: "He'll come right home—this will bring him."

"To see Vereker, you mean?"

"To see Vereker—and to see *me*. Think what he'll have to tell me!"

I hesitated. "About India?"

"About fiddlesticks! About Vereker—about the figure in the carpet."

"But, as you say, we shall surely have that in a letter."

She thought like one inspired, and I remembered how Corvick had told me long before that her face was interesting. "Perhaps it can't be got into a letter if it's 'immense.'"

"Perhaps not if it's immense bosh. If he has hold of something that can't be got into a letter he hasn't hold of *the* thing. Vereker's own statement to me was exactly that the 'figure' *would* fit into a letter."

"Well, I cabled to George an hour ago—two words," said Gwendolen.

"Is it indiscreet of me to ask what they were?"

She hung fire, but at last brought them out. "'Angel, write.'"

"Good!" I cried. "I'll make it sure—I'll send him the same."

VII

My words however were not absolutely the same—I put something instead of "angel"; and in the sequel my epithet seemed the more apt, for when eventually we heard from our traveller it was merely, it was thoroughly to be tantalised. He was magnificent in his triumph, he described his discovery as stupendous; but his ecstasy only obscured it—there were to be no particulars till he should have submitted his conception to the supreme authority. He had thrown up his commission, he had thrown up his book, he had thrown up everything but the instant need to hurry to Rapallo, on the Genoese shore, where Vereker was making a stay. I wrote him a letter which was to await him at Aden—I besought him to relieve my suspense. That he had found my letter was indicated by a telegram which, reaching me after weary days and in the absence of any answer to my laconic dispatch to him at Bombay, was evidently intended as a reply to both communications. Those few words were in familiar French, the French of the day, which Corvick often made use of to show he wasn't a prig. It had for some persons the opposite effect, but his message may fairly be paraphrased. "Have patience; I want to see, as it breaks on you, the face you'll make!" "*Tellement envie de voir ta tête!*"—that was what I had to sit down with. I can certainly not be said to have sat down, for I seem to remember myself at this time as rattling constantly between the little house in Chelsea and my own. Our impatience, Gwendolen's and mine, was equal, but I kept hoping her light would be greater. We all spent during this episode, for people of our means, a great deal of money in telegrams and cabs, and I counted on the receipt of news from Rapallo immediately after the junction of the discoverer with the discovered. The interval seemed an age, but late one day I heard a hansom precipitated to my door with the crash engendered by a hint of liberality. I lived with my heart in my mouth and accordingly bounded to the window—a movement which gave me a view of a young lady erect on the footboard of the vehicle and eagerly looking up at my house. At sight of me she flourished a paper with a movement that brought me straight down, the movement with which, in melodramas, handkerchiefs and reprieves are flourished at the foot of the scaffold.

"Just seen Vereker—not a note wrong. Pressed me to bosom—keeps me a month." So much I read on her paper while the cabby dropped a grin from his perch. In my excitement I paid him profusely and in hers she suffered it; then as he drove away we started to walk about and talk. We had talked, heaven knows, enough before, but this was a wondrous lift. We pictured the whole scene at Rapallo, where he would have written, mentioning my name, for permission to call; that is *I* pictured it, having more material than my companion, whom I felt hang on my lips as we stopped on purpose before shop-windows we didn't look into. About one thing we were clear: if he was staying on for fuller communication we should at least have a letter from him that would help us through the dregs of delay. We understood his staying on, and yet each of us saw, I think, that the other hated it. The letter we were clear about arrived; it was for Gwendolen, and I called on her in time to save her the trouble of bringing it to me. She didn't read it out, as was natural enough; but she repeated to me what it chiefly embodied. This consisted of the remarkable statement that he'd tell her after they were married exactly what she wanted to know.

"Only *then*, when I'm his wife—not before," she explained. "It's tantamount to saying—isn't it?—that I must marry him straight off!" She smiled at me while I flushed with disappointment, a vision of fresh delay that made me at first unconscious of my surprise. It seemed more than a hint that on me as well he would impose some tiresome condition. Suddenly, while she reported several more things from his letter, I remembered what he had told me before going away. He had found Mr. Vereker deliriously interesting and his own possession of the secret a real intoxication. The buried treasure was all gold and gems. Now that it was there it seemed to grow and grow before him; it would have been, through all time and taking all tongues, one of the most wonderful flowers of literary art. Nothing, in especial, once you were face to face with it, could show for more consummately *done*. When once it came out it came out, was there with a splendour that made you ashamed; and there hadn't been, save in the bottomless vulgarity of the age, with every one tasteless and tainted, every sense stopped, the smallest reason why it should have been overlooked. It was great, yet so simple, was simple, yet so great, and the final knowledge of it was an experience quite apart. He intimated that the charm of such an experience, the desire to drain it, in its freshness, to the last drop, was what kept him there close to the source. Gwendolen, frankly radiant as she tossed me these fragments, showed the elation of a prospect more assured than my own. That brought me back to the question of her marriage, prompted me to ask if what she meant by what she had just surprised me with was that she was under an engagement.

"Of course I am!" she answered. "Didn't you know it?" She seemed astonished, but I was still more so, for Corvick had told me the exact contrary. I didn't mention this, however; I only reminded her how little I had been on that score in her confidence, or even in Corvick's, and that moreover I wasn't in ignorance of her mother's interdict. At bottom I was troubled by the disparity of the two accounts; but after a little I felt Corvick's to be the one I least doubted. This simply reduced me to asking myself if the girl had on the spot improvised an engagement—vamped up an old one or dashed off a new—in order to arrive at the satisfaction she desired. She must have had resources of which I was destitute, but she made her case slightly more intelligible by returning presently: "What the state of things has been is that we felt of course bound to do nothing in mamma's lifetime."

"But now you think you'll just dispense with mamma's consent?"

"Ah it mayn't come to that!" I wondered what it might come to, and she went on: "Poor dear, she may swallow the dose. In fact, you know," she added with a laugh, "she really *must!*"—a proposition of which, on behalf of every one concerned, I fully acknowledged the force.

VIII

Nothing more vexatious had ever happened to me than to become aware before Corvick's arrival in England that I shouldn't be there to put him through. I found myself abruptly called to Germany by the alarming illness of my younger brother, who, against my advice, had gone to Munich to study, at the feet indeed of a great master, the art of portraiture in oils. The near relative who made him an allowance had threatened to withdraw it if he should, under specious pretexts, turn for superior truth to Paris—Paris being somehow, for a Cheltenham aunt, the school of evil, the abyss. I deplored this prejudice at the time, and the deep injury of it was now visible—first in the fact that it hadn't saved the poor boy, who was clever frail and foolish, from congestion of the lungs, and second in the greater break with London to which the event condemned me. I'm afraid that what was uppermost in my mind during several anxious weeks was the sense that if we had only been in Paris I might have run over to see Corvick. This was actually out of the question from every point of view: my brother, whose recovery gave us both plenty to do, was ill for three months, during which I never left him and at the end of which we had to face the absolute prohibition of a return to England. The consideration of climate imposed itself, and he was in no state to meet it alone. I took him to Meran and there spent the summer with him, trying to show him by example how to get back to work and nursing a rage of another sort that I tried *not* to show him.

The whole business proved the first of a series of phenomena so strangely interlaced that, taken all together—which was how I had to take them—they form as good an illustration as I can recall of the manner in which, for the good of his soul doubtless, fate sometimes deals with a man's avidity. These incidents certainly had larger bearings than the comparatively meagre consequence we are here concerned with—though I feel that consequence also a thing to speak of with some respect. It's mainly in such a light, I confess, at any rate, that the ugly fruit of my exile is at this hour present to me. Even at first indeed the spirit in which my avidity, as I have called it, made me regard that term owed no element of ease to the fact that before coming back from Rapallo George Corvick addressed me in a way I objected to. His letter had none of the sedative action I must to-day profess myself sure he had wished to give it, and the march of occurrences was not so ordered as to make up for what it lacked. He had begun on the spot, for one of the quarterlies, a great last word on Vereker's writings, and this exhaustive study, the only one that would have counted, have existed, was to turn on the new light, to utter —oh so quietly!—the unimagined truth. It was in other words to trace the figure in the carpet through every convolution, to reproduce it in every tint. The result, according to my friend, would be the greatest literary portrait ever painted, and what he asked of me was just to be so good as not to trouble him with questions till he should hang up his masterpiece before me. He did me the honour to declare that, putting aside the great sitter himself, all aloft in his indifference, I was individually the connoisseur he was most working for. I was therefore to be a good boy and not try to peep under the curtain before the show was ready: I should enjoy it all the more if I sat very still.

I did my best to sit very still, but I couldn't help giving a jump on seeing in *The Times*, after I had been a week or two in Munich and before, as I knew, Corvick had reached London, the announcement of the sudden death of poor Mrs. Erme. I instantly, by letter, appealed to Gwendolen for particulars, and she wrote me that her mother had yielded to long-threatened failure of the heart. She didn't say, but I took the liberty of reading into her words, that from the point of view of her marriage and also of her eagerness, which was quite a match for mine, this was a solution more prompt than could have been expected and more radical than waiting for the old lady to swallow the dose. I candidly admit indeed that at the time—for I heard from her repeatedly—I read some singular things into Gwendolen's words and some still more extraordinary ones into her silences. Pen in hand, this way, I live the time over, and it brings back the oddest sense of my having been, both for months and in spite of myself, a kind of coerced spectator. All my life had taken refuge in my eyes, which the procession of events appeared to have committed itself to keep astare. There were days when I thought of writing to Hugh Vereker and simply throwing myself on his charity. But I felt more deeply that I hadn't fallen quite so low—besides which, quite properly, he would send me about my business. Mrs. Erme's death brought Corvick straight home, and within the month he was united "very quietly"—as quietly, I seemed to make out, as he meant in his article to bring out his *trouvaille*—to the young lady he had loved and quitted. I use this last term, I may parenthetically say, because I subsequently grew sure that at the time he went to India, at the time of his great news from Bombay, there had been no positive pledge between them whatever. There had been none at the moment she was affirming to me the very opposite. On the other hand he had certainly become engaged the day he returned. The happy pair went down to Torquay for their honeymoon, and there, in a reckless hour, it occurred to poor Corvick to take his young bride a drive. He had no command of that business: this had been brought home to me of old in a little tour we had once made together in a dogcart. In a dogcart he perched his companion for a rattle over Devonshire hills, on one of the likeliest of which he brought his horse, who, it was true, had bolted, down with such violence that the occupants of the cart were hurled forward and that he fell horribly on his head. He was killed on the spot; Gwendolen escaped unhurt.

I pass rapidly over the question of this unmitigated tragedy, of what the loss of my best friend meant for me, and I complete my little history of my patience and my pain by the frank statement of my having, in a postscript to my very first letter to her after the receipt of the hideous news, asked Mrs. Corvick whether her husband mightn't at least have finished the great article on Vereker. Her answer was as prompt as my question: the article, which had been barely begun, was a mere heartbreaking scrap. She explained that our friend, abroad, had just settled down to it when interrupted by her mother's death, and that then, on his return, he had been kept from work by the engrossments into which that calamity was to plunge them. The opening pages were all that existed; they were striking, they were promising, but they didn't unveil the idol. That great intellectual feat was obviously to have formed his climax. She said nothing more, nothing to enlighten me as to the state of her own knowledge—the knowledge for the acquisition of which I had fancied her prodigiously acting. This was above all what I wanted to know: had *she* seen the idol unveiled? Had there been a private ceremony for a palpitating audience of one? For what else but that ceremony had the nuptials taken place? I didn't like as yet to press her, though when I thought of what had passed between us on the subject in Corvick's absence her reticence surprised me. It was therefore not till much later, from Meran, that I risked another appeal, risked it in some trepidation, for she continued to tell me nothing. "Did you hear in those few days of your blighted bliss," I wrote, "what we desired so to hear?" I said "we" as a little hint; and she showed me she could take a little hint. "I heard everything," she replied, "and I mean to keep it to myself!"

IX

It was impossible not to be moved with the strongest sympathy for her, and on my return to England I showed her every kindness in my power. Her mother's death had made her means sufficient, and she had gone to live in a more convenient quarter. But her loss had been great and her visitation cruel; it never would have occurred to me, moreover, to suppose she could come to feel the possession of a technical tip, of a piece of literary experience, a counterpoise to her grief. Strange to say, none the less, I couldn't help believing after I had seen her a few times that I caught a glimpse of some such oddity. I hasten to add that there had been other things I couldn't help believing, or at least imagining; and as I never felt I was really clear about these, so, as to the point I here touch on, I give her memory the benefit of the doubt. Stricken and solitary, highly accomplished and now, in her deep mourning, her maturer grace and her uncomplaining sorrow, incontestably handsome, she presented herself as leading a life of singular dignity and beauty. I had at first found a way to persuade myself that I should soon get the better of the reserve formulated, the week after the catastrophe, in her reply to an appeal as to which I was not unconscious that it might strike her as mistimed. Certainly that reserve was something of a shock to me—certainly it puzzled me the more I thought of it and even though I tried to explain it (with moments of success) by an imputation of exalted sentiments, of superstitious scruples, of a refinement of loyalty. Certainly it added at the same time hugely to the price of Vereker's secret, precious as this mystery already appeared. I may as well confess abjectly that Mrs. Corvick's unexpected attitude was the final tap on the nail that was to fix fast my luckless idea, convert it into the obsession of which I'm for ever conscious.

But this only helped me the more to be artful, to be adroit, to allow time to elapse before renewing my suit. There were plenty of speculations for the interval, and one of them was deeply absorbing. Corvick had kept his information from his young friend till after the removal of the last barrier to their intimacy—then only had he let the cat out of the bag. Was it Gwendolen's idea, taking a hint from him, to liberate this animal only on the basis of the renewal of such a relation? Was the figure in the carpet traceable or describable only for husbands and wives—for lovers supremely united? It came back to me in a mystifying manner that in Kensington Square, when I mentioned that Corvick would have told the girl he loved, some word had dropped from Vereker that gave colour to this possibility. There might be little in it, but there was enough to make me wonder if I should have to marry Mrs. Corvick to get what I wanted. Was I prepared to offer her this price for the blessing of her knowledge? Ah that way madness lay!—so I at least said to myself in bewildered hours. I could see meanwhile the torch she refused to pass on flame away in her chamber of memory—pour through her eyes a light that shone in her lonely house. At the end of six months I was fully sure of what this warm presence made up to her for. We had talked again and again of the man who had brought us together—of his talent, his character, his personal charm, his certain career, his dreadful doom, and even of his clear purpose in that great study which was to have been a supreme literary portrait, a kind of critical Vandyke or Velasquez. She had conveyed to me in abundance that she was tongue-tied by her perversity, by her piety, that she would never break the silence it had not been given to the "right person," as she said, to break. The hour, however, finally arrived. One evening when I had been sitting with her longer than usual I laid my hand firmly on her arm. "Now at last what *is* it?"

She had been expecting me and was ready. She gave a long slow

soundless headshake, merciful only in being inarticulate. This mercy
didn't prevent its hurling at me the largest finest coldest "Never!" I
had yet, in the course of a life that had known denials, had to take
full in the face. I took it and was aware that with the hard blow the
tears had come into my eyes. So for a while we sat and looked at
each other; after which I slowly rose. I was wondering if some day
she would accept me; but this was not what I brought out. I said as
I smoothed down my hat: "I know what to think then. It's nothing!"
     A remote disdainful pity for me gathered in her dim smile; then
she spoke in a voice that I hear at this hour. "It's my life!" As I stood
at the door she added: "You've insulted him!"
     "Do you mean Vereker?"
     "I mean the Dead!"
     I recognised when I reached the street the justice of her charge.
Yes, it was her life—I recognised that too; but her life none the less
made room with the lapse of time for another interest. A year and a
half after Corvick's death she published in a single volume her
second novel, "Overmastered," which I pounced on in the hope of
finding in it some tell-tale echo or some peeping face. All I found
was a much better book than her younger performance, showing I
thought the better company she had kept. As a tissue tolerably intricate it was a carpet with a figure of its own; but the figure was
not the figure I was looking for. On sending a review of it to *The
Middle* I was surprised to learn from the office that a notice was
already in type. When the paper came out I had no hesitation in at-
tributing this article, which I thought rather vulgarly overdone, to
Drayton Deane, who in the old days had been something of a friend
of Corvick's, yet had only within a few weeks made the acquaintance
of his widow. I had had an early copy of the book, but Deane had
evidently had an earlier. He lacked all the same the light hand with
which Corvick had gilded the gingerbread—he laid on the tinsel
in splotches.

X

     Six months later appeared "The Right of Way," the last chance,
though we didn't know it, that we were to have to redeem ourselves.
Written wholly during Vereker's sojourn abroad, the book had been
heralded, in a hundred paragraphs, by the usual ineptitudes. I carried it, as early a copy as any, I this time flattered myself, straightway

to Mrs. Corvick. This was the only use I had for it; I left the inevitable tribute of *The Middle* to some more ingenious mind and some less irritated temper. "But I already have it," Gwendolen said. "Drayton Deane was so good as to bring it to me yesterday, and I've just finished it."

"Yesterday? How did he get it so soon?"

"He gets everything so soon! He's to review it in *The Middle*."

"He—Drayton Deane—review Vereker?" I couldn't believe my ears.

"Why not? One fine ignorance is as good as another."

I winced but I presently said: "You ought to review him yourself!"

"I don't 'review,'" she laughed. "I'm reviewed!"

Just then the door was thrown open. "Ah yes, here's your reviewer!" Drayton Deane was there with his long legs and his tall forehead: he had come to see what she thought of "The Right of Way," and to bring news that was singularly relevant. The evening papers were just out with a telegram on the author of that work, who, in Rome, had been ill for some days with an attack of malarial fever. It had at first not been thought grave, but had taken, in consequence of complications, a turn that might give rise to anxiety. Anxiety had indeed at the latest hour begun to be felt.

I was struck in the presence of these tidings with the fundamental detachment that Mrs. Corvick's overt concern quite failed to hide: it gave me the measure of her consummate independence. That independence rested on her knowledge, the knowledge which nothing now could destroy and which nothing could make different. The figure in the carpet might take on another twist or two, but the sentence had virtually been written. The writer might go down to his grave: she was the person in the world to whom—as if she had been his favoured heir—his continued existence was least of a need. This reminded me how I had observed at a particular moment—after Corvick's death—the drop of her desire to see him face to face. She had got what she wanted without that. I had been sure that if she hadn't got it she wouldn't have been restrained from the endeavour to sound him personally by those superior reflexions, more conceivable on a man's part than on a woman's, which in my case had served as a deterrent. It wasn't however, I hasten to add, that my case, in spite of this invidious comparison, wasn't ambiguous enough. At the thought that Vereker was perhaps at that moment dying there rolled over me a wave of anguish—a poignant sense of how inconsistently I

still depended on him. A delicacy that it was my one compensation
to suffer to rule me had left the Alps and the Apennines between us,
but the sense of the waning occasion suggested that I might in my
despair at last have gone to him. Of course I should really have done
nothing of the sort. I remained five minutes, while my companions
talked of the new book, and when Drayton Deane appealed to me for
my opinion of it I made answer, getting up, that I detested Hugh
Vereker and simply couldn't read him. I departed with the moral
certainty that as the door closed behind me Deane would brand me
for awfully superficial. His hostess wouldn't contradict *that* at least.

I continue to trace with a briefer touch our intensely odd succes-
sions. Three weeks after this came Vereker's death, and before the
year was out the death of his wife. That poor lady I had never seen,
but I had had a futile theory that, should she survive him long
enough to be decorously accessible, I might approach her with the
feeble flicker of my plea. Did she know and if she knew would she
speak? It was much to be presumed that for more reasons than one
she would have nothing to say; but when she passed out of all reach
I felt renouncement indeed my appointed lot. I was shut up in my
obsession for ever—my gaolers had gone off with the key. I find
myself quite as vague as a captive in a dungeon about the time that
further elapsed before Mrs. Corvick became the wife of Drayton
Deane. I had foreseen, through my bars, this end of the business,
though there was no indecent haste and our friendship had rather
fallen off. They were both so "awfully intellectual" that it struck
people as a suitable match, but I had measured better than any one
the wealth of understanding the bride would contribute to the union.
Never, for a marriage in literary circles—so the newspapers described
the alliance—had a lady been so bravely dowered. I began with due
promptness to look for the fruit of the affair—that fruit, I mean, of
which the premonitory symptoms would be peculiarly visible in
the husband. Taking for granted the splendour of the other party's
nuptial gift, I expected to see him make a show commensurate with
his increase of means. I knew what his means had been—his article
on "The Right of Way" had distinctly given one the figure. As he
was now exactly in the position in which still more exactly I was not
I watched from month to month, in the likely periodicals, for the
heavy message poor Corvick had been unable to deliver and the responsibility of which would have fallen on his successor. The widow
and wife would have broken by the rekindled hearth the silence that

only a widow and wife might break, and Deane would be as aflame with the knowledge as Corvick in his own hour, as Gwendolen in hers, had been. Well, he was aflame doubtless, but the fire was apparently not to become a public blaze. I scanned the periodicals in vain: Drayton Deane filled them with exuberant pages, but he withheld the page I most feverishly sought. He wrote on a thousand subjects, but never on the subject of Vereker. His special line was to tell truths that other people either "funked," as he said, or overlooked, but he never told the only truth that seemed to me in these days to signify. I met the couple in those literary circles referred to in the papers: I have sufficiently intimated that it was only in such circles we were all constructed to revolve. Gwendolen was more than ever committed to them by the publication of her third novel, and I myself definitely classed by holding the opinion that this work was inferior to its immediate predecessor. Was it worse because she had been keeping worse company? If her secret was, as she had told me, her life—a fact discernible in her increasing bloom, an air of conscious privilege that, cleverly corrected by pretty charities, gave distinction to her appearance—it had yet not a direct influence on her work. That only made one—everything only made one—yearn the more for it; only rounded it off with a mystery finer and subtler.

XI

It was therefore from her husband I could never remove my eyes: I beset him in a manner that might have made him uneasy. I went even so far as to engage him in conversation. *Didn't* he know, hadn't he come into it as a matter of course?—that question hummed in my brain. Of course he knew; otherwise he wouldn't return my stare so queerly. His wife had told him what I wanted and he was amiably amused at my impotence. He didn't laugh—he wasn't a laugher: his system was to present to my irritation, so that I should crudely expose myself, a conversational blank as vast as his big bare brow. It always happened that I turned away with a settled conviction from these unpeopled expanses, which seemed to complete each other geographically and to symbolise together Drayton Deane's want of voice, want of form. He simply hadn't the art to use what he knew; he literally was incompetent to take up the duty where Corvick had left it. I went still further—it was the only glimpse of happiness I had. I made up my mind that the duty didn't appeal to him. He wasn't interested, he didn't care. Yes, it quite comforted me to believe him too stupid to have joy of the thing I lacked. He was as stupid after as he had been before, and that deepened for me the golden glory in which the mystery was wrapped. I had of course none the less to recollect that his wife might have imposed her conditions and exactions. (I had above all to remind myself that with Vereker's death the major incentive dropped.) He was still there to be honoured by what might be done—he was no longer there to give it his sanction. Who alas but he had the authority?

Two children were born to the pair, but the second cost the mother her life. After this stroke I seemed to see another ghost of a chance. I jumped at it in thought, but I waited a certain time for manners, and at last my opportunity arrived in a remunerative way. His wife had been dead a year when I met Drayton Deane in the smoking-room of a small club of which we both were members, but where for months—perhaps because I rarely entered it—I hadn't seen him. The room was empty and the occasion propitious. I deliberately offered him, to have done with the matter for ever, that advantage for which I felt he had long been looking.

"As an older acquaintance of your late wife's than even you were," I began, "you must let me say to you something I have on my mind. I shall be glad to make any terms with you that you see fit to name for the information she must have had from George Corvick—the information, you know, that had come to *him*, poor chap, in one of the happiest hours of his life, straight from Hugh Vereker."

He looked at me like a dim phrenological bust. "The information—?"

"Vereker's secret, my dear man—the general intention of his books: the string the pearls were strung on, the buried treasure, the figure in the carpet."

He began to flush—the numbers on his bumps to come out. "Vereker's books had a general intention?"

I stared in my turn. "You don't mean to say you don't know it?" I thought for a moment he was playing with me. "Mrs. Deane knew it; she had it, as I say, straight from Corvick, who had, after infinite search and to Vereker's own delight, found the very mouth of the cave. Where *is* the mouth? He told after their marriage—and told alone—the person who, when the circumstances were reproduced, must have told *you*. Have I been wrong in taking for granted that she admitted you, as one of the highest privileges of the relation in which you stood to her, to the knowledge of which she was after Corvick's death the sole depository? All *I* know is that that knowledge is infinitely precious, and what I want you to understand is that if you'll in your turn admit me to it you'll do me a kindness for which I shall be lastingly grateful."

He had turned at last very red; I dare say he had begun by thinking I had lost my wits. Little by little he followed me; on my own side I stared with a livelier surprise. Then he spoke. "I don't know what you're talking about."

He wasn't acting—it was the absurd truth. "She *didn't* tell you—?"

"Nothing about Hugh Vereker."

I was stupefied; the room went round. It had been too good even for that! "Upon your honour?"

"Upon my honour. What the devil's the matter with you?" he growled.

"I'm astounded—I'm disappointed. I wanted to get it out of you."

"It isn't *in* me!" he awkwardly laughed. "And even if it were—"

"If it were you'd let me have it—oh yes, in common humanity. But I believe you. I see—I see!" I went on, conscious, with the full turn of the wheel, of my great delusion, my false view of the poor man's attitude. What I saw, though I couldn't say it, was that his wife hadn't thought him worth enlightening. This struck me as strange for a woman who had thought him worth marrying. At last I explained it by the reflexion that she couldn't possibly have married him for his understanding. She had married him for something else.

He was to some extent enlightened now, but he was even more astonished, more disconcerted: he took a moment to compare my story with his quickened memories. The result of his meditation was his presently saying with a good deal of rather feeble form: "This is the first I hear of what you allude to. I think you must be mistaken as to Mrs. Drayton Deane's having had any unmentioned, and still less any unmentionable, knowledge of Hugh Vereker. She'd certainly have wished it—should it have borne on his literary character—to be used."

"It *was* used. She used it herself. She told me with her own lips that she 'lived' on it."

I had no sooner spoken than I repented of my words; he grew so pale that I felt as if I had struck him. "Ah 'lived'—!" he murmured, turning short away from me.

My compunction was real; I laid my hand on his shoulder. "I

beg you to forgive me—I've made a mistake. You *don't* know what I thought you knew. You could, if I had been right, have rendered me a service; and I had my reasons for assuming that you'd be in a position to meet me."

"Your reasons?" he echoed. "What were your reasons?"

I looked at him well; I hesitated; I considered. "Come and sit down with me here and I'll tell you." I drew him to a sofa, I lighted another cigar and, beginning with the anecdote of Vereker's one descent from the clouds, I recited to him the extraordinary chain of accidents that had, in spite of the original gleam, kept me till that hour in the dark. I told him in a word just what I've written out here. He listened with deepening attention, and I became aware, to my surprise, by his ejaculations, by his questions, that he would have been after all not unworthy to be trusted by his wife. So abrupt an experience of her want of trust had now a disturbing effect on him; but I saw the immediate shock throb away little by little and then gather again into waves of wonder and curiosity—waves that promised, I could perfectly judge, to break in the end with the fury of my own highest tides. I may say that to-day as victims of unappeased desire there isn't a pin to choose between us. The poor man's state is almost my consolation; there are really moments when I feel it to be quite my revenge.

Broken Wings

*C*ONSCIOUS as he was of what was between them, though perhaps less conscious than ever of why there should at that time of day be anything, he would yet scarce have supposed they could be so long in a house together without some word or some look. It had been since the Saturday afternoon, and that made twenty-four hours. The party—five-and-thirty people and some of them great—was one in which words and looks might more or less have gone astray. The effect, none the less, he judged, would have been, for her quite as for himself, that no sound and no sign from the other had been picked up by either. They had happened both at dinner and at luncheon to be so placed as not to have to glare—or to grin—across; and for the rest they could each, in such a crowd, as freely help the general ease to keep them apart as assist it to bring them together. One chance there was, of course, that might be beyond their control. He had been the night before half-surprised at not finding her his "fate" when the long procession to the dining-room solemnly hooked itself together. He would have said in advance—recognising it as one of the sharp "notes" of Mundham—that, should the gathering contain a literary lady, the literary lady would, for congruity, be apportioned to the arm, when there was a question of arms, of the gentleman present who represented the nearest thing to literature. Poor Straith represented "art," and that, no doubt, would have been near enough had not the party offered for choice a slight excess of men. The representative of art had been of the two or three who went in alone, whereas Mrs. Harvey had gone in with one of the representatives of banking.

It was certain, however, that she wouldn't again be consigned to Lord Belgrove, and it was just possible that he himself should not be again alone. She would be on the whole the most probable remedy to that state, on his part, of disgrace; and this precisely was the great interest of their situation—they were the only persons present without some advantage over somebody else. They hadn't a single advantage; they could be named for nothing but their cleverness; they were at the bottom of the social ladder. The social ladder had even at Mundham—as they might properly have been told, as indeed practically they *were* told—to end somewhere; which is no more than to say that as he strolled about and thought of many things Stuart Straith had after all a good deal the sense of helping to hold it up. Another of the things he thought of was the special oddity—for it was nothing else—of his being there at all, being there in particular so out of his order and turn. He couldn't answer for Mrs. Harvey's turn and order. It might well be that she was *in* hers; but these Saturday-to-Monday occasions had hitherto mostly struck him as great gilded cages as to which care was taken that the birds should be birds of a feather.

There had been a wonderful walk in the afternoon, within the limits of the place, to a far-away tea-house; and in spite of the combinations and changes of this episode he had still escaped the necessity of putting either his old friend or himself to the test. Also it had been all, he flattered himself, without the pusillanimity of his avoiding her. Life was indeed well understood in these great conditions; the conditions constituted in their greatness a kind of fundamental facility, provided a general exemption, bathed the hour, whatever it was, in a universal blandness, that were all a happy solvent for awkward relations. It was for instance beautiful that if their failure to meet amid so much meeting had been of Mrs. Harvey's own contrivance he couldn't be in the least vulgarly sure of it. There were places in which he would have had no doubt, places different enough from Mundham. He felt all the same and without anguish that these were much more *his* places—even if she didn't feel that they were much more hers. The day had been warm and splendid, and this moment of its wane—with dinner in sight, but as across a field of polished pink marble which seemed to say that wherever in such a house there was space there was also, benignantly, time—formed, of the whole procession of the hours, the one dearest to our friend, who on such occasions interposed it, whenever he could, between the set of impressions that ended and the set that began with "dressing." The great terraces and gardens were almost void; people had scattered, though not altogether even yet to dress. The air of the place, with the immense house all seated aloft in strength, robed with summer and crowned with success, was such as to contribute something of its own to the poetry of early evening. This visitor at any rate saw and

felt it all through one of those fine hazes of August that remind you
—at least they reminded *him*—of the artful gauze stretched across
the stage of a theatre when an effect of mystery or some particular
pantomimic ravishment is desired.

Should he in fact have to pair with Mrs. Harvey for dinner it
would be a shame to him not to have addressed her sooner; and
should she on the contrary be put with some one else the loss of so
much of the time would have but the greater ugliness. Didn't he
meanwhile make out that there were ladies in the lower garden, from
which the sound of voices, faint but, as always in the upper air of
Mundham, exceedingly sweet, was just now borne to him? She might
be among them, and if he should find her he'd let her know he
had sought her. He'd treat it frankly as an occasion for declaring
that what had happened between them—or rather what had *not*
happened—was too absurd. What at present occurred, however, was
that in his quest of her he suddenly, at the turn of an alley, perceived
her, not far off, seated in a sort of bower with the Ambassador. With
this he pulled up, going another way and pretending not to see
them. Three times already that afternoon he had observed her in
different situations with the Ambassador. He was the more struck
accordingly when, upwards of an hour later, again alone and with
his state unremedied, he saw her placed for dinner next his Excellency. It wasn't at all what would have been at Mundham her right
seat, so that it could only be explained by his Excellency's direct request. She *was* a success! This time Straith was well in her view and
could see that in the candle-light of the wonderful room, where the
lustres were, like the table, all crystal and silver, she was as handsome
as any one, taking the women of her age, and also as "smart" as the
evening before, and as true as any of the others to the law of a marked
difference in her smartness. If the beautiful way she held herself—
for decidedly it *was* beautiful—came in a great measure from the
good thing she professionally made of it all, our observer could reflect that the poor thing *he* professionally made of it probably affected his attitude in just the opposite way; but they communicated
neither in the glare nor in the grin he had dreaded. Still, their eyes
did now meet, and then it struck him her own were strange.

II

She, on her side, had her private consciousness, and quite as full a one, doubtless, as he, but with the advantage that when the company separated for the night she was not, like her friend, reduced to a vigil unalloyed. Lady Claude, at the top of the stairs, had said "May I look in—in five minutes—if you don't mind?" and then had arrived in due course and in a wonderful new beribboned gown, the thing just launched for such occasions. Lady Claude was young and earnest and delightfully bewildered and bewildering, and however interesting she might, through certain elements in her situation, have seemed to a literary lady, her own admirations and curiosities were such as from the first promised to rule the hour. She had already expressed to Mrs. Harvey a really informed enthusiasm. She not only delighted in her numerous books, which was a tribute the author had not infrequently met, but she even appeared to have read them—an appearance with which our authoress was much less acquainted. The great thing was that she also yearned to write, and that she had turned up in her fresh furbelows not only to reveal this secret and to ask for direction and comfort, but literally to make a stranger confidence, for which the mystery of midnight seemed propitious. Midnight was indeed, as the situation developed, well over before her confidence was spent, for it had ended by gathering such a current as floated forth, with everything in Lady Claude's own life, many things more in that of her adviser. Mrs. Harvey was at all events amused, touched and effectually kept awake; so by the end of half an hour they had quite got what might have been called their second wind of frankness and were using it for a discussion of the people in the house. Their primary communion had been simply on the question of the pecuniary profits of literature as the producer of so many admired volumes was prepared to present them to an aspirant. Lady Claude was in financial difficulties and desired the literary issue. This was the breathless revelation she had rustled over a mile of crimson velvet corridor to make.

"Nothing?" she had three minutes later incredulously gasped. "I can make nothing at all?" But the gasp was slight compared with the stupefaction communicated by a brief further parley, in the course of which Mrs. Harvey had, after an hesitation, taken her own plunge. "*You* make so little—wonderful *you?*" And then as the producer of the admired volumes simply sat there in her dressing-gown, with the saddest of slow headshakes, looking suddenly too wan even to care that it was at last all out: "What in that case is the use of success and celebrity and genius? You *have* no success?" She had looked almost awestruck at this further confession of her friend. They were face to face in a poor human crudity, which transformed itself quickly into an effusive embrace. "You've had it and lost it? Then when it has been as great as yours one *can* lose it?"

"More easily than one can get it."

Lady Claude continued to marvel. "But you do so much—and it's so beautiful!" On which Mrs. Harvey simply smiled again in her handsome despair, and after a moment found herself again in the arms of her visitor. The younger woman had remained for a time a good deal arrested and hushed, and had at any rate, sensitive and charming, immediately dropped, in the presence of this almost august unveiling, the question of her own thin troubles. But there are short cuts at that hour of night that morning scarce knows, and it took but little more of the breath of the real to suggest to Lady Claude more questions in such a connexion than she could answer for herself. "How then, if you haven't private means, do you get on?"

"Ah I don't get on!"

Lady Claude looked about. There were objects scattered in the fine old French room. "You've lovely things."

"Two."

"Two?"

"Two frocks. I couldn't stay another day."

"Ah what's *that?* I couldn't either," said Lady Claude soothingly. "And you have," she continued, in the same spirit, "your nice maid—"

"Who's indeed a charming woman, but my cook in disguise!" Mrs. Harvey dropped.

"Ah you *are* clever!" her friend cried with a laugh that was as a climax of reassurance.

"Extraordinarily. But don't think," Mrs. Harvey hastened to add, "that I mean that that's why I'm here."

Her companion candidly thought. "Then why are you?"

"I haven't the least idea. I've been wondering all the while, as I've wondered so often before on such occasions, and without arriving at any other reason than that London's so wild."

Lady Claude wondered. "Wild?"

"Wild!" said her friend with some impatience. "That's the way London strikes."

"But do you call such an invitation a blow?"

"Yes—crushing. No one else, at all events, either," Mrs. Harvey added, "could tell you why I'm here."

Lady Claude's power to drink in (and it was perhaps her most attaching quality) was greater still, when she felt strongly, than her power to reject. "Why how can you say that when you've only to see how every one likes and admires you? Just look at the Ambassador," she had earnestly insisted. And this was what had precisely, as I have mentioned, carried the stream of their talk a good deal away from its source. It had therefore not much further to go before setting in motion the name of Stuart Straith, as to whom Lady Claude confessed to an interest—good-looking, distinguished, "sympathetic" as he was—that she could really almost hate him for having done nothing whatever to encourage. He hadn't spoken to her once.

"But, my dear, if he hasn't spoken to *me*—!"

Lady Claude appeared to regret this not too much for a hint that after all there might be a difference. "Oh but *could* he?"

"Without my having spoken to him first?" Mrs. Harvey turned it over. "Perhaps not; but I couldn't have done that." Then to explain, and not only because Lady Claude was naturally vague, but because what was still visibly most vivid to her was her independent right to have been "made up" to: "And yet not because we're not acquainted."

"You know him then?"

"But too well."

"You mean you don't like him?"

"On the contrary I like him to distraction."

"Then what's the matter?" Lady Claude asked with some impatience.

Her friend hung fire but a moment. "Well, he wouldn't have me."

" 'Have' you?"

"Ten years ago, after Mr. Harvey's death, when if he had lifted a finger I'd have married him."

"But he didn't lift it?"

"He was too grand. I was too small—by *his* measure. He wanted to keep himself. He saw his future."

Lady Claude earnestly followed. "His present position?"

"Yes—everything that was to come to him; his steady rise in value."

"Has it been so great?"

"Surely—his situation and name. Don't you know his lovely work and what's thought of it?"

"Oh yes, I know. That's why—" But Lady Claude stopped. After which: "But if he's still keeping himself?"

"Oh it's not for me," said Mrs. Harvey.

"And evidently not for *me*. Whom then," her visitor asked, "does he think good enough?"

"Oh these great people!" Mrs. Harvey smiled.

"But *we're* great people—you and I!" And Lady Claude kissed her good-night.

"You mustn't, all the same," the elder woman said, "betray the secret of *my* greatness, which I've told you, please remember, only in the deepest confidence."

Her tone had a quiet purity of bitterness that for a moment longer held her friend, after which Lady Claude had the happy inspiration of meeting it with graceful gaiety. "It's quite for the best, I'm sure, that Mr. Straith wouldn't have you. You've kept yourself too; you'll marry yet—an ambassador!" And with another good-night she reached the door. "You say you don't get on, but you do."

"Ah!" said Mrs. Harvey with vague attenuation.

"Oh yes, you do," Lady Claude insisted, while the door emphasised it with a little clap that sounded through the still house.

III

The first night of "The New Girl" occurred, as every one remembers, three years ago, and the play is running yet, a fact that may render strange the failure to be deeply conscious of which two persons in the audience were guilty. It was not till afterwards present either to Mrs. Harvey or to Stuart Straith that "The New Girl" was one of the greatest successes of modern times. Indeed if the question had been put to them on the spot they might have appeared much at sea. But this, I may as well immediately say, was the result of their having found themselves side by side in the stalls and thereby given most of their attention to their own predicament. Straith showed he felt the importance of meeting it promptly, for he turned to his neighbour, who was already in her place, as soon as her identity had flushed well through his own arrival and subsidence. "I don't quite see how you can help speaking to me now."

Her face could only show him how long she had been aware of his approach. "The sound of your voice, coming to me straight, makes it indeed as easy for me as I could possibly desire."

He looked about at the serried rows, the loaded galleries and the stuffed boxes, with recognitions and nods; and this made between them another pause, during which, while the music seemed perfunctory and the bustle that in a London audience represents concentration increased, they felt how effectually, in the thick preoccupied medium, how extraordinarily, they were together.

"Well, that second afternoon at Mundham, just before dinner, I was very near forcing your hand. But something put me off. You're really too grand."

"Oh!" she murmured.

"Ambassadors," said Stuart Straith.

"Oh!" she again sounded. And before anything more could pass the curtain was up. It came down in due course and achieved, after various intervals, the rest of its motions without interrupting for our friends the sense of an evening of talk. They said when it was down almost nothing about the play, and when one of them toward the end put to the other, vaguely, "Is—a—this thing going?" the question had scarce the effect of being even relevant. What was clearest to them was that the people about were somehow enough taken up to leave them at their ease—but what taken up with they but half made out. Mrs. Harvey had none the less mentioned early that her presence had a reason and that she ought to attend, and her companion had asked her what she thought of a certain picture made at a given moment by the stage, in the reception of which he was so interested that it was really what had brought him. These were glances, however, that quickly strayed—strayed, for instance (as this could carry them far), in its coming to one of them to say that, whatever the piece might be, the real thing, as they had seen it at Mundham, was more than a match for any piece. For Mundham *was*, theatrically, the real thing; better for scenery, dresses, music, pretty women, bare shoulders, everything—even coherent dialogue; a much bigger and braver show, and got up, as it were, infinitely more "regardless." By Mundham they were held long enough to find themselves, though with an equal surprise, quite at one as to the special oddity of their having caught each other in such a plight. Straith said

that he supposed what his friend meant was that it was odd *he*
should have been there; to which she returned that she had been im-
puting to him exactly that judgement of her own presence.

"But why shouldn't *you* be?" he asked. "Isn't that just what you
are? Aren't you in your way—like those people—a child of fortune
and fashion?"

He got no more answer to this for some time than if he had fairly
wounded her. He indeed that evening got no answer at all that was
direct. But in the next interval she brought out with abruptness,
taking no account of some other matter he had just touched:
"Don't you really know—?"

She had paused. "Know what?"

Again she went on without heeding. "A place like Mundham is,
for me, a survival, though poor Mundham in particular won't, for
me, have survived that visit—on which it's to be pitied, isn't it?
It was a glittering ghost—since laid!—of my old time."

Straith, at this, almost gave a start. "Have *you* got a new time?"

"Do you mean you yourself have?"

"Well," said Straith, "mine may now be called middle-aged. It
seems so long, I mean, since I set my watch to it."

"Oh I haven't even a watch!" she returned with a laugh. "I'm beyond watches." After which she added: "We *might* have met more
—or, I should say perhaps, have got more out of it when we *have*
met."

"Yes, it has been too little. But I've always explained it by our
living in such different worlds."

Mrs. Harvey could risk an abruptness. "Are you unhappy?"

He gave her a mild glare. "You said just now that you're beyond
watches. I'm beyond unhappiness."

She turned from him and presently brought out: "I ought absolutely to take away *something* of the play."

"By all means. There's certainly something *I* shall take."

"Ah then you must help me—give it me."

"With all my heart," said Straith, "if it *can* help you. It's my feeling of our renewal."

She had one of the sad slow headshakes that at Mundham had been
impressive to Lady Claude. "That won't help me."

"Then you must let me put to you now what I should have tried
to get near enough to you there to put if I hadn't been so afraid of
the Ambassador. What has it been so long—our impossibility?"

"Well, I can only answer for my own vision of it, which is—which always was—that you were sorry for me, but felt a sort of scruple of showing me you had nothing better than pity to give."

"May I come to see you?" Straith asked some minutes after this.

Her words, for which he had also a while to wait, had in truth as little as his own the appearance of a reply. "*Are* you unhappy—really? Haven't you everything?"

"You're beautiful!" he said for all answer. "Mayn't I come?"

She demurred. "Where's your studio?"

"Oh not too far for me to go to places. Don't be anxious; I can walk, or even take the bus."

Mrs. Harvey once more delayed. Then she said: "Mayn't I rather come there?"

"I shall be but too delighted."

It was spoken promptly, even eagerly; yet the understanding appeared shortly after to have left between them a certain awkwardness, and it was almost as if to change the subject and relieve them equally that she suddenly reminded him of something he had spoken earlier. "You were to tell me why in particular you had to be here."

"Oh yes. To see my dresses."

"Yours!" She wondered.

"The second act. I made them out for them—designed them."

Before she could check it her tone escaped. "You?"

"I." He looked straight before him. "For the fee. And we didn't even notice them."

"*I* didn't," she confessed. But it offered the fact as a sign of her kindness for him, and this kindness was traceably what inspired something she said in the draughty porch, after the performance, while the footman of the friend, a fat rich immensely pleased lady who had given her a lift and then rejoined her from a seat in the balcony, went off to make sure of the brougham. "May I do something about your things?"

" 'Do something'?"

"When I've paid you my visit. Write something—about your pictures. I do a correspondence," said Mrs. Harvey.

He wondered as she had done in the stalls. "For a paper?"

"*The Blackport Banner.* A 'London Letter.' The new books, the new plays, the new twaddle of any sort—a little music, a little gossip, a little 'art.' You'll help me—I need it awfully—with the art. I do three a month."

"You—wonderful you?" He spoke as Lady Claude had done, and could no more help it again than Mrs. Harvey had been able to help it in the stalls.

"Oh as you say, for the fee!" On which, as the footman signalled, her old lady began to plunge through the crowd.

IV

At the studio, where she came to him within the week, her first movement had been to exclaim on the splendid abundance of his work. She had looked round charmed—so struck as to be, as she called it, crushed. "You've such a wonderful lot to show."

"Indeed I have!" said Stuart Straith.

"That's where you beat *us*."

"I think it may very well be," he went on, "where I beat almost every one."

"And is much of it new?"

He looked about with her. "Some of it's pretty old. But my things have a way, I admit, of growing old extraordinarily fast. They seem to me in fact nowadays quite 'born old.'"

She had after a little the manner of coming back to something. "You *are* unhappy. You're *not* beyond it. You're just nicely, just fairly and squarely, in the middle of it."

"Well," said Straith, "if it surrounds me like a desert, so that I'm lost in it, that comes to the same thing. But I want you to tell me about yourself."

She had continued at first to move about and had taken out a pocket-book, which she held up at him. "This time I shall insist on notes. You made my mind a blank about that play, which is the sort of thing we can't afford. If it hadn't been for my fat old lady and the next day's papers!" She kept looking, going up to things, saying "How wonderful!" and "Oh your *way!*" and then stopping for a general impression, something in the whole charm. The place, high hand-some neat, with two or three pale tapestries and several rare old pieces of furniture, showed a perfection of order, an absence of loose objects, as if it had been swept and squared for the occasion and made almost too immaculate. It was polished and cold—rather cold for the season and the weather; and Stuart Straith himself, buttoned and brushed, as fine and as clean as his room, might at her arrival have reminded her of the master of a neat bare ship on his deck and awaiting a cargo. "May I see everything? May I 'use' everything?"

"Oh no; you mayn't by any means use everything. You mayn't use half. *Did* I spoil your 'London Letter'?" he continued after a moment.

"No one can spoil them as I spoil them myself. I can't do them— I don't know how, and don't want to. I do them wrong, and the people want such trash. Of course they'll 'sack' me."

She was in the centre, and he had the effect of going round her, restless and vague, in large slow circles. "Have you done them long?"

"Two or three months—this lot. But I've done others and I know what happens. Oh, my dear, I've done strange things!"

"And is it a good job?"

She hesitated, then puffed prettily enough an indifferent sigh. "Three and ninepence. Is that good?" He had stopped before her, looking at her up and down. "What do you get?" she went on, "for what you do for a play?"

"A little more, it would seem, than you. Four and sixpence. But I've only done as yet that one. Nothing else has offered."

"I see. But something *will*, eh?"

Poor Straith took a turn again. "Did you like them—for colour?" But again he pulled up. "Oh I forgot; we didn't notice them!"

For a moment they could laugh about it. "I noticed them, I assure you, in the *Banner*. 'The costumes in the second act are of the most marvellous beauty.' That's what I said."

"Oh that'll fetch the managers!" But before her again he seemed to take her in from head to foot. "You speak of 'using' things. If you'd only use yourself—for my enlightenment. Tell me all."

"You look at me," said Mrs. Harvey, "as with the wonder of who designs *my* costumes. How I dress on it, how I do even what I still do on it—on the three and ninepence—is *that* what you want to know?"

"What has happened to you?" Straith asked.

"How do I keep it up?" she continued as if she hadn't heard him. "But I *don't* keep it up. *You* do," she declared as she again looked round her.

Once more it set him off, but for a pause again almost as quick. "How long have you been—?"

"Been what?" she asked as he faltered.

"Unhappy."

She smiled at him from a depth of indulgence. "As long as you've been ignorant—that what I've been *wanting* is your pity. Ah to have to know, as I believed I did, that you supposed it would wound me, and not to have been able to make you see it was the one thing left to me that would help me! Give me your pity now. It's all I want. I don't care for anything else. But give me that."

He had, as it happened at the moment, to do a smaller and a usual thing before he could do one so great and so strange. The youth whom he kept for service arrived with a tea-tray, in arranging a place for which, with the sequel of serving Mrs. Harvey, seating her and seeing the youth again out of the room, some minutes passed. "What pity could I dream of for you," he demanded as he at last dropped near her, "when I was myself so miserably sore?"

"Sore?" she wondered. "But you were happy—then."

"Happy not to have struck you as good enough? For I didn't, you know," he insisted. "You had your success, which was so immense. You had your high value, your future, your big possibilities; and I perfectly understood that, given those things, and given also my very much smaller situation, you should wish to keep yourself."

"Oh, oh!" She gasped as if hurt.

"I understand it; but how could it really make me 'happy'?" he asked.

She turned at him as with her hand on the old scar she could now carry. "You mean that all these years you've really not known—?"

"But not known what?"

His voice was so blank that at the sound of it, and at something that looked out from him, she only found another "Oh, oh!" which became the next instant a burst of tears.

V

She had appeared at first unwilling to receive him at home; but he understood it after she had left him, turning over more and more everything their meeting had shaken to the surface and piecing together memories that at last, however darkly, made a sense. He was to call on her, it was finally agreed, but not till the end of the week, when she should have finished "moving"—she had but just changed quarters; and meanwhile, as he came and went, mainly in the cold chamber of his own past endeavour, which looked even to himself as studios look when artists are dead and the public, in the arranged place, are admitted to stare, he had plenty to think about. What had come out—he could see it now—was that each, ten years before, had miserably misunderstood and then had turned for relief from pain to a perversity of pride. But it was himself above all he now sharply judged, since women, he felt, have to get on as they can, and for the mistake of this woman there were reasons he had to acknowledge with a sore heart. She had really found in the pomp of his early success, at the time they used to meet, and to care to, exactly the ground for her sense of failure with him that he had found in the vision of her gross popularity for his conviction that she judged him as comparatively small. Each had blundered, as sensitive souls of the "artistic temperament" blunder, into a conception not only of the other's attitude, but of the other's material situation at the moment, that had thrown them back on stupid secrecy, where their estrangement had grown like an evil plant in the shade. He had positively believed her to have gone on all the while making the five thousand a year that the first eight or ten of her so supremely happy novels had brought her in, just as she on her side had read into the felicity of his first new hits, his pictures "of the year" at three or four Academies, the absurdest theory of the sort of career that, thanks to big dealers and intelligent buyers, his gains would have built up for him. It looked vulgar enough now, but it had been grave enough then. His long detached delusion about her "prices," at any rate, appeared to have been more than matched by the strange stories occasionally floated to her—and all to make her but draw more closely in—on the subject of his own.

It was with each equally that everything had changed—everything but the stiff consciousness in either of the need to conceal changes from the other. If she had cherished for long years the soreness of her not being "good" enough, so this was what had counted most in her sustained effort to appear at least as good as he. London meanwhile was big, London was blind and benighted; and nothing had ever occurred to undermine for him the fiction of her prosperity. Before his eyes there while she sat with him she had pulled off one by one those vain coverings of her state that she confessed she had hitherto done her best—and so always with an eye on himself—deceptively to draw about it. He had felt frozen, as he listened, by such likenesses to things he knew. He recognised as she talked, he groaned as he understood. He understood—oh at last, whatever he hadn't done before! And yet he could well have smiled, out of their common abyss, at such odd identities and recurrences. Truly the arts were sisters, as was so often said; for what apparently could be more like the experience of one than the experience of another? And she spared him things with it all. He felt this too, just as, even while showing her how he followed, he had bethought himself of closing his lips for the hour, none too soon, on his own stale story. There had been a beautiful intelligence for that matter in her having asked him nothing more. She had overflowed because shaken by not finding him happy, and her surrender had somehow offered itself to him as her way—the first that sprang up—of considering his trouble. She had left him at all events in full possession of all the phases through which in "literary circles" acclaimed states may pass on their regular march to eclipse and extinction. One had but one's hour, and if one had it soon—it was really almost a case of choice—one didn't have it late. It might also never even remotely have approached, at its best, things ridiculously rumoured. Straith felt on the whole how little he had known of literary circles, or of any mystery but his own indeed; on which, up to actual impending collapse, he had mounted such anxious guard.

It was when he went on the Friday to see her that he took in the latest of the phases in question, which might very well be almost the final one; there was at least that comfort in it. She had just settled in a small flat, where he recognised in the steady disposal, for the best, of various objects she had not yet parted with, her reason for having made him wait. Here they had together—these two worn and baffled workers—a wonderful hour of gladness in their lost battle and of freshness in their lost youth; for it was not till Stuart Straith had also raised the heavy mask and laid it beside her own on the table that they began really to feel themselves recover something of that possibility of each other they had so wearily wasted. Only she couldn't get over it that he was like herself and that what she had shrunken to in her three or four simplified rooms had its perfect image in the specious show of his ordered studio and his accumulated work. He told everything now, kept no more back than she had kept at their previous meeting, while she repeated over and over "You—wonderful you?" as if the knowledge made a deeper darkness of fate, as if the pain of his having come down at all almost quenched the joy of his having come so much nearer. When she learned that he hadn't for three years sold a picture—

"You, beautiful you?"—it seemed a new cold breath out of the dusk
of her own outlook. Disappointment and despair were in such relations contagious, and there was clearly as much less again left to her
as the little that was left to him. He showed her, laughing at the
long queerness of it, how awfully little, as they called it, this was. He
let it all come, but with more mirth than misery, and with a final
abandonment of pride that was like changing at the end of a dreadful day from tight shoes to loose ones. There were moments when
they might have resembled a couple united by some misdeed and
meeting to decide on some desperate course; they gave themselves so
to the great irony—the vision of the comic in contrasts—that precedes
surrenders and extinctions.

They went over the whole thing, remounted the dwindling stream,
reconstructed, explained, understood—recognised in short the particular example they gave and how without mutual suspicion they
had been giving it side by side. "We're simply the case," Straith
familiarly put it, "of having been had enough of. No case is perhaps
more common, save that for you and for me, each in our line, it did
look in the good time—didn't it?—as if nobody *could* have enough."
With which they counted backward, gruesome as it was, the symptoms of satiety up to the first dawn, and lived again together the unforgettable hours—distant now—out of which it had begun to glimmer that the truth had to be faced and the right names given to the
wrong facts. They laughed at their original explanations and the
minor scale even of their early fears; compared notes on the fallibility
of remedies and hopes and, more and more united in the identity
of their lesson, made out perfectly that, though there appeared to
be many kinds of success, there was only one kind of failure. And yet
what had been hardest had not been to have to shrink, but in the
long game of bluff as Straith called it, to have to keep up. It fairly
swept them away at present, however, the hugeness of the relief
of no longer keeping up as against each other. This gave them all the
measure of the motive their courage, on either side, in silence and
gloom, had forced into its service.

"Only what shall we do now for a motive?" Straith went on.

She thought. "A motive for courage?"

"Yes—to keep up."

"And go again for instance, do you mean, to Mundham? We
shall, thank heaven, never go again to Mundham. The Mundha
are over."

"Nous n'irons plus au bois;
Les lauriers sont coupés,"

sang Straith. "It does cost."

"As everything costs that one does for the rich. It's not our poor relations who make us pay."

"No; one must have means to acknowledge the others. We can't afford the opulent. But it isn't only the money they take."

"It's the imagination," said Mrs. Harvey. "As they have none themselves—"

"It's an article we have to supply? We've certainly to use a lot to protect ourselves," Straith agreed. "And the strange thing is they like us."

She thought again. "That's what makes it easy to cut them. They forgive."

"Yes," her companion laughed; "once they really don't know you enough—!"

"They treat you as old friends. But what do we want now of courage?" she went on.

He wondered. "Yes, after all, what?"

"To keep up, I mean. Why *should* we keep up?"

It seemed to strike him. "I see. After all, why? The courage *not* to keep up—!"

"We have *that* at least," she declared, "haven't we?" United there at her little high-perched window overhanging grey house-tops they let the consideration of this pass between them in a deep look as well as in a hush of which the intensity had something commensurate. "If we're beaten—!" she then continued.

"Let us at least be beaten together!" He took her in his arms, she let herself go, and he held her long and close for the compact. But when they had recovered themselves enough to handle their agreement more responsibly the words in which they confirmed it broke in sweetness as well as sadness from both together: "And now to work!"

The Stor

THE weather had turned so much worse that the rest ᴏ ᴛʜe day
was certainly lost. The wind had risen and the storm gathered
force; they gave from time to time a thump at the firm windows and
dashed even against those protected by the verandah their vicious
splotches of rain. Beyond the lawn, beyond the cliff, the great wet
brush of the sky dipped deep into the sea. But the lawn, already
vivid with the touch of May, showed a violence of watered green;
the budding shrubs and trees repeated the note as they tossed their
thick masses, and the cold troubled light, filling the pretty saloon,
marked the spring afternoon as sufficiently young. The two ladies
seated there in silence could pursue without difficulty—as well as,
clearly, without interruption—their respective tasks; a confidence
expressed, when the noise of the wind allowed it to be heard, by the
sharp scratch of Mrs. Dyott's pen at the table where she was busy
with letters.

Her visitor, settled on a small sofa that, with a palm-tree, a screen,
a stool, a stand, a bowl of flowers, and three photographs in silver
frames, had been arranged near the light wood-fire as a choice "corner"—Maud Blessingbourne, her guest, turned audibly, though at
intervals neither brief nor regular, the leaves of a book covered in
lemon-coloured paper and not yet despoiled of a certain fresh crisp-
ness. This effect of the volume, for the eye, would have made it, as
presumably the newest French novel—and evidently, from the attitude of the reader, "good"—consort happily with the special tone of
the room, a consistent air of selection and suppression, one of the
finer esthetic evolutions. If Mrs. Dyott was fond of ancient French
furniture, and distinctly difficult about it, her inmates could be fond
—with whatever critical cocks of charming dark-braided heads over
slender sloping shoulders—of modern French authors. Nothing had
passed for half an hour—nothing, at least, to be exact, but that each
of the companions occasionally and covertly intermitted her pursuit
in such a manner as to ascertain the degree of absorption of the other
without turning round. What their silence was charged with, there-

was not only a sense of the weather, but a sense, so to speak, of its own nature. Maud Blessingbourne, when she lowered her book into her lap, closed her eyes with a conscious patience that seemed to say she waited; but it was nevertheless she who at last made the movement representing a snap of their tension. She got up and stood by the fire, into which she looked a minute; then came round and approached the window as if to see what was really going on. At this Mrs. Dyott wrote with refreshed intensity. Her little pile of letters had grown, and if a look of determination was compatible with her fair and slightly faded beauty, the habit of attending to her business could always keep pace with any excursion of her thought. Yet she was the first who spoke.

"I trust your book has been interesting."

"Well enough; a little mild."

A louder throb of the tempest had blurred the sound of the words. "A little wild?"

"Dear, no—timid and tame; unless I've quite lost my sense."

"Perhaps you have," Mrs. Dyott placidly suggested—"reading so many."

Her companion made a motion of feigned despair. "Ah, you take away my courage for going to my room, as I was just meaning to, for another."

"Another French one?"

"I'm afraid."

"Do you carry them by the dozen—"

"Into innocent British homes?" Maud tried to remember. "I believe I brought three—seeing them in a shop window as I passed through town. It never rains but it pours! But I've already read two."

"And are they the only ones you do read?"

"French ones?" Maud considered. "Oh, no. D'Annunzio."

"And what's that?" Mrs. Dyott asked as she affixed a stamp.

"Oh, you dear thing!" Her friend was amused, yet almost showed pity. "I know you don't read," Maud went on; "but why should you? *You* live!"

"Yes—wretchedly enough," Mrs. Dyott returned, getting her letters together. She left her place, holding them as a neat, achieved handful, and came over to the fire, while Mrs. Blessingbourne turned once more to the window, where she was met by another flurry.

Maud spoke then as if moved only by the elements. "Do you expect him through all this?"

Mrs. Dyott just waited, and it had the effect, indescribably, of making everything that had gone before seem to have led up to the question. This effect was even deepened by the way she then said, "Whom do you mean?"

"Why, I thought you mentioned at luncheon that Colonel Voyt was to walk over. Surely he can't."

"Do you care very much?" Mrs. Dyott asked.

Her friend now hesitated. "It depends on what you call 'much.' If you mean should I like to see him—then certainly."

"Well, my dear, I think he understands you're here."

"So that as he evidently isn't coming," Maud laughed, "it's particularly flattering! Or rather," she added, giving up the prospect again, "it would be, I think, quite extraordinarily flattering if he did. Except that, of course," she threw in, "he might come partly for you."

" 'Partly' is charming. Thank you for 'partly.' If you *are* going upstairs, will you kindly," Mrs. Dyott pursued, "put these into the box as you pass?"

The younger woman, taking the little pile of letters, considered them with envy. "Nine! You *are* good. You're always a living reproach!"

Mrs. Dyott gave a sigh. "I don't do it on purpose. The only thing, this afternoon," she went on, reverting to the other question, "would be their not having come down."

"And as to that you don't know."

"No—I don't know." But she caught even as she spoke a rat-tat-tat of the knocker, which struck her as a sign. "Ah, there!"

"Then I go." And Maud whisked out.

Mrs. Dyott, left alone, moved with an air of selection to the window, and it was as so stationed, gazing out at the wild weather, that the visitor, whose delay to appear spoke of the wiping of boots and the disposal of drenched mackintosh and cap, finally found her. He was tall lean fine, with little in him, on the whole, to confirm the titular in the "Colonel Voyt" by which he was announced. But he had left the army, so that his reputation for gallantry mainly depended now on his fighting Liberalism in the House of Commons. Even these facts, however, his aspect scantily matched; partly, no doubt, because he looked, as was usually said, un-English. His black hair, cropped close, was lightly powdered with silver, and his dense glossy beard, that of an emir or a caliph, and grown for civil reasons, repeated its handsome colour and its somewhat foreign effect. His nose had a strong and shapely arch, and the dark grey of his eyes was tinted with blue. It had been said of him—in relation to these signs—that he would have struck you as a Jew had he not, in spite of his nose, struck you so much as an Irishman. Neither responsibility could in fact have been fixed upon him, and just now, at all events, he was only a pleasant weather-washed wind-battered Briton, who brought in from a struggle with the elements that he appeared quite to have enjoyed a certain amount of unremoved mud and an unusual quantity of easy expression. It was exactly the silence ensuing on the retreat of the servant and the closed door that marked between him and his hostess the degree of this ease. They met, as it were, twice: the first time while the servant was there and the second as soon as he was not. The difference was great between the two encounters, though we must add in justice to the second that its marks were at first mainly negative. This communion consisted only in their having drawn each other for a minute as close as possible—as possible, that is, with no help but the full clasp of hands. Thus they were mutually held, and the closeness was at any rate such that, for a little, though it took account of dangers, it did without words. When words presently came the pair were talking by the fire, and she had rung for tea. He had by this time asked if the note he had despatched to her after breakfast had been safely delivered.

"Yes, before luncheon. But I'm always in a state when—except for some extraordinary reason—you send such things by hand. I knew, without it, that you had come. It never fails. I'm sure when you're there—I'm sure when you're not."

He wiped, before the glass, his wet moustache. "I see. But this morning I had an impulse."

"It was beautiful. But they make me as uneasy, sometimes, your impulses, as if they were calculations; make me wonder what you have in reserve."

"Because when small children are too awfully good they die? Well, I *am* a small child compared to you—but I'm not dead yet. I cling to life."

He had covered her with his smile, but she continued grave. "I'm not half so much afraid when you're nasty."

"Thank you! What then did you do," he asked, "with my note?"

"You deserve that I should have spread it out on my dressing-table —or left it, better still, in Maud Blessingbourne's room."

He wondered while he laughed. "Oh, but what does *she* deserve?"

It was her gravity that continued to answer. "Yes—it would probably kill her."

"She believes so in you?"

"She believes so in *you*. So don't be *too* nice to her."

He was still looking, in the chimney-glass, at the state of his beard —brushing from it, with his handkerchief, the traces of wind and wet. "If she also then prefers me when I'm nasty, it seems to me I ought to satisfy her. Shall I now, at any rate, see her?"

"She's so like a pea on a pan over the possibility of it that she's pulling herself together in her room."

"Oh then, we must try and keep her together. But why, graceful, tender, pretty too—quite or almost as she is—doesn't she re-marry?"

Mrs. Dyott appeared—and as if the first time—to look for the reason. "Because she likes too many men."

It kept up his spirits. "And how many *may* a lady like—"

"In order not to like any of them too much? Ah that, you know, I never found out—and it's too late now. When," she presently pursued, "did you last see her?"

He really had to think. "Would it have been since last November or so?—somewhere or other where we spent three days."

"Oh at Surredge? I know all about that. I thought you also met afterwards."

He had again to recall. "So we did! Wouldn't it have been somewhere at Christmas? But it wasn't by arrangement!" he laughed, giving with his forefinger a little pleasant nick to his hostess's chin. Then as if something in the way she received this attention put him back to his question of a moment before. "Have you kept my note?"

She held him with her pretty eyes. "Do you want it back?"

"Ah don't speak as if I did take things—!"

She dropped her gaze to the fire. "No, you don't; not even the hard things a really generous nature often would." She quitted, however, as if to forget that, the chimney-place. "I put it *there!*"

"You've burnt it? Good!" It made him easier, but he noticed the next moment on a table the lemon-coloured volume left there by Mrs. Blessingbourne, and, taking it up for a look, immediately put it down. "You might while you were about it, have burnt that too."

"You've read it?"

"Dear yes. And you?"

"No," said Mrs. Dyott; "it wasn't for me Maud brought it."

It pulled her visitor up. "Mrs. Blessingbourne brought it?"

"For such a day as this." But she wondered. "How you look! Is it so awful?"

"Oh like his others." Something had occurred to him; his thought was already far. "Does she know?"

"Know what?"

"Why anything."

But the door opened too soon for Mrs. Dyott, who could only murmur quickly—"Take care!"

II

It was in fact Mrs. Blessingbourne, who had under her arm the book she had gone up for—a pair of covers showing this time a pretty, a candid blue. She was followed next minute by the servant, who brought in tea, the consumption of which, with the passage of greetings, inquiries and other light civilities between the two visitors, occupied a quarter of an hour. Mrs. Dyott meanwhile, as a contribution to so much amenity, mentioned to Maud that her fellow-guest wished to scold her for the books she read—a statement met by this friend with the remark that he must first be sure about them. But as soon as he had picked up the new, the blue volume he broke out into a frank "Dear, dear!"

"Have you read that too?" Mrs. Dyott inquired. "How much you'll have to talk over together! The other one," she explained to him, "Maud speaks of as terribly tame."

"Ah, I must have that out with her! You don't feel the extraordinary force of the fellow?" Voyt went on to Mrs. Blessingbourne.

And so, round the hearth, they talked—talked soon, while they warmed their toes, with zest enough to make it seem as happy a chance as any of the quieter opportunities their imprisonment might have involved. Mrs. Blessingbourne did feel, it then appeared, the force of the fellow, but she had her reserves and reactions, in which Voyt was much interested. Mrs. Dyott rather detached herself, mainly gazing, as she leaned back, at the fire; she intervened, however, enough to relieve Maud of the sense of being listened to. That sense, with Maud, was too apt to convey that one was listened to for a fool. "Yes, when I read a novel I mostly read a French one," she had said to Voyt in answer to a question about her usual practice; "for I seem with it to get hold more of the real thing—to get more life for my money. Only I'm not so infatuated with them but that sometimes for months and months on end I don't read any fiction at all."

The two books were now together beside them. "Then when you begin again you read a mass?"

"Dear, no. I only keep up with three or four authors."

He laughed at this over the cigarette he had been allowed to light. "I like your 'keeping up,' and keeping up in particular with 'authors.'"

"One must keep up with somebody," Mrs. Dyott threw off.

"I dare say I'm ridiculous," Mrs. Blessingbourne conceded without heeding it; "but that's the way we express ourselves in my part of the country."

"I only alluded," said Voyt, "to the tremendous conscience of your sex. It's more than mine can keep up with. You take everything too hard. But if you can't read the novel of British and American manufacture, heaven knows I'm at one with you. It seems really to show our sense of life as the sense of puppies and kittens."

"Well," Maud more patiently returned, "I'm told all sorts of people are now doing wonderful things; but somehow I remain outside."

"Ah, it's *they*, it's our poor twangers and twaddlers who remain outside. They pick up a living in the street. And who indeed would want them in?"

Mrs. Blessingbourne seemed unable to say, and yet at the same time to have her idea. The subject, in truth, she evidently found, was not so easy to handle. "People lend me things, and I try; but at the end of fifty pages—"

"There you are! Yes—heaven help us!"

"But what I mean," she went on, "isn't that I don't get woefully weary of the eternal French thing. What's *their* sense of life?"

"Ah, *voilà!*" Mrs. Dyott softly sounded.

"Oh, but it *is* one; you can make it out," Voyt promptly declared. "They do what they feel, and they feel more things than we. They strike so many more notes, and with so different a hand. When it comes to any account of a relation say between a man and a woman —I mean an intimate or a curious or a suggestive one—where are we compared to them? They don't exhaust the subject, no doubt," he admitted; "but we don't touch it, don't even skim it. It's as if we denied its existence, its possibility. You'll doubtless tell me, however," he went on, "that as all such relations *are* for us at the most much simpler we can only have all round less to say about them."

She met this imputation with the quickest amusement. "I beg your pardon. I don't think I shall tell you anything of the sort. I don't know that I even agree with your premiss."

"About such relations?" He looked agreeably surprised. "You think we make them larger?—or subtler?"

Mrs. Blessingbourne leaned back, not looking, like Mrs. Dyott, at the fire, but at the ceiling. "I don't know what I think."

"It's not that she doesn't know," Mrs. Dyott remarked. "It's only that she doesn't say."

But Voyt had this time no eye for their hostess. For a moment he watched Maud. "It sticks out of you, you know, that you've yourself written something. Haven't you—and published? I've a notion I could read *you*."

"When I do publish," she said without moving, "you'll be the last one I shall tell. I *have*," she went on, "a lovely subject, but it would take an amount of treatment—!"

"Tell us then at least what it is."

At this she again met his eyes. "Oh, to tell it would be to express it, and that's just what I can't do. What I meant to say just now," she added, "was that the French, to my sense, give us only again and again, for ever and ever, the same couple. There they are once more, as one has had them to satiety, in that yellow thing, and there I shall certainly again find them in the blue."

"Then why do you keep reading about them?" Mrs. Dyott demanded.

Maud cast about. "I don't!" she sighed. "At all events, I shan't any more. I give it up."

"You've been looking for something, I judge," said Colonel Voyt, "that you're not likely to find. It doesn't exist."

"What is it?" Mrs. Dyott desired to know.

"I never look," Maud remarked, "for anything but an interest."

"Naturally. But your interest," Voyt replied, "is in something different from life."

"Ah not a bit! I *love* life—in art, though I hate it anywhere else. It's the poverty of the life those people show, and the awful bounders. of both sexes, that they represent."

"Oh now we have you!" her interlocutor laughed. "To me, when all's said and done, they seem to be—as near as art can come—in the truth of the truth. It can only take what life gives it, though it certainly may be a pity that that isn't better. Your complaint of their

monotony is a complaint of their conditions. When you say we get
always the same couple what do you mean but that we get always
the same passion? Of course we do!" Voyt pursued. "If what you're
looking for is another, that's what you won't anywhere find."

Maud for a while said nothing, and Mrs. Dyott seemed to wait.
"Well, I suppose I'm looking, more than anything else, for a decent
woman."

"Oh then, you mustn't look for her in pictures of passion. That's
not her element nor her whereabouts."

Mrs. Blessingbourne weighed the objection. "Doesn't it depend
on what you mean by passion?"

"I think I can mean only one thing: the enemy to behaviour."

"Oh, I can imagine passions that are on the contrary friends to it."

Her fellow guest thought. "Doesn't it depend perhaps on what you
mean by behaviour?"

"Dear, no. Behaviour's just behaviour—the most definite thing
in the world."

"Then what do you mean by the 'interest' you just now spoke of?
The picture of that definite thing?"

"Yes—call it that. Women aren't *always* vicious, even when
they're—"

"When they're what?" Voyt pressed.

"When they're unhappy. They can be unhappy and good."

"That one doesn't for a moment deny. But can they be 'good' and
interesting?"

"That must be Maud's subject!" Mrs. Dyott interposed. "To show
a woman who *is*. I'm afraid, my dear," she continued, "you could
only show yourself."

"You'd show then the most beautiful specimen conceivable"—and
Voyt addressed himself to Maud. "But doesn't it prove that life is,
against your contention, more interesting than art? Life you em-
bellish and elevate; but art would find itself able to do nothing with
you, and, on such impossible terms, would ruin you,"

The colour in her faint consciousness gave beauty to her stare.
" 'Ruin' me?"

"He means," Mrs. Dyott again indicated, "that you'd ruin 'art.' "

"Without, on the other hand"—Voyt seemed to assent—"its giving
at all a coherent impression of you."

"She wants her romance cheap!" said Mrs. Dyott.

"Oh, no—I should be willing to pay for it. I don't see why the

romance—since you give it that name—should be all, as the French
inveterately make it, for the women who are bad."

"Oh, they pay for it!" said Mrs. Dyott.

"*Do* they?"

"So, at least"—Mrs. Dyott a little corrected herself—"one has
gathered (for I don't read your books, you know!) that they're usually shown as doing."

Maud wondered, but looking at Voyt. "They're shown often, no
doubt, as paying for their badness. But are they shown as paying
for their romance?"

"My dear lady," said Voyt, "their romance *is* their badness. There
isn't any other. It's a hard law, if you will, and a strange, but goodness has to go without that luxury. Isn't to *be* good just exactly, all
round, to go without?" He put it before her kindly and clearly—
regretfully too, as if he were sorry the truth should be so sad. He and
she, his pleasant eyes seemed to say, would, had they had the making
of it, have made it better. "One has heard it before—at least *I* have;
one has heard your question put. But always, when put to a mind not
merely muddled, for an inevitable answer. 'Why don't you, *cher
monsieur*, give us the drama of virtue?' 'Because, *chère madame*, the
high privilege of virtue is precisely to avoid drama.' The adventures
of the honest lady? The honest lady hasn't, can't possibly have, adventures."

Mrs. Blessingbourne only met his eyes at first, smiling with a certain intensity. "Doesn't it depend a little on what you call adventures?"

"My poor Maud," said Mrs. Dyott, as if in compassion for sophistry
so simple, "adventures are just adventures. That's all you can make
of them!"

But her friend talked for their companion and as if without hearing. "Doesn't it depend a good deal on what you call drama?" Maud
spoke as one who had already thought it out. "Doesn't it depend on
what you call romance?"

Her listener gave these arguments his very best attention. "Of
course you may call things anything you like—speak of them as one
thing and mean quite another. But why should it depend on anything? Behind these words we use—the adventure, the novel, the
drama, the romance, the situation, in short, as we most comprehensively say—behind them all stands the same sharp fact that they
all, in their different ways, represent.

"Precisely!" Mrs. Dyott was full of approval.

Maud however was full of vagueness. "What great fact?"

"The fact of a relation. The adventure's a relation; the relation's an adventure. The romance, the novel, the drama are the picture of one. The subject the novelist treats is the rise, the formation, the development, the climax, and for the most part the decline, of one. And what is the honest lady doing on that side of the town?"

Mrs. Dyott was more pointed. "She doesn't so much as *form* a relation."

But Maud bore up. "Doesn't it depend again on what you call a relation?"

"Oh," said Mrs. Dyott, "if a gentleman picks up her pocket-hand-kerchief—"

"Ah, even that's one," their friend laughed, "if she has thrown it to him. We can only deal with one that *is* one."

"Surely," Maud replied. "But if it's an innocent one—?"

"Doesn't it depend a good deal," Mrs. Dyott asked, "on what you call innocent?"

"You mean that the adventures of innocence have so often been the material of fiction? Yes," Voyt replied; "that's exactly what the bored reader complains of. He has asked for bread and been given a stone. What is it but, with absolute directness, a question of interest, or, as people say, of the story? What's a situation undeveloped but a subject lost? If a relation stops, where's the story? If it doesn't stop, where's the innocence? It seems to me you must choose. It would be very pretty if it were otherwise, but that's how we flounder. Art is our flounderings shown."

Mrs. Blessingbourne—and with an air of deference scarce supported perhaps by its sketchiness—kept her deep eyes on this definition. "But sometimes we flounder out."

It immediately touched in Colonel Voyt the spring of a genial derision. "That's just where I expected *you* would! One always sees it come."

"He has, you notice," Mrs. Dyott parenthesised to Maud, "seen it come so often; and he has always waited for it and met it."

"Met it, dear lady, simply enough! It's the old story, Mrs. Blessingbourne. The relation's innocent that the heroine gets out of. The book's innocent that's the story of her getting out. But what the devil—in the name of innocence—was she doing *in?*"

Mrs. Dyott promptly echoed the question. "You have to be in, you know, to *get* out. So there you are already with your relation. It's the end of your goodness."

"And the beginning," said Voyt, "of your play!"

"Aren't they all, for that matter, even the worst," Mrs. Dyott pursued, "supposed *some* time or other to get out? But if, meanwhile, they've been in, however briefly, long enough to adorn a tale—"

"They've been in long enough to point a moral. That is to point ours!" With which, and as if a sudden flush of warmer light had moved him, Colonel Voyt got up. The veil of the storm had parted over a great red sunset.

Mrs. Dyott also was on her feet, and they stood before his charming antagonist, who, with eyes lowered and a somewhat fixed smile, had not moved. "We've spoiled her subject!" the elder lady sighed.

"Well," said Voyt, "it's better to spoil an artist's subject than to spoil his reputation. I mean," he explained to Maud with his indulgent manner, "his appearance of knowing what he has got hold of, for that, in the last resort, is his happiness."

She slowly rose at this, facing him with an aspect as handsomely mild as his own. "You can't spoil my happiness."

He held her hand an instant as he took leave. "I wish I could add to it!"

III

When he had quitted them and Mrs. Dyott had candidly asked if her friend had found him rude or crude, Maud replied—though not immediately—that she had feared showing only too much that she found him charming. But if Mrs. Dyott took this it was to weigh the sense. "How could you show it too much?"

"Because I always feel that that's my only way of showing anything. It's absurd, if you like," Mrs. Blessingbourne pursued, "but I never know, in such intense discussions, what strange impression I may give."

Her companion looked amused. "Was it intense?"

"*I* was," Maud frankly confessed.

"Then it's a pity you were so wrong. Colonel Voyt, you know, is right." Mrs. Blessingbourne at this gave one of the slow soft silent headshakes to which she often resorted and which, mostly accompanied by the light of cheer, had somehow, in spite of the small obstinacy that smiled in them, a special grace. With this grace, for a moment, her friend, looking her up and down, appeared impressed, yet not too much so to take the next minute a decision. "Oh, my dear, I'm sorry to differ from any one so lovely—for you're awfully beautiful to-night, and your frock's the very nicest I've ever seen you wear. But he's as right as he can be."

Maud repeated her motion. "Not so right, at all events, as he thinks he is. Or perhaps I can say," she went on, after an instant, "that I'm not so wrong. I do know a little what I'm talking about."

Mrs. Dyott continued to study her. "You *are* vexed. You naturally don't like it—such destruction."

"Destruction?"

"Of your illusion."

"I *have* no illusion. If I had, moreover, it wouldn't be destroyed. I have, on the whole, I think, my little decency."

Mrs. Dyott stared. "Let us grant it for argument. What, then?"

"Well, I've also my little drama."

"An attachment?"

"An attachment."

"That you shouldn't have?"

"That I shouldn't have."

"A passion?"

"A passion."

"Shared?"

"Ah, thank goodness, no!"

Mrs. Dyott continued to gaze. "The object's unaware—?"

"Utterly."

Mrs. Dyott turned it over. "Are you sure?"

"Sure."

"That's what you call your decency? But isn't it," Mrs. Dyott asked, "rather *his?*"

"Dear, no. It's only his good fortune."

Mrs. Dyott laughed. "But yours, darling—your good fortune: where does *that* come in?"

"Why, in my sense of the romance of it."

"The romance of what? Of his not knowing?"

"Of my not wanting him to. If I did"—Maud had touchingly worked it out—"where would be my honesty?"

The inquiry, for an instant, held her friend; yet only, it seemed, for a stupefaction that was almost amusement. "Can you want or not want as you like? Where in the world, if you don't want, is your romance?"

Mrs. Blessingbourne still wore her smile, and she now, with a light gesture that matched it, just touched the region of her heart. "There!"

Her companion admiringly marvelled. "A lovely place for it, no doubt!—but not quite a place, that I can see, to make the sentiment a relation."

"Why not? What more is required for a relation for *me?*"

"Oh, all sorts of things, I should say! And many more, added to those, to make it one for the person you mention."

"Ah, that I don't pretend it either should be or *can* be. I only speak for myself."

This was said in a manner that made Mrs. Dyott, with a visible mixture of impressions, suddenly turn away. She indulged in a vague movement or two, as if to look for something; then again found herself near her friend, on whom with the same abruptness, in fact with a strange sharpness, she conferred a kiss that might have represented either her tribute to exalted consistency or her idea of a graceful close of the discussion. "You deserve that one should speak *for* you!"

Her companion looked cheerful and secure. "How *can* you, without knowing—?"

"Oh, by guessing! It's not—?"

But that was as far as Mrs. Dyott could get. "It's not," said Maud, "any one you've ever seen."

"Ah then, I give you up!"

And Mrs. Dyott conformed, for the rest of Maud's stay, to the spirit of this speech. It was made on a Saturday night, and Mrs. Blessingbourne remained till the Wednesday following, an interval during which, as the return of fine weather was confirmed by the Sunday, the two ladies found a wider range of action. There were drives to be taken, calls made, objects of interest seen at a distance; with the effect of much easy talk and still more easy silence. There had been a question of Colonel Voyt's probable return on the Sunday, but the whole time passed without a sign from him, and it was merely mentioned by Mrs. Dyott, in explanation, that he must have been suddenly called, as he was so liable to be, to town. That this in fact was what had happened he made clear to her on Thursday afternoon, when, walking over again late, he found her alone. The consequence of his Sunday letters had been his taking, that day, the 4.15. Mrs. Voyt had gone back on Thursday, and he now, to settle on the spot the question of a piece of work begun at his place, had rushed down for a few hours in anticipation of the usual collective move for the week's end. He was to go up again by the late train, and had to count a little—a fact accepted by his hostess with the hard pliancy of practice—his present happy moments. Too few as these were, however, he found time to make of her an inquiry or two not directly bearing on their situation. The first was a recall of the question for which Mrs. Blessingbourne's entrance on the previous Saturday had arrested her answer. Had that lady the idea of anything between them?

"No. I'm sure. There's one idea she has got," Mrs. Dyott went on; "but it's quite different and not so very wonderful."

"What, then, is it?"

"Well, that she's herself in love."

Voyt showed his interest. "You mean she told you?"

"I got it out of her."

He showed his amusement. "Poor thing! And with whom?"

"With you."

His surprise, if the distinction might be made, was less than his wonder. "You got that out of her too?"

"No—it remains in. Which is much the best way for it. For you to know it would be to end it."

He looked rather cheerfully at sea. "Is that then why you tell me?"

"I mean for her to know you know it. Therefore it's in your interest not to let her."

"I see," Voyt after a moment returned. "Your real calculation is that my interest will be sacrificed to my vanity—so that, if your other idea is just, the flame will in fact, and thanks to her morbid conscience, expire by her taking fright at seeing me so pleased. But I promise you," he declared, "that she shan't see it. So there you are!" She kept her eyes on him and had evidently to admit, after a little, that there she was. Distinct as he had made the case, however, he wasn't yet quite satisfied. "Why are you so sure I'm the man?"

"From the way she denies you."

"You put it to her?"

"Straight. If you hadn't been she'd, of course, have confessed to you—to keep me in the dark about the real one."

Poor Voyt laughed out again. "Oh, you dear souls!"

"Besides," his companion pursued, "I was not in want of that evidence."

"Then what other had you?"

"Her state before you came—which was what made me ask you how much you had seen her. And her state after it," Mrs. Dyott added. "And her state," she wound up, "while you were here."

"But her state while I was here was charming."

"Charming. That's just what I say."

She said it in a tone that placed the matter in its right light—a light in which they appeared kindly, quite tenderly, to watch Maud wander away into space with her lovely head bent under a theory rather too big for it. Voyt's last word, however, was that there was just enough in it—in the theory—for them to allow that she had not shown herself, on the occasion of their talk, wholly bereft of sense. Her consciousness, if they let it alone—as they of course after this mercifully must—*was*, in the last analysis, a kind of shy romance. Not a romance like their own, a thing to make the fortune of any author up to the mark—one who should have the invention or who *could* have the courage; but a small scared starved subjective satisfaction that would do her no harm and nobody else any good. Who but a duffer—he stuck to his contention—would see the shadow of a "story" in it?